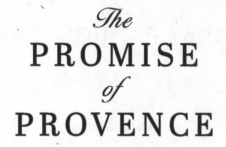

The
PROMISE
of
PROVENCE

The
PROMISE
of
PROVENCE

Book One in the
Love in Provence Series

PATRICIA SANDS

LAKE UNION
PUBLISHING

Text copyright © 2013 Patricia Sands

Published by Lake Union Publishing, Seattle

www.apub.com

Amazon, the Amazon logo, and Lake Union Publishing are trademarks of Amazon.com, Inc., or its affiliates.

ISBN-13: 9781503945647
ISBN-10: 1503945642

Cover design by Mumtaz Mustafa
Artwork by Scott Collie

Printed in the United States of America

In memory of Elizabeth Landman, who taught me to believe that every day is a gift.

1

Stepping out the front door into a wash of cool autumn air, Katherine closed her eyes and inhaled its crispness.

It doesn't get much better than this, she thought, walking briskly through the leafy neighborhood. Little did she know how this day would end.

Her usual 7:00 a.m. route to work caught the city in its final stretch of waking up. She loved the sense of lingering quiet while a blanket of calm lay gently in the air. Even the traffic seemed to move sleepily, preceding the honking, gesturing, and gridlock that would evolve as rush hour developed.

From her townhouse in the Annex to the prewar gray stone office building behind Toronto General Hospital took just half an hour. The tree-lined side streets stretching through the university campus and into Queen's Park were now a riot of gold and scarlet as autumn established its presence.

Crossing the last major intersection, Katherine looked down the street to check the weather beacon atop the wedding-cake-shaped insurance building. A Toronto landmark, its predictions were seldom wrong. The day was looking good.

On the corner, Benny paused in the setup of his back-bacon sandwich cart to flash his customary toothy grin.

"Good morning, missus!"

She had stopped reminding him of her name years earlier, accepting this was his preferred greeting. Waving, she smiled back.

The last stop on her route was the independent coffee shop on the ground floor of her building.

"Morning, Mrs. P. Your usual?"

"Thanks, Barb," Katherine replied. "Gotta have it!"

"Extra-large nonfat half-sweet extra-foam no-whip caffe mocha, to go, please," Barb called to an obviously new *barista*, who was looking a little perplexed and stressed as the line grew.

"A day without one of these is a day without sunshine," Katherine said, attempting to make the young girl behind the coffee machine feel better. She was rewarded with a hurried smile as the trainee pulled levers and banged the espresso filter to attend to her next order.

Silently Katherine thought how she would be terrible at that job and seriously dislike it. *Stress free and structured*, she thought, *that's how I like my life to be.*

Finally she climbed the stairs to the third floor of the historic building, whose original design did not include an elevator.

For fifteen years she had been a research assistant for Dr. Carl Henderson, a specialist in the study of pain. Katherine's PhD in health psychology and long years devoted to study had prepared her for the demands of analyzing statistics and test results, and she loved the work.

Dr. Henderson was an energetic seventy-two-year-old who inspired loyalty and a strong desire to succeed among his staff. The office atmosphere was upbeat as feedback indicated they were making headway in their field. That was a good thing, but every year they held their breath waiting for confirmation the necessary government funding was being renewed.

As she settled at her desk, Dr. H. approached with a small box in his hand that Katherine immediately recognized. As busy as he was, he never failed to acknowledge the birthdays and anniversaries of his staff of seven. Four Laura Secord truffles were his signature gift. Not sharing them was his respected rule.

"Congratulations and best wishes, my dear! Twenty-two years of marriage is a great accomplishment!" he boomed with his usual gusto.

A flush crept up Katherine's cheeks as she accepted the chocolates and exchanged a quick hug with her boss. "I was thinking about those on the way to work!"

"Got some plans for tonight?"

Nodding, she reminded him of the standard anniversary dinner at the Old Mill, where she had also been married. James would not hear of planning anything else.

The doctor chuckled. "Well, in three more years it will be the big twenty-fifth. I'll bet there will be a special celebration for that one."

"Maybe," she replied with a smile. She didn't mention how she had already been considering several different scenarios in anticipation of that anniversary—even though she had little confidence James would agree.

Stopping at the liquor store after she left work, she splurged on a chilled bottle of Dom Pérignon, smiling broadly when the cashier rolled her eyes at the price.

"Must be a very special occasion, huh?" said the young clerk as she handed back the credit card.

Katherine nodded, her eyes sparkling, as she placed the box in a pocket of her computer backpack and hurried off to the subway. She would ride home tonight to arrive a bit earlier than usual and fix some hors d'oeuvres to accompany the champagne. James would have made their traditional reservation for 8:00 p.m.

On the quick ten-minute walk from St. George Station, she cranked up her iPod, listening to whatever tunes she chose instead of the classical pieces James always wanted. A mix of her favorite Charles Aznavour songs carried her back to memories of France.

Was it really so long ago? Thirty years?

A six-week immersion course in storybook Villefranche-sur-Mer when she was just twenty-five years old. She felt her face burn at how she had fallen madly in love—with that town, the Mediterranean, the scenery, the language, the history, the food, everything—even Marc-André, although she had never told anyone that part. Her plan to return hadn't happened. She met James instead. Then came more grad school, her career, marriage, and the fact James wouldn't set foot on an airplane or cross the ocean in any manner.

The only way she ever revisited France was during extended soaks in the bath, when she often let her imagination slip into the framed map of the Côte d'Azur on the wall at the foot of the tub.

The late-afternoon chill caused her to quicken her pace even as memories of France warmed her from within.

Katherine was mildly surprised that James's car wasn't in the driveway. Their anniversary was the one day he promised not to work late, and without fail he had kept that vow.

Great! she thought, knowing she was a bit early. *Maybe I'll have time to shower and put on my new outfit before he gets here. We might even have sex tonight.*

Although their social life was mainly restricted to functions that revolved around his law practice and their biking club, Katherine knew how much James appreciated the way she looked when she put some effort into it.

At fifty-four she'd kept trim thanks to cycling, which was her passion, next to her job. Her figure was still a little fuller than she wanted, although at five-foot-seven she could carry it off. Add some four-inch heels and a pencil skirt, and magic happened—at least, that's what James often told her.

"Damn!" she muttered as she turned the key in the lock and bumped the side entrance door with her hip. Making a mental note to get that warped door fixed, she walked up the short flight of stairs into the kitchen.

Placing her purse and computer bag on the granite counter, as usual, she opened the wine fridge door and set the champagne in its special cooling section. Turning around, she inhaled as deeply as she possibly could and smiled at the same time. On the island was the standard anniversary bouquet of Perfume Delight roses. Twenty-two this year, if she counted them, and they presented a spectacular cloud of deep pink. The fragrance filled her head.

Obviously James had been home and gone out for something. Leaning against the vase was a card-sized envelope, also part of the tradition. *Some things never change*, she thought, without regret.

Holding the envelope in her hand, she paused for a moment. Breathing in the sweet perfume of her beautiful bouquet, Katherine felt a rush of affection tingle through her body right down to her fingertips.

Realizing she had forgotten something, she dropped the envelope on the counter and dashed upstairs to her desk. Taking an anniversary card and a small gift box for James out of the top drawer, she placed them on the vanity beside his bathroom sink. They had begun this tradition with the cards on their first anniversary: hers next to the flowers, and his on the vanity, where he would go to shave before they went out.

Taking the stairs back down two at a time, she hurried to the kitchen to open her card before hitting the shower.

Rather than a card, she pulled a folded piece of paper from the envelope.

Ohhh! He's planned something different. A flutter of excitement mixed with pleasure as she opened the note.

Time stopped.

Her head jerked as if recoiling from a punch.

Squeezing her eyes shut and shaking her head in an attempt to collect herself, she leaned on the kitchen counter for balance.

Slowly she slid to the floor.

This can't be happening . . . something gasped from within her.

Seconds passed before she became aware she was not breathing, as if she'd been punched in the solar plexus.

With effort, she inhaled. Struggling at first, she finally began to breathe, gulping for air. She forced herself to look at the message still held tightly in her grasp.

Read the first line again.

And now the next.

Keep reading.

Nausea and dizziness took over. It felt as if the blood in her body were draining to her feet, leaving her cold and weak.

This cannot be . . . her heart was screaming as she sat on the floor and opened the paper again.

Dear Katherine,

There's no simple way to say this without hurting you, and I'm sorry. I am leaving our marriage.

For a time now I have felt there was something very important missing from our life together. I'm guessing you will agree.

Here are the facts—I am in love with Ashley Johnston and wish to marry her. We are expecting a child together.

I cannot imagine what you are feeling as you read this, and I'm a coward for telling you this way, but I think it is the best.

I have taken most of my things out of the house today and will come back to clear my belongings from the garage in a few days, or when you say I may.

I want to talk to you whenever you are ready. This isn't your fault. It's no one's fault. It's just something that happened.

I'm grateful for everything we shared. In time I hope you will forgive me.

James

Numb, she stretched out on the cool limestone tiles, unable to process anything.

However long she lay there was of no consequence. Trying to understand what or how she was feeling was impossible. There were no tears, no sounds. There was nothing. For however long it was, there was nothing.

Aware that dusk was filtering in through the windows, she vaguely acknowledged the ringing of her cell phone. She felt a brief urgency to see if it was James. James calling to say he had made a terrible mistake. James calling to say of course he loved her. But then it might be James calling to see if she was okay after reading his note. That she could not bear.

She pushed herself up to a sitting position, her back supported by the elegant cherrywood cabinets. Dusk was changing to dark. No tears. No sounds. Nothing.

Finally she stood and flicked on the nightlight over the stove. The note lay abandoned on the floor, almost disappearing into the earthen shades of the tiles.

As if to confirm the truth of what seemed to be happening, she moved trancelike up the stairs. In the master bedroom she opened the doors to the walk-in cupboard and stared at the vacant space where his clothes had hung, always so neatly. She opened all his orderly drawers in the bedroom, the bathroom, the office.

Empty.

He was gone.

Filled with a sudden heaviness, she returned to the kitchen and took the champagne from the fridge. As she popped the cork, the cold wetness fizzled down the side of the bottle and over her hands, dripping onto the granite.

Raising the bottle to her lips with both hands, she drank deeply. She closed her eyes and held the cool bubbles in her mouth, savoring the special quality of this slightly sweet golden liquid before she swallowed.

Stifling the thought that this was their special celebration beverage, she moved to the bar and picked up a delicately etched Waterford crystal champagne flute. A wedding gift, she noted with a wince.

The light had almost faded from the living room as she stumbled through to her favorite spot. Her hand rested briefly on the silky alpaca velvet fabric before she slipped onto the plump cushions. She loved this chair, which seemed to invite her now to be comforted. What she wanted was to sink right through it and slip down the rabbit hole, like Alice.

Kicking magazines off the top, she propped her feet on the leather ottoman.

Robotically refilling her glass, she stared through the window into the darkened garden. Still there were no tears. No sounds apart from the fizzing of the champagne. Nothing except an unstoppable rush of thoughts flooding over and through her, cresting and threatening to pull her under.

Am I crazy? she wondered. *I feel crazy . . . can't grab onto a thought that makes sense. Have I been blind and stupid? What did he see that was missing in our life together . . . that hadn't always been missing . . . and we had accepted . . . or so I thought. He never wanted to talk about "problems." He always shrugged and said everything was fine . . . everything is fine. We're fine. That's what he always said . . . so I believed him . . . even when everything didn't seem fine to me . . . I accepted this was the norm. We had so many good things . . . didn't we . . . don't we . . . ? When did it stop being good for him and not stop for me . . . ?*

She parsed through those good things as they tumbled from her memory.

She thought all the way back to when she had first met James, a serious articling student competing for recognition in a large law firm, to the seven years they had dated without ever breaking up while she lived at home with her parents, through the twenty-two years in which they had built a life together.

They were both workaholics and didn't mind. In any spare time they shared a love of reading and cycling. The bike thing turned into a focus for them early in their union, as they got serious and in shape and joined a club. Wednesday nights and three weekends a month. They loved it. Grimacing, she thought how James was even somewhat socially relaxed with that group.

Including Ashley Johnston. How could she? How could he? How could they? She's young enough to be his daughter. How the hell . . . what the hell . . . when the hell . . . what is everyone going to say . . . to think? I'll never be able to be part of the club again . . . that bastard . . .

The champagne glass slipped from her hand to the carpet as she doubled over, wrapping her arms across her stomach. She ached at the thoughts that followed and remembered all the years they were certain it would happen for them.

He's going to be a father. Oh my God, he's having a child . . . with her. We tried for so long . . . had all the tests . . . I felt so guilty, so inadequate . . . he felt the same . . . time went by. He said it was okay. . . it didn't matter . . . after a while we just stopped talking about it . . . he said everything was fine and he loved me . . . I loved him . . . I do love him . . .

Running her hands over her body, around her breasts, and down her thighs, without thinking she let them rest in the warmth between her legs.

Did it make me less of a woman to him . . . less attractive . . . less desirable . . . what else would it be . . . it's my fault . . . how can he just walk away from all those years we've shared . . . how . . . why . . . I'm not sure I can do this . . . not sure I want to do this . . . I don't even know what "this" is . . . is it my fault? . . . what the hell is happening . . . ?

Tilting the bottle to empty the last few drops directly into her mouth, she wondered why she wasn't crying. She felt like it. But she wasn't.

Just minutes ago I loved James and now . . . I want to kill him . . . how does this happen . . . ?

Staggering into the kitchen, she fumbled in her purse for her cell phone and dialed James as she stumbled up the stairs to the bedroom. She had no idea what she would say, but she needed to say something.

No answer.

She felt mortally wounded. And very, very drunk. Passing out would be her salvation tonight.

⚜

The alarm clock broke through her fog: 5:30 a.m. For a moment her only awareness was of a terrible hangover.

Reaching over to the emptiness next to her, she remembered. *James has left me.*

Sobbing filled the room and grew into piercing wails. She clutched her pillow and, shoulders heaving, buried her face into the soft down. Dampness spread around her head.

Hurt mingled with sorrow, then anger. At times a sense of panic intruded as she pounded the bed with her fist.

She cried for her broken life, her broken dreams, and her broken heart. She cried until she ran out of tears and lay empty, it seemed, of everything.

Painful as it was to lift her head, she reached for the phone and hit the speed dial to her office. Knowing it was too early for anyone to answer, she left voicemail. "Sorry, I've got a terrible case of stomach flu and won't be in today. Probably not tomorrow either, the way I feel right now. I'll let you know."

She already knew she would take these two days off before the weekend. Her hangover was just the beginning of her agony.

Turning over, she fell back to sleep until the phone woke her at noon. As fragile as she felt, she saw her mother's name on call display and knew she had to answer. Her mom was eighty-five, with a heart condition, and Katherine was always a little nervous when the phone rang.

"Katica, *edesem*, I just called your office. When did you get sick? Was it something you ate last night at the Old Mill?"

Knowing she could not begin to address the truth, Katherine gave a convincing performance as she described a flu bug. "I'll call you tomorrow, Anyu. I'm sure I'll be feeling better. Are you okay?"

"*Igen*, I'm fine, but I'm worried about you."

"Don't worry. You know how these things are. A day in bed will fix it."

"Well, James will take care of you when he comes home."

It was such a stabbing pain, Katherine could barely hold the telephone.

"Bye."

Turning the ringer off as she hung up, Katherine lay still while the room spun around her.

"Oh no, not the whirlies . . ." she groaned. Closing her eyes, she willed herself not to throw up.

"I am breathing in. I am breathing out," she whispered until she felt herself get a grip. *This simply does not compute. My entire life has been predictable. This cannot be happening.*

Her parents had placed great importance on a simple, predictable life as they rebuilt theirs in Toronto as Hungarian immigrants in 1949. Katerina Elisabeth Varga was born in Toronto on the eleventh day of the eleventh month in the year 1955, Remembrance Day in Canada. They had always reminded her of this special coincidence. This day symbolized peace, and she had brought peace into their lives.

She had grown into a quiet and somewhat serious adult although under the surface there was a distinct sense of humor and avid curiosity about life. She had boundless energy, much of which she put into her love of cycling beginning with her bright-red Radio Flyer scooter at age four. With James, the cycling evolved into a passion and consumed most of their recreational time.

What the hell happened?

Lying in the softly luxurious bed, which she always hated to leave, she felt no pleasure today. Her head hurt. Everything hurt.

Gingerly sliding her legs over the side of the bed, she sat with her head in her hands, hoping the nausea would pass. After a few long minutes she went across the hall to her desk. For a moment she contemplated phoning James again but just as quickly decided against it. Pride, anger, hurt prevailed.

First she decided she needed to call a locksmith, one who would be there that day. Next, a lawyer. She recalled a card she had in her drawer. A friend of Molly's needed a divorce lawyer a while ago, and James had suggested this one, who it turned out was away until Monday. Katherine wondered whether hiring her was really a good idea but couldn't think of anyone else. Then again, with a touch of irony she thought, the woman *was* highly recommended.

She lay back in bed for half an hour, numb, and then threw on some workout clothes before halfheartedly running a comb through her shoulder-length blond hair.

In the kitchen, a wave of nausea washed over her again—partly from the hangover but more so from the gut-wrenching anguish that hit her as she stared at the roses on the island and the note on the floor. Feeling faint, she picked the biggest glass from the cupboard. Pressing the crushed-ice button on the fridge door, she half filled the glass and then topped it up with water.

She drained it in a few gulps. The cold began to clear her head and, with deep breaths, she felt some balance returning. Pouring a refill, she jumped as the doorbell rang.

Moving about his work very efficiently, the locksmith took just over an hour to replace three locks and show Katherine how to reset the combination for the garage.

Turning her new front door lock, she watched him drive off, then without a thought, climbed the stairs to the bedroom, fell into bed, and pulled the covers over her head. Tomorrow would be here all too soon.

❖

Around noon the next day, Katherine dragged herself out from under the duvet and lay staring at the ceiling. Still in her workout clothes, she had slept fitfully for almost twenty-four hours, alternately quietly crying during her wakeful times or simply feeling drained.

She knew she wanted to get up but couldn't think of a good reason why. *What's the point?* she asked as she slowly sat up.

Picking up the phone, she heard the insistent beeping that indicated messages were waiting.

She called the office first, confirming she was still not well.

Her mom needed to know she was okay. That would be her next call after she listened to the messages.

Her cousin Andrea, who was also her very dear and only truly close friend, had left a message. "Hey there, lovebirds! Hope you had a beautiful anniversary evening at the Old Mill. Don't forget we're expecting you for lunch on Sunday. Are you bringing your bikes? We thought we might drag you over to a neighbor's pumpkin patch so you can help pick out the perfect ones to carve for Halloween."

She swallowed hard, fighting that stabbing pain again. She would have to respond.

The final message was from her next oldest and only other friend, Molly (the Moaner, as James had dubbed her, and not without reason), apologizing for forgetting their anniversary, and sending belated good wishes.

"Oh God," Kat groaned, realizing she was soon going to have to find words to tell those closest to her what had happened.

Briefly she again considered talking to James. It felt instinctive, like the right thing to do. She shook that thought off. The finality of his words in that damn note cut through, and she knew there was no going back.

Taking a deep breath, she counted to ten to slow her heart rate. Then she forced some normalcy into her voice and phoned her mother.

"Hi, Anyu."

"Katica, how are you now?"

"I'm feeling much better today, but I'm not going to work. I thought I might pop over later this afternoon."

"Of course, come for tea. Come whenever. If James is working late, stay for dinner."

"I'll come around four and we'll have tea."

Swinging her feet gently to the floor, she pushed herself up, stretched long and hard, and headed for the shower.

⚜

Before Katherine got into her car, she took a quick inventory in the garage. She couldn't believe James hadn't taken his prized possession with him: the S-Works Venge road bike that he spent hours tuning and cleaning every week. He loved that bike. She noticed the car rack was still hanging on the wall and figured he had run out of time packing up his things before she came home.

Obviously that's what he was talking about in the note . . . that self-serving, self-centered note . . . and he'll come back for it . . . "When I say he may," she said out loud, her face tight with anger.

She slammed the door to her silver Toyota harder than she ever had before. The usual twenty-minute drive to her parents' home in the west end of the city seemed to take forever as she put all thoughts into how she would break her news. Taking deep breaths, she tried to stop crying before she arrived, knowing that would only upset her mother more.

More than once she pulled over to sob, beating her hands on the steering wheel.

Anger as much as anything fueled the outbursts now.

James was a liar and a cheat—this she knew. She wondered if she had really loved him or just loved the idea of being married. They had known each other for so long and become each other's habit before they ever married. She was beginning to feel like a fool. The midafternoon sky was low and gray. A light but steady drizzle infused a sense of gloom beyond the rhythmic slapping of the wipers.

How is it that less than forty-eight hours ago I thought I loved my husband and he loved me, and now I feel . . . hatred? Is that what it is? I'm not sure it's hate . . . I hate what's happening . . . I can't seem to think past that. How can I suddenly hate him? How could he do this?

She knew it was too much to comprehend at this point.

Just deal with it.

Pulling into the driveway of the small, Tudor-accented house in which she grew up, she sat for a few minutes to gather her thoughts. Katherine's mother in all honesty had not been very fond of James. Still, this would not be easy.

2

Elisabeth Varga was sitting in her most comfortable chair by the bay window in the living room, a place where she had spent many hours watching life pass by. When she saw her daughter's car turn into the driveway, she slowly made her way to the front door.

At eighty-five she grudgingly admitted her body was letting her down. Macular degeneration was stealing her eyesight, and her doctor had made it clear that her once-strong heart might not have much left to give her. A widow for just over eight years, a part of her was more than ready to join her beloved Joey. After all they had shared in life, his absence caused an almost constant ache.

The one balm that relieved the hurt was her darling daughter, Katerina. A happy, safe home had been their wish for their daughter, and as the years had passed without a sibling joining her, they focused every effort on being good parents to their only child. From the moment they arrived in Canada, their philosophy revolved simply around one belief: every day is a gift. This they knew only too well.

It was in this refuge Katherine knew she would find solace today. How much good it would do, she wasn't certain.

The door opened and she fell straight into the waiting arms she knew would be there. Mother and daughter hugged longer than usual, and Elisabeth sensed immediately all was not well. The strong, taut frame pressed against her, but something was very broken.

"Are you still feeling ill?"

Shaking her head and leading her mother to the sofa, Katherine felt the words she had tested on the drive over slip away as she struggled to keep her composure. Within seconds she was weeping as her mother held her tightly.

"*Na, na,*" Elisabeth whispered as she patted Katherine's back and rocked her gently.

Feeling strength flow from her mother's embrace, Katherine eventually pulled her shoulders back, wiped her face, blew her nose, and began to recount the unbelievable.

Elisabeth's hands trembled as Katherine held them in hers. Her skin was so thin now, like delicate, fragile porcelain to be treasured and protected.

Her mother's blue eyes, almost a pale turquoise, radiated concern. Katherine looked at her face, knowing every line held a memory of her long life, some of the deeper ones hiding pain too intense to acknowledge. She had been through so much herself and gone on to make such a fine life for her family. Love had motivated her mother in absolutely every action.

This news wasn't fair to her.

At length Elisabeth pulled a fine cotton handkerchief from the sleeve of her sweater to wipe the tears covering her cheeks, paled by sadness. She patted back her hair, which was pulled into a bun. Once a dark walnut brown, now still thick and the whitest white, this was a nervous habit her daughter knew well for as long as she could remember.

Elisabeth's disbelief erased the comforting words she had been offering. She sat in silence for some time, looking intensely at Kat or down at her lap, listening to a story she didn't want to hear.

Katherine talked nonstop, somehow finding the strength to control her voice when it caught. She had moved through a startling range of emotions. Right now she was angry. Totally pissed off.

"I just keep thinking of all the years we were together. Really from the autumn of 1981 until now he has been the only man in my life."

Elisabeth nodded, remembering those early days clearly. "You weren't crazy about James at first, *nem*? It seems to me you took your time warming up to him."

"Think back, it's not like I had been a big-time dater. I didn't have a lot of boyfriends in high school or during my undergrad. I was a bookworm, remember? I liked studying more than dating!"

The conversation took them through the period of Katherine's dating James to their moving in together in 1982.

"Your dad and I were not happy about that."

"I know. I felt badly about disappointing you, but we thought we were very cool. Marriage was old-fashioned and unnecessary."

"What was it young people like you were called then?" asked Elisabeth. "Poppies? Puppies? . . ."

Katherine had to laugh. "Yuppies—young urban professionals."

But her eyes welled up immediately as she went on to talk about them choosing to get married so they could have a family. They weren't *that* cool, they decided.

"Oh, *Anyu*, I've always wondered why it never happened. Why I never became pregnant when no specialist could give us a reason."

Elisabeth put her arms around her daughter and pulled her close. "Just let the tears come. You need to do that. I know it was such a disappointment."

"And now James is rubbing my face in it," Kat sobbed, her voice muffled as she buried her face in her mother's shoulder.

Elisabeth hugged her more tightly. She had no words for that pain. It would simply all have to work its way out in time.

Two pots of tea later, they sat at the kitchen table alternately looking into each other's eyes and passing a comment or watching the downpour run out of the eaves trough into the rain barrel by the porch. Elisabeth would take her daughter's hand from time to time and simply hold it during the silences.

"Stay for dinner, Katica. Keep your old mama company."

Hesitating for a few seconds, Katherine said, "That's a good idea. Honestly I don't feel like going home . . . yet . . ."

"I took some chicken out of the freezer just in case, and if you didn't stay I would simply have cooked it up and saved it for you."

While Katherine chopped onions, adding them to the paprika-laced butter melting in the pot, her mother mixed up the batter for her delicious *spaetzle*. The tiniest hint of garlic was her secret. She sieved the flour and whisked the eggs with her deft light touch before combining the ingredients. The little dumplings would be dropped into boiling water just before the meal was ready to be served.

Chicken broth was added to the sautéing onions, and then chicken breasts and thighs to simmer for just over a half hour. Familiar mouth-watering aromas soon filled the house, and before serving came the final touch of flour-thickened sour cream with a sprinkle of cayenne. Her mother's chicken paprikash, with its delicately seasoned creamy sauce, was the ultimate comfort food.

From a very early age, Katherine had sensed how meaningful it was to her mother to cook and bake old familiar Hungarian recipes. Many strong memories revolved around food and meals. Traditions passed down through generations. Although her mother never discussed the war years, she often told her daughter stories of her happy childhood and loving family before it all ended. It was as if a blade dropped, cutting the threads of a beautiful tapestry, leaving jagged and dangling edges that were beyond repair.

Katherine had often gently prodded her parents to write their stories so they would not be forgotten. "What happened will never be forgotten, but to give it life through words is impossible for us," her mother would respond with sadness.

The last thing she ever wanted was to bring more unhappiness into her mother's life.

Sitting at the table with her mother now and savoring every mouthful of the familiar meal, Katherine realized how ravenous she was. They attempted to concentrate on eating with a few quiet exchanges about nothing in particular. She knew the shock had been huge for her mother—*uh, as it was for me*, she thought with a pang. Another reason to want to hate James.

They had shared tears and consolation as best they could. Elisabeth would have her private moments to deal with her confusion and sadness over this loss, this hurt of her daughter's. Now she would give everything she could, as she always had, to provide love and reassurance about the future. Mothers who had this gift never lost it, no matter what the age, unless a health issue stole it away.

"*Na*, will you stay tonight? Snuggled down in your old bed?"

The thought of not returning to the townhouse alone was suddenly appealing. It was raining harder than ever now, a good night to stay put.

"*Anyu*, there's nowhere else I would rather be right now."

Mother and daughter clung to each other again for a very long while, rocking gently.

Lying in her old bed a short while later, Katherine couldn't stop thinking about her relationship with James. She felt they had truly been in love. *But then again*, she thought, *what is love?* They started off with attraction and interest, added lust, which turned to passion, built respect, and—she had assumed—actually liked each other. They enjoyed each other's company, wanted to be together, planned a life together. Why did it change for him and not her? When did it change? It was difficult to move past all the questions.

The morning dawned bright and clear. *A perfect day for a long bike ride*, Katherine thought with an overwhelming bitterness. She wasn't certain she would ever get on a bicycle again. At the same time a strong urge overtook her, something foreign to her nature but absolutely right under the circumstances.

Walking into the kitchen, she inhaled the pleasant breakfast bouquet in the air. *How does toast smell* so *good in the morning?* As she devoured a piece of buttered toast and a bowl of warm oatmeal served by her mother, the cinnamon scent revived more childhood memories. *Note to self,* she thought, *I must get back to oatmeal instead of yogurt and berries every day.*

"*Anyu,* I'm so sorry I had to unload all this on you. I know you and Papa didn't feel James was the right man for me. I guess I should have listened to you in the beginning."

Her mom wiped her hands on her apron and shook her head. Her voice filled with sympathy.

"My *angyalom,* we never know what life will throw at us. I'm so sorry for you to have your heart broken, but I know we will all survive it. You especially. One day at a time."

"I know you're right. Thank you for being you." Putting every ounce of strength and resolve into her voice, Kat wanted to give her mom reason to believe she was dealing with the situation.

As she drove home, the open windows created a breezy cross draft—anything to help her feel less numb. After making such an effort to reassure her mother, she felt empty, drained of energy and emotion.

Normally she loved to cycle on mornings like this, when the overnight rain had cleansed the air and soaked the earth so deeply that you could almost feel the energy coming from everything green. The sky was impossibly blue, inviting her to be outdoors. Today that invitation lay unopened in Katherine's mind.

How is it, when my heart is so broken, the world can still be such a beautiful place? It isn't right. It isn't appropriate or fair. Everyone and everything should be suffering like I am.

Resentment set in. Trying not to think of James—particularly his fathering a child—was an impossible task. Feeling an ache deep inside her, she lightly rubbed her hand across her abdomen.

A surprisingly nasty seed had begun germinating in her mind shortly after she had awakened. As she drew closer to home, the plan became clearer and stronger. By the time she pulled into her driveway, the intensity of it was almost overpowering.

Activating the garage door opener, she parked her car in the driveway and walked into the almost empty space. Along the back wall was a painstakingly organized worktable with all the tools James used to tune their bikes.

With determined movements Katherine lifted James's most valued possession down off its rack. She marveled for a moment at the lightness and beauty of the elite bike he had treasured with good reason.

Pulling on her leather-palmed gardening gloves, she picked up a Phillips screwdriver and began her task. First she dismantled the electronic components. Wielding a hammer, she smashed some parts on the worktable to ensure the system would be of no use to anyone ever again. She wanted every blow to injure him as he had her. Next the wire cutters were put to work as she cut all the spokes and cables and slashed the tires. With each clip of the cutters, she felt a sharp pain in her heart, but did not stop. A hacksaw would complete her task, cutting through the tire rims and carbon fiber frame again and again. There was no pleasure in this for her, but there was a clear sense of purpose. She had to hurt him back, and with each push and pull of the saw, she hoped she was doing just that.

Stuffing the pieces into a large plastic garbage container, she set the sorry mess in the driveway just outside the garage door.

Going into the house to get a black Sharpie, she printed "RE" in front of the "VENGE" and carefully laid that section of the frame on top of the pile.

Next on her agenda were the two phone calls she absolutely had to return. Molly would be busy giving piano lessons at this time on a

Saturday afternoon, so she could delay that call. But Andrea must be told. She was expecting Katherine and James to be at her place in St. Jacobs tomorrow. The conversation was brief.

"No, no, no! Kat, this is horrible. I can't believe it."

"Believe it," Katherine replied, surprised at her composure. "It's a fact."

"I'm coming over. I'll be there within two hours after I get things organized here, and that's all there is to it."

"Really, Andrea, I'm okay. I'm fine. I'm dealing with it."

"No way," Andrea insisted. "And *I'm* not fine. I'm not dealing with it. I've got to see you. I'll stay overnight and help in whatever way I can . . . or you can help me . . . good Lord, this is a nightmare!"

Knowing there was nothing she would like better than having Andrea with her, Katherine gave in.

She had never been one for getting involved with girlfriends. Molly and she had known each other since public school, living on the same street and somehow just always being around each other. Katherine always felt she was Molly's rock, there to talk during the many ups and downs of Molly's disorganized and unhappy life. Molly had lived on the wild side during high school, while Katherine had immersed herself in her studies.

Andrea was actually more like the sister she never had. They had grown up together. Their fathers had been brothers, and Uncle Andrew had immigrated with Jozsef and Elisabeth. He married a Canadian girl, and the cousins had been born within weeks of each other. Uncle Andrew had moved to Kitchener with his family when Andrea was in first grade, but the two families had maintained the tradition of spending every second Sunday together, alternating homes, which were a quick hour's drive apart.

Andrea, her husband, and their three children had lived on a small farm in the Mennonite area outside St. Jacobs, just north of Kitchener, for twenty-five years. Katherine and James visited often, and Katherine in particular had a close relationship with the three grown children. James had never shown a strong affection for any children, although he liked them well enough.

Katherine felt a hint of relief now. Andrea better than anyone would have a shot at helping her begin to sort through the tangle of emotions.

"I made some beef-and-veggie potpies this morning and tried a new bread recipe, so I'll bring dinner. I'll just go and find Terrence out in the garden and be on my way," Andrea offered, still sounding grim. "Kat, I don't know what to say. I'm so sorry. I'm just stunned . . ."

"Me too, Andie. 'Stunned' is the word. I keep bouncing between disbelief, sadness, and rage. I'm glad you're coming down."

"Make sure there's white wine in that fridge. Lots of it!" Andrea instructed.

⚜

Katherine pulled open a cupboard so the trash container slid out, and she dumped the entire magnificent bouquet of roses into the bag in one swoop—vase, water, and all. As she tied the bag, a cloud of fragrant perfume wafted up, causing her to pause briefly, shocked at her callous behavior. *What a shame*, she thought. Then she took the bag to the large garbage bin in the garage.

The phone was ringing as she came back into the kitchen; the display indicated it was Molly. *Better get it over with*, she told herself.

"Kat! I'm so glad I caught you!" Molly cut in, halfway through Katherine's hello. She had a loud, raspy voice that took on the softest tone, almost a whisper, when she taught piano to children, and transformed into a soulful, smoky singing voice when she worked her weekend gigs at the Blue Note.

"Where the hell have you been, lady? You didn't answer my call from two days ago! You won't believe the day I've had . . . Oh, crap, sorry I was a tad tardy with the anniversary wishes, but ya know me! Better late than never! Anyhoo, did you have a nice time celebrating your twenty-two years? At the Old Mill, as always! Same as ever?"

Katherine swallowed hard.

"Katski, are you there?"

A sound not unlike a squeak escaped Katherine's lips as she desperately tried to form a word and not a sob.

"Ka-ther-ine! What the fuck's happening? Oh my God, something's wrong. You're crying. Tell me you're okay . . ."

Sniffing loudly, Katherine gulped and cleared her throat as she began. "Don't interrupt . . . please. Just let me get through this, okay?"

Molly had to work at it but managed to remain quiet until Katherine indicated she was through with the details.

At that point, Molly was uncharacteristically at a loss for words as she blew out a loud burst of air. When she did find her voice, a string of curses exploded. "Un-fucking-believable . . . Oh, Kat, I'm so, so sorry. I'm just leaving for the Note, but I can come over right after the last show. Shit! I wish I could come right now. I just frickin' can't believe this!"

"It's okay," Katherine said softly through more tears. "Andrea is on her way and going to stay overnight."

"That's good," Molly said with a sigh of relief. "Nobody better. She's the Goddess of Serendipity, and I mean that sincerely."

Katherine nodded into the phone. "Why don't you come for breakfast with us tomorrow? I'll be in better shape by then . . . maybe. It's hard to think straight, but crazy as it sounds, I'm actually having some lucid moments. It's just totally bizarre."

"Fuckin' right it's bizarre, and a whole lot worse!" Molly added, issuing some highly unpleasant suggestions about James's health and safety before they said good-bye.

That was done. Her mom, Andrea, and Molly knew. Somehow it made the whole mess seem more real.

No one else really mattered. The neighbors on both sides of the townhouse were young married couples who seemed busy with their lives. They occasionally enjoyed a drink on one patio or another from time to time, and she figured they would eventually realize what had happened. There were people at the cycling club she knew well who would be placed in the most horrid position with this affair. She would prefer not to have to talk to anyone there for quite a while and hoped no one would call too soon.

Of course she would have to say something at work, even though no one there had ever met James. Dr. Henderson treated his staff extremely well, but didn't believe in socializing with them, so there were no personal connections there. He had once explained how years earlier, before her time, he had found it simply too upsetting to get to know spouses who were later replaced by others. At the time she had agreed wholeheartedly, even though her experience in that regard had been limited to a few of James's colleagues. It was awkward and weird.

Now it was happening to her, she considered with a sorrow that felt like grief as she flopped onto the couch. She was being replaced. Slumped in the cushions for quite a while, that single thought rolled around in her head.

Slowly she began to do something her mother had taught her long ago. As a youngster, if she was unhappy or crabby, Elisabeth would hand her a pencil and a piece of paper with a line drawn vertically down the middle. Katherine would make a list on the left side of all the things that were bugging her and on the other, all the good things in her life.

The good list was always much longer.

Tearing off a sheet from the grocery list pad, she wrote:

Fifty-four not young	*Healthy*
About to be divorced	*Capable*
Alone	*Have a wonderful mother*

James has left for a younger woman and is having a child	*Financially fine, no debt*
Wounded	*Menopause over, no hot flashes*
Angry	*Andrea and Molly*
Deceived	
Confused	
Frightened	
Heartbroken	

The good side isn't outweighing the bad at the moment, she berated herself. *I'm obviously having a bit of trouble seeing the positives. Will I ever? Are there any?*

Squeezing her eyes shut, she tried to will herself not to cry but knew it wasn't going to work. *Maybe it's best anyway to get rid of these tears before Andrea gets here.* She lay on the couch as the wetness slowly washed over her face, streaming down her neck and onto the cushion behind her. There was almost a sense of calm that came with them this time. A letting go of something, although she wasn't sure what.

Her mother's words came filtering through the debris floating around in her head. *Every day is a gift.*

The past few days didn't feel as if they had been gifts or anything close to that, she thought.

I've got a lot of work to do.

After a while, she went upstairs to the office and sat at her computer. She hadn't checked e-mails for the three days since her world had fallen apart. Normally she only looked at them in the evening anyway, as she didn't have much of a contact list. In fact, James, Molly, Andrea, the Toronto West Cycling Club, a couple of charities for which she volunteered, her yoga studio, and her colleagues at work were the only people who had her address.

A message from James was waiting. She chose not to open it. *Later.* Instead she read the messages from her colleagues at the office asking how she was feeling and sending a few files for her to take a look at when she felt up to it. They hoped she would be back with them on Monday.

I will, she told herself. *Life goes on.*

Opening iTunes, Katherine considered listening to some music, but every selection brought too many memories. *Too soon for that,* she muttered as she closed it.

Next she clicked on the local newspaper websites, attempting to focus on something beyond her own life. Katherine was an admitted news junkie. She began and ended every day with the local online newspapers, as well as the CBC, BBC, and Al Jazeera. It would not be difficult to put in time until Andrea's arrival. How much of what she was reading today would sink in was entirely another story.

Random thoughts mixed with doubt, uncertainty, fear, and shock, pushing everything else aside. Concentration wasn't happening.

Life can change in an instant, she knew—accidents, test results from your doctor, heart attack, murder, *your spouse announcing your marriage is over*—but when it actually happened, acceptance was a process more anguishing than she could have imagined.

3

The doorbell rang and Andrea walked in the front door. Standing in the hall, her eyes met Katherine's for a split second before they wrapped their arms around each other.

Andrea burst into tears.

Katherine did not, astonished at her erratic emotions.

The first bottle of wine emptied in no time. Andrea pulled herself together and listened in amazement as Katherine related every detail of Wednesday's events, leaving nothing out. Suddenly, Katherine's resolve broke and she sobbed, through a flood of tears, the question she simply could not reveal to her mother.

"What's wrong with me, Andie? This all somehow has to be my fault. What did I do wrong?"

Andrea grasped her by the shoulders and gave her a gentle shake.

"This absolutely is *not* your fault, so don't start beating yourself up. That's a natural reaction, but let's just take a look at the facts. You'll see you are not to blame for anything."

The raw shock Kat had suppressed at her mother's was finally exposed. Like an open wound that had been festering for days, she needed to find a balm for it. Something that might stop the toxins from taking over.

Andrea listened quietly, sharing that pain as Katherine poured her heart out. How she felt deceived and betrayed. How she railed against the unfairness of her infertility and how her body had failed her. Pounding her fists on the table at times and at others burying her face in her hands, she wondered how she would ever climb out from under the devastation.

Much later in the evening, Andrea insisted they eat, although neither was really in the mood. Andrea's potpie with its light, flaky crust accompanied by her sweet and savory flaxseed bread, were nothing less than delicious. *"Schmeckt gut!"* Katherine murmured with an appreciative look.

Andrea smiled back upon hearing those familiar words of Elisabeth's, glad to see that Katherine's mood had altered somewhat.

"You and Mom both know how to prepare food that gets right to your soul," Kat said.

The wine was making her mellow but not maudlin.

Slurring ever so slightly, she predicted, "I'm not going to let this beat me down. I feel like I've been hit by a bus, but I know I'm strong enough to get through this."

Andrea calmly agreed. "I know that too, and even though it won't be easy at first, you will come through this just fine. I guess it doesn't really help at this point, but two women in my bridge group have had their marriages end in the past couple of years, and they're both doing well. Great, in fact."

"It's such a bloody shock, that's the kicker. I mean, James never stopped acting like things were fine. He's obviously been deceiving me for a very long time. It makes me feel like our whole marriage was a sham."

She sat, quiet and still, as tears streamed down her cheeks again.

Andrea reached to take her hand, squeezing it gently.

"Kat, that's a normal reaction. You had some very good years, and I bet this hasn't gone on for long." *That was a dumb thing to say. What do I know? Comfort isn't always easy to dispense*, Andrea thought.

They sat like that for several minutes. Andrea felt awkward about giving Katherine another hug, as Kat's body language seemed to say she didn't want one at that point. Kat wiped her tears with the back of her hand and sniffed loudly, taking the tissue box Andrea handed to her and blowing her nose. She hadn't really been crying, she realized. The tears just forced their way out, and she didn't feel like trying to stop them.

"Let's try to get some sleep. I actually am feeling quite exhausted now. I'm glad I stayed at Mom's last night, but I feel like I didn't sleep much."

Crawling into bed, she turned off her reading light as reality settled in once more. Stretching her arm across the sheet, she could almost feel the warmth of James lying there. A memory opened of how good it was to spoon herself up behind his strong, lean body. He would reach back and take her hand in his, making her feel safe and secure. Often they fell asleep like that. The emptiness felt like an enormous chasm.

This is the way I will go to sleep for a very long time, she thought, *possibly the rest of my life. In fact, yes, the rest of my life, I will never fall in love again. Never.*

Lying awake in the darkness, Katherine breathed deeply, feeling as though she had never truly grasped the meaning of the word *"alone"* until this moment. Her whole body ached from the inside out.

Then an agonizing thought came: Had the tender love he felt once for her been given to this other woman? Did he hold the other woman close and dance with her the way they had? Did he take her hand and kiss it and tell her how much he loved her, looking deeply into her eyes? Did he hold her in a strong embrace and say she was the best thing in his life?

Gone. James was gone. Her marriage was gone. The future she had thought lay ahead of her was gone. She felt like she was gone too.

She was awake before dawn. Sleep was not bringing her much respite. Dressing quietly and leaving a note by the espresso maker on the kitchen counter, Katherine slipped out to walk through the familiar neighborhood that was just beginning to show signs of life. Here and there a light appeared as others began to prepare for their day.

The warm shades of the brick Victorian and Edwardian mansions appealed to her sense of style and history. Most were now divided into multiunit dwellings and townhouses, and a sense of community had developed.

Twenty years have passed in a flash, she thought.

By 8:00 a.m. the area would come alive with bikes, in-line skates, and Vespas. University of Toronto students and staff made up a significant portion of the neighborhood, along with young families, professional couples, and retirees.

Katherine had always felt safe here, as if she belonged, but this morning she suddenly felt displaced.

Replaying her evening with Andrea, she hoped it helped her cross a hurdle that was critical to finding her footing. She knew there would be missteps and untold moments of despair, disappointment, and anger to come.

What choice do I have? she questioned with a shrug. *It's not like I'm the first person this has happened to. I've joined the crowd.*

Molly would be another challenge. Her friend's fiery temper would erupt, and there would be a lot of nasty talk. Shaking her head at the thought, she was glad Andrea would be there.

⚜

It went much as Kat had anticipated. Molly burst into the house with expletives flying and stomped around the kitchen for several minutes cursing James and Ashley to hell and beyond.

Katherine and Andrea stood leaning against the counter until Molly stopped, took a breath, and pulled Katherine into her arms. Bursting into tears, she whispered her sorrow into Kat's ear and then they all cried. Even Andrea was drawn into the moment and knew it couldn't be helped. She put her arms around the other two as they all tried to find comfort.

They cried as they shared Kat's pain and disappointment.

At length, Andrea filled the coffeemaker as tissues were passed around. Molly surprised them by becoming very calm and quite logical and empathetic as they talked.

Getting closer to noon, pretty much everything had been said. Andrea whipped up a quick omelette for brunch and toasted some of her delicious bread as Molly regaled them with a few stories from the previous night at the Blue Note. Never a dull moment there, and just the comic relief they needed.

As Molly cleaned up, they made a list of what steps needed to be taken over the next few days.

Katherine would call the lawyer back the next morning. She had already decided she would go into work at noon so she could set a few things in motion first without having them weigh on her mind at the office. Not having the stomach to do it herself, she asked Andrea to open the e-mail from James and read it out loud. Molly perched on the edge of the desk while Katherine paced.

Thankfully it was brief and to the point. "Kat, I hope you are doing okay. Again, I'm sorry. Please call or e-mail me as soon as you can."

She decided she was not up to hearing his voice and responded just as briefly. Andrea stayed at the keyboard as Kat dictated.

"I'm waiting to hear from my lawyer."

". . . you fucking asshole," Molly interjected.

"I put your things from the garage by the side of the driveway."

". . . you dumb prick," Molly added as Kat and Andrea burst out laughing.

Katherine continued, "You can pick them up anytime."

She paused for Molly to have her say.

". . . you shit-for-brains bastard."

"Please don't try to see me if I'm home. The locks have been changed."

". . . you shameless, lying, deceitful loser."

Andrea clicked on "Send" forcefully.

"Ha!" Molly exclaimed and then snorted. "I saw what's left of his precious bike in that garbage can outside the garage door. You really did a number on it, Katski! Good job!"

"What? I must have missed it," said Andrea. "I was in such a hurry to get in the house I didn't notice anything outside. What's Molly talking about?"

Katherine looked slightly abashed. "I worked myself into such a rage on Saturday I did the only thing I could that I knew would really, really upset James. I totally destroyed his bike."

"Holy crap!" Molly muttered.

Andrea rolled her eyes and nodded. "That would do it, Kat. Wow!"

"I can't tell you how good it felt. It was a very mean, vengeful, vindictive act—and I don't have an ounce of regret about it. I needed to do something."

Molly laughed cynically. "Never underestimate the therapeutic powers of revenge. James is going to shit his pants when he figures out what's in that garbage can! I'd love to be peeking out the window."

"Serves him right," Andrea agreed.

"I can't believe I did it," Katherine said, shaking her head.

⚜

After a tall soy latte, grande caffe mocha, and venti green tea at the Starbucks around the corner, Andrea convinced the others to walk over to the Royal Ontario Museum, a nice stroll away. Some kind of distraction was what she had in mind.

Katherine still had difficulty accepting the beautiful weather when she felt so stripped of the ability to appreciate it. In spite of the best efforts of Andrea and Molly, she continued to feel dead inside, simply empty.

"*The Warrior Emperor and China's Terracotta Army*," Andrea read aloud as they approached the ticket window, "'an exhibition of objects from the tomb complex of Ying Zheng, first emperor of China, from 259 BC.' It was only discovered in 1974. Imagine! I've been dying to see this!"

"Me too," Katherine agreed, trying to summon enthusiasm.

"Oh, brother," moaned Molly, "it's not exactly how I planned to spend my day off."

"Thanks, Molly, I'm glad you're hanging out with us. I appreciate it," Kat reassured her friend.

The exhibit covered one thousand years of war and peace and profound societal change in China. The sheer beauty of the craftsmanship was remarkable. The sixteen life-size warrior figures and two horses on display cast an eerie time-travel vibe.

Katherine entertained thoughts about time traveling out of her present life.

"Twenty-two hundred years old," Molly commented. "There were thousands of statues found, and each face was different. That's frickin' amazing, isn't it?"

Katherine nodded, still without much feeling. She was going through the motions but not connecting. Andrea put her arm across her shoulder as they wandered through the display.

"You know, from the back, you two could be twins," Molly observed, pulling up the rear.

"Oh yeah," replied Andrea, "but not when you turn us around. I got the freckles and big boobs!"

"Not to mention that her hair is short and a totally different color," Kat added. "But you're right, Molly, we are the same height!"

They all laughed at that.

Picking up a pizza on the way back to the townhouse, they spent another hour quietly chatting before Molly got up to leave.

"Molly, thanks for today," said Katherine. "It was good to have you here, and don't feel you have to go."

"No problemo!" Molly replied in her raspy voice, hoping to sound upbeat and encouraging. Then her face softened and her voice dropped several notches as she looked intently at Katherine. "I'm so, so, so sorry this has happened. I would stay, but we've got a special choir practice at church this evening." Then she crossed her eyes and crossed herself.

The others had to laugh.

"Don't forget," she continued, hugging Katherine one last time, "call me anytime. Whenever, for whatever. We will get through this."

Andrea walked Molly to the door and stepped onto the porch with her, hoping to get out of earshot of Katherine. "Molly, keep checking on Kat, please. I'm concerned about how she is taking this. She really doesn't have anyone, apart from her mother, to talk to except you and me."

Molly nodded and whispered back, "I will, for sure. I can pop by any day on my way home from school. It's right on the subway line. I always suspected she didn't have any close girlfriends. James kept pretty tight control of their lives. Kinda weird, now that I think about it."

"You know, we never really talked about it. It just was the way it was," Andrea said. "Funny how we simply accept some things and then in retrospect wonder why."

"Don't worry," Molly assured her. "I'll keep in close touch and let you know if I have any worries."

They hugged good-bye and Andrea returned to the kitchen.

Once Molly was gone, Andrea and Katherine spent some time talking about their concerns about Elisabeth's health. It was a feeble attempt at diversion, and it didn't work for long.

Finally Katherine said, "Andrea, it's time for you to go. I'm so glad you came to stay with me. I needed you! And Molly too. Honestly, you were both so helpful. Now I need to be alone and you need to get back to your family."

Andrea put her arms tightly around her cousin one more time and then began to collect her things to leave.

Katherine admitted she was still having trouble not blaming herself for the whole mess. "It's going to take me a while to work through that, you know," she confessed.

"I understand, Kat, I truly do. I don't know what more I can say about it except that it's not your fault and you have to come to terms with that."

"Oh, I know that, intellectually. But emotionally it's another story. I feel destroyed."

"I can stay tonight, Kat," Andrea offered without hesitation.

"No, really, I'll be okay. I just needed to say that to you. It helps to say it out loud."

"Call me. Any time. You know that."

"Of course I do, and I will. I have no doubt about that. You've been a rock, as always."

They both teared up slightly and then gave each other a shake.

"Enough already," said Katherine. "I'm done for now."

They had decided Katherine and her mother would go up to St. Jacobs the following weekend, and Kat would focus on that. It would be Canadian Thanksgiving, her family's favorite celebration. James had even enjoyed it. That was going to be a tough one.

In the bedroom, she stripped the sheets from the bed, gathered all the towels from the bathroom, and stuffed everything in the washing machine. His scent was everywhere, despite her efforts to ignore it. The freshly showered and shaved smell she knew so well. His allergies kept any fragrances out of the house.

She had loved how he smelled. Now she wanted to be rid of it.

Immersing herself to her neck in a steaming bubble bath, she distracted herself by staring at the map of the Riviera at the foot of the tub. She thought about some of the French perfumes she had enjoyed wearing before she met James and his allergies. Maybe it was time to enjoy them again.

Sipping a mug of warm milk in bed afterward, she found the sleep she had been seeking.

⚜

Shortly after noon on Monday, Katherine walked into the office and broke the news, apologizing for not being honest when she called in sick.

Sitting on the edge of her desk, she could easily connect with everyone in the small open space. "I have something to tell you and don't want to have to say it individually, so please bear with me. James and I are divorcing, and that's why I was away."

Sympathetic responses and shocked expressions were the collective reactions.

"Let us know if there is anything any of us can do," Dr. Henderson said as he went over and put his arm around her shoulder.

Katherine clutched tissues and swallowed hard, nodding silently for a few seconds. "Right now the best thing for me to do is to get back to work and think about something other than myself. I really appreciate your support."

Laura put on the kettle and suggested a cup of tea, which Katherine gratefully accepted.

Later, Lucy came over to hug her and deliver a note that included some Chinese characters intended to be empowering and energizing. She offered to help in any way she could. *Typical Lucy*, Katherine thought appreciatively.

She was glad everything else in her life was under control.

At least I have plenty of work to keep me busy.

⚜

Looking back on it a month later, Katherine was astounded at how quickly everything about the separation and divorce proceedings was organized. With no children involved and all financial and property holdings in both their names, it was a straightforward arrangement: cut it all right down the middle.

There had been one brief, awkward telephone conversation that had ended with Kat hanging up in tears. Then there was the voicemail tirade he left upon discovering the remains of his bicycle. In fact, she had not even needed to see James in person. The thought of it made her feel ill, so the few issues they needed to discuss were handled by e-mail. It was all kind of surreal, but it worked.

Katherine and her mother had spent Thanksgiving weekend at Andrea's farm. It had poured rain most of the time and they passed the time reading, cooking, and playing board games. It had certainly not been the usual happy time, but they had made the best of it. Andrea's three kids were around and helped to keep the energy levels from flagging.

The wheels had been quickly set in motion by Kat during the week before they went out to St. Jacobs.

The townhouse was up for sale.

Katherine had no desire to stay on and be surrounded by memories that now felt tainted and false.

They had agreed on the division of furniture, and James had gone over with movers to remove what was his. There had been no disputes. Katherine discovered she was able to step back and not feel emotional about any material things.

"Really," she said to Molly over a mocha at Starbucks, "in the grand scheme of things, what does any of that stuff mean now?"

"Well, *I* would take the bastard for everything I could," Molly answered, "especially if I knew there were things he might really want. Then I would give it all to Goodwill!"

Kat choked on her last gulp of coffee, laughing at the same time.

"Seriously," Molly continued, "you've been way kinder about this split than I ever would have been! I know I would have been mean. I think there's something very satisfying about looking into the eyes of someone who has inflicted pain on me and saying 'gotcha!'"

"I hear you. I think I accomplished that when I demolished his beloved bike."

"Oh yeah, that was a good one. But I would definitely want a face-to-face confrontation. At least, that's what I needed with every one of my breakups," Molly said.

"Nope, not for me. I just want it over. I think James is hurt that I don't want to see him, and that's given me some satisfaction."

Molly nodded slowly, considering Kat's point.

"Dealing with my damaged ego and broken heart is another matter. Honestly, I feel like I would just like to punch the living daylights out of James if I had the chance."

"Kick him squarely in the balls," Molly offered.

"That too."

As expected, the townhouse sold quickly. The closing was fast, but Katherine had no problem dealing with that, as she was sending everything of hers to storage.

There had been one more unpleasant surprise. Unbeknownst to her, James had made some high-risk investments on a margin account, using the house as collateral. She had signed the papers at the time, but he had always assured her the investment was doing well, and she had no reason to doubt him.

When the house was sold, Katherine shook her head as she picked up her check from the lawyer's office. "I guess I have no recourse here, right?" she asked, and her lawyer confirmed that.

The final nail in the coffin, Katherine thought. *I really have no respect or feelings for the man now in any way. It's as if he is a completely different person to the one I thought I knew.*

"Asshole!" Molly spat out when Katherine told her.

"Well said," Kat agreed.

⚜

"*Anyu*, I know what you're going to say before I even ask this question, but I want you to at least think about it," Katherine had instructed her mother over dinner the night the house went on the market.

"So you know I'm going to say yes, no matter what it is. Why should I think about it?" Elisabeth replied, her eyes crinkling with laughter.

Shaking her head, Kat smiled lovingly. "You are the best." Within days she had moved into her old room and set up an office in the spare room.

Her quick retreat from the townhouse had helped put some things in perspective. Change was here, and this she was learning to accept. Her feelings of guilt, remorse, anger, and confusion were another story. The future looked blank. It wasn't as if she and James had talked a lot of about retirement and what came after. In fact, they actually hadn't, as they were both so focused on their careers. But certainly she had never considered life without him.

The thought of being a single woman at fifty-five was dragging her down. The sadness and emptiness were unrelenting, and she wondered if depression might be setting in. This frightened her for a lot of reasons she couldn't quite articulate. Andrea and Molly, as well as her mom, had suggested the possibility of some counseling, and she promised to look into it.

⚜

"So how's it going, Kat, really?" Andrea asked. They were walking down the snow-covered lane through Andrea's country property in the aftermath of their first real winter storm. The fields sparkled as if sprinkled with silver sequins.

It had been almost two months since the anniversary disaster.

Squinting in the brightness, Katherine replied quickly, "Mom is so happy to have me with her. I think she feels safer now, more secure, as she becomes frailer, and I'm happy to be able to help her and have this time with her."

"Yup, that I can see, but that's not what I meant and you know it."

Katherine bit her lower lip as she considered her reply. "I'm not feeling good yet. I'm still dealing with a lot of unpleasant emotions, but the counseling is helping. Thanks for pushing me to go."

"What's the worst part right now?"

Katherine took her time responding, picking up a handful of snow and scattering it as she walked.

"Two things. Uncertainty and identity—at least, that's what we've narrowed it down to in counseling. I have no sense of the future at the moment, where I'm going to live, what I'm going to do when I'm not at work. I can't live with Mom forever. I feel like I'm stuck in limbo right now."

"It's early days," said Andrea. "Everything happened so fast."

"Right, for sure," Katherine agreed. "But that doesn't stop the fear of the unknown, and that kind of ties into the second part. I feel like I've lost my identity somewhat. I'm not Mrs. Katherine Price anymore. I mean, I am, but I'm not. Like a lot of women, I kind of got tied up in James's identity. Y'know, the successful, smart lawyer . . ."

"But you're successful and smart too, Kat. You know that."

"That was partly tied up with the security I got from being married to James too. No financial worries, respect and recognition from his colleagues when we socialized—which was fairly often. I know it sounds kind of petty, and it's hard to explain. When I say it out loud, I think it just sounds stupid."

"No, no, no. Not stupid at all. Quite normal, I would imagine. It's a big shift."

"Yeah, a big shift, and I'm still just kind of in shock . . . I think."

"It came at you out of nowhere."

"Well, I've done a lot of thinking about it, and looking back I can see clues that we were drifting apart. I just didn't pay any attention to them."

"Aha! It's the old couldn't-see-the-forest-for-the-trees story . . ."

"Exactly," agreed Katherine. "We had our routines . . . and I was okay with them. Obviously he wasn't but never said anything."

Andrea laughed cynically. "Communication, good old communication . . . it's the key to everything. So simple and yet so difficult for so many."

"For sure, I guess we might have dealt with whatever the issues were if we had talked about them. But I'm also feeling like I was traded in for a new model—not much I can do about that . . ."

Her voice trailed off and she gave Andrea an exasperated look before continuing. "So here I am—single, fifty-five years old, more wrinkles appearing every day—not exactly sought-after dating material. Which really doesn't matter, because I'm not the least bit interested in dating. The thought of it repulses me! But still, the prospect of aging alone isn't particularly joyful."

Andrea listened quietly to this point. "And what does your counselor say about that?"

Katherine gave a snort. "Can you believe she actually insisted I go to my doctor and get an AIDS test?"

Andrea looked astonished. "And her explanation was . . . ?"

"It makes sense, actually. She explained that James put me at risk because he slept with someone else at the same time he was sleeping with me, and we have no idea of her sexual history."

"Smart thinking," Andrea agreed.

"I still felt very weird speaking to my doctor about it," Katherine said, biting her lip and scrunching her face to express her displeasure.

"I hear you. But it's all valid stuff that you have to keep working through. Just don't forget to think about the positives in your life too—remember your mother's famous piece-of-paper therapy!"

Katherine chuckled. "Don't worry. I've got pages all over the place. I'm working on it."

Andrea had often thought about Katherine missing out on having a houseful of kids and all the activity and energy that goes with that. Her own kids adored Aunt Kat, and the feelings were very obviously returned as she spent so much time with them through the years. Andrea knew how much her cousin had hoped for a family in the early years of her marriage.

"It's hard to understand how things work sometimes, but isn't it nice that you have your mom right now and she is such good company?"

Katherine nodded, looking serious. "That she is, thank goodness. You know, we'd become a bit distant after she suggested a few years ago that James was turning me into a different person. I got my back up and defended him and accused Anyu of being overly critical. That in itself was such a wrong thing to say on my part."

"Yeah, you know she's the last person to be like that."

"I've felt terrible ever since, but I still had to be loyal to James. Ha! I'm glad we've had this time together to patch things up."

"She cracks me up on a regular basis," agreed Andrea, "and she's so interested and informed about everything. The cup is always half full with her."

"She's still sharp as a tack, that's for sure. She appreciates every day, and I know she's trying, in her own way, to help me do the same. This whole split upset her terribly, but she has dealt with it. She tells me she doesn't have the luxury of time to let it consume her."

Andrea nodded. "Absolutely right too. We all should think that way no matter what our age, but we get too caught up in our dramas."

"She keeps saying how wonderful it is to know I'm going to be there every day. It has made me realize how lonely she was. I'm getting a whole new perspective on what it means to be old and alone. It's not as if I didn't think about it before and try to be attentive, but I'm truly understanding it now, and it is a powerful experience. It's a strong reminder how important a simple phone call can be."

"And yet," said Andrea, "she insisted you come up here alone this weekend even though I invited her too."

"Well, that's classic Elisabeth, isn't it? She knew it would be good for me to have time to just hang with you."

Andrea's voice took on a serious, softer tone. "I know you and I have shared this thought all of our lives, but I can never get it out of my head. After all the horror your parents and my father experienced during the war, they came out the other side of it with such grace and positive appreciation of life. It's been their greatest gift to us. Gosh, I miss my dad . . . and yours . . ."

"So true," Katherine said, sighing. "I miss them too. You know, Mom has actually made a few comments to me about the war years during these past weeks. I'm hoping she may finally talk with me about it. We've always wanted to know their stories, to keep that alive. Your kids should know."

"Yes, we all should. That carpet of your mom's that hangs on the wall, I know there's a real history to that, but she hasn't told you the details ever, has she?"

"There is a story, and I should know it. All she has told me is her father gave it to her for her seventh birthday. That would have been 1932. It's a Persian carpet with the Tree of Life pattern, full of animals and very sweet. How she saved it through the war is a mystery."

"That village, like so many over there," Andrea said softly, "where the large Jewish community was virtually decimated in the latter years of World War Two. This we know. Somehow she survived . . ."

"By hiding in plain sight. I heard that comment once from Dad and never forgot it. It sent chills down my spine . . ." said Katherine, her eyes welling up. "No wonder she can't bear to speak of it . . ."

The air was quiet and still, as it can be after a wild storm, and the women's breath hung in the air as they spoke. Turning back toward the house, the smell of smoke from the wood-burning stoves made them quicken their pace.

"Pancakes and that scrumptious Mennonite sausage are calling. With any luck, the kids will have them started."

"I always loved that weekend tradition here!" Katherine said, putting her arm around Andrea's shoulder. "The kids have grown into such fine young people. I'm so proud of them and the great job you and Terrence have done raising them!"

"Thanks! Hey, I'm supposed to be the one doing the hugging!" They stopped to give each other a long squeeze.

✤

As Christmas approached, Katherine wrestled with her emotions. She typically loved that time of year and all the traditions. Although her mother was Jewish and held close the traditions with which she had been raised, she had not practiced her faith since the war. She always told Katherine the roots of her upbringing would stay with her forever, as being Jewish was so much more than a religion. Faith, however, was not an active part of her life. It was complicated, she would say, before the sorrowful expression on her face and break in her voice ended the conversation.

Katherine's father had been raised a Roman Catholic, but typical of most Hungarians at the time, religion was not a big part of their life. As he had explained to her many times, the war caused him to walk away from many of his beliefs as they were ignored, trampled upon, and twisted, causing more pain and horror than he could have imagined. When the topic of religion arose, he would be overcome with emotion and the discussion would abruptly stop.

In spite of all this, as long as Kat could recall, Christmas had been celebrated as a joyful time of year, albeit a private one, with just Uncle Andrew and his family involved.

The small special Christmas tree her father put up on those first Christmas Eves when she was little eventually became an enormous tree covered in homemade decorations and others collected on special vacations as the years went by. Jozsef called it a memory tree.

The celebration would begin with the first Sunday of Advent, four weeks before Christmas. Andrea's family would share in the tradition as they made an Advent wreath from evergreen boughs. That first evening, after dark, a candle would be lit and fixed on the wreath as they sang a Christmas carol. The same procedure would occur on the remaining three Sundays before Christmas, and the wreath would be the centerpiece of the Christmas feast. On the Eve of St. Nicholas Day (December 6), Katherine would put her best, newly polished shoes outside her bedroom door. She would fall asleep wondering if Mikulas (St. Nicholas) would leave her sweets or stones, although she was always such a good child there was little doubt which it would be. Nevertheless, that small doubt made the anticipation exciting to a child.

Every day after that, more decorations were added to the house. A pine bough here, a painted bell there, ceramic Christmas figures, and beautiful tablecloths and runners stitched and embroidered by Elisabeth's talented fingers.

Until she was eight years old, her father would disappear into the living room, which had been curtained off on *Szent-este*, Christmas Eve. While Katherine helped her mother in the kitchen making *palachinta*, the delicious sweet crepes stuffed with apricot preserve, he worked his magic.

The melodic tinkling of little bells would signal Kat's permission to come to the living room. Pulling aside the curtain, she never ceased to be astonished and delighted at the beauty of the tree with its candles, lights, and sweets hung in bright foil wrappings. She was saddened when she was old enough to realize it was her father and not angels who delivered the tree, as he had always assured her.

A few simple gifts would be under the tree, and they would open them that evening as they enjoyed their Christmas cookies and crepes.

Hanukah was remembered as well, with a beautiful but simple menorah on the mantle and a candle lit every day of that holiday. As joyful as her parents made the season for her, the lighting of each of these candles was tinged with sorrow she could feel and see in her parents' eyes. It wasn't until she was a teenager that she began to understand.

Even though the holiday time was bittersweet, it was the positive that Elisabeth and Jozsef unfailingly emphasized.

"Anyu," said Katherine one evening as they rolled out cookie dough, "I know I don't say this out loud often enough. Thank you for all the memories you have given me . . . my entire life. I want you to know how much I treasure them."

"It's the greatest gift a parent can offer a child. Good memories build strong foundations. What do you think keeps me going?"

The conversation returned to recipes as Elisabeth went on to demonstrate her expertise in mixing the shortbread dough. Somehow hers always turned out better, Katherine told her.

"You don't have to spend every evening with me, you know," her mother told her. "If you want to go to a party or something, you should be doing that."

To Elisabeth's surprise, Katherine's eyes suddenly teared up.

Her mother immediately put her arms around Kat, holding her dough-covered hands at an awkward angle.

"My Katica. I know this hasn't been easy for you."

Katherine looked at her mom, wiping her tears on her shoulder. "Sorry, I just lost it for a sec. Every once in a while it still happens. Honestly, there's nowhere I would rather be than here with you."

Giving her daughter another hug, her mother whispered in her ear, "Remember, what doesn't kill us makes us stronger. Always."

Nodding, Katherine had heard those words from her mother her entire life. She knew her mother lived by them.

"Honestly, I am fine."

Katherine explained she didn't miss the round of cocktail parties the law firm held each year. "I'm happy to be here with you. There are no parties I feel like going to, nor have I been invited to any. So there you go."

When she analyzed it, the Christmas traditions she and James had observed had more to do with her family than their relationship. James had never really shown much Christmas spirit. He had merely tolerated her putting out her beloved Santa collection and other decorations and filling the house with boughs and poinsettias.

She had, in fact, received one invitation, but she didn't mention that. The secretary of the cycling club had called personally to extend an invitation for Katherine to come to the annual Christmas party. May McNeilly was one of the women Katherine had known well in the club. She had called about a month after "la Katastrophe," as Molly referred to the anniversary disaster.

The conversation had been awkward at first, but May was a straightforward type and quickly got to the point. She'd told Katherine that James and Ashley no longer belonged to the club, and the members were hoping Katherine would come back in the spring, as she was missed. They also hoped she would consider attending the party.

"May, thanks so much. I appreciate your call and the invitation. I'm simply not ready to party. I still feel awkward about coming back to the club, and I think I'll need more time, but I truly appreciate your support and the invitation."

She needed more time for sure, she had told herself as she hung up. The thought of being the single divorcée at social functions was not a scenario she relished.

4

A week before Christmas, Katherine and Molly had tickets for the Tafelmusik Baroque Orchestra and Chamber Choir's sing-along *Messiah* concert at Massey Hall.

"Be prepared to sing your heart out!" Molly encouraged as they walked from the subway to the much-loved old concert hall with its outstanding acoustics. "A little trivia for you. *The Messiah* was the first production here when the then Massey Music Hall opened in 1894. How about that?"

"Molly, I don't know anyone who knows more music trivia than you!"

Katherine was excited about the evening because of the concert, but also because it was her first real night out since the split. Molly had warned her they would have to stand in line, since only general admission seating was available. Keeners who wanted particular seats came early to line up, some with an appropriate warm beverage.

Obviously Molly knew the drill, taking a thermos and two cups out of her large shoulder bag.

"Oh, great idea! I could use a coffee," Katherine thanked her.

"Katski, I love how shit-straight you are. It's cocoa and Kahlua, and you'll enjoy it even more than a coffee right now. Besides we need to toast the occasion."

"You're too much! But this is a good occasion to toast!"

"Well, actually, what we should toast is the fact that this is the first frickin' time you and I have done something like this in about twenty years!"

"You're exaggerating, my friend," Kate retorted.

"Nope, I'm not. Just think about it and you will see I'm right."

They toasted and sipped the delicious beverage while Katherine considered what Molly had said. *Really? How had she allowed her life to be controlled and isolated in so many ways?* This was becoming apparent to her the more she lived life without James.

The concert was an event Katherine had longed to attend for years, but James thought it was "stupid," an affront to the classical music he loved. So she had never pursued it.

Finally getting to their seats, Katherine burst out laughing when Molly pulled off her wool hat and a wild mane of uncontrolled curls exploded from her head.

"My God, Molly! You usually have your hair pulled back. I haven't seen it like this for years! You look fabulous! It's so long!"

Molly smiled and blushed. "I always pull it back into a twist for school and my weekend lessons—prim and proper Ms. Malone, the music teacher!"

"So you only have it down for your singing gigs? Yikes, that tells you how long it has been since I was to one of those. I'm going to fix that!"

Katherine caught a look in Molly's eyes that hinted there was another side to the story about her hair—*her big sexy hair*, she thought. But just then the orchestra stood as the maestro made his entrance, and Molly put her finger to her lips to end the chat.

"Honestly, Kat, you're going to be blown away when you hear how kickass-amazing we all sound," she whispered. "The Tafelmusik choir and orchestra get just as pumped about this as the audience, and the enthusiasm is contagious."

Katherine smiled and felt more excited than she had in some time.

As they joined in the standing ovation after the final notes rang through the hall, Katherine hugged Molly. "Thanks! This was everything you promised and more!"

Having taken the subway downtown, they splurged on a taxi back. The plan was for Molly to stay overnight.

"*Tessék*, Molly. It's so nice to see you again," Elisabeth said, after a warm hug in the living room. "You haven't dropped by for a while."

Note to self, Molly thought. "You're right, Elisabeth, and I'm ashamed of that. I got a little caught up in life, but that's no excuse for not popping by. I always enjoyed our chats, and I'll start coming by more often again. It's good to see you looking so well."

"*Na*, Molly, I didn't mean to make you feel badly. I just wanted you to know I missed you—and your funny stories."

"Well, I can see you have certainly been busy decorating!" Molly exclaimed, taking it all in.

Elisabeth glowed. "Katica has made this season so special. We retrieved our old decorations from their storage boxes—many I haven't seen for years, and for sure since Jozsef left us. We have only recalled happy memories. There've been some painful moments, but we've tried to find the good in even those."

Katherine moved behind her mother, putting her hands gently on her shoulders. "We decided that nothing was going to spoil the time we're sharing right now."

Molly raised her eyebrows quizzically at Katherine while Elisabeth wasn't looking. Kat responded with a move of her hand that indicated they would talk later.

Stifling a yawn, Katherine suggested they all get to sleep. "*Anyu*, I can't believe you stayed up this late!"

Her mother smiled, a gentle look in her eyes. "Just like when you girls were teenagers, *nem*?"

"Except this time, I'm not sharing a bed with Katherine so we can yak until the early hours!" Molly said. "I need to sleep!"

In the morning, after a typically delicious breakfast, Katherine walked Molly out to her car.

"For Christ's sake, Kat, are you really handling things as well as your mom makes it sound?"

Putting her hand on Molly's arm, Katherine spoke with assurance.

"Molly, I'm not saying this is easy or that I'm not hurting, but one night when I was at my lowest point, I went for a long walk. I thought about this mess and decided I only had one way to go—up! I felt I couldn't get dragged down any further, and I was darned if I was going to let James ruin the rest of my life—"

"The shit-for-brains bastard . . ." Molly interjected.

"Exactly!" Katherine agreed. "I've spent every minute from that evening on attempting to move forward, and I have to tell you, my mother has been my biggest inspiration. I look at her every day and think about what she had to move on from in her life. Then I realize my problems are nothing compared to that. It's that simple."

Molly shook her head, followed by a look of pure admiration. "I don't know how you can do it, Kat. You know how I used to go off the deep end whenever I had a fucking breakup—hence my aversion to any kind of relationship . . ."

"Excusez-moi," said Katherine. "What exactly is your . . . let's see . . . how many years . . . ?"

"Seven," muttered Molly, looking up at the gathering snow clouds with a grumpy expression.

"Okay, I would say seven years qualifies as a relationship . . ." Katherine replied. "With the enigmatic Antonio."

"Friends with benefits—that's what it's called these days. They just made a movie about that," Molly curtly informed her. "We see each other maybe once a week—and it's strictly physical."

"Ha! It's got to be more than strictly physical if it's gone on that long."

As Molly always did when the conversation turned to this secretive affair, she changed the subject. "Wait a frickin' second, we're talking about you, not me! I just wanted to say that I think you're doing a helluva job dealing with everything. And the fact that your eighty-five-year-old mom is such a positive influence is a bonus. She's a great lady, and you're lucky to still have her."

Hugging, they wished each other a Merry Christmas. Molly had a busy singing schedule through the holidays, and Katherine knew that somehow the trysts with her elusive suitor also factored in.

She is a character, Katherine thought as Molly hopped into her Zipcar and backed out to the street. She often wondered what on earth Molly's secret might be.

⚜

Christmas Eve was on a Saturday, making it very convenient for Katherine and her mother to visit the local tree lot at the nearby Anglican church. The pickings were slim, but they were happy to choose a needy-looking little blue spruce to be delivered that afternoon.

Warmly bundled up, they slowly strolled the few blocks in the sunshine, Elisabeth's arm securely tucked in Katherine's.

"It feels good to be out this morning with everyone dashing about taking care of last-minute details," Elisabeth noted. "I miss that hustle and bustle. It's just not the same watching it out my window!"

By dinnertime, the tree was magical in their eyes.

Mother and daughter chatted and laughed. Later, with the box of treasured decorations between them, Katherine handed them one by one to her mother. The colorful ornaments and delicate angels, all of fragile painted glass, were hung with care, along with the traditional sweets wrapped in shiny gold, red, and green foil. Last came small white candles set in brass holders, which cast a sparkling glow when carefully lit by Kat.

When Elisabeth rang the tiny bells gently, their eyes locked in a look of remembrance, a mixture of sweetness and sadness.

"Life seems to pass in a heartbeat," Elisabeth whispered, her voice filled with melancholy.

They reminisced for a long while, sometimes laughing, sometimes shedding a few tears as old memories surfaced. As they sat in the candlelight and nibbled on Elisabeth's *palachinta*, they listened to a CD Katherine had made for her mother of her most treasured seasonal music and Hungarian carols. That had been the first gift from under the tree.

This year they had agreed to exchange three gifts with the most meaning and little cost as possible. In the past Katherine and Elisabeth had set aside a day or two to shop together, but this year Elisabeth said she was organized and it would not be necessary.

Her first gift to her daughter was one that held no mystery. The green-and-red-striped cookie tin had been passed between them since the first year Katherine was married and not living at home. It was filled with a selection of the delicious seasonal cookies and sweets that Elisabeth baked every year beginning well before December.

In return, Katherine purchased for her mother the largest box of Laura Secord chocolates available, putting them in a similar tin. The tins were passed between them every year. She knew her mother treated herself to one piece a day until they were gone—and then a replacement box would magically appear. The dates were well marked in Katherine's day timer.

Mother and daughter appreciated each other's weakness for sweets.

Elisabeth's next gift to Katherine was a wooden box, which looked vaguely familiar but very new. She recognized the lid as bird's-eye maple and then realized she had certainly seen the box many times before, sitting in her mother's closet.

"When your father and I were first getting settled in Canada, we often went to auctions to find affordable things. He bought this box for my birthday the first year we were here. We had no idea how special the wood was at the time. Imagine! Dad gave it to me to keep my treasures through the years. Cards, photos, letters, poems I would copy. Although it wasn't a hope chest, it did hold many of my hopes and dreams. It was a reminder to me of what mattered most."

"But *Anyu*, there is still time for hopes and dreams in your life."

"*Nem*, as I see it, the hopes and dreams should now be yours, and I want you to realize they still lie ahead in your life. You can collect them and save them in this special box, as I did."

Katherine knew there was no option for refusal, although she really did not foresee having much to put in the fine-looking box. Hopes and dreams felt dashed to her, and the future was not something she could even begin to visualize, apart from being alone. She definitely was not going to admit this to Elisabeth. "It looks magnificent. Someone has refinished it."

"Yes, Andrea took it to a Mennonite woodworker who lives near her. He did a fine job!"

Chuckling, Katherine told her mother they had both gone to the St. Jacobs area in their gift search. "I went to a local market with Andrea last month and found this next gift for you."

Elisabeth unwrapped a beautiful pale-turquoise shawl of the softest wool. "It was woven by hand. The woman even keeps her own angora rabbits and spins the wool herself. Have you ever felt anything so exquisitely soft?"

"It's beautiful, and just what I need for the hours I spend in my chair by the window. You noticed the one I have is getting a little worn, didn't you? And such a perfect color!"

When Elisabeth handed Katherine her last present, she kept her hand on it as she spoke. "Katerina, *angyalom, szeretlek*. I love you more than you can possibly understand. That's the way it is between parents and children. You have been my pride and joy."

"*Anyu*, we have been a wonderful family." Katherine struggled to keep her composure as her eyes welled up. "I know how much you miss Father, as do I."

"*Igen* . . . but hush . . . there have been too many tears. This gift is something you have been asking for over many, many years. It is something I was unable to give to you for a long time. Impossible. *Lehetetien.*"

Katherine had no idea what was coming.

Elisabeth continued, not lifting her hand from the beautifully wrapped present. "Watching you work through your heartbreak, I realized I had an important message for you that only this gift would help you understand. It is time."

"I'm sure whatever it is, is wonderful. Are you actually going to give it to me? You have quite a grip on it."

A strange look crossed Elisabeth's face as she passed the gift to her daughter, still keeping her hands on it. As they both held it, she issued one final instruction, her voice breaking slightly. "There is just one condition that accompanies this gift, my darling. You may not open it until I have passed from this earth."

Katherine's eyes widened.

"*Anyu?*"

"This is our story. The story of my family, and your father's, during the war. The story your father and I shared with each other and never anyone else in this country. Of course, Uncle Andrew was also part of it. I have never regretted that decision, but I know my days here are not long and then it will be important for you to know."

Bursting into tears, Katherine wrapped her mother in her arms. "Please don't talk like that. You have a good, long life ahead of you. But thank you for writing this. It's important to me and to Andrea and her family, and we will be eternally grateful. I will respect your wishes, so I believe it will be a very, very long time from now until I see it."

Elisabeth held her tightly and said. "I hope I don't have long, my Katerina. I am ready to join my Jozsef, and I feel my body slipping . . . I feel it. So don't be sad. You are making these days of mine so full of happiness, and let us just continue. So no more tears! I am not crying, and I don't want you to either."

That night, the lights were out early, as Elisabeth said she was exhausted and needed to rest for their trip to St. Jacobs the next afternoon.

Katherine sat on her bed for a long while, holding the precious gift she had received from her mother and realizing what a sacrifice she must have made to force all those memories out of storage and onto paper. How typical of her mother to do it because she thought she could help her daughter through her own experience.

She just never stops giving, Katherine thought as she drifted off to sleep.

5

The holidays passed with Katherine spending more time than she wanted working through lingering anger at James and how her life had changed in just a few short months. She had promised herself that she would not allow him to spoil her holiday any more than he already had. It wasn't always easy, but she blocked him out as best she could and kept the periods of sadness and depression well hidden.

I'll save it for my next counseling session with Dr. Olson.

Christmas and Boxing Days with Andrea and her family in St. Jacobs had been busy and noisy with all three of the children home. They were eighteen, twenty, and twenty-four and even when other friends of theirs weren't over visiting, the house felt full of life. They loved having their Aunt Kat and Neni Elisabeth share the holidays with them.

The whole family had worked on convincing Katherine and her mother to return for New Year's Eve and their annual sleigh ride and bonfire because it looked like it would be a good year for it, weather-wise. And so they did, much to everyone's surprise.

Standing by the bonfire, Andrea said, "It's so wonderful to see the happy times you and your mom have shared these past few months."

"It's been quite awesome in a lot of ways," Katherine agreed, adding with a bit of a snort, "Too bad it took my marriage blowing up to make it happen."

"Too bad indeed. How are you doing now?"

Katherine blew out a long sigh. "Not great. I'm so thankful for this time with Mom, but I know I have to start thinking beyond it. I've really got my head in the sand."

"Well, I know it sounds a bit cheesy, but a new year begins at midnight, and my wish for you is that this will be the beginning of your new life as well."

Katherine muttered a muffled "Mm-hmm."

❧

By the end of January, Katherine was feeling more settled into her new routine. Elisabeth, an early riser, would have breakfast ready when Kat came downstairs. Kat missed her long morning walk, so she had begun to go to yoga with Lucy twice a week. Yoga was new to her, as was the experience of having a regular commitment with a girlfriend now that James no longer controlled her agenda.

"Thanks for pushing me to do this. It's been a good way to fill my evenings."

Lucy smiled at her. "Obviously I don't know how painful divorce is, but we have a saying: 'One joy scatters a thousand griefs.'"

Katherine nodded. "I need to remember that one."

Lucy had suggested they go to this class and was a devotee to yoga, which Katherine found very helpful. Even with the clear instructions of the teacher, she felt like a klutz half the time.

There were days when Katherine still felt empty and without a vision for her future. There were days when she struggled with the feeling she was a loser and blamed herself in every way for James leaving.

The counseling therapy had helped. Dr. Olson was quietly intuitive, and Katherine liked her. The doctor had pushed Katherine to piece together the mosaic of her marriage, which Kat had so violently smashed on the floor of the garage as she dismantled James's bike that day.

"I literally kicked it into a thousand pieces. I didn't want any memory to remain intact," Kat confessed.

She had been encouraged to recognize the good that had existed during her years with James as well as the hurt she had endured. There were some truths she acknowledged and hung on to. Yes, she conceded, there had been many years of love and respect in her marriage. Yes, she had been deceived and hurt, but she had not been physically or verbally abused. She had not been left poverty-stricken. *Focus on the positive.*

Once-a-month maintenance appointments would help if she faltered. The forward momentum was difficult, she often admitted to herself.

There were times she thought she saw James in front of her in a crowd. She would recognize his height, broad shoulders, the back of his head, or maybe his familiar gait and catch her breath not knowing if she wanted him to see her. She knew she did not want to talk to him. She might punch him—or worse. But then she would see the profile and feel relieved she was mistaken.

6

Katherine hadn't seen it coming, but she sensed Elisabeth had. Thinking back, there had been plenty of warning.

The winter was cold and snowy, and getting her mother out for a walk was more and more difficult. At the beginning of February, Katherine hired a kind and cheery caregiver. She popped in every morning for a few hours to do a bit of housework, pick up some groceries from the list Katherine posted in the kitchen, and keep Elisabeth company while she prepared lunch for her.

Katherine and her mother both realized the help was necessary. Elisabeth's strength was waning noticeably, and it troubled her that Kat was working all day and coming home to clean as well as do everything else. This had been the compromise, and Elisabeth admitted to Kat that she looked forward to Hilda's visits. Elisabeth enjoyed the lovely Scottish lilt to her voice as she related the latest gossip about the royal family and other people in the news.

After a little initial resistance, Kat rented a hospital bed and set it up in Elisabeth's main-floor sewing room so the stairs were no longer an issue. Elisabeth had a trunk full of delicate linens that had belonged to her family for generations. The trunk was saved by a faithful family friend during the war and returned to Elisabeth before she left the horror behind.

Elisabeth had not used them in decades, but Kat convinced her to bring them out of their wrapping and take pleasure from them once more. Elisabeth told her several times how happy she was to see the pillow covers and hand towels in use again.

The most important issue of the relocation, as Elizabeth referred to the move downstairs, was bringing down the ceramic urn that contained Jozsef's ashes. This sat on the table by the side of the bed he had occupied throughout their life together. Elisabeth insisted on this and said her last words every evening to her beloved before she fell asleep.

"You know, we never spent a night apart after the war ended," she had reminded Katherine. "And we never will."

Elisabeth's other request had been about the carpet that hung on her bedroom wall. She was apologetic for asking, but it was important to her that it be moved to where she was sleeping.

Katherine was unaware that every night her mother pressed her forehead and palms against the soft—and in some places threadbare—Persian rug, connecting as best she could to all that she had lost so long ago.

Most evenings, Katherine and her mother played cribbage or honeymoon bridge, sharing a pot of warm milk and Elisabeth's delicious cookies before they turned in early, Elisabeth falling into contented slumber and Katherine drifting off later, her book slipping from her hands. Sleep was still not her friend, and unpleasant dreams often caused her to lie awake.

One morning in early February, Katherine did not hear the familiar sounds of her mother in the kitchen or smell the tantalizing breakfast aromas that normally wafted up to her. Somehow she knew, as she hesitantly went down the stairs to her mother's room.

⚜

"Her heart simply stopped," Dr. Howitt said to Katherine as he rested his hand on her shoulder. "It was worn out—and, to be honest, it gave her more time than I thought it would. She told me recently she was waiting until she knew you were going to be fine."

Katherine's eyes filled with tears.

"I had the pleasure of being her doctor, and your dad's, for over forty years. They were fine people. I miss your father and I will miss your mother now too. It's the hardest part of getting old, watching the people around you slip away."

"I know how much Mother valued your care . . . and your friendship," said Katherine.

They had this conversation when Katherine took a gift to his office a few days after her mother's private family funeral. She was in fact following some wishes Elisabeth had left in a file for Katherine.

"Mom left her little list of things she wanted me to do after she died," Katherine said to Molly over coffee on her way home from Dr. Howitt's office.

Molly nodded. "I'm so impressed that she talked to you about this—starting years ago. What a great attitude. I can appreciate how satisfying it is to know you are doing what she wanted. I wish I had been that fortunate."

"Molly, your parents' accident was a totally different situation. Your mother never recovered from her coma to express any wishes. It was a tragedy."

Molly nodded stiffly and changed the subject as she usually did, keeping her innermost emotions tightly under control. "I better hit the road. I've got a full schedule of lessons booked this afternoon. Sometimes I could kick myself for giving up my frickin' Saturdays!"

Katherine laughed as they put on their coats. "I've been listening to you complain about that for years! You know you love giving free lessons to those kids. They would never have this experience otherwise!"

Molly rolled her eyes and shrugged.

"It's a wonderful thing you do, Molly Malone. I'm very proud of you—always have been, but maybe I never said it before."

After a knuckle-bump and a grin, they headed off in different directions.

Once home, she shuddered slightly at the empty feeling in her heart as well as in the house. *I still can't think of it as mine.*

Putting on the kettle for tea, she felt her mom's presence. Tea with honey and lemon had been Elisabeth's antidote for all ailments—emotional or physical.

Katherine had decided that she was ready to open the special box her mother had given her for Christmas.

7

I should probably be pouring myself something stronger than tea, she thought, making herself comfortable on the couch with the gift beside her.

Her gaze moved to the carpet hanging on the wall in the room across the hall from her. Somehow her mother's spirit seemed to be woven into the threads now, adding a luster and richness to the golden shades.

Her hand rested on the ornate wrapping paper as she considered how difficult it must have been for her mom to write this. She knew reading it would not be easy.

Gently removing the paper and lifting the lid of the box, Katherine's eyes immediately moistened. Elisabeth had taken an old linen tea towel from her cherished box and sewn it to fit over the cover of one of Katherine's small loose-leaf binders from high school.

There are still all those boxes of my childhood bits and pieces in the basement. That's my next job to tackle.

On the front, in her uniquely beautiful style, Elisabeth had embroidered her initials and Jozsef's. At the bottom was "For our Katica, with love."

Inside, the pages contained her distinctive script, a combination of learning cursive in a different language such a long time ago and her natural artistic talent. There was a delicate beauty to it, and the slightly shaky effect of age only enhanced that.

My darling Katica,

I only want you to know enough, not every detail. I can tell you facts, not feelings, otherwise these pages would dissolve from my tears.

I know you understand that terrible things happen in life.

I know, like everyone else, you have learned of the horrors of the war years. I believe it is important when I am gone that you and Andrea know our family's story so you can pass it on to future generations. I want, most of all, to leave you with the assurance that everyone can find ways to move past whatever their hurts are and rebuild their lives.

You were the proof to your father and me . . .

As I often told you, my childhood was a happy time in a safe and loving place. We spoke Yiddish and Hungarian at home, and I spoke Czech at school. Ours was a big town for those days, with a population of about 30,000. The Jewish community made up approximately half of that, and everyone was friendly, tolerant, and respectful of each other. I never once had a sense of being different because of my religion.

My family was not as religious as some. It was more a way of life. We celebrated Shabbat and the holidays like everyone else, but my father did not go to the synagogue to pray every day as some men did.

My father was a lawyer. He had been born and educated in Budapest. He met my mother when she was visiting relatives in Budapest, and he moved to our town to court her and marry her. My mother, like most other women, worked in the home and used her talents, sewing and cooking, to help others. She often was asked to embroider wedding dresses or alter clothes, and she did so happily. She taught me her skills and I loved to sit stitching beside her.

We had a modest lifestyle, but others thought us "comfortable" because we had our own home with a small garden where we grew vegetables and fruit. We had electricity sometimes but mostly used oil lamps. We were fortunate to have our own pump so we didn't have to line up to carry water from the communal well. We had an icebox, a woodstove, and an outhouse. At night we used a chamber pot.

When we weren't at school, the children played outside and could go anywhere in the town. We all knew and looked after each other. We were never afraid of anything, and even though life was not easy, everyone laughed and did their chores with a good attitude. It was our life. Everyone helped everyone.

And now a brief history reminder:

In 1933, Hitler came to power in Germany.

In 1935, he enacted the Nuremberg Laws in Germany that did not affect other countries but made Jews everywhere nervous and unsure of the future as word slowly spread.

October, 1938, more than 12,000 German Jews expelled to Poland.

November, 1938, Fascist Hungary took over our region. Fear and uncertainty spread through our Jewish community and we began to be treated with disrespect.

November 10, 1938, Kristallnacht in Germany and part of Austria. Life changed dramatically for Jews in Eastern Europe.

Remember that news did not spread quickly, and often we did not believe the bad stories because it did not make sense and was so against the life we knew.

From 1938, when I was thirteen, life quickly changed. It was unbelievable.

At first we thought having the Hungarians take over our part of the country again would be a good thing, like it was the last time they were in power. We soon realized the Fascist Hungarians were a different breed and completely under Hitler's spell. Jews were not allowed to travel. They were not allowed to own their own business or go to school. Gentiles were not allowed to sell us food.

My father could only offer his services to Jews, and no one had any money to pay once they lost their business. Non-Jews, people who had been friendly before, began to insult us. The other children were taught bad things about us in school. Lies. We had to stay within our neighborhoods or be beaten for going elsewhere to try and find food. My father and my brother, who was five years older than me, were conscripted into a "special" army unit. There were only Jews in this unit and, unarmed, they were sent ahead of regular troops to clear minefields. Of course we did not know this and always thought they would return. They didn't.

Everyone was afraid and confused and did not understand what or why this was happening. Our rabbis told us to pray and God would make things right. My mother's parents moved in with us, as they lost their home to non-Jews. There were no explanations for these actions. If the Hungarians wanted something, they took it. Jews had no status now. No recourse.

We were thankful for our little garden, as food was so scarce, but we also shared what we could, so really no one had much of anything. My grandfather, on this side of the family, had a plumbing business but had to sell it, by law. Jozsef's father was an employee and our family's good friend, so it was sold to him and we were able to keep getting a little money from him until the authorities started snooping. That family kept trying to help however they could, smuggling food to us and to others.

Secretly, slowly, we buried plumbing pieces and jewelry in the dirt cellar under our house. Then we filled it with rocks, wood, and more dirt. We didn't know why but it seemed like we had to try to plan for the future.

Fear was our constant companion.

During the winter of 1943, Jews were told they must go to the municipal office to register for new identification papers. We did not realize this was how the Nazis were confirming their lists of Jews.

March, 1944: Drummers went through town and police put up posters stating all Jews over the age of six must wear a yellow patch on our clothes that was a Star of David, with the word "Juden" in the middle, and move to a ghetto area. I remember how humiliated everyone felt and even many Gentiles fought against that and put on yellow patches and scarves. Some were shot right in front of everyone for this. If a Jew was caught without the star or if it was creased or pinned on, they were beaten and sometimes shot, depending on the whim of the soldier.

There was no justice. We were treated worse than animals. The rabbis kept telling us to pray and God would be with us. But where was He?

The soldiers went around the entire town with guns and dogs and forced all Jews into the ghetto area, which was two long streets. Any Jew who lived somewhere else had to leave their home and move in here.

They forced us to take down the fences between our houses and build one big fence around the ghetto near the edge of town. There was mass confusion. On the way, the soldiers stopped people and went through their bags, taking jewelry and money and anything else they wanted. They pushed and shoved people, even children, and often used whips.

Our house was on one of those streets, so we didn't have to move, but now we had twenty people living in it. The rooms were small and we had to take turns lying down. The garden was jammed with people as well.

The Jews had no stores now, as we were all locked up and no one else was allowed to sell us anything. Some good people still tried to smuggle things to us. Jozsef and his brother would leave bread and fruit from their trees in a secret place for us. We all had to be very careful.

The situation was dehumanizing. Five families were moved into one apartment. Food was running out for most of the people that had to move, and we children were looking for food in garbage piles. Wood for cooking and heating was also running low. Water was in short supply.

Everything happened so quickly. I cannot describe to you some of the unthinkable things we were forced to do.

There are some things that can never be forgiven.

Our people kept saying, "Don't give up hope."

How could we find hope?

In spite of all this, mother would always hug me and say, "Hope survives."

Just before we were herded into the ghetto, Jozsef's parents came to my mother with a plan. They had a sister who was a nun in a convent a few hours away and they were trying to protect some Jews. When a nun died, they did not report or record it with the authorities as they did before. Someone could forge papers for me and they would smuggle me clothes and take me to the convent.

I did not want to leave what was left of my family and my friends. When we were forced into the ghetto, my mother and grandparents insisted it had to be now.

I argued to stay but they would not hear of it.

I was eighteen.

We hugged good-bye but we believed we would all be together again. The Nazis were telling us we would be moved into the brickyard by the railroad tracks and taken on trains to be relocated. Perhaps a better life waited for us. Perhaps there was a reason for all of this. Everyone was collecting the few valuables they had left and preparing for the trip. It was almost a relief. But most of us were still very afraid. We just didn't know of what.

So the plan was set. Some of us kids had figured out a way to sneak in and out of the ghetto at night through the sewers. It was horrible, but we were desperate. It was impossible to escape but we could forage for food scraps and bits of wood.

That night Andrew was waiting at an appointed spot with clothes for me without the star. I put them on. He told me not to look at anyone and walk quickly. When a soldier stopped us, Andrew said we had gone to throw stones into the ghetto and taunt the Jews. It was an unspeakable moment. The guard laughed and told us to hurry home.

A wagon was set up behind their house

with a secret compartment. After I
climbed in, it was covered with dirt topped
with horse and donkey manure. Jozsef
and Andrew would pretend to deliver this
to the convent for their gardens. The
moisture from it seeped through the cracks
of my hiding place. I had to hide there all
night. We could not go out on the road until
dawn. It was difficult to be quiet and not
choke. They were stopped by soldiers on the
road but the smell was so bad, they waved
us on. I thought I would die in that cart,
because dust came in from the bottom
and terrible seepage came from the top.
What saved me was a small cloth sack my
mother had made, filled with herbs, which
I held to my nose. With every jostle of
the cart, every clop of the donkey's hooves,
pain shot through my heart.

We went into a barn behind the
convent, where the nuns rushed me into
a stall to put on a habit. I never got to
say thank you or good-bye to the brothers.

Until May, 1945 I lived as a nun. It
was hard to be around anything religious
because I felt God had forsaken the Jews.
The words of prayer meant nothing to
me, and I sang them merely phonetically.
Religion became a mockery for me.

The nuns were able to take in two other
Jewish girls and we knew each other from

town. It was a comfort to have each other, but we shared the sorrow and fear of being separated from our families. There were also fifteen much younger Jewish boys and girls hidden in the cellars behind the catacombs.

We had to pretend in every way to be part of the chapter. We were always afraid. That feeling never left. The nuns were kind and did their best and sacrificed tremendously. Soldiers often came to take food. They took everything we grew except for what they allotted us and what we could hide. They kept track of what we were growing, so we had to be very sneaky and we were.

Sometimes we had to sew their uniforms. They would walk closely around us and leer at us during prayers to make sure we really were singing and not faking.

They said that Hitler was getting rid of every single Jew. They were all being killed. How could that be true? We felt sick to look at them or hear them, but we didn't believe it.

I worried about my family all the time. I cried at night not knowing how they were or where they were. Once they even took the Mother Superior out to the courtyard and threatened to shoot her if she did not admit she was hiding Jews. She denied it over and over, and eventually they left after hitting her in the head with the rifle butt.

In May, 1945—I don't remember the date, as days meant nothing to us—Russian soldiers appeared and told us the war was over. We did not believe them, until people from the nearby village came the next day to say it was true.

No one knew what to do. I was desperate to leave and go back to my family, but we were still afraid to do anything.

Then Jozsef and Andrew arrived to collect me a few days later. I cannot say anything more about that. It was overwhelming saying hello to them and good-bye to the nuns. I still did not realize they had all saved my life. I had no idea what I had missed.

We returned to town in a cart pulled by a very skinny donkey that had somehow not been eaten. We rode mostly in silence, as no one was able to talk about the horror that had occurred during the months since I left. There seemed to be no Jews in town now. I saw none I knew or anyone who even looked remotely Jewish. Strangers were living in all of our houses. When we went to my home, the people thought they were seeing a ghost when I stood in front of them. Jozsef told them to get out and they did. We waited while they moved their things but most of what they were using was ours.

I kept walking through the house and out into the little garden over and over. Everything was a mess. Where was my family? When would I see them?

In the weeks that followed, people would leave things at my door that they had taken from our house. They thought we would never return. Most things were lost forever. My mother's best Gentile friend, Mrs. Sandor, brought me the Persian rug my father had given me for my room on my seventh birthday. Before the ghetto, when things were getting bad, my mother had given her the carpet and a box of linens to keep for us. You know they have been my most prized possessions, and I hope will be yours.

Slowly we began to hear the horror of what had happened after I went to the convent. I don't know if anyone has ever found the words that express the moment when one's spirit is completely crushed, as mine was then. There is a numbness. Somehow your body still functions but thoughts cannot connect. Disbelief. A suspension of all that was real or true before that moment.

What I learned was this. In May, right after I went to the convent, everyone in the ghetto was moved to the brickyard and every day trains came and took them away. No one knew to where. The soldiers told the Jews they were just being relocated. We learned even Eichmann was there directing things. All the Jewish people had been sent to Auschwitz.

The will to live is a force of immense strength. Even when your heart is broken into a million pieces and feeling beyond repair, there is something in the human spirit that keeps going. From this time, I understood whenever I read about someone else expressing this. Whether I wanted to or not, I was going to keep living. As Nietzsche said, "That which does not kill us makes us stronger." I learned this philosophy many years later but I know this was the force that drove me. I realized that I was alone. I knew that in my aloneness I had to learn to be strong, to live for the others who did not survive. And I began from that moment.

No one had been safe from the Nazi terror. Jozsef's and Andrew's father had been hanged in the square with seven other men after they were accused of helping Jews. The Nazis made everyone come to the square to watch and no one was allowed to remove the bodies. His business was given away. Their mother became very ill after that and passed away. They were orphans, as I seemed to be too.

Why had we been spared? Why had the others been taken? Were our people so terrible they needed to be exterminated? How could this have happened? While the world watched?

The Russian Communists were now in control and life was not good. They were not like the Nazis, but still they made life difficult for everyone.

Jozsef, Andrew, and I quietly worked in the basement at night by candlelight and dug up the plumbing pieces. We had to sell them a few at a time and hoped we would not be reported. When we saved enough money, we started a bakery in my house. We sold bread, biscuits, and palachinta, because I could make so many paper-thin crepes. I also took in sewing. That's how we survived.

Jozsef and Andrew helped in every way and went to Budapest to buy flour and sugar on the black market. They also worked in the lumberyard.

Every day I hoped someone in our family would appear. I never gave up hope. Hope survives, my mother had said.

None returned. A few members of the Jewish community did make their way back. They had either been hidden like me or survived the horror of Auschwitz and were like ghosts. One woman had been in the same cattle car as my mother and grandparents.

I cannot begin to describe how I felt. The loss, the anger, the sorrow . . .

Jozsef and I fell in love. Now it didn't matter if a Jew married a Gentile. We both felt we had no religion anyway. God had forsaken all of us. After two years we decided to leave. Over many months we had slowly exchanged our money for diamonds in Budapest. Jozsef and Andrew would always go together, each time to a different trader, and it was a very risky undertaking.

We also took the small gems from the jewelry we had buried before the war. I sewed tiny secret compartments into your father's underwear to hide them. This was our little nest egg to try and begin our lives again. It wasn't a lot, but it was enough. I took the carpet and the box of linens to Mrs. Sandor, as my mother had done.

We had one mission before we left. I feel no shame in telling you this, but know you will be shocked. People in the village had talked about the collaborators and traitors, and your father discovered who had betrayed his father. He and his brother vowed revenge. We had to move quickly when we were suddenly told we would make our escape to Austria the next night.

I baked my palachinta with an extra ingredient in the apricot preserves filling and had them ready for the vulgar, loud carpenter who came by every day, always demanding a discount. His name was Miklos Nemecht. We never knew if the rat poison did its job, but we had to try. It was a small act of revenge for a horrific betrayal, and we felt no regret.

We snuck out secretly the next night, hiding in the back of a truck under a pile of debris. It was dusty and uncomfortable and fear was our companion once again. This time I had my Jozsef to comfort and calm me, but the memories of the past years stayed very close to the surface. It was a terrible night. Near the Austrian border we were taken down an abandoned logging road and dropped off. We had to walk for several hours following faint yellow marks on trees, which were difficult to see in the dim light of near dawn.

We came upon a roughly built cabin, where we had been told to wait. Inside there was bread and water in the cupboard and soon a couple arrived in a very old car. They took us to a safe house in Vienna. After a few days we were given new identity papers but with our proper names. We would work in a factory there until the plans were set for us to leave for Canada.

A woman there contacted Mrs. Sandor for us, and she delivered the carpet and linens to me after a month or so. She came on the train to Vienna and I met her at the station. She said she would never forgive herself for not doing something, anything, to save Mother and her parents. She said many, many people were struggling with this. I told her I knew there was nothing anyone could do against that evil. She was a true friend, and we cried as we parted.

When we came to Canada, the carpet and linens were all I had to remind me of the life I left behind. The life that was so horrendously stolen from me, and so many millions of others. We vowed not to speak of it and we didn't. In Canada we had love on which to build our new life and that's what we did.

After a while we felt safe. Canada was a good place to begin again. Soon Andrew came too and we were the only family we had. And we had hope. And then we had you—the joy of our life.

Katica, do not ever fear being alone but rather find your strength within. You will build a new life and you will love life again too. You will figure out what matters most. I know you will always feel our love filling your heart wherever you are.

always feel my arms around you, my darling daughter.

Anyu xoxoxo

Katherine closed her eyes. Leaning her head back against the cushions, she waited for the tears to end without attempting to stop them. *Let them come,* she thought, *tears for so many innocent people . . . for man's inhumanity to man . . . for my beautiful parents . . .*

Filled with despair and completely drained, she sat with the book closed on her lap.

Visions of her parents filled the spaces of her mind. She had so much to be thankful for. Gratitude, appreciation, and optimism had driven them. She wondered how they ever managed to rise above the horror they had survived to become the people they were. They were her heroes, like thousands of other survivors were to others all over the world. She wanted to hold her mother and father and Uncle Andrew. She wanted to cry with them and tell them how sorry she was. She knew they had not wanted that.

Getting up after a long while, Katherine walked over to the carpet hanging on the wall of the small room where her mother last slept. She put her cheek up against the silky threads in rich but worn shades of gold, brown, green, and red, and closed her eyes. Running her fingers over the softness, she envisioned her mother sitting playing on it as a child, joyfully pointing out the colorful animals so skillfully woven into the pattern. She felt a chill at the sadness and fear that would have filled the house as the carpet was rolled up and secreted to Mrs. Sandor to escape being stolen or worse.

What happiness and sorrow this carpet had known. Her mother's history lived on in its threads. It would always be there to remind her of this—and to remind her that her problems were not as big as they seemed.

8

It had already been a month since her mother's quiet family funeral. Elisabeth's belongings had been shared among Katherine and Andrea's family, with the remainder going to charity. Katherine converted the small sewing room that had, in the final months, been her mother's bedroom back into an office. Otherwise the house was left much as it had been.

"There's no reason to rush around making changes," Katherine said to Andrea when she spent a day with her a few weekends later. "Besides, I like the feeling that this is how Mom and Dad wanted it. I'm not ready to let go of that."

Andrea nodded. Katherine went on.

"Through my counseling I read some helpful books about the process of loss. It never really occurred to me that what I was feeling after James left was initially grief as well—not necessarily for the loss of James, but for everything else that went with our life together."

"Do you think that's helping now with losing your mom?"

"Definitely. But there's something else that is dragging me down, and I've got to share it with you. It's part of your history too—and I've been putting it off."

Katherine walked to the dining room table, where she still had a few items of her mother's that required attention. Andrea wore a puzzled expression as she was handed the linen-wrapped binder.

❧

On a Saturday morning later in March, Katherine turned off the main highway just past Kitchener and Waterloo. She never tired of the familiar maze of country roads that wound through abundant farmland leading to Andrea and Terrence's home.

Dried brown stubble poked through spots of lingering snow and the feathery plumes on strawlike stems of last year's pampas grass waved gently in the spring breeze. Driving slowly, she passed several Mennonites in their horse-drawn carriages. *A sure sign of spring,* she noted, passing many open buggies along with the enclosed models.

Driving up the narrow laneway to the century farmhouse, Katherine spotted other signals that might not be noticed in the city. The distinctive leaves of skunk cabbage were beginning to unfurl in patches here and there. Clumps of pussy willow planted years before by Andrea and her daughter, Kate, glistened silver when caught by the sun. Snow was melting in patches throughout the forested areas, while the soil in the fields gave the appearance of being almost ready to plow. The heavy snowfalls of the winter had provided for deep watering as they melted, and the furrows of autumn beckoned to be turned as they dried in the sun.

After a stroll through the property, Andrea and Katherine sat in the warm sun on the front-porch stairs.

"Okay, Kat," said Andrea, her voice full of energy and affection, "it's time to give some serious thought to the future."

Rolling her eyes, Kat squinted at her cousin. "I knew this was coming sooner or later."

Andrea nodded. "It's later and it's time!"

They sat quietly for a few seconds.

"The last six months of your life have been . . . um . . . rather dramatic."

"To say the least," Katherine replied, shaking her head.

"You keep saying you are doing okay, but somehow I sense you aren't. Talk to me, Kat. Tell me how you're really feeling. Please!"

After a lengthy hesitation, Andrea slipped her arm around her cousin's shoulders as Katherine softly spoke. "I'm really down. With Mom gone now, I have truly been feeling alone. I'm trying to convince myself I'm okay alone, that I can do this for the rest of my life. I'm just not feeling good about it."

"I know you haven't been to the counselor recently. Do you think you should go back to her?"

Nodding, Kat continued, "I might have to. I can't go on like this."

"So, Terrence and I have been talking about it, and we think you should take a vacation. Just get out of town. Go somewhere and have a complete change of scene! What do you think?"

Katherine stared intently at her cousin for quite a while and slowly nodded, eyebrows raised.

"I think that might be an idea. Hadn't really considered it, but y'know, the counselor did tell me I should consider doing something outside my comfort zone. That would qualify." She paused for a few seconds and added, "Do you know, crazy as this sounds, except for the odd conference in Montreal or Vancouver, I have never gone away without James . . . in twenty-two years . . ."

"Yes, as a matter of fact, that's exactly what we were talking about. You need your own life," Andrea exclaimed. "Trust us, Kat, you are w-a-a-a-y overdue!"

They sat in the kitchen at the long handcrafted pine table that wore its hundred and fifty years proudly, while Andrea made a mocha and a latte with her new coffee machine and tossed ideas around.

A beach vacation on a Caribbean island?

A hiking holiday?

Andrea gingerly broached the subject of cycling.

"Don't even go there," said Katherine.

Suddenly Andrea leaped up to grab her laptop from her desk.

Returning to the table, she opened her computer and pulled up her bookmarks.

"I've just had a brainwave, Kat! Do a home exchange! Here's the website we use. It's the perfect idea for you!"

Laughing at her cousin's enthusiasm, Katherine looked at her in disbelief. "Don't be crazy!"

Shaking her finger, Andrea replied, "Absolutely not. People often think it's a big deal until they try it. Trust me, it's the best way to travel!"

Katherine pulled her chair alongside her cousin.

"Here's how it works. It's so simple, it's unbelievable, and we are going to register you right now! That way you can take your time and look at the properties at your leisure and think about where you might want to go."

"And I can see you aren't taking no for an answer," Kat said, laughing.

Andrea was unstoppable. "Your parents' house—I mean, your house, because that's what it is now—is the perfect exchange property. It's got enough space for a family, and the location couldn't be better, with shops and a subway stop just a few blocks away. Trust me! This is going to be good! Let's take a virtual trip right now! If you could choose one part of the world, any place you want, where would it be?"

Katherine closed her eyes and nodded her head as a smile slowly spread. "The South of France, no question . . . the South of France . . ."

"Of course! That's where you took the language course a zillion years ago! I remember that! Brilliant . . . here we go!"

Andrea clicked on the map. First Europe, then France, next the Côte d'Azur, and then a long list appeared on the screen.

"All of those properties are available for exchange?" Katherine asked in amazement.

"Oui!" Andrea shouted. "See what I said? There are so many possibilities! Of course, you need to take a look at each listing to see what appeals to you and also to be certain your listing is what that person wants. Let's narrow it down to a specific town."

"I stayed in Villefranche-sur-Mer. That's where the language school was, and I know it's still there, because I've looked it up online a few times just to give myself a thrill," Katherine said with a wry grin.

"Too bad you never got back there when you enjoyed it so much."

"You know, since James left, I've thought over and over again how I allowed myself to be controlled by him. I'm not blaming him—it was always ultimately my choice—but for me not to go back to Europe for twenty-two years because he didn't want to fly is so lame, I can't believe it."

Andrea nodded. "We often make choices in life that amaze us when we consider them later. As they say, hindsight is twenty-twenty, huh?"

"Twenty-twenty indeed! You can't imagine how much my vision has improved in the last few months! Thank you for doing this. I know how I'll spend my spare time for the next while."

Grinning at each other, they looked up as Andrea's husband, Terrence, came into the kitchen from the garden, where he had been taking stock of the winter's effect. As he washed his hands in the mudroom adjoining the kitchen, Andrea told him what they had been doing.

Terrence chuckled. "Andrea should be receiving a commission from that website. I can't tell you how many of our friends she's signed up."

Andrea laughed along with him, her head bobbing with excitement. "As if Kat doesn't know that. She's been listening to me go on about our great home exchanges for years."

"Yup," agreed Katherine. "James always thought you were crazy for allowing strangers to stay in your place. He wouldn't have considered it in a thousand years."

"Isn't it nice you can make up your own mind about these things without having his overbearing influence?" Terrence asked. "Sorry, Kat, perhaps I shouldn't have said that, but honestly, the more I hear how he controlled your lives, the happier I am you are out of that marriage. You have a lot of living to do!"

Katherine stood and hugged him.

"I'm not sure about the 'lot of living' part, but I have to admit I'm not having a hard time accepting that I'm the one who makes all the decisions about my life now. There's no question I really miss my mom, but I do not miss my former husband. Period. Full stop!"

It had taken Katherine almost six months to say that out loud, and as soon as she did, it felt right. Not that it removed the hurt, but she felt a certain degree of success at being able to banish good memories of him from her thoughts.

Pausing briefly as her words sunk in with everyone, Katherine turned the subject back to home exchange.

"Putting Andrea's chronic optimism aside—seriously, Terrence, how do you feel about these exchanges? Any problems ever?"

"Nope," he answered without hesitation. "Each one has been great, although there's no question you have to be flexible."

"Meaning?"

"For example, our first exchange was to Portugal—a holiday house in the Algarve, with a pool—we always look for a property with a pool. The exchange family went to the condo we have at Blue Mountain. They wanted to go in the summer to see that part of Canada after they visited relatives in Toronto."

Andrea added, "But remember, this was in 2000, and they didn't have all the listings on the Internet yet, so we just saw photos in the catalogue. Most communication then was by fax or phone! Seems kind of archaic now, doesn't it?"

"Right," Terrence continued, "it's so much better and easier today since you can see exactly what you are getting."

"So what was the problem?" Katherine asked.

"Well, it turned out there wasn't a comfortable chair to sit in anywhere! It was all wicker with thin cushions! Looked nice, but felt terrible!"

"And the bed in the master bedroom had a sag in the middle so enormous we would immediately roll into it."

Terrence and Andrea both laughed at the memory.

"So we went to the nearest local housewares store and bought a couple of fat cushions! Besides, the weather was so fantastic we were out by the pool or at the beach most of the time anyway."

"Not a big deal," Andrea said, "and we fixed the problem with the bed easily by stuffing our empty suitcases under the sag.

"Anyhow, today when you go online you'll read other people's experiences. You can check with others who have exchanged at the property you are considering for a referral too."

"I was skeptical when Andrea first suggested we do it." Terrence said. "The reality is we have remained in touch with every single family or couple we exchanged with—seven so far. Maybe just an e-mail or Christmas card, but the connection remains. It's a nice feeling."

Andrea beamed now. "The best thing about house exchange to me is that this reaffirms my belief that most people are good, kind, and honest all over the world. You rarely hear of a problem!"

Katherine and Terrence smiled at each other and nodded. That was Andrea all right!

"Molly is right," Katherine said to both of them, "when she calls Andrea the Goddess of Serendipity."

Terrence put his arms around his wife, giving her an encompassing bear hug, and said, "Just one of the many reasons I love her."

James always said too much hugging just makes it meaningless, Kat was reminded, looking on with envy before she banished the thought.

"Okay," said Terrence, "if the home exchange promotion is over for the moment, let's have lunch and get out to the sugar bush to empty the sap buckets."

The afternoon was spent emptying the sap into the large cans on the back of the tractor that Terrence then transferred to the boiling vats in the sugar shack. Once that task was completed, they spent several hours raking the dead grasses and clearing dried remnants from the raised-bed gardens.

As the sun was sitting lower in the sky, Terrence suggested they go into St. Jacobs for dinner at one of their favorite spots. "Let's just see which place is the least busy and pop in. It's a little early for tourist season, and since we don't have any kids at home this weekend, the bill will even be manageable!"

"Great idea," said Katherine. "My meal preparation hasn't been stellar this past month. I could go for some of that delicious Mennonite cooking."

More home exchange stories were the focus of conversation during dinner. Katherine had thought about it for a good part of the afternoon.

Terrence insisted it was time to take a break and make their dessert choice.

"Shoofly pie for me," Katherine requested, "with just a dab of vanilla ice cream, please."

"Make that two," said Terrence. "I only have it when you're here, you know, Kat. You're a bad influence when it comes to sweet stuff."

Katherine nodded in agreement, happy to own up to that charge.

"Okay, I'm becoming warily convinced about exchanges and feeling just a tad excited about the possibilities with this," Katherine admitted.

9

Since Andrea had signed Katherine up on the home exchange website, she had been receiving a couple of inquiries each week. Many of them would not work for her, time-wise, or were in locations other than France, and she had decided she was going to focus on making that French dream come true.

Andrea had also recommended that Kat include her listing in the "short notice" category.

"Most people begin to organize their holiday many months before. You want to catch the last-minute planners too," she had explained.

Sure enough, Katherine quickly received an inquiry marked "Urgent" from a couple in Chicago who wanted to make a spur-of-the-moment trip to Toronto for Easter weekend. They offered a modern two-bedroom apartment in a downtown high-rise overlooking Lake Michigan.

Molly had taken to dropping in on Katherine every week or so if she saw lights on in the house, calling her cell first.

They also managed to plan dinner at least once a month now.

Katherine poured them each a glass of pinot grigio and put some cheese and olives on the coffee table as they sat in the living room.

"You know, I really like it when you pop in like this."

"Me too," Molly agreed. "I'm sorry your marriage fell apart, but it's been great to spend more time with you." She picked up her wine and reached over toward Katherine.

As they clinked their glasses, Molly toasted, "Here's to our friendship. I really appreciate it."

"Ditto."

"Almost fifty years of you listening to me complain!" Molly said, "Hard to believe!"

Katherine laughed. "French immersion kindergarten with Madame LaChapelle. That's where it all began. She was so nice."

Molly snorted, "I'll never know why my mother signed me up for that. At least you hung in right through high school and didn't drop out like I did."

"You stayed through grade eight. That was pretty good. Lots of kids dropped out of French then."

"I didn't have the interest in it, and the performing arts academy was a temptation that went straight to my heart."

"I can remember how excited we all were when you got accepted into the music program! What a day that was!"

They toasted again to that memory and continued reminiscing.

The music program had given Molly a sense that she had a place in the world. Her parents had divorced when she was six, and Molly and her younger brother had never been well treated. Their father in particular had been verbally abusive and swore constantly.

Both parents badmouthed each other to the two kids, leaving them confused and fragile.

"You know, Kat, I often think how odd it is that I chose to put myself in front of an audience when I suffer from such insecurities. Curious, isn't it?"

"Maybe that's how you get the love you felt was missing."

They mulled that over for a while. "At least I managed to keep a grip on reality, unlike Shawn."

Molly's heartache was palpable when she brought up this subject. Her brother, three years younger, had battled drug addiction most of his life and hadn't been heard from in two years despite Molly's best efforts to track him down. The coup de grâce for them had occurred when Molly was a year away from graduating university and her brother was in first year. Their parents had driven together to the funeral of a mutual friend on a day when the weather was very stormy. Forensics tests had indicated her father was well over the alcohol limit when he caused the accident that claimed his life and left their mother in a coma for several years.

Abandoning her hopes for a music career, Molly had acquired her real estate license so she could maintain a flexible schedule to help with the care of her mother in the seriously understaffed nursing home. She learned some important lessons during those years about the need for an elderly patient to have someone advocating for them. Every minute of her spare time was spent making certain her mother was kept clean, well nourished, and hydrated. This was not a given without daily vigilance. The reality of the nursing home had been shocking, and she learned to keep an eye on other patients nearby who had no one to help.

Molly and Shawn had struggled for years to pay bills and keep their lives moving forward. When their mother passed away, they inherited a small insurance fund. Molly went back to university to complete an education degree and became a music teacher at a venerable Catholic private school. She buried herself in her work. Weekend nights she had been the featured singer at the Blue Note for the last ten years.

Sadly, Shawn chose hard drugs, bouncing in and out of rehab.

Katherine's heart went out to Molly all over again as they worked their way through her history. "Molly, you should feel proud of every effort you made to meet the challenges through the years. It hasn't been easy."

"You are so fuckin' right about that, my friend."

Katherine always wondered if Molly's bad language was somehow her way of dealing with her frustrations. She had never been a smoker or a drinker, so maybe swearing was her outlet. Oddly, it never bothered Katherine. She just accepted it as Molly's bad habit, like chewing fingernails, and she realized Molly only swore around certain people, never strangers or at work.

As she refilled their glasses, Katherine rolled her eyes when Molly declared their evening was turning into a bit of a pity party.

"Sometimes life is just plain exhausting," said Katherine. "That's never been more evident to me than in the last six months. My energy level has tanked. My doctor says I don't have depression, but I'm definitely 'down' and need to ramp up the vitamin D."

Molly nodded. "I've noticed you haven't been brimming with your usual positive attitude, but it will take time, Kat. Trust me on that." Snorting, she added, "I've never been positive, so I don't have to worry about getting that back!"

"So what did you think of the e-mail I sent you this morning?" Katherine asked, happy to change the subject. "You didn't respond."

"That's why I dropped in tonight. I've been thinking about it all day," Molly replied, her voice dropping a notch. "It's a great idea, but I have a problem." Putting her glass down, she took a deep breath and looked down at her lap. "I can go if we drive, but I can't afford to fly."

Katherine was surprised with Molly's obvious embarrassment. "Gosh, there's not really time to drive, Molly. That would take up two days of the trip."

"Yeah, I realize that . . . just thought I would run it by you. I can't afford the airfare. I'm humiliated to admit it, actually."

"Molly, what's happened? I mean, I know you've had a tight budget paying off Shawn's bills, but I thought it was manageable. I'm so sorry. Did you tell me before and I forgot?"

"No," Molly said softly, dropping her eyes as her face reddened. "I didn't want to say anything with all you've been going through, but I've had a financial disaster."

"Oh no! Tell me what—"

Molly interrupted as she stood and began pacing, "You know how the fucking stock market has been all over the place? Well, I just happened to have the bulk of my investments in a stock that bit the dust. It's been solid for years, paying a good dividend. It's not really anyone's fault. The money manager I used was doing a good job and just didn't see this coming."

"Oh, Molly, that's awful! Will you be able to manage?"

"It's been two years since Shawn checked himself out of rehab and disappeared and the bills just keep rolling in," Molly sighed. "I'm feeling the pinch and have to keep myself on a strict budget."

Katherine reached over. "Listen, I checked Porter Airlines today and they have great rates to Chicago. Let me pay. Please! You've been such a big help to me these last few months. Let this be my treat."

Molly's face flushed with embarrassment, but before she could object, Katherine pleaded once more. "Trust me, Molly. I really want you to come with me. Please say you will."

"I just don't feel right about it."

"Let me put it this way. This is the first thing I've felt something like excited about since 'la Katastrophe,' as you call it. I won't go by myself and I don't want to ask anyone else. How's that?"

Closing her eyes, Molly let the words sink in.

"Okay, I'm in, thanks! Let's go! I'll treat us to dinner Saturday night, although it might just be pizza."

Katherine grinned and they high-fived. "Fantastic! Now I have to get back to the woman who sent the inquiry and confirm it. I told them I was interested and would let them know by tomorrow."

"The question is, can you put up with me twenty-four-seven?" Molly said.

"It's only a four-day exchange, so I think I can handle it," Katherine chuckled.

"Kat, seriously, you know I'm not always the best company. I'm moody, anal, unpredictable . . ."

Interrupting her with a shush, Katherine looked intently at her friend. "Do you think I don't know that after all these years?"

"If you're willing to take a chance, so am I. And over Easter weekend too! How convenient is that?"

"Exactly! We don't even need to take time off work."

Now that Molly was keen to go with her, Katherine finalized the arrangements and got busy making a booklet about her own house with guidance from Andrea. As well as instructions on how to operate the various appliances, she included public transit information, doctor, dentist, hospital details, her neighbor's phone number, and the location of various shops and also downloaded a map of the area.

She popped into her local bookstore and picked up two books about Toronto and the surrounding area. At the travel agent's down the street, she collected brochures about sightseeing.

Placing all the information in a wicker basket on the dining room table, she added a bottle of wine and a note saying there were special cheeses in the fridge.

Katherine was ready for her first exchange.

⚜

Molly had been right in her prediction. She wasn't the best company.

The weekend had started off well. The flight early Friday morning was quick and efficient and before noon they were settled into the condo. The concierge was aware of their pending arrival and had the keys ready for them.

The apartment was immaculate. A bottle of wine and an information book were sitting on the coffee table, along with a box of chocolates from a local chocolatier, with a note addressed to Katherine.

"Nice touch," Molly commented as Katherine opened the box. "Here's to your first exchange, Katski."

The condo was a short walk from Chicago's renowned shopping

area, the Magnificent Mile, and they decided to hit that first for lunch and some browsing. With Molly's budget issues, they had agreed they were not shopping but had just as much fun checking out the area after all they had read about it.

"I'm in such a funk about my finances. The very idea of shopping turns me off," Molly confessed.

"Well, I don't feel I need any new clothes because nothing new is happening in my life. So there you go—retail therapy is not working for us at the moment."

Seeing such famous structures as the Wrigley Building, Tribune Tower, and the Old Chicago Water Tower District was a thrill. The Mag Mile did live up to its reputation.

Twice during the afternoon Molly's cell phone had rung, with the other party hanging up after a brief period of silence. Or so she said. She looked troubled but brushed it off.

By the time they got back to the condo, Molly was complaining that her feet hurt and she felt a headache coming on, and went to lie down.

"Do you want me to wake you up for dinner?" Katherine asked.

Molly muttered she would be up in time without a problem.

She wasn't.

Tiptoeing into the darkened room a half hour before their reservation time, Kat whispered Molly's name. Molly rolled over and groaned her apology. Disappointed but sympathetic, Katherine canceled their reservation and walked down the street to a nearby deli for a couple of takeout corned beef sandwiches.

She watched television for an hour or so while she ate alone and put Molly's sandwich in the fridge.

The view across the vast city sparkled and twinkled as far as she could see from their twenty-second-floor perch. Looking around at the ultramodern decor and furnishings, she considered how different the choices were from the ones that she made for her home. There were moments it seemed rather odd knowing she was in another person's home.

As she climbed into bed with her book, she hoped Molly would feel better in the morning. It wasn't exactly the way they had planned to spend the evening.

Saturday morning they had eleven o'clock tickets for the architectural tour by boat that had been highly recommended by Dr. Henderson. The tour itself was interesting and educational, but the blustery weather made the ride turbulent. Molly was turning green, and just before they docked she dashed to the ladies' room.

"Oh God, Kat," Molly sputtered when she finally emerged, "I am so seasick. I don't think I can walk."

Leaning on Katherine, Molly hobbled down the gangplank and they hailed a cab.

Molly went back to bed and Katherine walked down to the Art Institute on her own.

Katherine was impressed with the building and its vast collection. Lingering where she chose, she couldn't help being reminded how she once would have moved about galleries as James had wished.

Molly had gathered her strength by the evening. They had dinner at a wild Russian restaurant where the excellent meal was served by bustling waiters, each determined to outdo the other's personality. A jazz club around the corner offered fine entertainment before Molly began to fade and they called it a night.

Sunday morning felt right for sleeping in, followed by a bus tour.

Monday they left the apartment as spotless as they had found it. Molly apologized a half-dozen times on the way home, and Katherine surprisingly realized she might be very happy traveling on her own.

The thought was one that simply had never crossed her mind.

10

Apprehensive, Katherine walked into her house and looked around. Everything appeared just as it had before she left.

On the kitchen table sat an envelope with her name on it. Katherine gulped as she felt the sharp jab of a bad memory. Closing her eyes and shaking her head, she cleared it quickly away and opened the thank-you note.

Smiling, she thought, *Andrea is right. Home exchange is very cool.*

After unpacking her things and calling Andrea to give her a detailed report on the weekend, Katherine heated up some soup. Taking it with her to her desk, she sat down, turned on her computer, and signed in to the home exchange website. She was hooked.

Scrolling through the properties—everything from castles to apartments to modern homes and ancient village and farm properties—she didn't find any in France that indicated a desire to visit Toronto. In spite of that, it was great fun just looking at the listings.

As she settled into bed later, she smiled sleepily. *Now I have something worth dreaming about . . .*

⚜

Walking across the street to yoga with Lucy after work on Tuesday, Katherine told her all about the weekend trip.

Lucy thought for a minute and then suggested, "Here's how I see it. The exchange experience was perfect. Molly's company, not so much."

"That's about it," Katherine agreed, "although it wasn't really her fault. She just seems to be dealing with a lot of issues, some of which I was completely unaware. I wish I could help her."

"If you feel like telling me more about it sometime, Katherine, perhaps I can suggest something. Obviously I don't know the details."

Katherine nodded. This whole experience of spending time with girlfriends was very new to her. She had always confided in James, and she wasn't used to talking to anyone else about someone's personal life.

"I guess I am being a bit vague, but I kind of feel uncomfortable talking about Molly's issues. Let me think about it, but thanks, Lucy. I know you want to help."

"We have a saying: 'Life is simple, but we insist on making it complicated.' Maybe what's troubling Molly is not as complicated as it seems."

"I hope you're right. I feel concerned, but then, I've never spent that kind of time with her, so it was a surprise. I might be overreacting. Oops, we'd better get into class!"

❧

Later that evening Katherine stared into the bathroom mirror as she massaged a night cream over her face and down her neck. She had been thinking about Molly ever since her yoga class. Something just didn't feel right.

On Wednesday morning, Molly left a voicemail message apologizing, again, for not being the best company in Chicago. Katherine left one in return suggesting they have a quick lunch on Saturday.

Ordering a chicken pad Thai and green mango salad to share, they stared glumly out the window at the early April snow shower.

"I so frickin' did not want to see snow again," groaned Molly.

"We really have had more than our share of it this winter," Katherine agreed. "I love it, but I'm ready for spring. A few weeks ago up in St. Jacobs, I thought it was here!"

All talk of weather vanished as they savored the tantalizing spicy, slightly sweet, and richly flavored dishes before them, fragrant with exotic turmeric and tamarind.

"Who knew mango and onion would complement each other," Katherine said, helping herself to another serving of green mango salad.

"Man! I love this food!" Molly said. "Excuse me for talking with my mouth full—it's so-o-o delish!"

Katherine laughed and nodded her agreement, but as time passed she felt Molly was not herself.

"Molly, are you okay?"

"What do you mean?"

"I don't know. I sensed something was bothering you last weekend. You were so excited about going to Chicago and then Saturday afternoon your mood changed dramatically—like something happened. But what?"

"Nope, nothing happened. I just got one of my horrible headaches. Bad timing. Like I said, I really am sorry. I didn't mean to spoil the weekend."

"You didn't," Katherine hurried to assured her. "Not at all. It was still a lot of fun and we crammed a lot into a short time! I'm so glad you . . ."

The ringing of Molly's phone interrupted the conversation.

Molly hesitated with an apologetic look as Kat stared back at her. "Better take it. Might be one of my students," Molly mumbled.

Obviously it wasn't. Molly attempted to mask her look of concern as she put her phone away, having said nothing more than hello.

"Why don't you just keep your phone shut off and take the messages later?"

"I'm sorry, Kat. I just can't."

"And why not?"

"The first and most important reason is that I've never lost hope that one of those calls will be from Shawn. I never know what number he might call from, so I kind of have to answer every one. If he has to leave a message, he might not."

"And . . . ?"

"Well, when it's Saturday, it could be one of my students canceling at the last minute. God knows what phone they might be using."

"Makes sense," Katherine agreed, "under normal circumstances. This doesn't seem normal, somehow."

"It's not frickin' normal, I'll give you that. If I shut off the ringer and don't answer, whoever is doing this calls back until my voicemail is totally jammed. And they use different numbers all the time, so I can't even block a number!"

"Can't the phone service do something about this? That's awful!"

"It's really starting to get to me. I don't know what I'm going to do."

Molly went on to say that at first there would just be silence on the line. In the last few weeks that had changed, and now the caller was doing the classic heavy breathing and every once in a while would say her name. Her voice trembled. "It's horrible, Kat. I can't tell if it's a male or female voice. It's goddamn spooky."

"Oh, Molly. Something has to be done."

"I agree, but I feel stuck because I won't change my number . . . Shawn . . ."

The conversation veered to the subject of Molly's brother. Katherine knew how haunted Molly was by his disappearance and her feelings of inadequacy at being unable to track him down. Kat often wondered how someone could simply vanish as he seemed to have.

Molly looked heartbroken as she reminded Katherine how Shawn had loved to hear her sing from the time he was very young. "Sometimes I think that's what really helped me to develop as a singer before I even knew that's what I wanted to do. I used to sing to him for hours—especially when our parents were turning the air blue around us."

"Strange how things happen," Katherine agreed. "Let's trust you'll sing for him again. Don't lose that hope."

"Nope, I never will."

"By the way, next Saturday I'm coming to catch your show at the Blue Note. I promise. I've been meaning to for ages, and Andrea and Terrence said they'd like to come too. How does that sound?"

"Sounds fan-fucking-tastic!"

11

Katherine spent the remainder of Saturday afternoon in the basement. She had pulled boxes into the middle of the floor and was slowly going through them, saving what she wanted and purging the rest. A strong urge to simplify her life had resulted in her taking several large bags of papers to a recycling depot that morning, and she was determined to continue with her plan to adopt a minimalist style of living.

"The new me," she described to Andrea in an e-mail. "I want to keep every aspect of my life uncluttered from now on. No more hanging on to unnecessary stuff! I'm slowly beginning to climb from the bottom of the well, and I know my recent visits to my counselor have helped."

The rejection and lingering pain from the shock of James leaving still made its presence known from time to time, but overall she was coping. Nights were the worst. She had never minded having time to herself when James was working late, and she could always find ways to be amused—most of which revolved around a good book or the History Channel or cooking a new recipe from the Food Network.

Molly was pressuring her to hook up with her online and play bridge, but Kat hadn't tried that yet. In fact, she really hadn't played bridge since her university days, although her card evenings with her mom through the winter had revived her enjoyment in that.

Andrea, a keen bridge player since university, had also encouraged Kat to take up the game. "Not just because it's fun and something you can do everywhere, but it's also a great way to meet people . . . if you are so inclined . . ." she had said.

Katherine simply didn't feel like meeting people right now. She still found herself wondering if she would be on her own forever. At this point, in some ways it didn't feel like such a bad idea.

Never, she knew, did she want to be so vulnerable again. Through her counseling, a number of books helped put things in perspective. A line had recently resonated within her: *"Trust takes years to build and seconds to shatter."*

It had certainly only taken seconds for her to read that note and find her life shattered. Being deceived and betrayed had devastated her. But then she would be reminded of her mother and the trust that had vanished from Elisabeth's young world, the betrayal and horror she had endured, the lives that had been shattered. Katherine would give herself a shake. *No comparison, Kat, move on.*

Her strong connection with Andrea had gone a long way to keeping her sane through the worst days. Her friendships with Molly and Lucy were growing in their own unique ways.

Lucy had been instrumental in getting her plugged into yoga classes, and the time they shared there was meaningful, even though there wasn't the opportunity for a lot of conversation. Because of this, their exchanges at work had shifted slightly, and they often discreetly touched on personal issues. That had never happened before. Knowing each other better as individuals, there were lighter moments in the office, and that was fun.

And Molly. Well, she chuckled, Molly didn't realize what a close friend she was in spite of her issues. Somehow her idiosyncrasies made her all the dearer to Katherine, who felt good about being able to offer her support in return. She sensed she had only scratched the surface of what was going on in Molly's life.

Katherine was beginning to feel something closer to normal. She knew she didn't feel happy, but the anger and disappointment that had plagued her were diminishing. She missed her mother terribly, but she had moments of a sense of calm in her life.

Taking a break in the early evening, she contemplated dinner without much enthusiasm. Usually she settled for a quick and easy salad when she was in a mood like this, but tonight that didn't call to her. She knew there was only one solution.

Popcorn.

The old-fashioned hand popper from her childhood still hung in her mother's pantry, and they had used it often since Katherine had come to live with her. Many a bowl had been shared as they played their evening card games.

Shaking it over an element on the stove, Katherine also melted some butter in a small pot and within a few minutes the aroma filled the kitchen. A hot bowl of buttered popcorn was soon ready.

Placing it on the desk beside her computer along with a large glass of water, Katherine settled in with a smile on her face.

Checking her e-mail, which she did several times a day now that she was registered for a home exchange, she felt a little flutter as an unfamiliar and very French-sounding address appeared.

We are Madeleine and Jean-Pierre Lallibert. We are at last minute to try to plan our holiday. Would you like to visit to our little farmhouse for first two weeks June. We hope you like our pictures. We you wait the answer.

In the Mont Ventoux area, cozy 250-year-old farmhouse, big garden, in the Luberon, near Avignon in the beautiful Provencal landscape. We are just close to the little village Sainte-Mathilde. Walk to the boulangerie for café and croissant on your way to daily market.

> We are surrounded with beautiful villages and scenery
> from Mont Ventoux, local gorges and the Plateau de
> Sault which is covered with lavender fields until the end
> of July.
>
> You would enjoy our Provencal markets and festivals
> in the different villages and relax in this typical
> atmosphere . . . and lots of wines to taste. There is
> a bike and you can ride around the house in nearby
> vineyards.

The photos of the property were like something described in her favorite Peter Mayle books about Provence. The weathered stone house with blue shutters and door, worn terra-cotta roof, and several outbuildings surrounded by slightly overgrown gardens of the happiest looking perennials. Oh, and sunflowers! Just behind them she could see vineyards stretching to the distant hills.

Something told her this was meant to be. It wasn't supposed to happen so soon, and here it was. She couldn't wait to hear what Lucy would say about the meaning of it all.

She immediately googled the area and read more about it. Transportation was easy, with a flight to Paris and then the TGV, the high-speed train, to Avignon, where she would rent a car. She soon realized she already had it all planned.

"Andrea!" Katherine almost shouted into the phone. "You won't believe it, but I just got an exchange inquiry from France, and it's perfect. I can't believe it but it's perfect and I really want to go but I just don't know what to do and . . ."

"Whoa!" Andrea interrupted. "Are you excited or what? Slow down and start over, please!"

Calming down, Katherine told her the details before Andrea brought a little reality to the situation.

"That's just over a month away. Isn't that a bit of a rush? A bit too soon?"

"Too soon for what? I have enough vacation time, since all I've taken this year was a week after mom died. The house doesn't need to have anything done to it. Ever since my trip to France as a student, I've kept my passport up to date. All I have to do is book my ticket and pack my bags."

"Who is going to go with you?"

"No one."

There was silence from Andrea for a few seconds and then, tentatively, she asked, "Are you sure about that?"

"Never surer. I thought about this when Molly and I went to Chicago. I realized that I might want to travel alone. I can't ask her this time anyway because school will still be in. I can't ask you because I know what a busy time it is on the farm for you guys. I can't ask Lucy because she simply can't get away from her family obligations. So that leaves me, myself, and I."

Andrea was amazed at Katherine's assured tone of voice.

"I want to go on my own. It's important to me."

12

A week later, the ringing startled Katherine out of a deep sleep. Looking at her clock, she noticed it was 1:30 a.m. as she fumbled for her cell phone.

Her first thought, for a split second, was of her mother. *Some habits are hard to break.* Then Molly's terrified voice cut through the heaviness. "Kat, oh God, Kat!"

Sitting bolt upright, Katherine was fully awake. "Molly, what's wrong? What's going on?"

Sobbing into the phone, Molly struggled to speak.

"Are you okay? What's happening? Molly, talk to me!"

"Oh God, Kat. Can you come over? I am just freaking."

"Try to calm down and talk to me. Of course I'll come, but tell me what's wrong?"

"Uh, gross . . . just . . . gross . . ." Molly sputtered.

"What's gross? Please tell me first that you are all right!" Katherine demanded.

"Sorry, I'm okay . . . but . . . it's the phone calls . . . cranked up a fuckin' notch . . . it's gotta be . . ." Molly replied, slowly regaining some composure. "Okay . . . first of all, I've had calls every day this week. All different times, all different numbers. I actually did turn my phone off a couple of nights because I couldn't take it and I needed to try and sleep."

"And you never told me—"

"No, I know, but anyway . . ." She sniffed and blew her nose loudly. "Sorry . . . fuck . . . !"

"What the hell is going on?"

"I just got home, right? There was a florist's box in front of my apartment door. A nice white box with a gorgeous bow. When I opened it . . ." Molly coughed and gagged before continuing. "It was full of dead flowers and . . . a dead rat, like a rotting dead rat . . ." She gagged again on the last few words.

"Oh Molly," Katherine gasped, her mouth suddenly dry. "How awful."

Molly cleared her throat loudly. "Honestly, maggots and everything . . . I almost threw up right then and there . . ." A loud choking noise forced Kat to pull the phone away from her ear.

"Molly?"

"Sorry . . . I'm okay. Shit! I put it all straight down the garbage chute. I'm sitting here on the couch shaking . . ."

"I'll be right over," Katherine assured her, scrunching her face in disgust.

"Kat, I'm sorry." Molly sniffed. "I'm really losing it."

"Don't worry. We can keep talking while I drive over. I'll put you on speaker while I throw some clothes on."

"No, wait . . . wait . . ." Molly said after blowing her nose. "Just talking to you is helping. Really, I don't want you to come at this hour. I shouldn't have asked you to do that."

"No problem."

"Seriously, I'm feeling better having you at the end of the line."

"Good Lord," Katherine whispered. "Who is doing this to you? This is beyond awful."

"I called the super right away. He was freaked that I was so freaked, and then he was freaked when I described it. I'm sure he didn't

appreciate being wakened, but he went all around the lobby and outside and couldn't see anything. He offered to call the police, but . . ."

"But the security video camera in the lobby must have picked up
something," Katherine suggested.

"Ha! Remember, I'm not exactly in a luxury building. We don't
have one."

"I think you have to talk to the police. I really do."

They spoke for a few minutes more and Molly became calmer.
"I don't want to stay here. I'm just too spooked. Can I come to your
place?"

"I don't want you to go out by yourself. Call a cab. What about the
one you use to come home from the Note?"

"Yup. I'll call Fred. Shit, he just brought me home! He'll come right
to the lobby door."

"You buzz him right up to your apartment door. I don't want you
taking any chances!" Katherine warned.

"Good idea," Molly's voice broke and faded to a whisper. "This is
surreal. I can't frickin' believe it!"

Katherine shook her head at the other end of the phone. "Me
either . . . it's like a Stephen King story. I'll be watching out the window for you. Call me when you're in the cab—and don't open your
door for anyone else."

A half hour later, they were sitting at Katherine's kitchen table, each
having a scotch and water, a rare event.

"Christ! I needed this," Molly said, taking a deep swig. The ice
rattled in her glass as her hand trembled uncontrollably.

"Ditto," Katherine agreed, reaching over to guide Molly's glass to
the table. "What a night."

They sighed and gave each other a major eye roll. "You need to call
the police tomorrow. This is serious."

"That's what the super said too."

"First thing in the morning. Now let's try to get some sleep—and make sure your phone is off."

Sunday morning Molly called the police nonemergency number. She was assured an officer would be over to her apartment in the afternoon between 2:00 and 5:00 p.m.

"Okay," Katherine suggested, "let's go for a long walk after breakfast and then I'll drive you home and spend the afternoon with you. Oh, but first, let me show you the home exchange inquiry I received yesterday! You won't believe it!"

They spent a good while at the computer as they looked up details about the area, and Molly shared Katherine's excitement.

"I can't believe you're going on your own, Kat! Are you sure about that?"

Katherine nodded her head with so much assurance Molly had to laugh. "Fuckin'-A! I'm convinced! Good on you, girl! I mean it!"

"Well, I just made the decision last evening, so let's see how I feel as time goes by."

After finishing their breakfast of hot oatmeal and blueberries—part of Katherine's new morning regimen—they walked through the nearby park along the Humber River.

The rogue snow shower from the day before was forgotten as Sunday brought sunshine. Cyclists, dog walkers, and joggers joined the strollers, happy to feel that spring might be coming after all.

The river was running quickly, with the usual warning signs posted to keep children back from its banks.

Molly said she didn't want to talk about the delivery incident until they got back to her place.

"Really, I just want to enjoy the walk and the fresh air. Let's talk some more about your exchange and what you're going to do in *la belle France*. I'm so jealous!"

Katherine was only too happy to oblige.

It was close to one o'clock when they were driving back to Molly's place, just a five-minute drive from Katherine's house.

"Let's stop and pick up some Swiss Chalet chicken for lunch," Molly suggested. "As usual, there's not much in my fridge."

As they waited for their takeout order, Molly turned to the next person in line and handed him a coupon for a free Swiss Chalet dinner.

The stranger looked at her in puzzlement as she explained. "This coupon is for you. Seriously! The next time you get a coupon in the mail, save it and give it to someone else. Just for the heck of it. It's my good deed for the day."

The man smiled then, getting the message. "You gotta be kidding! Thanks! Very nice of you, and I will pay it forward," he ended with a wink.

Molly grinned back. "Right on!"

"What was that all about?" Katherine asked as they walked out to the car.

"I've been doing this for a few years now and it gives me such a buzz," replied Molly. "It's my random-act-of-kindness thingy."

"Huh?"

"A few years ago I read something online about a woman in Pittsburgh who spent a year doing anonymous little acts of kindness for strangers. She gave them a note asking them to do the same thing for someone else, and the whole thing took off on the Internet. Now people are doing it all over the world, including me. But I'm not organized enough to have a little note, so I just pass the message on verbally."

"Moll, that's so cool. So thoughtful. I want to do it too."

"Then you will," Molly assured her. "It's what we all should be doing."

Kat grinned. "You never cease to surprise me."

Once they were settled in Molly's apartment, Katherine felt it was time to press her on what was going on. "Okay, let's talk. Something is obviously going on in your life, and you don't seem to want to discuss it."

"Kat, I have no idea what this is all about. I swear!"

Feeling Molly's answer was a bit too quick and her expression not convincing, Katherine pushed her a bit more. "You know you can tell me anything and it won't go any further. You know that . . ."

Molly quickly stood on the pretext of going to the kitchen to get some plates for their chicken sandwiches. At the same time there was a knock on her door.

Startled, she looked at Kat with panic in her eyes. "Fuck! That scared me! Kat, will you see who it is? Nobody can just get in here, but maybe they walked in when someone else was coming in. Oh, man!"

"I got it. Don't worry."

The building superintendent was at the door, holding a large green garbage bag.

"Is Ms. Malone here?" he asked, peering in.

"Oh, hi, Mr. B. Yeah, I'm here. Sorry about waking you last night and being so freaked out," Molly apologized.

"No problem. That was some kind of weird, though. I went through the garbage after I left you last night and I managed to pick most of the stuff out."

"Omigawd, even the . . .?"

"Yeah, even the rodent. It's all here in the bag and I really think you should call the cops about it."

Molly explained that they were waiting for the police to arrive.

"Thanks, Mr. B. I'm so grateful for your help. Sorry again for this whole thing."

"Well, I'm sorry too," he answered, "but actually it might be a good thing for the building, because I'm hoping the owners will put a security camera in the lobby now. You've no idea what a help it will be. All sorts of strange shit . . . oh, excuse me."

Katherine had to turn her back, pretending to pick something up, so he wouldn't see her smirk at the idea of someone apologizing to Molly for swearing.

"Anyway," he continued, "lots of stuff happens around here, and a camera might just make the difference. If the cops want to talk to me, I'll be around all day. Just give me a shout."

Molly was not reaching for the bag, so he gingerly placed it on the floor just inside her entrance hall and backed out, waving.

Katherine picked up the bag quickly and put it out on the balcony. "Yuck. No need to have that inside," she said, scrunching her face.

Looking pale, Molly sat down. "I've lost my appetite, but you go ahead and have your sandwich."

"Um, I think I'll wait a bit too," said Katherine. They turned on the television and feigned interest in a home makeover show.

Katherine was trying to think of a way to get Molly to admit she was hiding something and wondering how she could help her.

Molly was trying to figure out who could possibly know her secret.

An hour later, two police officers arrived, a man and a woman. They were thorough and brief. Unfortunately they were also less than helpful. They said it appeared that someone had a grudge against Molly and was taking it to extremes. However, if she had no idea who it might be, there was little they could do, particularly without any video evidence. They suggested she speak to the phone company and keep a list of each number the caller used. It would be tedious, but each of those numbers could be blocked. They understood Molly's reasons for not changing her number.

The officers looked at the mess in the garbage bag, recoiling slightly at the increasing stench. Although they would give it to their lab, they did not hold out much hope of anything helpful coming of it.

"We're really sorry, Ms. Malone. You've had a terrible experience, and we will send this to our lab right away."

Handing her some brochures about personal safety, the officer continued, "Be very aware of who is around you and how they are behaving. This must be someone who knows you and has it in for you for some reason. Try and think about every aspect of your life right now and see if you can come up with anything."

Molly signed the complaint form they had filled out and promised to be vigilant.

Leaving a card with her copy of the form, the female officer said, "Don't hesitate to call this number if anything else happens. We are here to help."

Molly thanked the officers for their assistance and waited a moment after closing the door before filling the air with expletives.

Katherine calmly let her blow off steam, while she went to the kitchen and took out the chicken sandwiches and fries that had sat forgotten. Molly followed her.

"I'm going to give these a quick a zap in the microwave. We both need to eat. Then we can talk about this some more if you want to . . ."

The more Molly thought about the whole thing, the angrier she became. As she set the table, she moaned, "Honestly, Kat! There's no way I deserve this. I mean, no one does, but . . ."

The timer buzzed. Molly took over putting the food on plates while Kat poured them each a glass of wine and they sat down to eat. "I think we can both use a calming drink."

Katherine decided she was going to put pressure on her friend. "Molly, something is going on that you don't want anyone to know about. I've had inklings of it for a long time, but mostly in these last few months as we've spent more time together."

She held her hand up to silence her friend as Molly tried to disagree. "I can't put my finger on it, but I see it on your face and hear it in your voice from time to time. I've chosen to ignore it, but now I'm worried about it."

Molly looked down at her hands and was silent. She felt Katherine's eyes locked on her face.

"I know I'm right."

Molly bit her lip and said nothing, continuing to look down.

"Think about it, Moll. I only want to help you figure this out."

Nodding, Molly replied in a quiet voice, "Katski, you are my best friend—my only close friend, really—and we've become so much closer these past few months. You're right. I do have a secret."

Katherine waited.

"And it has to stay a secret, but I swear it's not something that is hurting anybody!"

"Are you having an affair with a married man?"

"No. Absolutely not."

"So your secret, mysterious lover is not attached to someone else?"

"Absolutely not. Pass the ketchup, please."

With a shrug, Katherine changed the subject and they finished eating without addressing it again.

As she got organized to leave, Kat hugged Molly. "Well, as the officers suggested, try to figure it out. I'm just a phone call away if you want anything. Do you want to stay at my place tonight?'

Molly thanked her, saying she would be fine and that she wasn't going to let some idiot turn her life upside down. "The shock is wearing off and now I'm just getting totally pissed off. You can bet I'm going to try to figure this out and get to the bottom of it. When I get my hands on whoever it is, there'll be hell to pay."

13

By noon on Monday morning, Katherine had confirmed her vacation dates with Dr. Henderson and Laura, the office manager. Everyone in the office shared her excitement as she described the home exchange details.

All she had to do now was keep her eagerness in check for four weeks.

Two weeks later, on Saturday evening, she invited Andrea and Terrence for dinner at her place before they went to hear Molly's ten o'clock show at the Blue Note.

May had become cool again in the middle of the month, as so often happened, and Katherine decided to cook a veal stew that was a favorite in her family. She hesitated at first when she recalled how James had loved the dish but then quickly put that thought out of her head. Reminders of James and their life together were taking far less of her energy now. It was what it was, she told herself. Divorce happens.

There was still pain, to be sure. *Wouldn't there always be?* she wondered.

Dinner conversation centered on some surprise news about Andrea and Terrence's oldest son.

Andrew had recently turned twenty-five. After graduating from the agricultural college at the University of Guelph, he had gone to Kenya for six months with a volunteer group to help establish small farm co-ops. Since his return he was quickly becoming an important part of the family's farming operation. His grandfather's namesake, he had astonished them with a recent announcement.

Andrea explained, "We gave Elisabeth's story to the kids to read. It was such a difficult experience for all of us . . . just so painful . . ."

"Kat, you know how deeply, deeply touched we all were," Terrence continued. "If only we had known—"

Andrea broke in, "I mean, we knew, but we didn't."

"I understand," Katherine said, "but they didn't want us to know. They didn't want us to carry that horror inside as we were growing up. I get where they were coming from."

Andrea and Terrence looked at each other, and he reached for her hand as Andrea spoke.

"Andrew has decided he is going to their birthplace to honor his grandfather and your parents."

They sat in silence for a moment.

"My goodness," Katherine whispered, "my goodness . . ."

"We were stunned too," Terrence said, dropping his head.

"Moved," Andrea added, her eyes welling.

"It's such a noble idea," said Katherine, still shocked, "but let's think about it. That area has changed completely, not just the town. I doubt there's much left from their time, and we don't even know exactly where they lived. I appreciate what he is feeling, but I wonder if he really should go."

"We've had the same conversation, Kat. He's determined."

"He's already begun planning, checking flights, accommodation."

They talked over all the pros and cons of Andrew's plan. The truth of the matter, they all agreed, was that it wasn't whether it made sense but rather how strongly Andrew felt about it.

While Andrea and Terrence, at their insistence, cleared away the dinner dishes, Katherine finished getting ready to go out.

Pausing, she leaned her head against her mother's carpet and rubbed her hands gently across the soft texture of the silk. *What would you think of all this, Anyu? Of my plans, of Andrew's . . .*

⚜

Terrence dropped the women off in front of the Blue Note and went to park. He was reminded of how long it had been since he had visited this part of the city and how much the Queen Street East area had changed.

The dearth of parking spots was just one example, he noted with mild frustration.

As property in the area became pricier than anyone would ever have imagined, the run-down tenement houses were slowly being replaced with high-end condos and townhomes. However, homeless people still tucked themselves into protected corners, and the odd overserved individual stumbled about.

In the area, a drop-in center was run by the Catholic church, providing food and shelter, although developers were strenuously campaigning to have it relocated. The Blue Note was a long-established, slightly tired bar that featured indie-type music during the week, switching to jazz every Friday, Saturday, and Sunday night. Molly had been a fixture on stage Saturday and Sunday for over ten years, at times sharing the bill with other vocalists. Her followers were loyal and the bar was usually packed by 10:00 p.m.

Terrence squinted as he entered and offered silent thanks for the city bylaw that no longer allowed smoking in bars. He remembered only too well the thick haze that used to hang in that room. Even so, it took a minute for his eyes to adjust. Wood-framed booths upholstered in comfortably broken-in black leather lined the sides of the room, with small round dark oak tables and chairs filling the center. Soft lighting from antique brass fixtures created a funky ambiance.

Most tables sat groups of four or fewer, but by the end of the night a few boisterous clusters of six or eight typically pulled chairs together to party more effectively. The atmosphere lent itself to friendly intimacy. The decor was as it had been since the bar opened in 1959.

Bing, the bartender, had been there forever and managed to control the balance in the room, cranking things up or cooling it down as needed. From behind the highly polished walnut bar nothing escaped him, and he made everyone feel they were longtime regulars from the minute they walked in.

Molly was sitting with Katherine and Andrea and gave Terrence a warm hug as he drew up a chair to join them. They chatted for a few minutes more before the band returned to the stage and Molly was introduced.

Voices dropped as the dusky tones of her voice filled the room. Her bluesy style was often compared to that of the great Peggy Lee, and as sultry as her sound was, her phrasing was magic. When Molly sang, Katherine always noticed how her entire body language transformed to suggest she was relaxed and happy.

A male vocalist joined Molly for a few duets before Molly stepped down and made her way back to their table. Just before she reached them, she signaled she would be a minute and went over to the bar.

In spite of the dim lighting, Katherine noticed Molly greeted with a light kiss on each cheek by an attractive, dark-haired man of an indeterminate age. They spoke for a moment before she returned to the table alone.

Brimming with curiosity, Katherine asked, "Did I notice a priest's collar under that handsome fellow's jacket?"

"You certainly did," Molly answered. "That's Father DeMarco. He's very involved in street ministry in this area, and he often drops by. Needless to say, weekends are his busiest time around this neighborhood."

"He's the priest from your church as well, isn't he?" asked Katherine, realizing where she had seen him before.

"Yup, that too."

Andrea chimed in, commenting on his rugged good looks. "What is a guy that hot doing as a priest? I'll bet his Mass is well attended by the ladies."

Terrence rolled his eyes as Katherine chuckled, and Molly squirmed ever so slightly before she smiled and nodded.

A plate of warm flatbreads accompanied by hummus, a hot pepper dip, and a bowl of olives arrived at the table while the band took a break.

"My treat, guys," Molly said, grinning. "Thanks for coming out tonight."

She accepted their murmurs of thanks and appreciation as they all dug in.

At midnight, after two more sets with sounds that just kept getting better, Molly stayed behind for one last set while the others went back to Katherine's, where Andrea and Terrence were staying overnight.

Lingering over breakfast the next morning, Katherine gave them a copy of her flight info and ran through her planned itinerary. She had a couple of contact phone numbers of people near the property in France who could be called for any reason.

"You were right about the great preparation and care people put into organizing their exchanges," she said to them.

"Kat, we're so excited for you!" Andrea exclaimed, tears filling her eyes, "This is going to be such an awesome experience. I just know it!"

Terrence nodded, adding in a worried tone, "I hope you won't regret going alone."

Shooting him a quick narrow-eyed look along with a shake of her head, Andrea pulled the conversation into positive territory again. "Oh, for heaven's sake, Terry, Kat's a big girl! She knows what she's doing and she'll be more than just fine!"

Kat laughed and hugged Terrence, thanking him for his concern. "You know, I've had moments of thinking I must be crazy to go alone, but honestly I do feel excited at the prospect now. Besides, I need to do this—for me."

14

The Friday morning of her departure, Katherine was up earlier than usual, filled with excitement. Mentally going through her checklist, she called the limo service for a 4:30 p.m. pickup.

With an early-evening flight, she had factored in the unknowns of rush-hour traffic.

"Better safe than sorry," Andrea had agreed when they talked about it on the weekend. "There's always a jam-up by the airport, even at the best of times."

Katherine was leaving the office at noon so she would have the afternoon for last-minute details. There was a meeting that morning she didn't want to miss or she would have taken the day off. But the truth was she didn't need to.

Ha, I've had my bags packed for a week!

Taking Katherine by surprise, Lucy made a presentation on behalf of the staff.

The others looked pleased as Katherine unwrapped a compact video camera.

"Oh my gosh! You shouldn't have. I'm really . . . quite, um, embarrassed . . . but thrilled. Thank you!"

Dr. Henderson put his arm around her shoulder. "This past year hasn't been the easiest for you, so we hope you enjoy every minute of this trip."

Blinking, Katherine smiled through her tears. "I plan to put every effort into doing just that."

⚜

It would be another hour before her flight was to board. She had checked approximately six times.

Not that I'm excited, especially with my new best friend in hand, she thought with a smile as she took out her e-reader. She had reread all of Peter Mayle's books about Provence during the past two months and downloaded his *Provence A to Z: A Francophile's Essential Handbook* to amuse herself on the flight.

Katherine had purchased her first e-reader for this trip after years of denying she would enjoy using it. Much to her surprise, she discovered she liked it very much, and she had enough material downloaded to last a very long time.

She had loved the entire experience of preparing for her adventure. She had spent the previous Sunday with Andrea and Terrence. To her delight, Andrew, Kate, and Jack were there for dinner, especially to say *bon voyage.* Andrew's desire to visit his grandfather's birthplace had only intensified since he first announced his plans. He was anxious to share his thoughts about it.

Katherine had called him the weekend his parents told her of his decision, and she realized then he would not be dissuaded.

He'd done an impressive amount of research already.

"There's an agricultural co-op just outside the town now that's focusing on organic products, so I'm going to spend some time there as well. I'm really hoping that by meeting some local people, I might even meet someone who has a link to the past."

Katherine was amazed at the local information he had acquired.

"It's all there online, Aunt Kat," he said, "including photos, videos.

It's so easy to find out about anything these days. You should take a look. Mom did."

Andrea looked at Katherine sadly and shook her head. "It's very, very difficult to read all the information from the war years, but there are photos, Kat. When you are ready, you should look at them. I cried the entire time, but somehow in the end it helped me to actually picture where they had lived before all hell broke out."

Katherine nodded and said she would, asking Andrea to send her the links.

As coffee was being served, the children presented Kat with a beautiful leather-bound journal and Montblanc pen.

"We know it's a German pen, but it sounds French!" they said, laughing and kissing her.

"Keep a journal, Aunt Kat. In fact, Mom is going to show you how to create a website tonight so we can follow your adventure that way!"

Molly had taken her out for dinner the night before she left.

"*Voilà, ma chère amie!*" Molly handed Kat a small, brightly wrapped package.

Katherine unwrapped a tiny iPod shuffle and looked at the attached piece of paper. "Fantastic! Oh, thanks, Moll! Piaf, Aznavour, Brel, Hallyday . . . oh, even Dalida!"

There was also some North African music and then a name that brought a quizzical look to Katherine's brow.

"Zaz . . . ?"

"Oh yeah! My new all-time favorite—Zaz. Kat, when you listen to her song 'Je Veux,' you won't be able to stop smiling or dancing around. You're going to love it."

"Such a thoughtful gift! Thank you so, so much! *Merci beaucoup!*"

Molly grinned back.

Katherine continued, "Oh, and thanks too for offering to pop in on the Lalliberts while they're at my house. I'm sure they will appreciate it. I've left them your phone number along with Michael and Susan's, and also Andrea's."

"That ought to cover everything," Molly confirmed. "Sounds like you are all set."

"I'm ready to go. I'm excited, and I don't think I'm ignoring any other feelings."

"Well, with everything that's happened to me lately, I'm feeling scared about you by yourself in a frickin' little farmhouse in the middle of nowhere."

"I'm not going to be as alone as you think. I told you that house is in a vineyard property and there are other people in the main house just five minutes away—five minutes' *walk*, not drive."

"Yes, but—"

"And the farmhouse has an alarm system. So I'm not exactly unprotected."

"Well, why do they have an alarm? Have they had problems? Did you ask?"

"They were very up front about it and said everyone in their area has an alarm, as there have been problems. Where aren't there these days? But they have never had anything happen."

Molly shrugged and talked some more about her concerns.

"Okay," said Katherine, "There's one more thing I haven't told you. I might be looking after their dog too. A yellow Lab."

This was a surprise. Kat explained that the dog was an option.

"At first I thought I would refuse but then decided it might be nice to have the company."

"But you've never had a pet!"

"I know. Crazy, huh? I'm not sure what's come over me, but I just want to do all these things I've never done before. They said the dog is happy to sleep outside or can stay at the main house—whatever that is—if I don't want him in the farmhouse."

Molly stared at Kat and shook her head. "Shut up! I can't wait for you to get home, to hear all your stories."

"I'll call you from there or Skype from the gas station! We'll just have to organize around the six-hour time difference, which could be a problem during the week when you're at work. Speaking of phone calls . . ." said Kat.

"Nothing since the lovely floral delivery," Molly said, looking a bit pale.

"Fingers crossed that's the end of it," Katherine toasted, raising her wineglass.

Recalling all this as she sat at the gate, Katherine felt slightly overwhelmed and very fortunate.

Putting her Kindle away when she heard the boarding announcement, she stifled a smug grin, joined the lineup, and was soon settled into Air France's business class. She had often wondered when she would get to use her travel points since James wouldn't fly. They'd collected a ton of them, only to use them for hotels. Now she was reaping the benefit—*and loving it*, she thought with a smile.

Too excited to sleep, she killed some time by watching a couple of movies before she finally closed her eyes in the comfortable fold-down-flat seats. The next thing she knew, lights were turned up and the cabin was full of activity as breakfast was served. Organizing her things, she prepared for arrival at Charles de Gaulle Airport.

France! I'm really here in France! was all she could think in the terminal as she let the sound of French voices and accents fill her head.

After collecting her luggage, she found the TGV easily enough thanks to the clear signage. She could board directly onto the train to Avignon from the airport without having to go into Paris.

After checking the departure notices, it was a short walk to the platform. Validating her ticket with the time-stamp punch in one of the yellow machines, she was glad she had read about this in advance. The machines weren't too easy to spot.

The 8:00 a.m. TGV left on the dot, as advertised. True to its name, the ride on Le Train à Grande Vitesse was a thrill, the countryside flying by as the train exceeded three hundred kilometers per hour. In well under three hours she arrived outside Avignon. The slick TGV station was located ten kilometers outside the town, with the car rental office conveniently next to it. Rolling her luggage along, she discovered a note on the office door.

"Fermé pour le déjeuner. Réouverture à 14h 30."

I'm in France! Open at two thirty after lunch, I'd forgotten about that. Now what do I do for three hours?

Back in the station she was surprised to discover that there was nowhere to store her luggage. For a moment, she felt a desire to not be so alone and for someone else to be making a decision.

How did I miss this information when I did my trip research?

Seeing a small bus, she waved to the driver, who stopped for her. Using hand signals and limited vocabulary eventually solved the problem. There were storage lockers in the *other* Avignon TGV station right in town and this bus would shuttle her there. Who knew? Trying not to berate herself too much, Katherine slowly shrugged off feelings of inadequacy and aloneness and began to see the delay as an opportunity to explore.

A ten-minute stroll through twisting medieval alleys brought her to Place du Palais. Katherine stood in awe at the beauty of the immense Palais des Papes, the Palace of the Popes, flanked by its four massive towers. Built in the 1300s, it was the size of four normal French cathedrals, and she could see why it was described as one of the most important Gothic structures in Europe. Breathtaking didn't describe it.

Fantastique!

She wrote postcards to Andrea, Molly, and Lucy as she sat in the square opposite the imposing palace. Her phone beeped to indicate a text coming in, and Katherine was thrilled to see that Andrea had received the text she sent her from the station saying she had arrived safely. At least they could communicate that way.

Feeling surrounded by history, she smiled with satisfaction as she treated herself to a *papaline*, a chocolate truffle filled with liqueur distilled from sixty locally picked herbs. *Having two would be decadent*, she told herself. So she did.

The friendly *navette* driver had informed her there was a thirty-minute bus tour around the town, which left from the square.

She found the history fascinating, listening to the English version on the headphones supplied. Until she read up on her history before leaving for France, she had forgotten that the seat of the Roman Catholic Church had actually moved from Rome to Avignon in the 1300s, remaining there about seventy-five years. It was surprising how much remained from that time.

The famous bridge was a disappointment. After singing "Sur le Pont d'Avignon" for so many years as a schoolgirl, she had expected it to be much larger. Only four arches remained of a bridge that once spanned the Rhone, but it was still exciting to see, she decided.

Drinking a *café crème* afterward, she recognized the first hurdle she would have to cross during her visit. No caffe mocha to be found! Everyone appeared to drink espresso or the standard French coffee, ordered as *café*. The waiter had been kind enough to suggest a *crème* might be what she wanted. With the addition of three sugar cubes, it would have to do.

I promise myself I won't even look for Starbucks while I'm in France. It just doesn't seem right.

It was three o'clock when Katherine picked up her rental car. The man in charge apologized for not speaking English, indicating his absent colleague did. Between them they managed to communicate with a mix of languages, smiles, and nods.

She quickly became aware that while her French immersion education from so many years ago had actually left residuals, her vocabulary was another story. At least it should make for some funny stories when she got back.

The paperwork was complicated and again Katherine wished she wasn't the one who had to fill it out. Once she had finally completed the information, the agent helped load her bags into the trunk. Wishing her a *bonne journée* with a wave, he went back to the next customer as she started her car. It was a peppy blue Citroën with a manual transmission, and even had a GPS system. Her excitement growing, she entered the village name and positioned her seat.

Sainte-Mathilde was located halfway between the villages of Gordes and Roussillon. Katherine felt as if she had already driven the route with all the time she had spent on Google Earth. She would be there in less than an hour, according to her directions. It looked like a beautiful drive, very straightforward, although there were a lot of squiggles on the map. After the earlier arrival fiasco, she hoped her research had been accurate.

Starting the car, she pulled onto the road with a lurch as she changed gears. She was overcome for a moment with memories of her dad teaching her to drive a stick shift. He had been so patient with her.

Once you learn to drive a manual transmission, you don't forget. She heard his words, smiling as she sailed smoothly along after she awkwardly finished the necessary gear shifting.

Leaving the more urban area, Katherine encountered her first challenge: roundabouts. *Ronds-points*, she reminded herself. *Think in French here!*

Holding her breath, she entered as confidently as possible and, as the GPS directed, made a left at the second exit. The vehicles already circling have the right of way, she had read. After a few more, Katherine felt she had them mastered.

Oops, perhaps not, she muttered as she found herself not quite sure of her exit in a later one. Shifting gears hesitantly and going around a second time, someone swerved in front on her right, cutting off her exit, and around she went again.

Oh brother, I'm having a Griswold moment, she sighed, remembering *European Vacation,* which she had watched with her nephews and niece many times.

Gripping the wheel, she took a deep breath as she swerved quickly, counted to the third exit, and veered off onto it.

Maybe I do need a bit more experience, she conceded, for a moment unsure whether to laugh or cry.

The roads gradually became narrower and less busy, which allowed her to take a longer look at the pastoral countryside. As she rounded a corner, cresting a small hill, she suddenly pulled the car to the side of the road and burst into tears.

In front of her was a postcard scene from Provence in June. An enormous field of golden sunflowers glistened with an intensity that was hard to believe, as if someone had plastered a "Visit Provence" poster smack in her face. To one side was the classic *mas,* with its outbuildings, the shades of the yellow-gray limestone farm structures softened by the midafternoon sun. Traditional weathered blue shutters on the south-facing windows and doors were flung open on this fine day. It was a scene Katherine had admired in so many books and movies. She couldn't begin to count the number of images exactly like this that had filled her computer screen in the past month. And now there it was. And there *she* was, overwhelmed by the moment.

She stepped out of the car and hollered at the top of her lungs, "I'm here. I've done it! *Je suis arrivée!*"

Grabbing her camera, she let the lens caress the fields, buildings, and sky, knowing this was just the beginning. The pleasure of composing each shot was like eating a divine piece of chocolate. She could almost taste it.

Katherine leaned against the hood of the Citroën, letting the reality sink in. Not simply the scenery but the truth of it all: she was in France, of her own doing, by herself. The "by herself" part at this moment felt a bit raw. For a moment she felt as if she were on a precipice, unsure of what was coming next in her life. But it wasn't danger or fear that she was experiencing. Rather, there was a sense of excitement and an urge to quickly proceed to see what lay ahead.

I'll deal with being alone. I can do it. This adventure is full on, she thought as she settled back into the car. Pulling off the grassy shoulder, she grinned, thinking, *I can't wait to see what happens farther down the road—in more ways than one.* Then she laughed out loud.

The traffic soon became more congested. Katherine read road signs indicating the turnoff for the hilltop village of Gordes a short distance away. Tourist season was already under way.

Then it appeared before her, perched like a sculpture carved out of the rocky outcropping, just like in the travel book photos. The cluster of buildings tumbling down the hillside was dominated by the majestic castle and cathedral, presenting an almost dreamlike apparition. The beige stone of the buildings glowed softly in the afternoon sun as the village seemed to blend into a solid unit from where she viewed it.

Katherine had a list of towns she planned to visit, and Gordes was near the top of the list. Resisting the urge to stop for another photo, she reminded herself there would be other opportunities, and the traffic wouldn't allow it anyway.

Five minutes later her GPS was telling her to turn right, but there appeared to be two options. At a fork, one road went left and two roads went right. Taking a chance and feeling only a little unsure, she took the first right.

"Recalculating," the GPS told her. "Make a U-turn when possible."

Katherine snorted, as the road had narrowed to the width of a single lane with deep ditches on either side. Driving slowly, she noticed some activity ahead. As she drew closer, a herd of goats was crossing the road from one field to the next. Young kids led the way, nimbly frolicking and nipping playfully at each other. The beiges and light cocoas, mixed with black and dark brown, presented a pleasing blend. Small buds of horns appeared on bigger members of the group, with many of the elder males sporting handsome horns that curved gracefully around.

Chuckling, she stopped to wait for them to pass, certain now someone must have scripted all this for her arrival. The lightness of their collective movement was joyful, she thought. The smell, not so much.

The herd was followed by a grizzled older man, who waved and approached her window. Having closed it to a crack, Katherine fumbled for her best French and explained, in a short sentence, she was looking for the village of Sainte-Mathilde.

His response was as undecipherable as anything she had ever heard.

He then smiled and made grand gestures with his arms, indicating she should turn around. Then using his hands he demonstrated a road, a corner, and a right turn. She got the message.

Turning into the lane the goats had used, with some effort she maneuvered the car through a U-turn, stalling only once, and drove back down to the turnoff. The GPS was happy with her again.

The fields turned into forest for a few minutes, and through her open window Katherine became aware of a most aromatic fragrance. Cedar she recognized, but she could not identify the rest. All she knew as she slowly cruised the tree-lined route was that it smelled divine.

A tight corner caused her to brake slightly. Without warning the car was hemmed in by village buildings where the woods ended as suddenly as they had begun. Her eye caught a narrow rectangular white sign with a red border. *Sainte-Mathilde!*

"I'm getting closer!" she said and slowly wound her way along the street as she noted the bakery, the wine store, the butcher shop, and, to her surprise, a casino. That didn't compute.

To one side she passed a sun-speckled open square surrounded by trees with trunks that appeared to be painted in a camouflage pattern. Pulling her car into a parking spot, she caught her breath before getting out.

A column with four spouts pouring water into its circular basin sat in the middle of the square. A few people could be seen outside some small cafés sitting on metal chairs, the tables covered with bright cloths.

Just beyond the square, a group of men stood on a long stretch of reddish-colored sand, hands clasped behind their backs as they watched others. Katherine recognized serious games of *boules* taking place and smiled, pleased that her fantasy continued to be coming true.

The Lalliberts had instructed her to introduce herself to the bar owner, Jacques, who would have the keys to the house. As she stood at the counter, all eyes turned toward her and the lively conversation faded.

"Bonjour, madame," greeted a severe-looking man with rolled-up shirtsleeves.

Katherine introduced herself, somewhat timidly, and explained the reason she was there. Jacque's stern look transformed almost into a smile.

Coming around the counter, he greeted her with a kiss on each cheek and welcomed her to the village.

"Bienvenue à Sainte-Mathilde!" he said with obvious pride.

The keys were presented with a flourish, and a hand-drawn map to the house accompanied them. Katherine graciously thanked him, refusing his offer of a welcome drink and promising to return another day. The warmth and sincerity of these few moments almost over-whelmed her. Everyone had warned her the French were rather cool and unfriendly. This had been anything but.

Next she asked where she could purchase groceries since she hadn't noticed a store. The bartender responded, *"Ah oui, Casino."*

Katherine, taken aback, smiled hesitantly, believing she had fumbled with her French vocabulary. She replied she didn't want to go the casino but would like to buy groceries. The bartender chuckled as did several others, and he explained that "Casino" was the name of a grocery store. Taking her arm and steering her to the open door, he pointed to the "casino" she had passed.

Feeling her face flush slightly, Katherine thanked him. As she responded to his *à bientôt, madame,* she heard the same farewell from the others in the bar.

Sweet, she thought, overcome with embarrassment.

In the grocery store, she tried not to dawdle as she admired the fruit and vegetables artfully displayed in wicker baskets. A straw-filled crate near the cash desk contained brown eggs that looked as if the farmer had just delivered them from the coop. Selecting a bottle of deep pink rosé, she paid and felt pleased with her ability to return the pleasantries of the woman behind the counter.

"Merci et bonne journée, madame."

Katherine responded in turn.

Quickly popping into the *boulangerie* next door, she knew she was in trouble. The selection of mouthwatering pastries demanded she not pass them by. But she resisted and planned to return the next day once she was settled. A simple baguette would suffice for today.

"Merci et bonne journée, madame."

Again Katherine responded, noting how polite everyone was.

The next stop was the *fromagerie* a little farther down the street. Once more she was greeted. The selection of cheese was mind-boggling. She chose a delicately soft Brie that was just beginning to show its age, and the shopkeeper nodded in approval while wrapping it.

"Merci et bonne journée, madame, et bon fromage!"

Katherine chuckled at the addition to the standard farewell. *"Bonne journée, madame!"* she replied. She was definitely liking this.

A tomato-and-Brie baguette sandwich was calling to her as she placed her purchases in the trunk.

Checking the map the Lalliberts had left for her, she confirmed their property was just outside the village, as they had described in their inquiry. She followed the narrow main street, lined with stone dwellings separated occasionally by a small courtyard or vacant lot. Cottages of cream and ochre stucco topped with terra-cotta tiles and sitting on small garden properties tempted her to reach for her camera yet again.

Later, later, she promised.

Grape-laden rows of vineyards stretched along both sides of the road. At a pale-yellow gatepost, she turned onto a dirt lane, the entrance to which was marked by mounds of lavender not quite bursting into color. A five-foot stone wall guarded the house, its gate hanging open as if it had not been closed for a very long time. Lanky bushes of plumbago, with blooms as blue as the sky, mixed with honeysuckle and other flowering shrubs as the driveway became a circle in front of the house.

Awed by the unfolding scene, Katherine slowed to a stop at the path leading to the front door, which appeared slightly ajar. The heavy-looking door opened and a white-haired woman walked down the path to the car. Her smile was as warm and wide as the spread of her arms. A yellow Lab, tail wagging energetically, ambled beside her.

Katherine parked the car and opened her door. Her first greeting was that of a wet nose and then a paw offered before the dog obeyed the command to *assis* from the woman.

Laughing, Joy Lallibert introduced Picasso, the dog, and then herself.

"He considers himself the official greeter no matter where he is!"

Joy was a charming Englishwoman, the sister-in-law of Katherine's exchange couple. Katherine guessed her to be in her midseventies. A well-preserved and elegant midseventies, she noted.

Katherine admitted, with relief, she was glad Joy spoke English.

"I've been reminded all day how stressful it is to try to communicate in a foreign language when it's not a classroom situation! I'm not sure I passed the test in the village!"

"Not to worry," Joy reassured her with a chuckle. "The villagers are always delighted when a visitor simply makes the effort. You will find most of them know a smattering of English. There are a lot of us *Anglaises* around!"

Joy reached down to scratch the top of the dog's head, saying his nickname was Pico. Katherine noted he continued to remain sitting while his tail eagerly swept the ground and his eyes pierced hers, insisting they be friends. As she returned his gaze, he lifted a paw to shake, and when she grasped it, an explosion of dust rose from his thumping tail. He had, Joy explained, made such messes when he was a pup they decided his results looked like Picasso's art—hence the name. Katherine laughed at the imagery.

Joy offered to help Katherine with her things, and soon they were putting away the groceries in the kitchen, Kat's suitcases sitting at the foot of a staircase. Joy suggested they leave the bags to take up later and plugged in the kettle when Katherine accepted her offer of a cup of tea.

"I should be offering you a *pastis* or glass of rosé at this time of day, but after all your travels, it seems like a cup of tea might be in order."

"Absolutely," Katherine agreed, wide-eyed but starting to feel a bit jet-lagged.

Although the Lalliberts had photos of every room of their home on their website, there was no comparison to actually being there. The thickness of the walls, the richness of the wood, the feel of the uneven floor tiles underfoot—everything surpassed the photos and their descriptions. There seemed to be an instant sense of familiarity despite the unfamiliar setting. Peter Mayle had done his job well.

After their cup of tea, Joy suggested they take a quick walk around the main floor and into the garden before darkness moved in. A large front hall, lounge, and dining room were separated by wide arches, allowing for easy movement from room to room. A magnificent fireplace with enormous mantle and hearth dominated the area. Large, comfortable-looking sofas and chairs invited casual lounging.

"I don't think I will be using this gorgeous table," Katherine commented with a chuckle as she ran her hand along the ancient-looking oak trestle table and twelve chairs. "The small table in the kitchen looks just my size!"

Stepping out onto a terrace, Katherine gasped audibly at the sight of the climbing rosebush in full soft-pink bloom that draped over a small stone structure Joy referred to as the potting shed. Brilliant purple and red flowering vines stretched across a stone archway, through which Katherine could see more gardens and walkways dotted here and there with stone benches and pottery.

Cicada songs filled the air as the two women strolled the little pathways through the gardens and around the back to a tumbling ruin of a former stable. "Many of the stones from this jumble are those you saw outlining some of the paths. There was really no reason to rebuild it, and to be honest, the ruin holds its own special character. I hope you don't find it unpleasant to look at."

Katherine assured Joy she did not, and in fact was already planning some photo angles.

As they walked back into the house, Katherine barely managed to stifle a yawn.

"You must be feeling quite tired. We have some dinner for you," Joy said as she produced a *cassoulet* that had been heating in the oven and took a simple green salad from the fridge.

Katherine invited Joy to dine with her and felt increasingly comfortable with her easy manner.

The fridge had been left well stocked, and several bottles of local wines—accompanied by a note inviting Katherine to enjoy them—were lined up on a rustic but elegant sideboard in the dining room. Wear marks on the wooden drawers and a missing handle simply added character to the piece.

Joy explained how she and Albert had raised their children in the larger home, the *manoir*, construction of which had begun by ancestors over three hundred years before.

"During the Revolution they fled to Italy, and there was much rebuilding to be done when the property finally was returned to the family in the mid-1800s."

She gave a brief history of how the land was transformed into a vineyard at that time and an overview of how the business functioned.

"How fascinating to know so much about your family and to have such a connection to the country's history," Katherine commented, her eyes bright with interest.

"You must come over for a tour. We love our home and our land and like to show it to others who appreciate its story."

"I would love to see it," Katherine replied.

"It is beautiful but enormous. We divided it so our two children could also live there after they married, and now I am surrounded by my four wonderful grandchildren. They are gradually away more and more but still are my *joie*, and we are a big happy family. My daughter, Marie, and her husband, Christian, work in the business. My son, Henri, is an artist and his wife, Sylvie, is a nurse-practitioner with a clinic in Roussillon."

"Sadly," she explained with downcast eyes, "Albert left this earth five years ago. I miss him terribly, but it was his time."

She went on to describe how Christian managed the financial side of the business and Marie oversaw the marketing. Jean-Pierre's son would eventually take over his father's role.

"And this house?" asked Katherine, enjoying hearing this family history so different from any other she knew.

"When Jean-Pierre married, he wanted to live in a smaller house—and truthfully, he and Albert did not get along that well. First of all Albert was eighteen years older, and that in itself created difficulties. They ran the business together well, but they had very different temperaments. Jean-Pierre wanted some space, you might say."

Katherine nodded and poured them each another glass of wine as Joy continued.

"He loves this *mas*. It needed quite a bit of work, but that was his pleasure to restore it. They raised their two children here, and he swears he and his precious Madeline will remain forever."

"I can understand why," Katherine observed. "This house has an instant magic to it. It feels like it has a history."

"Ah oui! This began as a shepherd's cottage, a *bergerie*, four hundred years ago, and is the oldest building on the property. That part is now the kitchen. In fact, we still allow a goat farmer to use part of the property to graze his herd. You will see them from time to time, but they will not interfere with your use of the yard in any way."

"Joy, I can't tell you how happy I am to be here. I was ready for a change in my life."

Truthfully, it was already much more than she had anticipated.

"How are you feeling about having the dog stay with you, Katherine? He appears to have made up his mind," she said, nodding at Picasso, who was settled happily at Katherine's feet.

"He seems to be a sweetheart," Katherine observed, adding with just the slightest hint of hesitation, "I think I would like to have him here."

His tail beat thickly on the floor, as if he understood.

"Obviously he is bilingual," said Joy. Katherine chuckled.

Walking over to the deep porcelain sink, Joy pointed to the wide window ledge above it.

"We have a habit here of using this ledge for messages if no one is home, so be sure to check it every day. You never know when one of us will drop by."

Picking up a notepad on the counter, she continued, "There is always someone at work on our property and our numbers are posted here. Call us for anything. Sadly we feel we need a person around twenty-four hours. At the same time it must be a good idea, as we have never had a problem—unlike some of our neighbors."

Katherine nodded. "Madeline told me there was an alarm system here, and I will use it, but I want you to know I'm not nervous."

Walking over to her luggage, she pulled the information she had been sent via e-mail out of her carry-on bag. Joy walked Katherine through the simple instructions for the system and flipped through the pages to see if anything else required explaining.

Included in the Lalliberts' very complete instruction booklet were Pico's meal details and a list of the commands with which he was familiar. A reasonably mature five-year-old with deep, dark eyes that missed nothing, his presence was actually comforting, Kat thought.

He happily followed the women upstairs after an assortment of cheese and a traditional plum tart had completed their meal. Joy deflected Katherine's compliments throughout the meal, insisting it was simple fare.

After Katherine insisted on clearing the dishes, Joy suggested the suitcases be taken upstairs to the hall while they toured all four bedrooms.

Kat had only seen rooms painted such shades in French home-decor magazines, and each delighted her more than the last. The linens were crisp, white, some with embroidered edges, and, as Joy explained, many had been in the family for generations.

"There is still an old-fashioned *salle de lavage*—washing room—in the *manoir* with a huge press for the sheets. You must come and see it. A woman comes every week to launder the linens, and I cannot bring myself to end the tradition."

"I may simply take turns sleeping in every one of these rooms," Katherine observed with a satisfied smile.

Forty years before, after learning at their father's side since childhood, Joy's husband, Albert, had taken over the vineyard with his brothers, Jean-Pierre and Christian.

Their father had, before them, inherited the vineyard from his father. Over one hundred and fifty years of love, toil, and sweat were soaked into the property of Le Manoir de Sainte-Mathilde, and their Côtes de Provence wines were well recognized.

Back downstairs, Joy suggested Katherine might be ready to think about sleeping with the long travel hours surely kicking in. She leaned toward Katherine and gave her the familiar French *bise* at the side of each cheek. Kat smiled at this; it was just so French to her.

Saying *bonsoir*, Joy hopped on a small motorbike to head back to the main house. Pausing, she mentioned one final, nearly overlooked detail. "There is an old *vélo*—excuse me, bicycle—inside the potting shed behind the house, my dear. Feel free to use it, such as it is," she said, noting Katherine's sudden downcast expression.

"It's rather old and looks a bit beat up, but is actually in good condition. It's great for going to market days on Monday and Thursday, when parking can be limited. You can ride it through the vineyards as a shortcut to our *manoir* too," Joy told her. "It's shorter to come through the vineyard than by car on the road. You know how it is around here. Driving, you have to go to the main road and then double back down the old road to our place."

Watching the taillight of Joy's motorbike disappear down the lane, Katherine waited for the dog to return from his nightly duty.

As spontaneously as they began, the cicadas abruptly ceased singing, and darkness dropped like a blanket over the landscape and around the house.

15

A gentle breeze rustled the curtains. Sunshine streamed through the uncovered bedroom window, causing Katherine to squeeze her eyes shut again after she first opened them.

Lying quietly for a few moments, her arms resting on top of the soft coverlet, she luxuriated in her current reality.

She barely recalled having a shower and falling into bed the night before. Sleep had immediately claimed her.

A sudden damp coldness on her hand popped her eyes wide open. Enormous dark eyes met her startled gaze as Picasso stood with his nose resting on the covers. Katherine laughed out loud and patted him on the head.

Sitting up and stretching, she caught sight of the orderly vineyard rows reaching as far as she could see through the French doors at the foot of the bed.

The window next to the bed offered more of the same view, but there was a field bordering the grapevines on this side, and she spied a herd of goats resting quietly. Rolling, purple-tinged hills created a back-drop, topped by a brilliant blue sky.

Slipping her light white cotton housecoat over the matching night-gown, she practically skipped down the stairs to open the front door and step outside.

On her heels, Picasso brushed by quickly through the open door and into the small thicket of trees by the driveway.

Directly in front of the house, the gravel drive circled around a perennial bed that was bursting with the liveliest mix of colors she could ever remember seeing in anything but paintings. Red and pink poppies, orange calendula, yellow strawflowers, purple phlox, blue and white hydrangeas—along with a number of other plants Katherine did not know—mixed together in wild abandon. Mounds of lavender bordered the drive, with clumps of shrubs and trees scattered on the lawns between the house and fence and the road beyond. Rows of lush grapevines rooted in rich red soil stretched in every direction beyond the farmhouse property.

Katherine sat on the stone steps, absorbing every detail of the view. Tears rolled down her cheeks. Making no attempt to stifle them she sniffed loudly.

For all her bravado and her happiness at making this fantasy come true, the other side of her reality took over. She was alone. In the midst of the beauty, the adventure, the dream—which begged for a husband, a partner, a lover, or at least a friend with whom to share it, there was none. *Nada*. Alone.

Burying her face in her hands, Katherine cried silent tears of sad emptiness for the moment.

Slowly aware of a warm presence by her side, she looked sideways to find Pico sitting next to her, lightly leaning on her and looking straight ahead.

Katherine slipped her arm around him. "Looks like it's you and me, pal," she said, moving her head just in time to avoid a sloppy lick, square on the mouth.

Laughing in surprise, she wiped her cheeks with the sleeve of her housecoat, gave a melancholic sigh, and got up, in serious need of a tissue. Picasso stood and stretched. Together they walked back into the house.

French doors, the classic blue paint slightly peeling, led from every room out to pleasingly jumbled gardens, gravelly patios, or newly mown lawns. Katherine opened all of them, lingering each time as soft morning light and fresh country air flowed around her and into the house. The mild day was perfect for her plan to explore the immediate surroundings and then go into town for a stroll.

A boiled egg for breakfast with some of the baguette she had purchased the day before would suit her just fine. Another lesson learned— yesterday's baguette was as hard as a rock!

Katherine was filling a pot with water when her eye caught sight of something on the window ledge. A small basket sat with a white cloth over it. Opening the window, she retrieved the basket and looked under the cloth to find two fresh croissants, a *pain au chocolat*, and a round pastry she recognized as a *pain aux raisins*.

A note tucked inside read "*Bon appétit*, Joy."

Sitting at a small metal-framed round table on the patio outside the kitchen, Kat lingered over each delicious bite as she lost herself in the view. Situated at the back of the farmhouse, the scenery was completely different as fields and pastures carried the eye across the Luberon Valley to the distant blue-tinged hills of the Vaucluse.

The tinkling of bells caught her attention as a sizeable herd of goats scrambled along a barely noticeable lane between the vineyard and fence on the east side of the property. Behind them, she recognized the same goat herder who had directed her to turn around when she chose the wrong road the day before. He waved as he passed. Katherine returned the gesture while Pico stood watching, his tail wagging lazily at a sight familiar to him. He ran over and accompanied the man partway up the lane, receiving many rubs and scratches on the head for his effort.

Watching the goats gambol up the lane and through the fence that was opened for them, Katherine stretched lazily, rose, and decided it was time to get moving.

Later, with a mixture of apprehension and curiosity, she showered and dressed quickly before walking to the potting shed behind the house. As Joy had promised, inside was a bicycle that had seen better days. A green Peugeot leaned against the wall with chipped paint, rust marks all over the chrome, a large light mounted over the front wheel, and a weathered wicker basket sitting on a frame over the rear.

Katherine blinked and then laughed out loud at the simple appeal of it as she ran her hand over the frame. It appeared someone had recently wiped it clean, and when she ran her finger over the chain, she could tell it had been newly oiled. *Very thoughtful,* she acknowledged.

After a long look at the bike, she turned around and began walking down the lane with Picasso racing ahead and then looking back to make certain she was following. Searching out the bicycle had been a response to something deep inside that she realized she was still attempting to keep buried. *Not yet,* she thought.

The walk into town was an easy fifteen minutes along a well-worn path beside the narrow road. With every step, Katherine reveled in the natural aromatherapy of the herbs and shrubs tumbling from the forest onto the edge of the path. Lavender was the most obvious scent in the air, and occasionally she breathed in wafts of thyme and rosemary.

Light clouds scudded across the periwinkle-blue sky, helping to keep the temperature just right. Feeling slightly lightheaded, she kept grinning.

It's like I'm dreaming. Everything is so perfect, so right, so just how I hoped it would be. I will be fine. I will be on my own and I will be fine.

Church bells rang out as she entered the village, signaling the end of Sunday morning Mass. A few of the faithful straggled out the beautifully carved wooden doors of the fifteenth-century church as the priest wished them good day from the steps. Katherine decided to have a *crème* at one of the spots in the square before she went to look inside.

Planning to have a quiet day settling in to her surroundings and adjusting to the time change, the view from the patio where she sat with her coffee was distracting her. She sipped slowly and tried not to think of a caffe mocha.

Amazing how the right atmosphere can convince me I like this drink.

She could see Gordes beckoning from its perch on the hill. It was too tempting. She knew she had to go there immediately. Joining the long line for the lunch baguette, she faced a decision she hadn't before considered. *"Baguette" isn't just baguette! Pointy ends, round ends, flat, thick, short, long, crisp or not—and people asking for baguette normale, ancienne, intégrale. Yikes—what do I choose? Besides, there are all sorts of other breads and fougasse, in all its variations, seems more popular here.* She had just spotted the display of those specialty flatbreads.

Large wicker baskets full of baguettes were coming, one after the other, from the wood ovens out back as customers left with two or more. The packets of bread were held together by a small square of paper, ends twisted expertly by the cashier to secure them. More often than not, as soon as the customer left the shop, the heel of the loaf was broken off and enjoyed immediately.

As she waited, her eyes swept the shop. Shelves and counters were filled with breads, cakes, and *patisseries* as well as mouthwatering sandwiches. The shop reminded Katherine of an art gallery rather than a bakery, with displays artistically arranged.

How could I forget my camera? she admonished herself. *Never leave home without it!*

As Katherine's turn approached, she listened to the words of the lady before her and repeated the order.

Looks good to me.

Picasso waited patiently outside the shop, happily receiving many pats on the head from villagers who obviously knew him well. Feeling like a local, Katherine munched on the heel of one of her two baguettes as they strolled back to the house.

Lunch consisted of cheese and sliced tomatoes to go with the delicious bread. Sitting in the garden, the clinking of the bells hanging on the goats' necks pleased her immensely.

Making a list, Katherine planned her menus for the next few days. Tomorrow was market day in the village.

This afternoon she would drive up to Gordes and possibly stay there for dinner.

Adding a French phone to her list, she also planned to check out the gas station for Internet access. At this point she wasn't missing it either, she realized with some surprise.

Washing up the dishes, she saw a visitor had dropped by and left a note on the windowsill. Thoughtful Joy suggested she would pick up Katherine the next morning at nine so they could go to the market together and she could show her around the area. Joy said if she didn't hear otherwise, she would consider it a date. Kat looked forward to it.

Leaving Picasso snoozing happily in the warmth of the midday sun on the front doorstep, Katherine hopped into her little Citröen, set the GPS, and drove up the road toward Gordes. As she approached the village, parking signs appeared, and she soon realized she would have to try and find a spot with the hordes of other visitors and tour buses already there.

Of course! It's Sunday. It will be crowded, but not as bad as midsummer, so I will not complain.

The walk from the lot into the village square was mere minutes. Uphill, of course, and lined by stone walls. Once she arrived at the square in front of the palace, that area was surprisingly flat and didn't seem as packed with bodies as she had anticipated. She thought she had never seen so much stone in her life. Her guidebook explained these building materials had originally been dug up from fields as agricultural activity increased during the eighteenth century. There were still *bories*, mortarless stone huts, from those early days just outside the town, which she planned to visit another day. Any new construction in France was strictly regulated, and in the Gordes area, stone must still be used along with terra-cotta roof tiles.

No wonder these villages are so visually pleasing, she thought as she lined up her next photo. There was something to be said for all the rules, *which must have driven the homeowners crazy.*

The immense castle and church dominated the village they once protected, as she had seen from the road. Below them spread a warren of crooked laneways filled with shops, cafés, and tourists. After browsing the traditional products offered in the shops, Katherine climbed the splendid spiral Renaissance staircase of the castle to see an art exhibit displayed throughout. The sheer presence of the architecture of this carefully preserved palace, which existed in 1031 and was rebuilt in 1525, set Katherine's imagination off with fantasies of sieges and battles.

Once again Katherine struggled with her emotions of being on her own. She wasn't missing James, but couples strolling arm in arm or exchanging intimate looks as they shared a glass of rosé were poignant reminders that she was alone.

As the afternoon wore on, her rumbling stomach reminded her she hadn't eaten much. Checking out the numerous restaurants, she chose a smallish bistro with a terrace overlooking an unending view back down to the flat terrain. A *salade de chèvre chaud* followed by a scrumptious lamb dish was as fine a meal as she had ever eaten, she decided. The relaxed ambiance of the al fresco dining suited her, and she studied more tourist information on her Kindle as she dined.

Before long, a British couple at the next table engaged her in conversation, curious about her Kindle and how she felt about it. They continued to regale her through dinner with tales of their motor trip and were entertaining company.

Sleep came quickly that night. The last sound she heard was Picasso's gentle snore as he lay outside her doorway. As she drifted off, a contented smile remained. *"It will be all right" will be my new mantra.*

⚜

Picasso bounded across the grass and skidded to a stop at Katherine's feet, dropping the stick he had been retrieving for the previous fifteen minutes. Tail wagging at warp speed, black eyes intently fixed on her hand as Katherine let the thick branch fly one more time, the Lab dashed after it again.

After only two days, Katherine was already feeling a connection to his loving, accepting personality. She had enjoyed the dogs Andrea had owned through the years, but having one around her all day was a new experience. Through some of the studies and papers at the office, she had occasionally read about the contribution pets made to the attitudes of people suffering from various pain issues. Now she had an understanding. When she had something to say, she told Pico, and as he cocked his head and made better eye contact than many people she had met, she was convinced he cared.

Joy pulled up the driveway and waved as she got out of her Smart Car. Katherine had seen them but never been in one and was thrilled at the prospect.

"Pico, *chien gâté*, you spoiled pup!" Joy said, laughing and giving him an affectionate rub as he greeted her excitedly.

"I see you two are bonding," Joy chuckled as she and Katherine exchanged *bises*.

Nodding with a grin, Katherine picked up her *panier*, a braided wicker market basket, from the front step and climbed into the car. Picasso looked questioningly at Joy and she pointed through the vineyard. *"Au village. Vite! Vite!"* With that he took off at full speed.

As Joy climbed behind the wheel, she explained to Katherine, "Pico will be there before we will—you'll see! I really can't fit him properly in this little car."

"Thanks for picking me up. I'm so excited to ride in one of these! I've seen the numbers slowly growing in Toronto but have never been in one."

"In my opinion they are the only car to have for local driving in this country, with our narrow roads and shortage of space in towns—particularly now that so many foreigners have moved here. But although some do, I don't take it on the *autoroute*."

"That makes sense to me too," Katherine agreed.

"So how are you doing, Katherine? Are you feeling comfortable here? What have you done?"

Katherine passionately relayed the details of the previous day, saying how she had loved her walk into Sainte-Mathilde and then later strolling around Gordes.

"Your voice betrays your emotions about being here. That's so lovely!"

In a few short minutes they were in the village. "Oh, *mon Dieu*, look at this spot I'm going to slip into. My parking *ange* is with us!"

Walking a couple of minutes down a winding, cobbled lane, Katherine's face lit up as they rounded the corner and entered the village square that was transformed into the twice-weekly market. Stalls of beautifully organized fruits, vegetables, herbs, and olives intermingled with those selling flowers, cheese, and meats. At the far end, she could see clothing and linens hanging and couldn't wait to discover what else.

Sitting patiently at the entrance with the nearest vendor talking to him was Picasso. Both women patted his head, and when Joy told him to wait there, he promptly flopped down.

"We're early, so let's begin at the far end and buy our food last," Joy suggested. Katherine was surprised to learn that the markets traditionally opened at 9:00 a.m. She had assumed it would be much earlier.

Joy explained how the market vendors arrived earlier and set up and then sat down for their own coffee and gossip before opening up.

As they passed the stalls, Katherine was reminded of how artistically everything was presented. It was the French way. Nothing was simply helter-skelter on the stands, but rather set out in a way that invited one to browse. Some vendors still used worn wicker baskets that took on richer tones as they aged, and the herb and spice display was nothing short of a prizewinning photo opportunity. The variety and mix of colors caught the eye and didn't let go. Exotic aromas and scents filled the air.

Katherine apologized for continually stopping to take photos, but Joy was only too happy to share in her appreciation of everything. The video camera Kat had been given at the office was being put to good use, along with her digital SLR.

The market spilled down narrow side laneways and there was little one could not find. The multicolored display of made-in-Marseille soaps with their delicate fragrances made choosing just one an almost impossible task. A crowd of women were sorting through racks of fashionably casual linen and cotton clothing. Katherine couldn't recall seeing more linen being worn anywhere else than in Gordes.

"I may pick up a few pieces," she considered, spotting an outfit she liked.

And then there was the hat vendor. *Click!* The stacks of delicately woven fine straw hats with huge brims were a mix of the most vibrant and unusual shades. Joy popped one on her head with a grin and demonstrated how the brims were easily adjusted into all sorts of attractive shapes.

"You must have one, Katherine! I doubt you will find these at home. They are from Italy, and all the tourists love them! And so do we—since we are so conscious of the sun these days."

Katherine agreed they were irresistible and after much deliberation settled upon a soft turquoise shade. Joy and the hat vendor exclaimed how the color complemented her skin and eyes as Katherine blushed.

They lingered over the household linens, admiring the quilts and the ever-popular Provençal tablecloths and placemats in the classic colors and patterns. Those had been the gifts Katherine had purchased so many decades before—*a lifetime ago, really*, she thought—when she was in Villefranche, and she knew she would want some again.

"I'm going to wait to buy things like that until I visit more markets," she said to Joy, who nodded.

Joy agreed they represented true traditions of Provence, even though they had become kind of touristy and displayed everywhere you turned. She warned Katherine to check labels to see if they were actually made in France. By law, everything made in France was so marked.

"There are so many knockoffs being produced in Asia and other places, and the quality is simply not as good. But don't worry about the hats; we know where they are produced in Italy, and again, they have been selling here forever."

"I know what you mean. We have the same problem at home and I always try to buy goods made in North America there. I only want to purchase things made in France while I'm here—or Italy," Kat added with a smile.

They continued browsing the stalls, with Katherine particularly drawn to the olive-wood items.

"I will take you to a smaller village one day if you like," said Joy, "where I know a craftsman whose family has been creating from olive wood for centuries. His prices and the selection of products cannot be matched."

"I would love that," Katherine replied, appreciating her good fortune at meeting this thoughtful woman.

When they returned to the food vendors, Katherine tried to control herself. Everything tempted. Joy was greeted by name by most of the vendors, and she took the time to introduce Katherine. Whenever she mentioned Kat was from Canada, bright smiles followed.

Purchasing just enough cheese, salad greens, and a roasted chicken for the next few days, Katherine calculated she would probably have one meal a day out somewhere as she explored. The selections of tomatoes amazed her, and on Joy's recommendation she purchased a very odd-looking variety. Plump and ribbed, they appeared slightly squashed, like none she had seen before.

"We English call them harem cushion tomatoes, and don't they just look like that?" Joy asked with a laugh. The vendor smiled as he weighed them and gave Katherine clear instructions how to serve them as Joy nodded in agreement.

"It's the only way," she smiled.

Olives, tapenade, lemons, and local olive oil were essential buys.

And of course, the daily baguette as well as two croissants, just because they looked as divinely delicious as she knew they would taste.

"If you would like to buy some wine, we will pass a *cave* on the way back to the car. We have many fine small local vineyards, ours included, that produce labels you will want to try. I promise you won't be disappointed."

Collecting Picasso as they left the market, they next stopped at Le Petit Café. Joy offered Katherine more history of the village and the area while they watched the bustling activity.

"This is the oldest café in our little village, owned by the same family for six generations! In the beginning it was also an inn for voyagers passing through, but that vanished along with the horse and carriage."

Katherine shook her head. "That's something that we would simply never find in North America. I can't believe how many small independently owned businesses there are in this area. I'm glad that the big-box invasion has not found you."

Joy looked confused, repeating, "Big box?"

Katherine explained how Super Walmarts and other huge merchandising outlets were destroying the main streets and small businesses of communities back home.

"Oh, there are some over by Avignon, but so far we are resisting."

Lingering over their drinks—*café* for Joy, *crème* for Katherine—they chatted easily as Picasso quietly rested his head on his paws under the table.

Katherine remarked how she admired the shopkeepers' attitudes toward dogs in their establishments. "That's another thing you will never see back home."

Joy looked puzzled, commenting that as far as she knew, every country in Europe had the same attitude toward dogs and treated them as guests. Water bowls and treats were everywhere.

Smiling at the thought, Katherine also mentioned how happy she was at the house and with Picasso keeping her company.

"That's wonderful, but you know he can stay with me, if you would rather."

Shaking her head, Katherine assured Joy that she truly was enjoying his personality and discovering that he was such good company.

"He's a special dog," Joy agreed. "And the goats? Have you met François yet?"

Katherine looked puzzled. "I guess not," she answered.

"Ah, he is *le berger des chèvres* . . . the shepherd of the goats, I guess you would say," she said, her English becoming more French for a moment. "He's actually a retired investment banker from Paris! His family has had goats here forever—they make *un bon chèvre*—fine goat cheese—and when he retired, this is what he wished to do. You will like him, and he speaks excellent English."

"I guess that's who I saw yesterday, and he waved," Katherine said. "But . . . wait . . . I also saw him when I got lost on the first day. He didn't speak English then!"

Joy had a sheepish grin as she told Katherine that François sometimes did that with tourists. "He will have to apologize."

Now Kat laughed. "Not at all. That made the experience even more authentic! I love the sound of the goats' bells and the gentle bleating of those sweet little kids. I feel like I'm living in a movie right now," Katherine said, beaming with delight.

Joy sighed. "I understand. I still feel the pleasure of living here, although we have had hardships through the years with drought and disease in the vineyard, and the French bureaucracy can make one crazy. Even so, I believe Provence is a special place and we who live here are blessed."

Stopping in at a small electronics shop that supplied *Orange* service, the French telephone and wireless supplier—Joy helped in choosing a simple, inexpensive pay-as-you-go phone. Katherine's Canadian phone was turned off and packed away until the return trip to Toronto.

The next stop was the Internet room at the gas station. Joy made introductions and Katherine was welcomed with quiet reserve. She was pleased to see there was a well-organized room with six computers, and gaining access was simple. Joy suggested Katherine take some time to send a few messages while Joy ran errands. There were inquiring e-mails from everyone, and Katherine responded with a short group message say she was "alive and well and living in paradise."

When Joy dropped Katherine at the house, Picasso raced to the car to welcome her back. Katherine grinned, impressed with his independence.

"Call me if you need anything, and let me know when you want to go to see the olive-wood shop. Also, I wish to invite you to lunch at my home on Sunday. It will be crazy, with lots of family, and they would all be so happy to meet you. What do you think?"

"Oh thanks! I'd love to," Katherine responded, feeling pleased.

The afternoon passed quickly. Lunch on a terrace by the back gardens was a celebration of delicious taste sensations as Katherine sampled her morning market purchases.

First she followed the directions the vegetable seller had given her when she purchased those most amazing tomatoes.

Slicing them, she drizzled olive oil and lemon juice before she sprinkled fresh basil, salt, and pepper all over. Accompanied by the crisp, fresh baguette, the result was indeed divine. She knew she would be preparing this many more times. A little *pâté*, some cheese, olives, and of course more baguette followed, accompanied by a glass of—Joy's recommendation—Bandol rosé. Yawning and stretching, *a nap on the chaise might be the perfect finish*, Katherine thought.

She could hear the goat bells faintly and noticed they were much farther away today. The sound of the cicadas was the only other accompaniment to the silence that surrounded her. Peace.

She relished the quiet and the time to gather her thoughts. *This whole experience is so much more than I expected it would be. I just wish I could tell Mom about it. Maybe she and Dad are watching . . .*

Turning on her Kindle, she pulled up travel information and planned more excursions. It was pleasant to have time to relax in her own space that was easily feeling like home.

Shaded from bright rays but still warmed by the midday sun, Katherine dozed off with her trusty canine snoring a few feet away.

Later, writing postcards she had purchased in Gordes, Katherine picked at the roasted chicken for dinner. Her messages to her office colleagues were brief but passionate expressions of her happiness with this adventure.

Anxious to use the rose-scented *savon de Marseille* and bath oil she had purchased at the market, she wrote her journal entry, then indulged in a long soak in the claw-foot bathtub. Climbing into bed, she turned to say goodnight to Picasso, who was standing in the doorway where he had been sleeping since she arrived. Somehow she sensed he was staring at the carpet beside her bed, so she invited him to come—*viens*—leaning down to pat the rug. Before she could blink, he was lying on the rug looking up at her with the kind of gratitude only a dog's eyes can offer.

16

Up with the sun, Katherine unfolded her bright-purple yoga mat and congratulated herself on having squished it into her suitcase. A last-minute decision when she packed the final few items on the evening before her departure, it had meant she had to sit on her bag to close it. Spreading the mat on a terrace in the early-morning light, she went through a one-hour yoga routine. Letting go had never been easier.

Picasso spent the entire hour moving from one side of the terrace to the other as he watched Katherine transition from pose to pose. Cocking his head with obvious curiosity, it appeared he wasn't going to rest until he had it figured out. Kneeling on her mat after she had cooled down and meditated, Katherine beckoned Pico to come to her. As he sat facing her, she rubbed his ears and bent her forehead to his in a quiet moment of connection that surprised her.

The plan was to head to Roussillon bright and early to avoid the worst of the crowds. She set the GPS and headed off. While Gordes had been close to the top of her must-see list, Roussillon was without question number one.

Through the rearview mirror, she watched Picasso settle onto the front step to await her return and felt a twinge of guilt for not bringing him along.

The color of the earth began to take on tones of reddish orange as Katherine drew closer to town. She had read that the ochre in the surrounding area was a natural pigment used in paints, and the quarry here was one of the most significant deposits in the world. The village perched on the ridge of a steep cliff, and Katherine was pleased to discover she could still find a parking spot in the lot partway up the hill.

As she had expected, her camera was out and in action the minute she exited her car. All the houses were painted ochre shades that varied subtly from light yellow to dark red. Brightly colored shutters and doors added to the striking appeal of this *plus beau village* from the base of the village right up to the summit of the Castrum.

The red, yellow, and brown shades of the earth created a striking contrast to the deep green pine trees and the vivid blue of the Provençal sky. The hours passed quickly as she indulged in the sheer beauty of it all.

The small square at the top of the village was lined with restaurants, and Katherine chose a small place with an enormous patio in the back that provided a full 360-degree view. The patchwork of orchards, vineyards, lavender, and wheat fields stretched across the valley to the Grand Luberon, the slopes of Mont Ventoux, and the plateau of the Vaucluse. It was a stunning panorama that she felt was hers alone as she ate her green salad and planned which ice cream flavor she would choose for dessert.

After relaxing, consumed by the vista, she pulled her old running shoes from her backpack and changed as she lined up for a ticket to the ochre mines. Now that the mines were no longer used, the tour was recommended as an excellent opportunity to understand how ochre was produced and the important role it played in the development of the area until the end of World War II.

As Katherine walked along the trail of multicolored sand, the well-signed path described the geology, the plants, and the history of the amazing deposit that dated back millions of years.

"A palette of flamboyant color," she read on the brochure in her hand. *Got that right.*

Driving back home with her now-orange shoes stashed in a bag, Katherine entertained romantic fantasies of running away to live in Roussillon. The village had an allure and gentle luminosity that was hard to resist, in spite of the tourists. Even so, she knew the crowds would be far worse a month from now and was glad to be there in June.

As she drove up the lane to her *mas*, Katherine blinked and shook her head in disbelief. Goats were everywhere. In the gardens. On the terraces. Lounging, grazing, wandering. Something was very wrong. Katherine also realized that Pico was nowhere to be seen, which was even stranger. Surely he would have been a little excited about this caprine invasion of his territory.

Walking around to the back of the house, she was greeted with even more goats. Laughing out loud as she spotted one on top of the potting shed, she jumped in surprise as she was lightly but firmly butted from behind. Animals were clustering around her and she couldn't help but smile at the sweet babies with their soft coats demanding to be touched and stroked.

She was about to open the kitchen door to get the list of family numbers, to call someone to help, when she heard a bark coming from down the lane by the adjoining field. Almost as far away as she could see, she could make out Picasso.

Calling him, she watched him come tearing toward her. Partway, he stopped—legs rigid—looked at her, and barked intensely, as if to announce this was not a game. Then he went running back. After he repeated this several times, Katherine hastened farther down the lane and saw Pico was worrying about something piled on the ground.

Breaking into a run, Katherine hurried to where Picasso was waiting and realized a person was lying in a heap. She recognized the goat herder's clothing and knelt down. He was barely conscious and spoke haltingly, *"Au secours . . . aidez-moi . . ."*

For a moment she was paralyzed into inaction before her mind kicked into gear with a plan. He didn't need CPR, she determined; he needed an ambulance. She wrestled with the question of whether she should help him up or not and was frustrated at not knowing the right choice.

He waved at her to go. *"Allez . . . allez . . ."*

Assuring him she would get help, she raced back to the yard and straight to the potting shed. Hopping on the bicycle, she pedaled as quickly as possible through the vines to the manor house, searching for the French words she would need.

She could see two men working among the vines.

"Allo-o-o-o," she called as she neared them. "Help! *Au secours, s'il vous plait. Au secours! Il y a un homme qui est blessé. Venez vite! Venez vite."*

The men raced to the house, shouting directions as others came outside and a car took off toward the road. Then they jumped on a motorcycle and roared to the scene. Katherine pedaled furiously behind them.

Within twenty minutes an ambulance left with François strapped to a gurney, weak but conscious. The fear was he might have suffered a stroke. Joy, along with a handyman who had been working at the house, had been in the car that took off. They had called the emergency services number at the same time, and the response had been rapid. A relative of François had been called and would be waiting at the hospital.

Now they all sat around Katherine's kitchen table, the men and Picasso having rounded up the goats and securely settled them in the field. Joy had produced a bottle of *pastis* from her brother-in-law's cupboard, and Katherine offered a bowl of olives and some nuts.

"My dear," Joy addressed her, "thank goodness you arrived home when you did. Who knows how long François would have lain there otherwise."

"Well, thanks to Pico," Katherine responded as she reached down to scratch his neck. "I never would have seen him were it not for this good boy."

Speculating about the destination of the ambulance, the consensus was it would be Avignon, as their medical facilities were the best.

The men spoke of their admiration for François and his love for how he spent his days there. Joy explained that he came to Sainte-Mathilde from Paris intermittently through the year and then for most of the summer. He usually passed the better part of his days with the goat herd.

Their expressions reflected their affection.

"In spite of his successful business life in Paris," Joy translated, "François is really a philosopher . . . a man of the earth . . . he loves nature."

Katherine listened, adding her hopes that he would recover well.

The conversation this time was more in French than English and with the excitement they had just experienced, it was often too fast for Katherine to follow.

Joy translated when she felt Katherine was getting lost, and the others apologized for speaking so quickly. Nothing really changed, though, and Kat was reminded of how much work she needed to do on her language skills.

Politely refusing an invitation for dinner, Katherine waved goodbye from the back terrace. Everyone watched their step in order to avoid the goat poop littering the yard, and Joy assured her they would send one of the field workers to clean it up.

As Kat climbed the creaky stairs to the bathroom, the only thing on her mind was a good long soak with more of her luxurious bath oil. As the water filled the deep tub, she went downstairs and poured a glass of sauvignon blanc, calling a reluctant Pico in from his evening rounds. The smells remaining around the yard by the goat invasion had left him plenty of spots to investigate.

Katherine set her iPod in the portable travel speaker; Ella Fitzgerald pieces played softly in the background. She turned the light off, moonlight filtering through the small window creating a delicate glow.

At the open door, she heard Picasso flop down with a deep sigh. He'd had quite an adventure himself.

Sinking under the water up to her neck was a blissful indulgence that calmed her after the stressful experience of finding François. One thing she missed in her parents' house was a deep bathtub and this reminded her she should seriously consider a bathroom renovation when she got back to Toronto.

Sipping her wine, she reflected on all that had transpired since she boarded the TGV in Paris on Saturday morning. The exchange was a big part of making this trip so special. Having a base that felt like a home added a different dimension to taking a trip. It was such fun to have all this space and not be confined to a hotel room. And Picasso—who knew? Also, she was incredibly fortunate to have met Joy, who made her feel as if she belonged there. As she counted her blessings, a feeling of shocked awareness overtook her thoughts.

"The bicycle. My God, I got on the bicycle," she said out loud. Eight months and a bit, she quickly calculated. That's how long it had been.

17

Katherine awoke to a loud knocking, followed by Picasso roaring down the stairs and barking ferociously. Throwing on her robe, she hurried down and peeked out the small window in the door to see a middle-aged woman waiting patiently.

"*Bonjour, madame. Je suis Marie-Claude, la femme de ménage.*"

"*Oui, bien sûr,*" replied Katherine, "*entrez, s'il vous plaît.*" Of course, she thought, *it's Wednesday*—she knew about a housekeeper coming on Wednesday and Saturday. The Lalliberts had told her in an e-mail, and it was also noted in the exchange booklet.

Katherine felt embarrassed that there wouldn't be much for the woman to do, but Marie-Claude was as cheerful as could be and quickly set about her work. Occasionally she would ask Katherine a question about how she was enjoying her visit, but otherwise she seemed to have no trouble keeping herself busy.

Surprised to discover she had slept until after 9:00 a.m., Katherine decided to go into town for a *pain aux raisins* and *café crème* rather than stay underfoot. She could stop at the gas station and catch up on e-mails too.

She would ride the bicycle to the village.

Looking at the map in the exchange booklet, she noted she could ride through the vineyard almost right to the village with only a short distance involving the road. Walking to the potting shed, Katherine felt a moment of hesitation.

In the early weeks after "la Katastrophe," she felt she would never ride a bicycle again. The memories she attached to cycling with James were simply too painful. Her mother had pointed out how Kat was sacrificing something important to her, but she was not to be dissuaded at the time. However, in an emergency situation where she had no time to question her actions, she had ridden a bicycle.

Now she moved the ancient Peugot into the sunshine and took a good look at it. The simplicity made her smile. With no gears to shift, this bicycle was as basic as they came. Hopping on, she headed toward the village, bumping through the vineyard with Picasso trotting along behind. When she reached the road, the dog immediately ran up onto the trail beside it. He knew what he was doing.

"Good boy!" Katherine called to him, feeling something like pride for this companion that was quickly claiming a piece of her heart.

Deeply inhaling, she marveled yet again at the abundance of fragrance in the air. Nothing was banal here. From a simple stroll or bike ride to standing on a hilltop looking out over a stunning vista, the senses were always engaged.

Leaving Pico outside the gas station with the bike, it felt wrong not locking it up.

Andrea had sent a long update on her family life, saying everything was in order and describing the busy activity at the farm, as always during the short growing season.

Lucy sent office news and said how she was reading all about Provence for the first time ever. She relayed greetings from the rest of the staff. Molly's message had a worrying undertone, although she didn't say anything specific was wrong. She mentioned she had apparently misplaced her purse at school, although she couldn't see how it had possibly happened. It was discovered in the women's staff powder room and returned to her by the math teacher, who said it was sitting on the counter. "Fuckin' bizarro" was her comment.

Sending a collective message to them first, she followed with a private one to Molly, assuring her that stuff like a misplaced purse happens to all of them. Suggesting they Skype on Sunday at 4:00 p.m. Provence time, which would catch Molly with some of her rare free time, Katherine thought they should talk.

Kat was increasingly aware of how personal her interactions with Molly had become and wondered if Molly had ever had other close friends with whom she shared her feelings. She really had no idea; Molly never spoke about any other girlfriends.

But then, neither did I, thought Katherine. *I told everything to James, and he always convinced me nothing was a problem. I never thought about how great girlfriends might be.*

Bidding the others in the room *"bonne journée,"* she walked to where she had left the bike leaning against the side of the building. Picasso lay next to it, indicating clear proprietorship. When Katherine had asked Joy about locking the bike, she had been answered with a look of surprise and told it simply was not necessary. Smiling, she now understood why.

Next stop was Le Petit Café for a *crème* and *a pain aux raisins.* Picasso lay by her feet munching a biscuit the waiter had given him, and Katherine chuckled, noticing other village dogs stopping by for a treat from time to time as they made their daily rounds.

With a sandwich and the local newspaper in the basket, along with her water bottle and camera, she headed home. The pavement felt like velvet after the lumps of the vineyard trail, and when she came to the turnoff to her house, Katherine simply kept on going.

Picasso stopped and yelped a warning. She looked back to see him standing and barking sternly at her to let her know she had missed the turn. When she continued, he hurried to catch up through the woods.

The warm morning breeze caressed her skin and ruffled her hair as her legs pumped rhythmically. The bike was as basic as one could find, and yet somehow a finely tuned machine. There was no need for gears with roads as flat as those nearby, and the odd incline presented a welcome opportunity to work a little harder. It had been a very long time since she had ridden like this—simply for the pleasure of it and on her own. *Well*, she smiled, *not exactly alone*. Picasso trotted barely ahead of her, just off the road, as if he knew precisely where she was headed.

The plane trees lining the narrow road provided a canopy of dappled shade. Traffic was light along this route except for two groups of bicycle tours that passed her, waving and calling *bonjour*.

I'm going to seriously plan to book a cycling tour in France. Maybe Andie will want to come with me.

The simple act of riding down a country road brought history to life as Katherine recalled all she had read about Napoleon ordering the planting of thousands of the trees throughout the country to shade his armies.

Taking in the details of the lush farmland, orchards, and olive groves she passed, the aromatic smells wrapping around her, and the effortless motion that carried her along, Katherine felt something building strongly inside her. *I am happy.* The feelings began in her heart and spread through her entire frame. *I am so happy.*

Pedaling on, she reached a small bridge crossing a shallow creek that bordered on a field of sunflowers blooming in full glory. The brilliant golden flower heads, bursting with dark seeds, raised up to the deepest blue sky. Brown-tinged leaves betrayed the lack of rain recently.

"Oh my, my, my," she said out loud.

On the other side of the bridge, Katherine stopped on the almost nonexistent shoulder of the road and pulled the bike up through the long grass to rest it on a wire fence. Picking up her camera, she lost herself in the setting. Picasso wiggled under the fence and kept busy investigating areas of interest while her shutter clicked away. Close-ups, landscape settings, every conceivable angle, and some shots of Pico poking around—she took them all.

Then she sat by the edge of the creek, the sunflower field her backdrop, and ate half of her baguette sandwich. Pico eventually joined her and was rewarded with a few nibbles. She considered the immense pleasure of doing what she felt like, when she felt like it. *So much for my organized, structured life.*

Wrapping the remaining half of her sandwich in its paper bag, she leaned back on her elbows with her eyes closed, basking in the warm sun and serenaded by the soothing sounds of the babbling brook. Her memories took her back to the day her life had changed, and slowly she worked her way through the months to this moment. She had been there many times before. Sometimes the process had been easier than others.

Thoughts of her mother filled her now. The serenity of this setting brought back memories of the gentle woman she had been. Katherine knew how *Anyu* would have approved of this trip. She heard her mother's gentle reminder after James had left: "What doesn't kill us makes us stronger." Katherine had been guided by those words her entire life, but now, knowing the details of her past, she realized the deep meaning they held for her mother.

Absentmindedly she reached over to stroke Picasso's back.

I am getting stronger.

It wasn't that James had walked all over her. He just liked to be in charge, and he did it well. He made all the decisions and she complied. He planned trips and Katherine made the bookings. It seemed to be teamwork. Now she realized it wasn't.

He moved me like a chess piece. His story became mine. Now I'm rewriting.

Riding back to the house, she kicked up her speed a notch. Nothing like the powerful bikes she had ridden for years, but still it was satisfying. She missed cycling, she had to admit, and this experience confirmed she would get back into it in Toronto.

The Peugeot survived the workout and in fact gave her a great ride. She gratefully gave it a pat as she put it back in the potting shed. Walking through the garden to the kitchen door, she noticed she had missed a visitor. On the windowsill sat a bouquet of flowers—a colorful and fragrantly exotic mix made up of possibly the most spectacular selection of blooms she had ever seen. She was not even certain what half of them were.

She had noted cleverly creative bouquets like this in shops in Gordes and Roussillon. With the stems gently twisted and tied, the bouquet sat in a water-filled colored plastic bag that gave the impression of a vase. Picking it up, she breathed in the fragrance and stood for a moment enjoying the blend of colors and textures. Taking the card she discovered tucked in the center, she went into the kitchen and set the flowers on the table. For a moment, but ever so briefly, she remembered the last bouquet she had received and then banished the thought.

The note was simply handwritten.

I am the nephew of François. He is becoming better, and we say merci mille fois. I would like to meet you and will be with the goats tomorrow morning. Philippe

Marie-Claude was gone and the house was spotless. Katherine had planned to do some laundry in the afternoon and was shocked when she saw her clothes neatly folded on the bed. Done.

The rest of the day was spent reading in the garden, where she immediately noticed the absence of the clinking goat bells. With some surprise, she realized she missed the sound and hoped it would soon return. As dusk fell, she moved to the comfort of the living room.

The evening was devoted to what she thought might be her new addiction: playing bridge on her laptop. Molly had lent her some beginner and intermediate bridge programs by Canadian bridge guru Audrey Grant, and Katherine discovered a keen enjoyment of the game. At home she had even gone so far as to play with real people in online card rooms but still didn't feel ready to sit down to a serious game otherwise.

After the events of the previous day, Katherine had felt she needed a quiet day off, and this one had been just fine.

18

After another sunrise yoga session in the garden, Katherine now looked out the bathroom window as she toweled dry her hair after her shower. Hearing the familiar bells, she hung farther out and could see goats grazing just across from the house in the lower field.

By the gate, a sleek racing bicycle rested against a tree.

Dressing quickly, Katherine stopped to take a few bites of a croissant in the kitchen before she walked out the front door.

Picasso came bounding around the corner of the house when she called him, stopping in front of her for a few seconds for a morning ear rub. Giving her a look, he disappeared back from where he had come.

Following around the corner, she saw her competition for Pico's affection. At the edge of the goat field—as she had now come to think of it—a slim young man in classic serious cycling gear sat on a boulder. Smoking and looking in the other direction, he turned when Picasso ran up to him.

Katherine noticed him give the dog a treat and wondered where on earth he had stored it, considering the tight fit of his bright yellow, red, and black spandex. The thought flitted away when he turned to look at her. She thought she had never seen a more unfriendly face.

Stepping toward him, she reached to shake hands as she would at home.

"*Bonjour*, you must be Philippe. I'm Katherine."

Standing quickly with a sullen expression that startled Katherine, the young man nodded and made a half bow in her direction. Clearly this was his way of greeting her. No hand was extended in return. Nothing further was invited.

"Thank you for the beautiful flowers. That was most thoughtful of you!"

Her words were received with a look of confusion and incomprehension. Taking a long drag from his cigarette, he looked away, blowing the smoke over his shoulder.

"*Oui, je suis Philippe, mais—pas en anglais.*" He raised his shoulders in the classic Gallic shrug, spreading his hands and scrunching his face as he added, "*Désolé.*"

Well, that was almost polite, Katherine thought, then spoke to him in her best French, asking about François.

Philippe's replies were short, fast, and definitely not encouraging of further conversation. He told her François had a "*crise cardiaque*" . . . and would be going home in a few days. He would go back to Paris for tests.

Once again Katherine thanked him for the flowers and received no response.

"*Vous êtes Anglaise?*" he asked without a smile.

"*Canadienne,*" she responded.

With a slightly softer shift of his face, he replied with a quiet "*Bienvenue.*"

Then, after one last quick drag, he flicked his cigarette to the dirt, ground it out with his toe, and walked over to the fence. Hopping over in one swift movement, he picked up his bike. Saying *au revoir* as he strapped on his helmet, he cycled off.

Katherine stood there for a few minutes. She felt confused at the young man's attitude but was relieved to hear François had suffered what she thought was a heart attack and not a stroke. She would confirm that with Joy.

Picasso dropped a stick at her feet. Picking it up, she threw it as far down the lane as she could as she considered the conversation. It was hard to believe this was the person who had left the bouquet. This young man had been the perfect stereotype of a sullen Frenchman. The first she had encountered anywhere on this trip.

"*C'est la vie,*" she said with a shrug of her own.

Thursday morning was market day again in Sainte-Mathilde, and Katherine thought a little retail therapy might be just the thing—a couple of linen items had caught her eye on Monday. She drove to the village so she would still be fresh for trying on clothes, leaving Picasso looking disgruntled on the front steps. Joy had called to suggest they meet at Le Petit Café at eleven, and Katherine took along the itinerary of a two-day road trip she had planned, to get some opinions from her.

Joy was absolutely right about the shortage of parking spots. Katherine had to circle the small lot at the edge of town a few times before someone left. Today she chose a different passageway to walk to the market and again lost herself in the simple beauty and charm of her surroundings.

Many of the houses on this street were ringed by ancient stone walls with flowering vines tumbling down from the top or climbing helter-skelter from where a small patch of dirt provided a rooting spot between the cobblestone lane and the wall. It seemed so natural and unplanned.

The market was vibrant and clamorous. Vendors hawked their wares with humor and enthusiasm, their stalls overflowing with local produce, cheese, wine, and oil. Katherine resisted making any of these purchases, as she was leaving the next morning for an overnight trip she had planned before she came to France.

Heading straight for the clothing stand, she checked through racks of linen and cotton skirts, dresses, pants, tops, and jackets. The selection of styles was as varied as the choice of colors, and today a very pale dusky-blue was calling to her.

With the help of an efficient but taciturn woman, she took a dress, capris, and cropped jacket into the changing area, which was simply a large sheet hung on a circular wire. *Different*, she observed, *but it works!*

Loving the feel and fit of the clothes, Katherine was quick to make her purchases. Gone were the days of haggling over prices, Joy had explained to her on Monday. With the economic crisis in France just as bad as it was in North America, that old tradition was now frowned upon. Everyone was struggling to make a living.

Katherine felt the prices were still reasonable and the quality of the linen like none she had seen at home. On the other hand, when was the last time she had even looked at linen in Toronto? It was a fabric that just seemed so right over here in the South of France, and she convinced herself she would wear the items at home as well.

Today she wandered around the periphery of the market, taking candid photos of the displays and vendors. She hadn't noticed before how many small cafés lined the street. Their tables were filled with coffee drinkers, smoking and chatting animatedly or reading the daily journals. It was quite amazing, she thought, how smoking was still a big part of this culture.

Losing herself in the satisfaction she found through her camera lens, Katherine suddenly realized it was almost eleven and hurried across the square.

Joy stood and waved as she reached the café. Greeting Katherine, she introduced her to a classically beautiful, tall, and slim fiftysomething French woman—dressed in well-pressed linen, Katherine noted.

"This is my dear friend, Mirella. I thought the two of you would enjoy meeting. Mirella knows everything there is to know about the Luberon—its history, what to see and what to miss, who's who, what concerts are on, and the bits of folklore and, shall we say, gossip?"

Mirella laughed easily and confidently in a quiet way. "Katherine, I'm so pleased to meet you. Joy told me about this wonderful home-exchange adventure, which intrigues me. I don't know anyone who has done this before, and it sounds like such a . . . *bonne idée!*"

They placed their orders, conversation then flowing as Mirella plied Katherine with questions about the exchange process.

"Ah, but now I understand you might have some questions. Joy told me you are taking a little motor trip tomorrow."

Katherine grinned with excitement as she took the papers out of her *panier*.

"I am a big Peter Mayle fan and have read all of his tales about Provence," she began, but then stopped as she noticed a look exchanged between Joy and Mirella.

"Oops . . . I'd heard there was some controversy as to how folks in Provence feel about his books," Katherine said, looking apologetic.

The Frenchwomen laughed. *"Non, non!"* Mirella said. "We enjoy his books too. But admittedly life did change here after he wrote them, and there was quite an inundation of British into the countryside of Provence. Some people like to blame him."

"We hadn't stopped to think he had made such an impact in North America too," Joy continued. "But . . . why not?"

"Well, many people I know are also fans of his," said Katherine, "and I have to tell you, I wouldn't know nearly as much about this area were it not for his stories. So, I did some research when I knew I was coming here. Tomorrow I am taking myself on an abbreviated road trip to just a few of the towns about which Mayle wrote. I'm going to explore and stay overnight, and I would love you to tell me if I have made good choices, or if I'm missing anything."

They studied the map with her highlighted route.

"Here's my plan. I'm going to leave early tomorrow morning and go to Bonnieux for the Friday market. Then I'll check into the inn I've chosen, which is just down the hill from the town. I am *so* excited about staying there!"

"Wait! Let me guess," interrupted Mirella. "I imagine you are going to stay at Le Mas des Oliviers! *Oui?*"

Katherine laughed. "Right you are!"

Joy looked at Mirella in amazement. "How did you guess?"

"Everyone I've spoken with lately has been dying to stay there. It's one of the Bonnieux hot spots at the moment."

Joy explained to Katherine that Mirella was an English teacher at a college near Avignon, and students often ask for recommendations.

"So then what's next?"

"I'm going to drive to Lourmarin, poke around, and have lunch before I go up to Ménerbes. I want to visit the village and see the *bories* and *dolmens* in that area. I might make a quick stop in Lacoste, although I understand there is not much there except the ruin of the castle of the Marquis de Sade. But I might save it for Saturday depending on my time."

Joy and Mirella both nodded in agreement.

"That will be enough sightseeing for me tomorrow, and if this weather continues, I should be able to enjoy some pool time before dinner. I hear the kitchen is beyond compare!"

"Food in France is serious business, as you know," said Joy.

Laughing, Mirella added, "But in Provence, it's close to sacred."

"I'm not even thinking what the scale will say when I get back home," Katherine assured them. "I'm going to enjoy every opportunity to eat while I'm here! Is there a restaurant you suggest for lunch in Lourmarin?"

"Here's my suggestions," offered Mirella. "Have lunch at L'Antiquaire in Lourmarin—"

Joy held her hand up to interrupt. "*Ah mon Dieu*, if their *daube* is on the menu, I highly recommend it. It's a traditional Provençal recipe, really authentic local cuisine. *Comme un rêve*, a dream, *vraiment*."

Nodding in agreement, Mirella added, "It's their specialty."

She paused as if to savor the thought before continuing. "When you're ready to leave the village, go just a few kilometers down the road to Cadenet and stop for a coffee at a bar across from Le Tambour d'Arcole."

Taking one of Katherine's papers with some blank space on it, she drew a simple map.

"Anyone can tell you how to find it if you still get lost, which we know is so easy to do here. This town is not so pretty, but very authentic, and you will love the story of this statue. It was cast in the 1800s in honor of a little boy from the village who was a drummer boy and a hero to Napoleon when a major battle was being fought in 1796. Any local serving you at the bar will be happy to tell you the story, as they are very proud of it. But to me, the best part is this: In 1943, when France was occupied by Nazis, they were taking every bit of metal they could to melt down for weaponry—statues, gates, art. It was horrible! A number of men in the village secretly dug a huge hole, and in the middle of the night, they carried the statue out of town and buried it. Few people knew of its whereabouts, so the secret would not leak to the Germans. When the war ended, the statue was returned triumphantly to the square."

Joy smiled broadly while Katherine sighed. "That is a beautiful story. I do want to go see it."

"Well," Joy said, "if you run out of time, you can always visit the Ménerbes area on Saturday too."

"For sure. I'm very flexible. I plan on Saturday morning to hike the three-kilometer trail through the cedar forest outside Bonnieux. After that, I'll have the rest of the day to do whatever. I'm thinking I'll arrive back home early Saturday evening."

"Don't worry about Pico. We'll look after him well, even though he does seem to prefer your company," Joy said with a smile.

Katherine laughed and replied shyly, "You have no idea what a gift he has been to me this week."

"Shall we order lunch, ladies? We seem to have a lot of chatting to do!" Mirella suggested, and the others agreed.

Katherine told Joy how happy she was to know François was doing well, and Joy confirmed that he was going back to Paris for tests.

"So you met Philippe?" Joy asked with an expectant smile.

Hesitating, Katherine smiled in return. "Yes." After an awkward silence, the waiter arrived with menus, and the conversation turned once more to a delicious discussion about local dishes.

When the ladies parted, Joy reminded Katherine how much her family was looking forward to meeting her at Sunday lunch at the *manoir*.

"One o'clock will be perfect. *À bientôt!*"

Katherine had one thing on her mind as she parked in her driveway and stepped out to be greeted by a joyful Picasso.

"Let me change, boy, and then we are off for a ride," she told him as she dashed into the house.

A short time later she was back outside, retrieving the Peugeot from the potting shed. For the first time, she saw a biking helmet hanging there and strapped it on.

"*Allons*, Pico," she called, and they set off down the road together.

Katherine still couldn't believe the joy she was feeling from cycling again. The memory flooded back of this indescribable sensation deep inside, something like nirvana, she had always felt on her bike. *It's liberating. It's joyful.*

She felt open, exposed, completely laid bare to the elements. Vulnerable but at the same time in charge, controlling whether she went fast or slow, where she turned, how far she rode. She was loving it again, on a simple basic bicycle. *Well, it* is *French*, she conceded. She knew when she returned to Toronto, she would be retrieving her bike from the garage, uncovering it, and riding once again. It didn't have to be about memories with James, she realized, and the epiphany was almost overwhelming.

She was feeling somewhat close to whole again.

"Who am I without him?" she had asked her therapist so many months ago. Now she was beginning to truly sense the answer to that question and realized words were not enough.

As she rode, Picasso ran along the edge of the road or in the woods where the undergrowth was low. The sense of companionship she felt with him continued to surprise her. The bounteous farmland drew her in with its gnarled vineyards, orderly orchards, lush low rows of greens and vegetables, the soft silver-green shades of the leaves of olive trees, and always the incredibly fresh aromatic air. All of it under an impossibly blue sky.

She knew every day wasn't necessarily like this. The winds of Provence were legendary, and a mistral, with its unkind reputation, completing its long journey from Siberia, could blow in when least expected. She had been blessed so far with the weather. Wind-sculpted trees dotted the landscape, along with tidy stone structures and abandoned ruins in various crumbling states. Limestone outcroppings provided dramatic contrast and perfect settings for perched villages, with rippled blue hills in the distance.

Katherine cycled for most of the afternoon, her legs surprising her. Stopping for breaks by lazy streams, Pico would lap eagerly while she used her water bottle. When she finally pedaled up her own driveway, she was feeling extremely pleased with herself and her stamina, considering her exercise regime had been less than stellar for the preceding months.

Heading straight for the bathtub, she knew her muscles would benefit from a long soak.

Later, as she organized to get an early start in the morning, she gave Picasso a tummy rub and realized she was sad to be leaving him for two days.

19

Midafternoon on Friday, Katherine turned into the lane leading to Le Mas des Oliviers with only one thought in mind. She would be in the pool as fast as humanly possible. It had turned into the hottest day of the week, and she was a mass of wrinkled linen after the fiasco she had just been through.

The day had begun perfectly. The Bonnieux market was setting up when she arrived just before nine, and she had lingered over a *crème* and a *pain aux raisins* on the terrace of a café near the "new" church. *"Only" 170 years old*, she thought with a chuckle, as she considered that would be ancient back in Toronto.

Beginning at the bottom of the town, she wandered through the small market that wended its way up the narrow streets to the square by the twelve-century-old church at the top of the hill. The food stalls toward the top of the market overflowed with temptations, but she knew most of those products would be found at her own market on Monday in Sainte-Mathilde.

Resisting the appeal of the displays and the cajoling of the vendors, Katherine finally faltered with a most delicious Cavaillon melon. The vendor offered a sample to taste, and that was that. *Sold!* To seal the deal, he assured her he would put bite-size pieces into a container so she could easily enjoy it all day. Juicy and sweet but not sugary, and so intensely full of flavor Katherine's taste buds felt as if they would pop. *No wonder you read of them in every book about Provence.*

The view from the top of the village displayed the patchwork landscape rolling right up to Mont Ventoux in the distance to the north, and to the west, the village of Lacoste perched on the next hillside. The ruin of the castle of the Marquis de Sade stood out like a beacon—she couldn't wait to visit.

Munching on the melon, Katherine had taken the quicker route of eighty-six steps down to the bottom of the village and back to her car. Taking her time driving, she was thankful the roads weren't busy this day and she could dawdle as she liked through the sensuous landscape.

Lunch in Lourmarin, set on the plains on the banks of the Aiguebrun River, had been all Mirella and Joy had promised. In the center of town where the roads converged, restaurants spilled their tables into the tree-lined square. Laughter and chatter filled the air. Carafes of rosé sparkled. Unable to resist stopping in a few of the shops, she discovered a glass bowl that would be the perfect gift to take to Joy's lunch. The clerk told her it was the well-known bubbled glass from Biot, a village featuring talented glassblowers, close to Nice. The shade of green and the flowing shape were unique, and Katherine could see a number of ways to enjoy using it.

She waited for it to be gift-wrapped, free of charge, a custom she found particularly charming.

L'Antiquaire had been a challenge to find, but the delicately seasoned stew was on the menu, the service casually efficient, and the ambiance as warm as she had been promised.

The village was yet another visual feast. The blue shutters and doors of so many houses, in a great assortment of shades and weathering, were captured from every angle by Katherine's camera.

Window boxes and flowerpots—the more cracked and chipped, the more beautiful to her—spilled over with vibrant color and artistic combinations of verbena, cosmos, daisies, lobelia, phlox, and so many others she couldn't identify. More than once she stopped to admire colorful geraniums, lush with greenery and enormously brilliant flower heads.

I could easily live here, she thought, as she wandered the narrow lanes. *I just feel it. There's something that speaks to my heart in all of these ancient towns.*

Mirella had promised Cadenet was ten minutes down the road and definitely worth the detour, but not so much for beauty. Katherine agreed. As predicted, the waiter at the bar opposite the drummer boy statue proudly recounted its history, with locals sitting nearby providing further comments. Katherine sat on the terrace for some time, absorbing the lines of the statue, the determined expression of the young boy as he beat his drum. The artist had sculpted a sense of movement into the metal, and Katherine felt a lump grow in her throat at everything it represented.

History is so alive here. I love how it surrounds me.

She also felt it was time to put her camera down, jump in a pool, and cool off. Guided by the map the innkeeper had e-mailed her, she soon found herself back in the center of Cadenet. Driving out of the village for the second time, she passed a small work crew of three men at an intersection where she had slowed down on her first attempt to leave. She smiled sheepishly as they appeared to give her a look of recognition.

The road wound around, as they did, before a bifurcation presented itself that was nowhere on her little map. Guessing as much as anything, she chose the road to the left and drove along, feeling unsure of her choice. She realized her error when she passed the same work crew but from yet a different direction. This time they waved and grinned. She was headed back into the village for a third time. Flustered, Katherine pulled over and managed to explain her dilemma to the workers. After the three men had an exchange that sounded like a serious argument, one took a pen from a clipboard and drew some additional lines on the map. Speaking slowly, accompanied with much gesturing, they gave her very straightforward instructions.

"Non, madame. Non, non, non!" Wagging fingers and shaking their heads when she picked up the GPS.

Katherine drove slowly with the map on the seat beside her. Frustrated and perspiring from anxiety, she was grateful for the help she had received. Seeing the road sign she had been seeking, she suddenly laughed out loud. *That was truly another Griswold moment!* In her former life, she would have had to put up with a profanity-laced tirade from James.

A narrow laneway was lined with mounds of lavender against a massive backdrop of pink, red, and white oleander. Large clusters of pale-mauve blooms gracefully drooped from an obviously well-established wisteria vine that trailed over the entrance to the inn, offering a spectacular show. The property gave the appearance of being deserted, apart from a small gravel parking area that held three other cars.

Katherine knew by now that this was the more exposed north side of the farmhouse. The other side of the structure would be a very different story. This *mas* was considerably larger than "her" farmhouse, but the visceral pleasure was much the same. The stone, the shutters, the tile and beams combined to create a feeling that was warm and welcoming.

Walking into the entrance foyer with her overnight bag, she discovered directions to pull the silk cord hanging nearby to ring a bell. Minutes later she was greeted by a young woman, who asked Katherine to sign in before leading her down a pristine hallway to a small circular stone stairway. At the top, a single door opened to her room.

Decorated entirely in blending shades of cream, off-white, and taupe, the tones complemented the pale stone walls and stripped blond wood beams of the whitewashed ceiling. The furniture was simple and sleek, matching in color to the rest of the room so everything blended in a cloud of soft, subtle refinement. Somehow the clean modern lines worked with the ancient setting.

Sunlight from a large window flooded the spacious minimalist bathroom, with its modern white porcelain fittings and immaculate tiles. Just walking into the room made Kat feel clean.

"Some of our guests are by the pool and at the bar on the terrace nearby, *madame*," said the young woman. "Please let us know if there is anything you wish."

Katherine thanked her, wondering how anyone could wish anything more than this.

French doors opened with a decorative railing stretched across the space. These early buildings in France were not built with balconies, she had read. That was, apparently, because the people spent so much time in the sun for centuries, they wanted to be protected from it once inside. Balconies were normally found only on structures built in the last one hundred years.

After hanging her few items in the closet, she relaxed in the serenity of the room for a few minutes, then showered and changed into her bathing suit and robe. Eager to have that first splash in the pool, she walked out to the terrace.

There were several empty lounges by the pool; five were occupied. Saying *bonjour* to the others, Katherine settled herself on a chaise that was somewhat isolated at the far end of the pool. Although she did not want to appear antisocial, she did wish to have some quiet time. Certainly there would be plenty of chatting at dinner.

She pulled another lounge close to her and placed her Kindle, towel, and sunscreen on it. Easing herself gently into the pool, her entire body responded to the refreshing cool softness of the salt water. After a few laps and some time simply floating in peaceful contentment, Katherine settled on her lounge, applied a generous amount of sunscreen, put on her sunglasses, and began reading.

She startled suddenly to a voice at her side and realized she had been dozing.

"I'm sorry. Do you mind if I take this chair?"

"Mmmm . . . no! Oh. Excuse me . . . of course. Please take it."

"Now my turn to apologize. I didn't realize you were sleeping! Those glasses camouflaged it well!"

Katherine flashed an embarrassed smile as she removed her things from the lounge and looked up at a ruggedly handsome man with a veneer-perfect grin.

"Seriously, I'm sorry to have disturbed your snooze. Could there be a better spot for one?"

Smiling back, Katherine explained, "My goodness, the pool area has become popular! When I arrived there were just a few of us here, so I took the liberty of spreading my stuff to this chair too."

"I guess everyone is back from a day of sightseeing." Offering his hand, he introduced himself. "Matt Robertson."

"Katherine Price," she replied, noting his American accent with its distinct Southern twang.

Moving the chair a few feet away, Matt explained he was on a business trip to Marseille and taking a few days to explore the countryside.

"Do you know this area very well?" he asked.

Katherine told him about her mini-Mayle motor trip. After sharing her experience so far that day, she asked a few questions about Marseille and then turned back to her book as he dove into the pool.

Checking her watch later, she was shocked to see she had slept for over an hour. The pool area had filled with two other couples and three teenagers, and she hadn't heard a sound. Before getting back to her reading, Katherine and Matt exchanged a few intermittent pleasantries about the inn and the area, and she soon heard him quietly snoring. He was still asleep as she tiptoed by to go to her room.

Admiring the freshly pressed linen dress she had brought for dinner, Katherine was glad she had made the purchase. A luminescent shade of the softest blue, it accentuated the striking blue of her eyes. The style, calf length with spaghetti straps, complemented her lean figure.

Leaner in the last six months, that's for certain, she thought as she studied herself in the mirror.

She was glad she was vain enough to still care how she looked. She knew that wasn't always the way divorce affected women—for a while, anyway.

When she had arrived back from the pool, a pitcher of water with lemon and lime slices in it and a small bowl of cherries were on the desk in her room. Now she poured a glass and ate a few cherries as she looked out over the pool and the olive grove beyond. Picking up the phone, she asked the young woman in reception if it might be possible for her to stay in her room for an extra night.

"I will check, *madame*. May I confirm with you later?"

"Thank you. I have a dinner reservation for eight p.m.," Katherine replied.

"*Très bien*, I will find you, *madame*."

Katherine surprised herself by deciding to go to the bar for a drink before dinner.

Must be the curative powers of Provence making me feel so relaxed.

Before going downstairs, there was time to go online to read her e-mails and send a group update as well as to remind Molly about their Skype date on Sunday. Just after seven, she walked into the intimate bar area, which extended onto a vast terrace accented with enormous terra-cotta planters overflowing with a riotous color mix of plants. Once she had her glass of sauvignon blanc, Katherine went over to confirm they were real.

"It's hard to believe they aren't artificial, isn't it?" a soft British-accented voice asked. Katherine turned to see a woman she had noticed that afternoon by the pool and a young girl who appeared to be in her early teens. They chatted about the flowers on the terrace and through-out the countryside for a few minutes. "Have you been down to the coast—to the Riviera?"

Katherine replied she had not been for a very long time.

"Well, the flowers there are even more abundant. The municipalities take great pride in their gardens, even on the islands on regular streets. In some of the roundabouts—er, traffic circles, as you say—the displays are amazing. Villages and towns compete each year for the coveted *ville fleurie* designation."

The woman was obviously a gardener, and Katherine was happy to learn the names of a few species, unknown to her, that she had seen.

It turned out all three teenagers from the afternoon belonged to this family; two sons drifted in with their father to join their mother and sister.

Introductions were made and pleasing conversation quickly followed. *The British are so very good at conversation*, Katherine thought. The children were equally stimulating conversationalists, and before long the family had invited Katherine to sit at their table for dinner.

Dinner would not be served until 8:00 p.m., and Katherine did not refuse when another glass of her wine materialized. The British were also masters of social graces.

When they were called into the dining area, the women gasped at the candlelit setting. Once again the colors were soft and earthen. The lighting was so cleverly blended, it was hard to believe that anything more than candles created the ethereal effect.

Everyone at the table chose the *specialité de la maison*. Katherine was surprised the teenagers were interested in such fine food, but they explained they had been holidaying in this part of Provence every summer for ten years. They were almost as knowledgeable about the food as their parents.

"That's so wonderful! Travel is the best educator, is it not?" Katherine commented, and they all agreed.

Not long afterward, Katherine noticed Matt come into the dining area and sit alone at a table for two. Looking around, he noticed her and waved with a smile. Katherine waved back, returning the smile.

Wine flowed through all five courses, shifting from sauvignon blanc to a full-bodied Bordeaux to complement the main course, *queue de boeuf à l'orange.*

The teens were anxious to get on to other activities once their meals were finished.

"Undoubtedly of a digital nature," muttered their father as they excused themselves and politely said goodnight to Katherine. The owners of the inn appeared in the dining area to invite the ten remaining guests to join them on the terrace for a *digestif*—a cognac.

"On the house, as you say in America," M. LaFontaine said with a grin. "*C'est offert par la maison . . . un cadeau . . .* a gift, if you please."

Although Kat felt she had consumed more than enough alcohol, the other guests cajoled her into one more. The next thing she knew, Matt was pulling out a chair for her at a long table where everyone was gathered and chatting amiably.

"How can you not want to sit and enjoy this amazing setting?" Matt asked as he sat next to her. "It's like something out of a magazine, isn't it?" Katherine nodded with an appreciative smile and agreed it truly was enchanting. Again, candlelight and torches in the garden accompanied the glow of a nearly full moon. Soft jazz played in the background, and conversation flowed easily as everyone introduced themselves.

Along with the British couple, there were two couples from Paris and another from Germany, with Katherine and Matt being the only North Americans. M. LaFontaine mentioned there was another couple from the United States staying at the inn.

Everyone was interested in hearing about Katherine's mini-Mayle motor trip that day. No one was aware of the story about the statue in Cadenet, and she enjoyed sharing it. Most of the guests had visited the area in the past, and there was much trading of restaurant names and helpful tips about lesser-known places to see. When Kat mentioned she was going to hike through the Cedar Forest outside Bonnieux on

Saturday morning, the British couple told her they had already done this, and described their experience.

"As you may know, since you seem to be a well-informed visitor, it's an easy walk, but lovely. Only one and a half hours full circle, but the views are expansive. There are signs throughout so you know what you are seeing, and we really appreciate that. It gives an excellent overview of the Petit Luberon."

One of the couples from Paris said they planned to do the walk and suggested Katherine might like to go with them. She replied it would be fun to have company.

Lucille and Hubert seemed a delightful couple. She was a tall, slim French beauty, blond with a flawless complexion, and he was a charming dark Italian with sparkling eyes that matched an infectious sense of humor. They were enjoying their first week away from their ten-month-old daughter, Alice, but at the same time suffering the pangs of withdrawal, as new parents do. Photos of the sweet child were passed around for everyone to admire.

"Well, if y'all don't mind," piped up Matt, his Southern drawl slipping in, "maybe I could tag along?"

"*Perché no . . . er, scusi . . .* as you say, why nota?" Hubert answered.

"The more, the merrier!" Matt exclaimed.

"Get an early start," advised M. Lafontaine. "Tomorrow is supposed to be as hot as today. Even though you will be sheltered in the forest, the heat will find you!"

The hikers agreed to meet in the lobby at 8:00 a.m., ready to leave, and Matt offered to drive.

"In that case, I'm going to stumble off to my room," laughed Katherine. "I've enjoyed way too much libation this evening!"

"That makes two of us. Allow me to escort you," said Matt, rising to leave with her.

At the foot of the staircase to Katherine's room, she turned and casually extended her hand. "Thanks. See you in the morning."

Taking her hand, Matt said, "*Merci beaucoup!* Let's be French." Leaning in, he grazed each cheek with his in the French way.

Caught a little off guard, Katherine smiled politely and turned to go up the stairs. His behavior seemed more pushy than gracious, she thought with displeasure.

"*Bonsoir,*" she said.

"*Bonsoir*, Kathy!" He didn't see Katherine wrinkle her nose in annoyance as she quickly opened her door. Inside her room, she rolled her eyes, wondering why some people automatically used common nicknames without asking.

Closing her door, Katherine discovered a handwritten note on the desk indicating she was more than welcome to stay another night in the room.

I'm okay traveling on my own, and every day seems to reaffirm that, she thought contentedly.

Sitting up, she filled out a menu form to hang on her door, ordering a glass of orange juice and croissants for breakfast, then slipped into her nightgown. Sinking into the luxurious comfort of the plump mattress and collection of plush pillows, a smile lingered as she fell asleep in an instant.

20

After a restful night with fresh air streaming through the windows and breakfast at a small table by the open French doors, Katherine arrived in the lobby to find Matt, Lucille, and Hubert ready for the hike. She apologized for keeping them waiting, but they assured her they had all just arrived that minute.

Instructions in hand, they climbed into Matt's car and headed off for the Cedar Forest. The morning was clear, but already a hint of the heat to come was in the air.

Three hours later the bedraggled foursome arrived back and in no time were submerged in the pool. It had been a hot morning for a hike—even an easy one—and the cool water was just the tonic before they continued with the agenda they had cooked up while walking. Katherine's plan was to visit Ménerbes, then explore the countryside, looking for the ancient stone *bories* and *dolmens*. On the way back to the inn she would stop at Lacoste. It was decided all four would go together, and Katherine was happy to have their company. They were delighted she had provided a tour.

After a light poolside salad, Katherine phoned Joy to let her know she was staying an extra night at the inn.

"Pico will be sad," Joy told her. "He keeps walking down to the farmhouse to see if you are there. But I'm so glad you are having such a lovely time. *À demain!*"

When the others had finished their meals, Matt offered to continue his chauffeur services, and they wound their way the short distance to the hilltop village of Ménerbes.

Once again, the views were breathtaking.

"This is the nature of Provence," explained Lucille. "One gasp after another and all in the name of beauty." She had grown up in Normandy, and her stories caused Katherine to decide she must visit that area one day.

Ménerbes was the town Peter Mayle first immortalized in his 1989 book *A Year in Provence*. He was so successful in painting an immensely appealing village and way of life with his words that he eventually was hounded by the tourists who sought out his house. He had done too good a job describing the joys of the area. Everyone felt he was just the type of person with whom it would be lovely to sit and sip wine while listening to his amusing tales. Katherine read aloud that since he had moved to a more private property, the town had returned—somewhat—to a quiet medieval village exquisitely poised over the Luberon Valley. Exploring the paths and laneways past grand village houses and up to the massive Citadelle provided wonderful views over the countryside.

Stopping at a café in the Place de l'Horloge for a break, they consulted travel information on Katherine's Kindle and decided to take a small detour out of town to the Musée du Tire-Bouchon, or Corkscrew Museum. It displayed more than a thousand corkscrews, and Matt wanted to buy a souvenir there.

The winding drive was thrilling, and Katherine had to admit Matt was doing a remarkable job of navigating the twists and turns.

"I love this kind of driving," he assured them with a wide grin. "You don't find roads like this in Florida. It's all flat swampland."

Next on the agenda was the village of Lacoste with the castle ruin of the Marquis de Sade, now owned by Pierre Cardin. Parking at the bottom of the hill, they stopped for a beer at the Café de France, with its popular hanging terrace. Then they continued past the *mairie* and back into the Middle Ages as they walked on the cobblestones through the Portail de la Garde, into the ancient heart of old Lacoste. There were no shops or cafés here, but a delightful jumble of ornately decorated doors, mullioned windows, and intriguing architectural details. And of course the castle.

Dominating the town at the top of the hill, the castle was still in partial ruin, although restoration had been ongoing since the 1950s. The town was busy with activity in preparation for the music festival held every summer in July and August. Looking over the schedule of concerts, the four visitors bemoaned the timing.

Watching Lucille and Hubert stroll hand in hand all afternoon with the occasional PDA, Katherine felt a pang of regret at her lack of romantic memories. James had considered any public show of affection to be juvenile.

Maybe I just don't inspire it.

The heat was getting to all of them, and an ice cream cone was deemed a necessity as they walked back down to the car. There were few villages where there was not a *glacier* selling its own brand of delicious ice cream.

"Katherine, I can't believe you would want to trade your nice modern facilities in Canada to live in a three-hundred-year-old house with bad plumbing and no air conditioning," Hubert commented.

"And who knows what other problems," added Lucille.

Katherine chuckled. "I guess when you have lived with these kinds of villages around you all your life, and so much history, you feel differently about them. Perhaps I'm not being realistic, but I have to say the attraction is overwhelming. I feel the challenge would be worth it!"

The young couple offered a viable argument about the negatives of taking on such a challenge, based on experiences of relatives and other friends living in such villages.

"It's not as romantic as tourists have a tendency to think."

"My head tells me you are undoubtedly right," Katherine agreed, "but my heart wants to think otherwise."

Matt added, "Y'all know this is my first trip overseas, and I think it's cool here—even though everything is so old. I mean, duh, of course it is. I like it too, but I don't think I'd want to live here."

They were all noticeably quieter on the return trip—tired but happy, as Matt said—and he suggested they go out together for dinner.

Lucille and Hubert had dinner reservations in Bonnieux. Although they offered to see if two more guests could be added, Katherine declined. She felt a strong desire for a long soak in the tub and then a quiet meal at the inn.

Matt suggested she join him to eat and she politely agreed, although in truth she would have preferred the evening to herself.

"Meet you at 7:30 in the bar?" he asked.

Katherine nodded and left for her room.

⚜

Matt was sitting in the bar when Katherine arrived, and she suspected he had begun without her. Ordering a Ricard, she took a satisfying sip of the refreshing anise-flavored drink and settled into a comfortable tub chair.

"That's one drink I've never particularly liked," Matt commented.

"I first tasted *pastis* over thirty years ago when I spent six weeks at an immersion school on the Riviera," Katherine told him. "I didn't like it the first time, but I slowly developed a taste for it. Now I love it, probably because it makes me think of France!"

Matt was drinking scotch, and he had two more while Katherine nursed her drink. Just after eight, they were told their table was ready. Feeling as if she had been eating her way through the last two days, Katherine decided to simply have the *sole meunière*. Matt ordered rack of lamb. Through dinner they chatted amiably about life in France, as they saw it, compared to life in North America. She already knew he was married with two grown children, and he knew she was divorced with no children. He had called her Kathy once more in the morning, and she had politely explained that no one called her that. He had said she could call him Matty if she wanted, and they had both laughed at that.

He was a nice enough guy, just a bit loud and opinionated, she had decided. He was certainly thoughtful about driving them around and seemed to appreciate the sightseeing as much as everyone.

Lucille and Hubert, after years in Paris, were more jaded about their culture. Katherine had enjoyed their company today, sharing opinions and experiences.

When Kat had first joined him this evening, Matt politely consulted with her about the wine list and ordered a bottle of Pouilly-Fuissé to accompany dinner. Very nice. The fact that he proceeded to drink most of it, not so much.

As the meal progressed, he became more flirtatious, making the odd comment with less than subtle sexual innuendo. To a point, Katherine was mildly pleased having dinner with a man who appeared to appreciate her, but little warning bells were going off, and it seemed like a good time to end what really had been a lovely day. Ordering a decaf cappuccino, Katherine decided to skip dessert, and Matt agreed that was a wise move. He ordered a cognac instead, and his slurring became more noticeable. Not wanting to appear rude, Katherine lingered just long enough over her decaf before saying she absolutely had to get to bed. This had caused his eyebrows to rise in a salacious manner, which Katherine chose to ignore, but he had remained a gentleman as he stood to say goodnight and walked her to the lobby.

"Let's be American tonight," he said, leering, as he swooped Katherine into a hug. She turned her head just in time as he landed a sloppy kiss on her cheek and released her, much to her relief. Katherine wasn't certain what to do, so she smiled and touched his arm as she thanked him for dinner, which he had insisted he pay for.

"This was a lovely day, Matt, and you were very kind to drive us around. It was good fun."

"It certainly was," he agreed, stumbling back slightly.

Katherine took advantage of that to head to her room, turning back to wave, which gave a certain note of finality to the evening. She would see the group over breakfast in the morning and say her good-byes then. As she closed her door, she blew out a sigh and wondered if she had overreacted to his behavior. It had been so long since she had even considered being in a situation like this, she wasn't sure she was really thinking clearly.

Standing at the balcony railing, she looked out over the pool, now deserted and washed with moonlight along with the fading glow from the garden torches. The air was hot, much more so than the evening before, and an impulsive idea took over. Changing into her bathing suit and robe, she decided she wasn't going to miss this opportunity.

As she walked quietly through the bar and out to the terrace, she noted that no one else was about. Going to the far end of the pool, she draped her robe over a chaise and slipped into the still water. Submerging, she swam underwater to the other end and then glided back and forth in laps, doing a smooth, silent breaststroke. The moonlight bathed her. Absolute silence surrounded her, with the exception of the small ripples of water as she swam effortlessly.

At some point she became aware that the garden torches had gone off completely.

Probably on timers, she thought.

Even though the garden was dark, the main rooms of the inn still glowed. Katherine thought it was probably about time she went in, but lingered at the deep end for a few minutes. Resting her chin on her crossed arms on the pool edge, she let her gaze float through the gardens and olive grove and up to the star-studded night sky.

Magic, she sighed.

A sudden movement of water startled her, and she realized she was no longer alone.

"Don't worry. It's just your pal Matty," she heard as she turned to look behind her. Seeing him already chest deep in the pool, she shook her head with annoyance.

"Well, you did give me a start," Katherine scolded.

"You looked so lonely out here, I thought I should keep you company."

"Nope! Not lonely at all. I was enjoying the peace and quiet."

By this time Matt had reached the end of the pool and was leaning on the edge beside her.

"You're right," he said. "It is peaceful . . ." He hiccupped. "Uh . . . *excusez-moi*, I think that last beverage did me in."

"Time for me to go in," said Katherine, hiding an uneasy feeling. She began to swim to the shallow end, adding, "But do stay and enjoy this."

Matt swam alongside her, causing her to move closer to the edge of the pool. As soon as she could touch bottom, she stopped to pull herself out of the water. Before she could, he was behind her, his arms trapping her on either side.

"C'mon Kathy, don't be in such a hurry. This is the perfect place for romance."

He ran his lips roughly over the back of her neck and locked his hands over hers so she couldn't find the leverage she needed to get out.

For a moment, Katherine was completely panic stricken, then sickened.

How the hell can he be so ignorant . . . so presumptuous?

Keeping her cool despite the flash of panic, Katherine said resolutely, "Don't be ridiculous! You're a married man and there's nothing between us."

With a bit of a snort he said, "Married, shmarried. Didn' we have a beautiful day together?" Pressing into her back, he added, "And there's somethin' between us now."

To her horror, Katherine realized he was naked and ready for action as he rubbed his hardness against her.

Her stomach tightened and her pulse began racing. This was not a good situation. He was drunk and he was strong. His hands had moved to her shoulders now, slipping the straps of her bathing suit down. He had her arms firmly in his grasp, so getting out was still impossible.

Her mind raced.

Fear enveloped her.

Screaming seemed like the only solution. *Do I worry about being embarrassed in a situation like this? What is stopping me?*

She couldn't believe he would really go through with taking her by force. Then she realized she was more angry than scared.

"Matt, be reasonable. Think about what you are doing," she demanded, as her anxiety morphed into strength. "This is crazy."

He was talking nonsense now and drunker than she had realized. "Crazy . . . I'm crazy about you. You're a shpessshul lady . . ."

"I'll scream if you don't let me go."

"Oh yeah, baby, I'll make you scream with pleasure," he slurred, breathing disgusting fumes into the air and grinding his erection into her buttocks.

A thought crossed her mind. She decided to go for it.

"Let me turn around," she said with a softer tone.

He loosened his grip on one arm and she turned, not caring that her suit was around her waist.

She leaned forward as if to kiss him and put her hands on his shoulders. Cupping his hands around her breasts, he relaxed as he moved to respond to her lips. Tightening the hold on his shoulders, which she hoped he would interpret as passion, she raised her knees, pushed back with her hands, and kicked her feet into his stomach with all the force she could muster.

Falling backward, he submerged briefly.

Katherine pulled herself out of the pool faster than she had ever thought possible. Grabbing her robe and holding it against her exposed chest, she raced across the terrace, tears streaming.

Pulling the key from her pocket in spite of her shaking hands, she was safely in her room when her anger exploded.

"What an asshole!" she said out loud. "Asshole, asshole, asshole . . ." she repeated as she stepped out of her bathing suit and stomped into the shower.

Shaking with a mix of powerful emotions, Katherine burst into tears as she willed the steaming hot water to wash off the stain of the uninvited touch, the sense of violation and betrayal.

Katherine tossed around all that night, unable to stop thinking of the incident and pondering why some men were guided by their dicks, as Molly would say. She was certain she had not led Matt on in any way.

The thought never crossed my mind! I didn't behave any differently to him than I did to anyone else here.

Yet somehow this man, a virtual stranger on the one hand but accepted as a friend on the other, had no qualms about assaulting her.

Goddamit! It was frightening, insulting, infuriating! . . . I'm proud of the way I handled the fear. Thank Christ my idea worked.

She was up early, feeling completely disquieted.

"Note to self," she muttered as she packed up her bag and slammed it shut, "let this be a reminder I have no need for a man in my life."

21

By 7:00 a.m. Katherine had paid her bill and thanked the owner, who was up to see off the departing guests.

She debated reporting the pool incident but felt she could prove nothing; it was her word against his. She knew the woman was always suspected of "asking for it." Who would care?

Matt's inexpensive rental car was parked next to hers by the tall hedge at the end of the small gravel lot.

Placing her bag in her backseat, she opened the driver's door and began to slide in when she was suddenly overcome with a memory: her revenge on James's bike and the satisfaction she gained from it.

Making sure she was alone, Katherine quickly crouched between the cars. Unscrewing the top of the tire valve on Matt's rear tire, she jammed small stones into it and listened for the release of air.

Hurray for gravel lots . . . there was no shortage of small, pointy pebbles.

Peeking up slowly to ensure no one was about, she crouched down again and moved to the remaining tires, repeating her actions as quickly as her trembling hands would allow.

As she drove away from the inn, a smirk forced its way onto her face while a thought repeated itself: *I can't believe I did that.*

Soon she was on her way "home," finding it hard to believe her happy interlude had come to such a distressing end. The episode had consumed her during the night, and she wanted to banish it. Emptying those tires had helped.

I refuse to let it spoil everything else, she thought, pursing her lips and scrunching her face in frustration. *He was a stupid guy who had too much to drink and made a very bad decision. I won't forget it . . . but I will get over it.*

Not only had she been delighted with the villages she visited, but Mirella had been right: the drummer boy statue in Cadenet had been worthy of a stop, and the hotel had been a dream, to say nothing of the cuisine. Everyone she met had been so interesting and pleasant until . . .

She shook her head and knew this was not going away so easily.

Robotically, she followed the GPS for some time, until the beauty around her once more worked its magic. The plane trees she was so fond of stood like sentinels along the narrow roads as the early morning light filtered through the leaves. Eventually she felt herself regain a sense of security.

In Sainte-Mathilde, she joined the lineup for baguettes, bought some *pain au chocolat* (*This morning calls for chocolate,* she thought) and exchanged a few *bon dimanche* greetings.

Instant therapy greeted her when she arrived at the farmhouse as Picasso bounced excitedly by the car door. Katherine knelt on the gravel, ignoring the sharp pebbles digging into her knees, and hugged him before he flopped over on his back for a tummy rub.

This is love, she thought, *pure and simple, without threat, without demands.*

Wandering around the house before she went out to the garden to enjoy her breakfast, she relished the sense of belonging. After just a week, the familiarity of these surroundings felt right. Her thoughts turned to Andrea as a feeling of gratitude washed through her.

Placing her *pain au chocolat* on a plate and pouring a glass of juice, she settled happily at the small round table on the back terrace, as she did most mornings. Bees buzzed around the lavender in the early sun, reminding her to buy a few jars of the local lavender honey to take home. She had sampled some in the kitchen and savored the delicately sweet flavor.

Glistening with sweat after a yoga session, she showered and dried her hair before she dressed in a favorite cotton sundress. Coming midway down her calves, pale yellow with delicate straps, it made Katherine feel cool just looking at it. She picked up a lightly woven silk shawl of cream and butter shades to take along in case she needed some protection from the sun. Her wide-brimmed hat from the market would be the final touch.

She knew James had liked her in this dress and thought fleetingly about that now. She had been determined not to toss out her entire wardrobe purely because some items carried such memories.

Ridding herself of the thought, she picked up the gift she had purchased in Lourmarin for Joy and opened the backseat of her car for Picasso. Today they would drive together.

"You're my escort," she told him, patting the nose that was poking over the top of her seat.

It was typical of the complicated system of roadways throughout France that it would take longer to drive to the *manoir* than it would to walk to it through the vineyard. At one point Katherine thought she might be lost and chuckled at the possibility. Driving was no easy matter in this country.

The lane leading from the road to the house was cut through a small patch of forest, and Katherine smiled with delighted awe as she pulled into the large courtyard. She had only seen the structure from the other side when she rode through the vineyard and was simply not prepared for the beauty before her.

Sitting on a slight rise, the large ochre-toned two-story rectangular structure was the epitome of Katherine's fantasy of a French manor house. A tower wrapped around the eastern corner, hinting at the early Italian influence. Blue-shuttered windows were placed asymmetrically the length of the manor with shuttered French doors beneath them. The enormous door of the grand central entrance stood open, and Katherine could hear Joy's greeting voice as she approached. A wrought-iron balcony above the door overlooked the elegant esplanade dotted with large glazed Anduze pots and lined by stately plane trees. The majestic fountain at the far end of the terrace, covered in moss and slightly crumbling, completed the sense of harmony and design.

Joy greeted Katherine warmly as she led her into the expansive foyer. She immediately opened her gift and was thrilled with the hand-blown glass bowl.

"Oh, Katherine, how did you guess? You will smile when you see my table set with only Biot glass. It has been my favorite since I first saw pieces fifty years ago. Thank you for being so thoughtful. I will treasure this."

Picasso had raced around to the back as soon as he was out of the car, as if he knew it was time for Sunday lunch.

"Come and meet everyone, *ma chère*, and we will tour the house later. If you would like to, of course."

"No question!" Katherine said with a widening smile. "I can't wait."

Joy led the way through an enormous room and then one slightly smaller from which French doors led out to a large fine gravel terrace, where a large animated group was chatting and laughing around a very long table.

The bright tones of yellow, blue, and green of the fabrics in the classic Provençal tablecloth and napkins were echoed in the distinctive Biot glassware, creating a symphony of colors.

Introductions were made by Joy, assisted by Picasso, who made his way around the table, greeted by squeals from the young children and affectionate words and rubs from the adults. His popularity was obvious.

"Of course, you know Mirella."

Mirella, looking cool in a crisp sleeveless pale-green linen dress, approached her immediately with a warm smile as they exchanged *bises*. "I'm so looking forward to hearing about your motor trip!"

Introductions went around the table, with each person standing to greet Kat with *bises*. Joy's son and daughter, each with their spouse; two of her four twentysomething grandchildren; as well as Mirella and her two youngest grandchildren, ages six and eight, had all taken their seats again when a man rose at the end of the table. Joy turned to Kat.

"My dear Katherine, this is Philippe Dufours. He is the nephew of François and the Philippe I thought you met the other day."

He smiled somewhat shyly and took Katherine's hand, bending over it in a most gracious and flattering manner as he murmured, *"Enchanté."* The gesture, unfamiliar to her, momentarily stunned her, and she blushed furiously.

"I'm confused," she said to Joy as she looked from one to the other. "Who was the Philippe I met?"

With a chuckle, Philippe explained the young man was the son of a friend in the village who had helped him out that day.

Katherine felt better having that perplexing encounter explained. She had been wondering why it had felt so bizarre.

"Well then, thank you so much for the beautiful bouquet you left on the windowsill. It was stunning!"

"De rien! It was my pleasure. We are all so grateful to you and Pico for saving François. It was such good fortune you were there," Philippe replied, his English accompanied by a charming accent.

Katherine's attempts to play down her role were waved aside.

Joy indicated Katherine should sit next to Philippe as she then took the chair on the other side of her.

Conversation flowed easily as champagne corks popped and flutes were placed on the table by a couple that appeared to help serve. When everyone's glass was filled, Joy stood and held her glass to make a toast.

"*Ma chère* Katherine, we are so pleased to welcome you here as a friend and hope by the time you leave, you will feel part of our family. Not only are you a lovely person, but now, you see, we feel you have saved our dear François, and we are forever in your debt. *Bienvenue et merci mille fois.*"

Everyone at the table raised their glass to join the toast while Katherine's face once again turned a deep pink.

Shyly, she lifted the slender flute. "*Merci beaucoup. Je suis très heureuse d'être ici, et vous êtes très gentils.* It is my honor to be here at your beautiful home. You make me feel very welcome."

Glasses were emptied and more corks popped. It would be a champagne beginning to the lunch, which consisted of bowls of olives, baskets of baguettes, platters of small sliced salami accompanied by bite-size tomatoes, and a selection of *pâté*. As a quiet elderly couple tended to filling glasses and keeping the little ones busy, Joy introduced them as Antoine and Hélène.

They beamed with pride when Joy said, "They are the third generation of their family to help us run the *manoir* and so are also very special members of our family. We could not manage without their talents."

Everyone was interested in hearing Katherine's opinion of the villages she had visited, and of course the inn that was getting so much attention. Recounting her adventures with great enthusiasm, she omitted the worst and realized she could completely isolate the bad from the good. Philippe had quietly listened, asking the odd question as Mirella and Joy pressed her for details.

She tried not to gush over everything, which was what she truly wanted to do. At length, Katherine pretended to take a deep breath, confessing she was talking too much. The others assured her she was not.

"It's a pleasure to listen to visitors that don't complain! Many have long lists."

She was relieved when someone else picked up the chatter so she could indulge in the melt-in-your-mouth *pâté*.

Philippe chuckled as he prepared a portion for her and passed it on a small plate. With a look of bemusement, he said, "I believe you have seen as much in a week as most people see over the course of several visits to the Luberon!"

"There's more on my list for this week, but I doubt if I will be able to see them all."

"If you were asked to choose one moment from those two days that really stood out, one thing that you saw, ate, heard, what would it be?" Mirella asked.

"Without question, I loved seeing the statue in Cadenet." They all nodded knowingly. "That tale struck a chord in my heart. I was most touched there—reminded of how terrible the war must have been here."

There was silence around the table briefly as Katherine's remark resonated. Then Joy's son, Henri, spoke up.

"My mother's generation does not speak of those times very often—"

Katherine interrupted, feeling flustered, "I . . . I'm sorry . . . of course, I should have thought before mentioning . . ."

Joy put her hand on Katherine's arm and patted it. "*Non, non.* It's not a problem, *ma chère.*"

Henri quickly continued, "*Non* . . . sorry, Katherine, I did not mean to make you feel badly. I actually wanted to say that my generation is trying to encourage my mother and others to tell their stories because they are important. So I'm very glad you brought that up."

"Yes," broke in his wife, Sylvie, "we must insist these stories are shared. You made a very good point right now about how meaningful they are . . . really, I'm so glad you did."

All faces were turned toward Joy and Mirella, who were looking into each other's eyes and nodding.

"*Nous vous écoutons* . . . we hear you," Joy replied quietly. Mirella nodded in agreement.

Katherine thought for a moment before speaking up. The champagne had relaxed her just enough to let the story spill from her lips.

"I had the same situation in my own family . . ."

She went on to tell Elisabeth's story in a shortened version and how finally she now had the written account in her mother's own words. "I cannot express how much it means to me. I so agree that these stories must be told."

There were sympathetic expressions around the table. Katherine could feel this was an important topic here too.

The moment was interrupted by platters of food, theatrically delivered from the kitchen by Antoine, Hélène, and Joy's daughter, Julie.

"Bravo! *Le grand aioli* especially for Katherine!" announced Henri.

Three large platters heaped with chunks of whitefish and a colorful array of beets, potatoes, cauliflower, artichokes, carrots, and beans were set on the table. Large bowls of freshly prepared chickpea sauce and aioli accompanied each platter.

Smaller plates with hard-boiled eggs and wedges of lemon also arrived as the eager diners waited to begin.

Carafes of rosé now replaced the empty champagne bottles.

"Bravo! *Mère*, you have prepared another feast for us!"

"Not without Hélène by my side, as you know!" Joy responded.

Turning to Katherine, she explained, "This is a very traditional summer recipe and possibly quite unusual for you. I hope you enjoy it."

"It's the aioli that makes it," Henri shouted from the other end of the table. "I guarantee it will cause you to swan."

Katherine looked puzzled until Mirella quickly corrected, "Swoon, Henri, you mean swoon."

Laughter filled the terrace once more as everyone began to fill plates.

"I cannot get over how everything tastes so much better here," Katherine commented to Philippe.

"Trust me, I can show you some places that might cause you to change your mind," he suggested. "But truly, you are right. Food is our religion. Everything is prepared to bring about the greatest pleasure in every sense."

Mirella leaned in to explain further, "You know, Katherine, we are masters of the art of *plaisir*. It is the underlying theme of life here. In spite of the many negatives in our society today, the French continue to strive to be artful, exquisite. It is a legacy we do not want to lose."

"It combines with the art of seduction . . . *la séduction*," Joy interjected, with a knowing smile. "It's a virtuous skill here to seduce and touch all the senses with fashion, cuisine, wine, scent, words . . ."

Katherine glanced at Philippe, who was gazing at the two women with bemused admiration.

Turning back to Katherine, he gestured toward them. "And here is a perfect example of how the women in France simply continue to improve with age."

The others around the table had moved on to politics and parenting, while Mirella and Joy were interrupted by the antics of Picasso and the young grandchildren.

Someone had obviously made a funny remark, as the far end of the table erupted in laughter.

Philippe was interested in Katherine's life in Toronto. He plied her with questions about the whole experience of home exchange, something unheard of to him.

In return he explained he was a *fromager* with a business selling cheese in the South of France near Nice.

"A *fromager* is a career you would not hear mentioned often in Canada. Please tell me about it . . . and excuse me, but I must say your English is excellent."

"Ah, *merci*, thank you," Philippe replied with a smile. He told her about living in England for several years as a teenager while his father worked with a British cheesemaker who wanted his goat-cheese expertise.

Katherine asked question after question about his family's history and found it mesmerizing.

Who knew the history of making cheese could be so interesting—or is it Philippe I'm finding so interesting? His voice is like velvet.

Philippe explained he had driven up to Sainte-Mathilde as soon as he received the phone call about François. He planned to stay for a few more days until arrangements could be made for the herd of goats to be cared for. He spoke fondly of his uncle.

"He has always been a fine man. He worked hard all of his life in investment banking in Paris, very successfully, and not without a great deal of stress, and provided for his family in a very good way. My father, his brother, died in a car accident shortly after our return from England, and my uncle did all he could to fill his shoes. I love him very much."

"And now he is a goat herder?" Katherine asked.

Philippe smiled broadly. "*Oui, un chevrier.* He loves the peace of the fields, the goats, and the fresh air. The goats do not need him, but he needs them. He spends the day meditating, thinking, reading, being at peace."

"*Plaisir,*" said Katherine. Philippe nodded.

Joy leaned in. "Did Philippe tell you that François knows the goats by name?"

"Just like his father and grandfather before him," he said, laughing. "It's a dying tradition that you still find on some farms in Provence."

Luncheon plates had been cleared, and a simple green salad arrived as the wineglasses disappeared.

"Wine with salad is not a choice we make here," Joy explained to Katherine.

Katherine noted how relaxed everyone was, taking in food and conversation in equal portions. Each course was lingered over, and murmurs of appreciation hung in the air.

When the salad was finished, selections of cheese were brought to the table on beautiful slabs of olive wood, along with heaping bowls of freshly picked cherries.

A variety of *digestifs* were offered, including *eau de vie*, a homemade pear-plum-cherry-raspberry liqueur. Everyone insisted Katherine try it.

Henri was speaking to Joy and Mirella about their stories of the war years.

"Katherine, thank you for giving us the opportunity to raise this topic again. Mère and Mirella both have tales to tell. Provence was a hotbed of the Resistance, and there are amazing stories of bravery and daring."

Katherine mentioned that a favorite poet she studied at university, René Char, had been involved in the Resistance in Provence.

Mirella shook her head in disbelief. "*Mon Dieu*, it's a small world indeed."

"During the war, M. Char lived in a house owned by Mirella's family," Joy explained. "He refused to allow his work to be published by the Germans and buried his papers in the basement of the house until the war ended."

"He often read us stories and helped us with our homework," Mirella added.

"His code name was Capitaine Alexandre, and he truly was a hero of the *Résistance*, commanding the famous Durance parachute drop zone," Philippe explained.

"Not just a *résistant*, but a fighter on a moral plane his entire life," said Mirella, her eyes shining with admiration. "None more famous than his protests against polluters or with Picasso in the sixties against the threatened nuclear installations on Mont Ventoux."

"The village where he lived, Céreste, is not far from here," said Joy. "But then, you can stop in any of these towns and villages and find stories of the *Résistance*."

"And of collaboration and betrayal and pain and loss," said Henri. "There's no question it was hell. But we must keep the stories alive."

"And so we will," Joy and Mirella both promised.

Katherine had been touched by the thoughtfulness shown by every person at the table as they each made time to speak with her. Some spoke English quite well and were happy to show off their ability. Others struggled, but in a good way, with good humor, laughs, and hand gestures.

Katherine made every effort to use her limited French vocabulary and was not surprised at how she enjoyed it. She had already decided to join a conversational French group when she got back to Toronto.

Farewells were now being shared and Katherine noted how the words sweetly meant "see you soon," *à bientôt*, rather than "good-bye"—and, of course, there were *bises* all around. Always *bises*.

Joy reminded Katherine she would tour her through the house, and Katherine asked if she might bring in her laptop to use the Wi-Fi and Skype her friend Molly.

"Of course, *ma chère*, as we discussed the other day. *Avec plaisir.*"

As this was all being organized, Philippe was chatting with the rest of the family. Now he returned to Katherine and asked if she would like him to drive her to Céreste on Monday afternoon to visit the tiny Char museum.

"It would be my pleasure to introduce you to some of our little short-cuts. Mirella would love to go as well and show us the house in which Char lived."

"I would very much like to do that," Katherine replied and Philippe arranged to collect her at 2:00 p.m.

22

Alone in the courtyard as the last car drove off, Katherine complimented Joy on her family.

Joy nodded. "They are the light of my life, and I feel blessed that they still love to come here and spend time with me in spite of their busy lives. It's how we mothers hope our families will be, but it doesn't always happen. Now come, let me show you some of the much older members of our family."

"It's like a private museum," Katherine said in awe. The family history in the area went back to the 1500s, and some of the buildings on the property dated back over three hundred years, Katherine's farmhouse being one.

Construction on the manor house had taken place in the late 1600s. The family had fled to Italy in 1789 in the early days of the French Revolution and did not regain ownership of the property until 1816, after the Napoleonic Wars had ended. The property had not been maintained properly then, and there had been much work to do afterward. Most of the valued furniture had been sold, burned, or stolen through those years. Incredibly, through many long years of searching, the odd original piece was traced and bought back.

With a typically Gallic shrug of her shoulders, Joy indicated it was what it was.

Three of the oldest oil portraits of ancestors had been saved, as they were rolled up and taken along to Italy when the family escaped there. Katherine listened, enthralled, as Joy shared stories in each room.

The enormous fireplaces in the main floor grand hall and the upper hall were still used, but much of the house was not heated or inhabited in winter.

"It is such an unusual experience to hear a history that is so old and yet still so much a part of your family's life today. We simply do not have those kinds of stories in North America—at least, not many of us do. Thank you for allowing me this intimate glimpse into the past."

Joy smiled graciously. "Time creates a collage with layers of history—family and events. Some of us feel privileged to have these works of art, these properties, entrusted to us, but often they present great difficulties to families and cannot be maintained. Taxes are atrocious!"

"I can imagine," Katherine said.

"Upkeep never stops, and as the years go by, the costs are becoming a burden, but we simply don't want to let our property go. Our grandchildren are already looking at business plans to turn the manor into a small hotel after I am gone, and I think that's a good idea."

"What about the vineyard?" asked Katherine.

"Oh, that will continue, from what I hear," Joy replied in a hopeful tone. "But nothing is guaranteed these days. So much is changing. In the last fifty years, three out of four farms in France have stopped functioning. It's a terrible shift in how our country operates, and we don't quite know how the economy and the general population will ultimately be affected."

Making certain Katherine was comfortably settled in the office, Joy said she would find her in the garden when she was through.

After reaching Molly on Skype, Kat insisted she share the latest in the ongoing mysterious and frightening incidents in her life.

"Come on, Molly, spill," Katherine said, saying she could see from her friend's face all was not well.

"Oh shit, Kat! I didn't want to say anything while you are having such a fantastic holiday. The calls are still coming . . . not quite as often, though . . . but something worse happened."

"Oh no. What now?"

"My car was keyed in the school parking lot. Badly!"

Katherine groaned.

"That was so bad in two ways," Molly said, fuming with anger. "One, because it was a Zipcar, and two, it means the person knows where I work."

"How do you know it was the same person?"

"They left a fucking phone message mocking me. It made me want to puke!"

"How awful! Did you report it?"

"Immediately," Molly said, calming slightly. "One of the officers we met before actually seems to be taking an interest in the situation."

"Well, that's good to hear. They will get to the bottom of this. I just know it," Kat said.

Molly plied her with questions about her life in Provence, and Katherine decided not to say anything about Matt the Asshole until she was back home with a glass of wine in her hand.

Molly reported that the Lalliberts loved Toronto. She had greeted them when they arrived at Katherine's house the first day, and on Friday had taken them to lunch at an Italian restaurant with a patio offering a view of the lake.

"Madeline has invited me to come for a French dinner next Wednesday. They are going to shop at the St. Lawrence market and show me what I'm missing!"

"Please give them my regards and tell them I have fallen in love with their country, their home, and their dog. Molly, you would adore it here—and of course, there is jazz everywhere."

They agreed to try to catch each other on Skype the following Sunday, when Kat would be in Paris.

23

Monday morning she wakened to the sun streaming through the open window. Lying in bed, she replayed the preceding three days, contemplating how she was wearing her independence.

Her stomach knotted as she thought about Matt's offensive behavior, but her head overcame the anxiety, as she felt strong and empowered by her actions.

In the village later for a *crème* at Le Petit Café, she still wasn't getting a smile from the waiter, but she sensed he recognized her even without Joy. Her goal there was to see a smile before her trip ended.

Well aware that the French did not really cotton to unsolicited smiles or offhand comments from strangers, she knew acceptance needed to be earned.

Mentally making a list of her plans for the rest of the week, she realized some things simply weren't going to happen.

Easy good humor filled the car that afternoon as they wound their way through the maze of narrow roadways. Philippe informed them which ones had begun as goat and donkey paths or the routes of invading enemies.

"Philippe, you constantly amaze me with all these details."

He gave her a modest smile and bowed his head. "We live with the stories and legends all around us and grow up hearing them from our elders. *N'est-ce pas*, Mirella?"

Mirella's intimate knowledge of Céreste and Char's stay there made it her turn to bring the history to life.

Before leaving the village, they sat at a small terrace and sipped pastis as they watched the afternoon pétanque players, smiling at the passionate and noisy debates over each game. Katherine had never realized what an important role this pastime played in the life of every village and town in France.

Once again she felt a sense of peace and comfort in the simple ambiance of such a village.

On the way home Mirella mentioned she was one of the conveners for a concert in the small, fifteenth-century chapel in Sainte-Mathilde on Wednesday evening.

"I would be honored if both of you would accept an invitation to be my guests."

⚜

Tuesday, Katherine thought she might drive to Aix-en-Provence for the afternoon.

Reading in the garden midmorning while Picasso stretched by her chair and lazily snapped at flies, she looked up at one point and noticed a figure standing in the far reaches of the goat field where it met the forest.

When she went into the house to refill the water pitcher, she saw a sleek touring bike leaned against the fence and figured the young, sullen Philippe was in the field. Puttering in the garden later that morning, she heard her name called and realized it was not the sullen Philippe but rather the charming, soft-spoken Philippe. He beckoned her to the fence and asked if she might like a short walk through the trees to see a special place that François had discovered years before. The invitation pleased her and aroused her curiosity.

"Let me put on some proper walking shoes instead of these sandals."

As she skipped up the stairs to her bedroom to find her shoes, Katherine had a moment of *déjà vu* as she flashed back to the disgusting and frightening episode with Matt the Asshole.

Philippe, on the other hand, seemed such a gentleman.

But then, she hadn't seen the assault coming from Matt either. Maybe she was just too naive. She had been wrapped up so safely in the cocoon of her marriage for twenty-two years that it had not occurred to her to be suspicious of men. Was that it?

Pausing for a moment at the top of the stairs as she was on her way back outside, Katherine made a judgment call that she had nothing to fear this time. To be on the safe side, though, at least in her mind, she stuck her pointy manicure scissors in her pocket.

Opening a gate for Katherine, Philippe invited Picasso along before the excited pooch dashed past them and took the lead.

"Why don't the goats simply clamber over? I mean, the fence isn't really that high, and I've certainly seen what good climbers they are." She recounted how they had invaded her yard the day of François's accident.

"They are insatiably curious creatures, very nosy but rather lazy," said Philippe. "They love their food and live to forage. The field and forest offer so much for them to eat, they can't be bothered to leave. I have a theory about why they were in your yard that day. I believe the leader of the herd sensed a problem when François collapsed. When he left the field to investigate, the others followed, and that attracted Pico's attention."

He continued to regale her with obscure information about goats, and had her chuckling with his wry observations about their quirky and affectionate personalities.

Following behind him, Katherine took stock. Just over six feet, with thick brown hair, combed straight back and curling behind his ears, he was neither slender nor stocky, with a solid build. Well-muscled arms and legs suggested a lifestyle that demanded fitness. He didn't appear to be much over forty, she thought. Not handsome, but very attractive in a French kind of way, with a slightly olive-toned complexion and strongly defined but not-too-big mouth, nose, and brow. Deep, dark eyes. *Nice butt.*

She smiled to herself, acknowledging she hadn't lost her appreciation of a good- looking man, particularly the latter detail.

After twenty minutes through the lightly forested woods, a pasture-like clearing opened up and Philippe stopped before what appeared to be a jumble of rocks.

Peering more closely, she could see order in the jumble as Philippe proudly told her these were the remains of a Roman wall and a secret that remained just in their family. François had made the discovery and painstakingly dug it out. Local historians had confirmed the authenticity and agreed it was not situated in an appropriate place for officials to make it accessible to everyone.

"How exciting to know that Romans once lived on your property!" Katherine exclaimed. "Although I guess it's not so unusual around here."

Philippe nodded, smiling at her enthusiasm.

Katherine continued, "When I get home I'm going to go to the library and take out some books on the ancient history of this area."

That list in my journal is getting so long it will keep me occupied for months, she thought.

The land sloped, opening up a vista stretching across orchards and fields, dotted with the familiar lines of farmhouses and outbuildings.

They sat on the grass chatting for some time with no shortage of topics while Picasso kept busy poking his nose in groundhog holes. Feeling no anxiety, her fingers played with the scissors in her pocket as she felt mildly foolish for having brought them.

She told Philippe she was driving to Aix for the afternoon, and he genuinely seemed disappointed that he had other commitments and could not go with her.

"Aix is one of my favorite towns, and there are many special places to discover. Follow the directions straight to Cours Mirabeau, the heart of the old town, and you will have a full afternoon ahead of you."

When they got back to the farmhouse, he looked at Katherine's guidebook and made some notes to prioritize her touring.

"Is that your bike?" Katherine asked.

Nodding, Philippe lifted his T-shirt slightly to show his cycling clothes underneath.

Katherine noticed then that his cycling shoes were tied around the handlebars.

"A serious cycler from the look of it," she commented.

"It's a passion," he smiled.

Katherine winced inside, remembering the passion she also once had for the sport, and changed the subject back to Aix.

With more information from him than she could possibly use in one afternoon, she thanked him again and went into the farmhouse to change and set off on her next adventure.

En route to the highway, Katherine stopped in at the manor. With no one in sight, she left a note. The message invited Joy and her family, as well as Antoine and Hélène and the vineyard helpers, to come to the farmhouse for an aperitif on Friday afternoon at 4:00 p.m. She asked that Mirella be invited as well.

Impulsively she had conceived the idea while she chatted with Philippe that morning.

"We call that a *buffet dînatoire*," he said. "You call it cocktails, right?"

Katherine nodded. "With a few hors d'oeuvres, nothing too heavy."

When he then said he was going to change his travel plans and stay for her party, Katherine felt a surge of pleasure.

Grinning now as she drove toward Aix with a jazz station blaring, she felt energized and incredibly content with herself. Everything she was doing in her life was the result of her decisions alone. No one was passing judgment or telling her what to do.

I thought I was coming on this exchange to run away from something, but now I feel I was really running toward something—a new me.

24

Wednesday morning Katherine began to organize her clothes and pack what she knew she wouldn't need until Paris.

In the late afternoon, Joy collected her, and they drove to a nearby but secluded studio where five generations of the gifted Lalonde family had worked with olive wood to create beautiful bowls, platters, cutting boards, and other items.

Walking into the shop, Katherine felt overwhelmed by the warm shades and textures of the wood filling the space, creating a sense of tranquility. The sizes and shapes of the bowls were surprising. It wasn't until she watched a video, playing on a flatscreen on the wall, that she understood how the initial crafting began with painstaking labor a hundred years ago, and more recently, with a chainsaw.

She chose a number of cheeseboards, each one an original piece of art in her opinion and yet so reasonably priced. They would be perfect gifts and easy to pack. Kat checked another item off her to-do list.

During the drive back, the women chatted easily.

Katherine's curiosity could not be contained as she asked, "Philippe has been very thoughtful. Does he have a family?"

"Philippe was widowed six years ago. His wife, Geneviève, battled a virulent strain of leukemia for many years, but sadly it took her. He has struggled with his grief as he devoted himself to raising their daughter, who was fifteen at the time. Now she is a university student in Paris and goes to England in the summers to work in a business owned by a family they have known for a very long time. She's a lovely young woman."

"I'm so sorry for his loss."

"He is a fine person," Joy continued, "who made an interesting choice as a young man to carry on the tradition of his father, and grandfather, and become *un fromager*. He went to university and could have chosen any career path, but this is his passion."

"Quite a fascinating choice," said Katherine, "but of course not unusual in France, I guess."

Joy laughed. "Precisely. You know the saying, I'm sure. The Holy Trinity in France is *le pain, le vin, et le fromage*. Some like to say *le pain, le vin, et le Boursin* because it rhymes. Boursin had a very clever advertising campaign like that years ago. But some cheese snobs turn their noses up at Boursin."

"Mmm, I love it!" Katherine said, and Joy nodded in agreement.

As Joy was dropping her off, Katherine mentioned that she was going to the concert at the church that evening, and Joy assured her it would be special.

"You will truly enjoy it. I usually attend but I have a conflict this evening, *désolée*."

Katherine drove herself to the chapel a half hour early and was surprised to see the large turnout, knowing there was little room for a crowd inside.

Mirella greeted her at the door of the chapel, where she was handing out programs, and responded to Katherine's puzzled question by explaining that the courtyard at the back of the church was opened on such occasions with outdoor seating, speakers, and a large flatscreen.

"Even here at a fifteenth-century chapel, the digital world has invaded," she said, sighing.

Philippe was already there and stood to greet her. The small wooden chairs, their frames rubbed smooth by the hands of the faithful through several hundred years of use, barely accommodated today's larger-framed bodies, but somehow they were still comfortable.

As the lights dimmed, Mirella slipped in beside Katherine and the music began, with candles casting an almost eerie glow.

The piano, Philippe had explained, once belonged to Pablo Picasso and now his daughter. She loaned it to the community every year for this concert. The visiting Russian pianist had been a guest artist for years and was much loved and respected. And talented.

The experience of sitting in this darkened chapel where people had prayed, mourned, and celebrated for almost six hundred years was nearly overwhelming. Despite her lack of religious beliefs, Kat was always touched by the atmosphere of such churches.

When the final notes were played, the crowd broke into enthusiastic applause that morphed into rhythmic clapping, traditional of French audiences wishing an encore.

The artist acknowledged the response and said he would like to invite a visiting friend to join him. This man was a well-known religious singer, also Russian, whose name was obviously familiar to many in the crowd. The applause was warm.

As the first notes played, Katherine knew what was coming and steeled herself. Now that she knew her mother's story, certain religious pieces moved her to tears as they had her mom, and this was one.

The singer's voice was magic. Pure, clear notes, sung in Latin, filled the entire chapel and seemed to embrace the congregation.

"Ave Maria, gratia plena, Maria, gratia plena . . ."

Katherine swallowed hard, blinking back tears, but emotion overtook her and she wept. Quietly. As she fumbled in her purse for a tissue, Philippe handed a handkerchief to her with a questioning look. She accepted the offer gratefully and nodded her head to indicate she really was not in distress. Rather than fight it, she allowed her tears to flow in appreciation of the depth to which she was touched by the experience.

As people began to file out of the chapel, Mirella and Philippe turned to Katherine with concern.

"I'm sorry. I cry whenever I hear such deeply religious music. It touches my soul and I weep. But I'm fine. Really. I just had to let it go because I knew I couldn't stop it."

Relieved there was no problem, Mirella suggested they go out to the square for a coffee or glass of wine. It seemed as though the entire village was out there, and the perfect evening air was filled with laughter and chatter.

"Mirella, thank you so much for the opportunity to hear this concert. It was a wonderful experience."

Philippe nodded in agreement. "No matter how often I attend concerts in these ancient churches, the effect is almost visceral—the acoustics, the ambiance, the centuries of history that cannot be denied, combined with the music . . . it touches the soul in a way that has nothing to do with religion."

"So true. These days, the prime function of most churches here is hosting musical events," Mirella told Katherine.

Over coffee, Katherine disclosed how her mother had often become teary when she heard religious music or tolling church bells.

"Until I read the story she wrote for me of her experience during the war, I had no idea why she reacted as she did. Now I understand, and I weep for her."

Mirella nodded. "Many of us carry scars from those years. We buried them or covered them with makeup rather than acknowledging the imprint they left on our souls. It seemed easier that way. You were right to remind us to record those stories. Since you told us your mother's story, I have begun to write the story of my own family during our dark time. Thank you for that."

Philippe looked at both of them. "Women connect about these issues. I'm impressed."

Mirella responded with a serious expression, "You know, Philippe, French women of my age do not tend to have close relationships. It was Joy and her English upbringing that brought such a friendship to my life, and what we have shared is irreplaceable!"

Katherine thought how she was just beginning to appreciate the deeper friendship of the few women in her life.

"It's too bad you haven't met her husband," Philippe told Katherine as he nodded his head toward Mirella. "He's a fine man, and together they provide the most entertaining times. They make a conversation about a potted plant an event!"

Chuckling, Mirella added, "But this is the point of conversation, *non?*" *There's that* plaisir *attitude again.*

Katherine knew Mirella's husband was in Asia on business, and they spoke a while about his travels. Then Philippe and Mirella commented on some local political issues, with regional elections approaching, before they wished each other *à bientôt* as they *bised* and left as they had come.

Picasso was on guard duty by the front door, and Katherine laughed out loud as she scratched behind his ears and hugged him. "Pico, how am I going to say good-bye to you? That is not going to be easy."

He cocked his head and perked up his ears, giving her the look that always made her grin.

25

Sad that this was her last visit to the local market, Katherine vowed to visit the St. Lawrence market at home more often.

Adding three jars of lavender honey to her basket, her next stop was the herb seller, whose long table blazed with vivid color and filled the air with a bouquet of fragrantly pungent smells that was almost hallucinogenic. Here she chose three mixtures prepared by the woman whose flamboyant makeup and dresses were as colorful as her wares. One packet was for preparing fish dishes, another for Mediterranean salads, and the last for lamb.

As she lingered, she was reminded of the word *"la garrigue,"* which Joy had used to describe the combination of earthy, herbal, floral, and other scents found in the Provençal markets. It was unique and something she felt she would not forget.

Her last stop was the soap vendor. Again, the vibrant and fragrant display of the famous *savon de Marseille*, oils and creams, caressed her senses. She wasn't certain how many dozens of photos she had taken here. It was difficult to control the impulse again as she added a dozen bars of her favorite soaps—honey, lavender, rose, jasmine—to the *panier*. Some would be for her and some for gifts.

I wonder if that will last until my next visit to France. She reminded herself that the way the world was now, she could buy those soaps at home too. *Not the same, just not the same* . . .

Taking her time to enjoy every detail of the vendors and stalls, each equally enticing, Katherine captured it all yet again with her camera. There were always new angles and different perspectives to discover. She planned to make a photo book.

The first book without James, she thought, gripped for a moment with an odd feeling that was somewhat like regret, which she quickly shook off . . .

A *crème* at Le Petit Café, delivered with a nod and a subtle smile from the waiter, made her morning.

After some journaling time and lunch in the garden, Katherine climbed on the rusting Peugeot. She had marked out a route on her map and, at roughly three hours including a lunch stop, this would be her longest ride.

Picasso had been pacing with anticipation. As soon as he saw the bike come out of the shed, he knew something was up.

Placing two water bottles, a container of water for the dog, and a tube of sunscreen in the rear basket along with a wedge of nicely ripe Brie and three figs, she was set.

"A few biscuits for Picoboy! *D'accord?*" she asked, causing warp-speed tail wagging.

A little concerned her legs were not in shape for this challenge, Katherine took time to stretch before she set off. This time she had her cell phone with Joy's number plugged into it, just in case. She knew now there were infrequent local buses with bike racks on the front, and she certainly did not discount this option.

The day was as perfect as the others had been. She counted the fine weather among the many blessings reflected upon as she pedaled. With the breeze caressing her on this relaxed first leg of her route, she ran her mind over each day since her arrival.

Everything in Provence seemed to speak directly to her heart. She felt different here, changed somehow, and removed from the sadness that still lived within her orbit in Toronto.

People here like me for me . . . as I am right now. They don't know my past, just my present.

She wondered if she should sell her parents' home. As much as she loved that sweet house and all the good memories of her childhood, sadness dwelt there too. Maybe it was time to move on, literally and figuratively.

Her job was satisfying and challenging. She would not change that.

Breathing heavily as she put greater effort into a series of small inclines, her mind continued to replay her life.

As the kilometers rolled by, so did her thoughts, leaving a trail of broken memories while she rode toward bright possibilities. It felt at first cleansing and then almost as if a door was opening to a future she could not see before, like some sort of epiphany. Somehow this trip was offering her the promise of a new beginning.

Cresting another hill, the perfect spot for a rest presented itself.

"Que penses-tu, Pico? C'est bien ici?" she asked.

Picasso followed Katherine onto a grassy patch and lapped his water with gusto after she put the container on the ground.

Katherine removed her helmet, giving her head a good scratch. Patting down the grass, she settled her back against a rock while Picasso had an energetic roll in the shade of a nearby plane tree.

She unwrapped her figs and cheese, and alternated bites, savoring the delicious combination. Until this trip, she had not been particularly fond of figs. What a discovery they had been here. Never fresher, their luscious velvety sweetness combined with the light crunchiness of the tiny seeds to produce a subtle flavor Kat decided was almost orgasmic.

Now, there's a word that hasn't crossed my mind for a very long time.

She thought about how she had put the prospect of making love out of her head for all those months. It's not like she never wanted it to happen again. She just couldn't imagine ever allowing herself to get that close to any other man. *Why risk the hurt?*

The warmth of the sun and the buzz she was feeling from cycling turned her thoughts to fantasy as she rested on the soft grass and breathed the fragrance of the air.

What a perfect place this would be . . . right here . . . this moment . . .

She surprised herself even more by enjoying the sensations spreading up her legs and inside her to a spot that was almost climactic. Running her hands over her breasts and down to rest between her legs, she finally admitted she missed making love. Letting out a long sigh, she reveled in the fantasy a few seconds more.

It would not have happened here with James. He had never been impulsive in that way. There might be bugs or dirt, or someone might have seen them. She could just hear him now.

The thought of him burst the fantasy bubble, and she popped the final piece of fig into her mouth, followed by a bite of cheese. The wedge of Brie had ripened even more in the warm morning sun as it sat in the basket. *Perfect.*

Philippe had recommended that particular Brie for figs and for a sensual moment she held on to thoughts of him as her fantasy was fading.

Too bad I'm leaving so soon.

Kat tossing Pico a biscuit from time to time, the two stayed as they were for some time.

I wonder when I'll be back here . . . if ever.

From somewhere inside, a little voice told her that the choice was hers. Hers alone. She liked it.

Licking the cheese from her fingers, she used some of her water to clean her hands and splash on her face.

Time to head back.

Consulting her map again, she was quite certain of the route after all the driving around she had done.

It was time for Zaz on the iPod.

The chorus resonated as Katherine kept hitting "Repeat" and sang along, her voice floating over the fields and through the woods.

Indeed she did wish for love, joy, good feelings. It wasn't money that made her happy. She was discovering her freedom. Forget the clichés.

Welcome to my reality, my new reality.

She sighed. *If only it were.*

26

My last day here, Katherine thought, stretching sleepily and feeling very much at home. *I'm going to miss this bed, this house—everything. Pico, oh, Pico . . .*

Having admonished herself during the past few days not to be melancholy, clearly she was ignoring that advice.

Leaning over the edge of the bed, she looked down at her new best friend. Picasso gazed back at her with his limpid dark eyes, not lifting his nose from the floor, gently thumping his tail.

Katherine reached down and scratched the top of his head. *Crazy,* she thought. *It is crazy to feel this way about a dog.*

Down to the back garden for an hour of yoga—*Lucy will be proud of me when I tell her*—and a restful half hour writing in her journal brought that up to date.

Breakfast was the last of yesterday's croissants with homemade strawberry jam. She washed her yoga clothes and her biking outfit from the day before and hung them on the line, knowing they would be dry within hours. This was something else she was determined to continue at home. There was a clothesline at her mother's that she never used.

With her suitcase and carry-on lying open on the floor of the bedroom across the hall, Katherine took everything out of the closet except what she would wear in the afternoon and for travel tomorrow.

Once her packing for the day was complete, she went down to the kitchen to make some preparations for her *buffet dînatoire*, grinning as she repeated the words, enjoying the sound.

It had been a surprise to learn from Joy and Mirella that, apart from little cubes on a toothpick with perhaps a cherry tomato, cheese was not served as an appetizer in France.

She had decided to make asparagus spears wrapped in prosciutto with a sliver of parmesan and curried chicken on endive and tuna-stuffed cherry tomatoes—typical North American hors d'oeuvres—as well as a small selection of the French standard salamis and olives. A small green salad and cold chicken were a tasty lunch as she read in the back garden and then spent some time editing photographs on her computer. Few things gave her more pleasure than looking through her travel photos—over and over. Her family always praised her photography skills, but she felt that it would be impossible to take bad pictures in Provence. Everywhere you looked offered a wonderful Kodak moment.

I guess that term will soon disappear, she thought sadly.

During the afternoon, her food preparations completed, Katherine and Picasso made one last tour through the gardens and around the property. On the path bordering the goat pasture, Katherine paused, remembering the frightening experience with François, and gave Pico a big pat on his back as he stood beside her.

"You've been my companion, friend, protector, roommate, and confidante, you gorgeous boy." As she kneeled down, he licked her cheek, and they sat together for a few minutes.

Back at the house, Katherine reorganized the flowers she had purchased at the market the morning before and took two arrangements out to the garden.

Pulling two of the small outdoor tables together, she laid tablecloths and placed the vases on them. Stepping back to admire the setting, she heard a car pull up her driveway.

"I thought you might like to have a little assistance," Joy said with a smile. "So I'm early. *C'est bien?*"

⚜

Katherine mentally patted herself on the back. *Sometimes it pays to be impulsive—another lesson I'm learning.*

Laughter and conversation filled the air as her guests arrived for the *buffet dînatoire*. Food and drink were consumed with gusto, and Katherine held back tears as she said her good-byes. Joy told her she would come by in the morning, so they could delay their farewell.

"Katherine, let me help you clear up," offered Philippe.

While Picasso took care of cleaning up any goodies on the ground, Philippe and Kat moved chairs and tables to where they belonged after clearing the last of the dishes. Joy had given strict instructions that dishes were to be left on the counter for Marie-Claude to take care of in the morning, saying the housekeeper would be unhappy if there was little for her to do.

"There's enough wine here to squeak out two more glasses," Philippe offered. "Shall we sit and enjoy it?"

"*Bonne idée,*" Katherine answered, smiling.

"A little longer here and you would be speaking fluently," Philippe complimented her. "Even though you're reluctant to speak French with me, I overheard you doing so with some of the family at Joy's brunch, and again today, and I was very impressed."

With a shy look, she admitted to an immature anxiety of making mistakes. He assured her that just making the effort was most appreciated and everyone understood.

"What do they say in North America? Just do it!"

With an air of comfort between them, they talked more personally now about their lives, but still there was much left unsaid.

"So do you enjoy your work, Katherine?"

"I do," she replied with a smile, "but there's a part of me that would like to run away to Provence forever. I didn't expect to be so captured!" Philippe nodded. "This part of the planet tends to cause that reaction in visitors."

"Unfortunately it's a little too far away for me to consider popping over for weekends," Katherine commented with a sigh.

Philippe chuckled. "A weekend would never be long enough. You will just have to plan an extended holiday next time."

"When will you return?" Katherine asked him.

"Life is getting busy on the coast now so, as long as François is in Paris, I won't return until the autumn. I won't have a reason to come."

There was an awkward silence before Philippe asked Katherine her plans for her three days in Paris. Chuckling at her agenda, he teased her about accomplishing so much on a trip.

"But here is one thing you have to know about Paris. You must be a *flâneur* and walk everywhere. Look down at the cobblestones and up to the zinc-and-slate rooftops and do not miss anything in between. Paris is made for strolling."

Offering her tips about some places she would never have known, they parted with a bet between them as to whether she would actually get through her list.

Exchanging e-mail addresses, Katherine promised to give him a full report. Blurting awkwardly as Philippe took her hand and bent over it, his lips gently brushing her skin, she blushed.

"It has been such a pleasure to meet you . . . *ah, plaisir,*" she said, chuckling softly, "and to appreciate the French definition of that word. I'm so grateful for all you have done for me."

Philippe smiled back. "*Oui . . . le plaisir . . .* it is all mine . . . but, if you like, I will come tomorrow and show you a faster road to the station."

Katherine felt a flutter of happiness at the thought of seeing him again.

⚜

Her bags were by the front door with Picasso stretched on the floor next to them. He knew something was up. Marie-Claude bustled around the kitchen, thrilled to have a cleanup for a change. As planned, Joy had arrived earlier. Chatting, she accompanied Katherine as she made one last tour of the house to make certain all was in order and nothing left behind.

Katherine had left a gift-wrapped book about Toronto, with an illustrated history, along with a thank-you note on the hall table for the Lalliberts to find upon their return.

Handing Marie-Claude an envelope that contained a thank-you note with a hundred euros, they *bised* and said a warm good-bye.

Walking out to the car together, Joy helped with the luggage.

Both women looked fondly at each other, blinking back deeper emotion.

"Joy, it has been a singular pleasure getting to know you. I cannot thank you enough for everything you have done for me, for the friendship and acceptance you have offered, for touring me about . . . I'm at a loss for words."

"Everything has been my pleasure, *ma chère*. We never know what to expect with each home exchange, and your presence here has been a very special experience for me as well. We will all miss you, and you must promise to stay in touch."

After they kissed each other's cheeks with more feeling than usual, Joy gave Katherine a very warm hug in a distinctly non-French way. "You bring out the British in me," she said with a smile.

At that moment, Philippe pulled into the driveway as planned. He was going to lead Kat to the TGV station through a much shorter but more complicated route than she had taken when she arrived.

Joy greeted him through his car window as Katherine started her engine.

"Come with us!" he invited. "We will wave good-bye to Katherine at the station like good hosts! Come, Joy—and Pico! You ride with her and I'll take the boy with me! It will be fun!"

Katherine had heard this through her open window and was eagerly nodding.

"This makes me feel like it's not over yet," she told Joy with an enormous grin as they drove out to the road.

⚜

Standing at the espresso bar in the station, they sipped the last of their coffee as the train pulled in. Katherine loved the fact that Picasso was welcome there too, and this spur-of-the-moment final farewell had put a more festive spin on her departure.

With *bises* all around once more, Katherine felt her eyes well with emotion as she said good-bye this last time. After a shake of the paw from Pico, Philippe loaded her bags onto the train and jumped off as the whistle blew to close the doors. French trains did not waste time lingering in stations, particularly the TGV.

Waving frantically through her window at her beaming friends, Katherine wiped her tears as she accepted this part of the adventure was over.

Gazing through her reflection on the window for a good hour, she recognized how this trip had opened so much for her. It wasn't a sudden realization but more an awareness that revealed itself as her thoughts peeled layers away. *Hard to believe two weeks could make such a difference.*

Now Paris beckoned, and her excitement turned to that.

27

Katherine had a plan for her arrival at the Gare De Lyon, and it involved three words: *Le Train Bleu.*

When Philippe had teased her about all she accomplished in her two weeks' stay at the farmhouse, she stated she had a full agenda for Paris. He had created a list for her, and a challenge had been set.

Item number one was to enjoy a *crème* and pastry at *Le Train Bleu.*

Leaving her luggage in the cloakroom, Katherine climbed the sweeping staircase to the restaurant. A survivor of France's *Belle Époque,* it was a reminder of a time when train travel was considered an exquisite luxury. Massive chandeliers illuminated brilliantly painted ceilings and walls, many with scenes from southern France, since most trains departed south from the station. Not one square centimeter was unadorned in the grandly romantic space, with gilded statuary flanking the enormous banks of windows. Inaugurated in 1901, today it was a classified historical monument and not to be missed.

Scratch number one off the list, she thought with satisfaction.

It was raining, but the taxi lineup was right outside the station door. She hurried quickly toward the sign, hoping to beat the rush off the TGV.

Checking in to the Hôtel Henri IV in the Latin Quarter, Katherine was pleased with the appeal of this seventeenth-century building the minute she stepped through the door into the intimate lobby.

The efficiently renovated room and bath felt cozy and, well, French. Unfolding her travel raincoat and running shoes, she was ready to explore and eat.

That small pastry had simply been a teaser.

Only 4:00 p.m., she knew her choices would be from one of the many student haunts in this lively area that was home to the Sorbonne. No serious French restaurant would be serving anything at that hour. It simply wasn't done.

Philippe had given her helpful tips along with the exact location of his favorite Latin Quarter shop to have *le snack*—a light bite of something to tide her over until her 9:00 p.m. dinner reservation at La Petite Chaise. This was Paris, after all, and she was determined to make every minute count.

Noticing a basket of umbrellas in the lobby, she was encouraged by the desk clerk to help herself.

Grinning, she stepped out onto the sidewalk, crossed the busy avenue, and headed down a narrow street teeming with life in spite of the weather. Often considered the heart of Paris and named for the days when the language of learning was Latin, this area buzzed with the energy of the young student population.

Exploring the maze of cobblestone alleys, the artistic history of the west bank came alive. *Hemingway, Stein, Fitzgerald, Sartre, de Beauvoir, Picasso, Matisse*—the endless list filtered through her thoughts.

Following her map, she wound her way to Place Saint-Germain-des-Prés. Touristy as it was, a glass of wine in Les Deux Magots was on her list as she envisioned the ghostly spirits of its famous past patrons. Her excitement was barely concealed.

I'm already in love with Paris!

Thankful for the umbrella's protection, Katherine began to make her way back toward her hotel. Almost there, she stopped and gasped. Rue de la Bûcherie!

I knew it was close but, there it is . . .

Shaking the rain from her umbrella, she leaned it under the protected canopy of the entrance and stepped into a wonderland of literary history. Browsing the overflowing shelves of the legendary Shakespeare and Company bookshop, she stayed far longer than she intended. Everything about the worn, comfortable ambiance invited her to sink into one of the armchairs with a book in her hands.

Checking another item off her list, she hoped she would have time for another visit before she left the city.

I simply have to come back to Paris . . .

The rain had turned to a drizzle as she strolled the short distance to her hotel. Kicking off her shoes, she sat down on the bed with her laptop to answer e-mails before she showered and changed for dinner.

She had told Philippe she wanted to eat in the oldest restaurant in Paris—if it was still reputable, of course. He explained that the famous La Tour d'Argent was hands down the oldest, dating back to 1582, and probably one of the most expensive. However, he had continued, La Petite Chaise was considered the winner because it was still in the original location. In fact, he added, it still had the same grillwork from 1680 when it opened. It was much smaller and less elegant, and Katherine decided to go there.

Philippe had called from the farmhouse right then and there and booked her reservation.

The rain had stopped when she headed out for dinner, directions clasped in her hand, drawn by the helpful young woman at the front desk.

As she ordered her French onion soup and roasted duck breast, Katherine thought of Philippe and how considerate he had been. The meal did not disappoint.

Walking back to the hotel, Katherine felt absolutely safe, enchanted by her surroundings and refreshed by the cool dampness hanging in the air.

Sunday morning dawned drizzly again. Undeterred, Katherine had a quick *pain aux raisins* downstairs in the breakfast room and headed down Avenue Saint-Philippe to Notre Dame, a few minutes' walk away.

The sky was brightening by the time she crossed the bridge. She sat on a bench for a while, taking in the splendid cathedral, and planned to take a tour later in the afternoon when services were not on.

Stopping at the Point Zéro marker in front of the church, she mentally checked that off her list as well. Her guidebook explained this was the point from which all distances in France were measured. Who knew?

Katherine strolled by the *bouquinistes'* stalls lining the street along the Seine, taking photos and looking through prints and books as well as original art.

Following her map, she arrived at the famous flower market, knowing that on Sundays the bird traders were also there.

Housed in iron pavilions with glass roofs since 1808, the colors and scents of the flower market drew her in like a bee. Never had she seen such a selection. Pleased with herself for remembering to recharge her camera battery overnight, she was quickly filling her chip.

From the hop-on/hop-off bus she received a full overview of the city. At noon in Montmartre the streets were full of activity and the Place du Tertre, the artists' square was bustling. Mindful of the scammers who would approach you to sketch your portrait, Katherine avoided eye contact and gave them a firm *non*. She noted there were several talented, serious artists and settled on a small watercolor of the rooftops of Paris as a treat for herself.

Stopping early for a lunch of steak tartare and a fine glass of red Côtes du Rhône, she sat on the terrace at Chez la Mère Catherine and chuckled, remembering how Philippe had warned her it was a tourist trap and suggested there were far better places down the side streets.

She had told him it didn't matter because she had read too much about this spot and wanted to go. Established just four years after the end of the Revolution, the story went that the use of the word "bistro" began here. In the 1800s, Russian soldiers occupying France after the Napoleonic Wars would pound on the tables and yell *"Bystro, bystro,"* which meant "hurry."

Philippe had assured her this was an urban legend, but she liked the story anyway.

Katherine stared for a while at the majestic Basilique du Sacré-Coeur before entering, thinking it was even more stunning in reality than in photos. Built in the late 1800s, although it did not share the mantle of history as so many other Paris attractions, its beauty was indisputable.

Taking the funicular down from the hilltop, she strolled the crowded street to Place Pigalle and hopped on the tour bus again.

Her next stop was the massive Arc de Triomphe, where she decided she did not have time to go to the top.

Crossing the Champs-Élysées, she strolled down Avenue Kléber.

After a half hour, she arrived at the Place du Trocadéro and bought a bottle of water from a snack truck. Finding a spot to sit behind the Palais de Chaillot, she overlooked the beautiful gardens and fountains and felt overwhelmed by emotion.

There it was. In real life. The Eiffel Tower.

The lawns of the Champ de Mar stretched beyond, filled with people of all ages enjoying the day. Strollers, dog walkers, children playing, people lounging on the grass. It was full of activity.

This moment had been a long time coming.

She had wondered if the tower would appear commonplace after the countless times she had seen images of it through her life. Somehow seeing it for real was breathtaking.

Making her way down through the gardens and across the bridge to the tower, her shutter clicked madly. Directly under the tower was a vantage point for some amazing shots.

The lineup for the elevator to the top was long, and Katherine decided that was one item on her list she would not get to check off.

You've really bitten off a bit more than you can chew, she admitted. If she wanted to tour Notre Dame, she couldn't continue walking, as she would run out of time. There was a small square near the church Philippe had suggested that she very much wanted to visit.

Hopping on the Métro, she was soon at the cathedral and glad she had made that choice.

The last tour of the day was with a small group and an excellent guide, just the way she liked it. It was almost unimaginable that construction had begun in 1163. Finished just under two hundred years later, Katherine couldn't help but think of the novel *Pillars of the Earth*—she'd read it three times—and how generations of families worked on building such magnificent structures.

Severely damaged during the Revolution, it had gone through some extensive restoration, resulting in the spire being added in the nineteenth century. The last work, done in the 1990s, paid close attention to preserving the historic architecture.

The rose windows sparkling like jewels, imposing sculptures, fantastically grotesque gargoyles—she was awestruck.

Exiting the cathedral, she took a piece of paper from her purse on which Philippe had written directions. Crossing Le Petit Pont from Île de la Cité to the Left Bank's Quai Montebello, a short walk brought her to the Square René-Viviani.

The view of Notre Dame from here was the best, and she was surprised at how few people were around.

Resting on a bench in the midst of lush gardens, she tried to absorb the fact that the tree in front of her, dramatically leaning and supported by concrete pillars, was believed to be the oldest in Paris. A variety of locust tree, healthy and flowering, it was planted in 1602 by Jean Robin, a gardener and herbalist to several French kings, who introduced this plant species to Europe. A plaque also informed it was hit by a shell in World War 1, which did nothing but shorten the height.

Discovering these surprises off the typical tourist path made Katherine's visit even more special. *Thanks to dear Philippe.*

In fact, he had told her about this park when she was sharing some of her mother's story. That had caused him to think of the special sculpture. Among other things, it showed infants with wings and others appearing lifeless that commemorated more than 11,000 Jewish French infants deported by the Nazis to Auschwitz. Many were from this *arrondissement*. Philippe had added that most guidebooks did not mention this component of the statue.

Feeling heartache, Katherine considered her mother and all the family she had lost. *I wonder if there is any sort of commemoration in her village. I guess we will find out after Andrew makes his trip there.*

So much history in such a small plot of land. It would require many visits to Paris for her to even begin to discover everything she wished.

⚜

Allowing herself the luxury of sleeping in until 8:00 a.m. Monday, she first slipped in to see the Church of Saint-Séverin, right across the street from her hotel. One of the oldest remaining churches on the left bank, the holy place had been there since before the Vikings. She read, to her delight, that among the bells to which she had wakened was the oldest in Paris, cast in 1412.

Meandering and window shopping through the Latin Quarter, she made her way once again to the Marché aux Fleurs.

Choosing something to take to François was no easy task.

She wandered through the whole area thinking how her mother would have loved to see this market.

Eventually Katherine retraced her path to one stall selling the most creative and beautiful bouquets. After much deliberation, she chose a spectacular but understated arrangement in shades of the palest pinks and soft greens that combined antique garden roses, orchids, pale-green dahlias, ranunculus, Queen Anne's lace, and seeded eucalyptus. Her photo of it ensured it would last forever.

Hailing a cab, Katherine realized she was hungry. She was also looking forward to meeting François under better circumstances than the last time.

The apartment was across the Seine, on the right bank, in the sophisticated sixteenth *arrondissement*, with its regal apartment buildings and parks. The ornately palatial building, dating from the nineteenth century, like many others now housed spacious apartments.

An imposing doorman dressed in a long military-looking coat and hat attended Katherine with a reserved look and directed her to the concierge desk, where a young woman telephoned her arrival to the apartment.

The mirror-and-gilt lobby resembled photos of castle salons Katherine had seen, and she wondered if the furniture was authentic or reproductions as she stepped into the rich wood-paneled elevator.

An older woman of unidentifiable age, wearing an outfit Katherine had only seen in movies, answered the apartment door. The classic black dress and white apron indicated she was . . . *what? A housekeeper, a maid? Do people even use that word anymore?*

Greeting her with a *"Bonjour, madame"* and a warm smile, she led Katherine into a large living area where François was seated in a wheelchair, a mohair throw draped over his legs. The view from the wall of windows stretched over the typically Parisian rooftops to Montmartre and Sacré-Coeur on its hilltop in the distance. A spectacular postcard panorama.

"Katherine! So here is the young lady who saved my life! Excuse me for not rising, but I am ordered to sit in this contraption for another month. Most annoying!"

"François, I'm happy to see you looking so much better. Thank you for inviting me. It was very kind of you."

After François gushed over the bouquet, Angélique appeared, to take care of the flowers, setting down a small tray of hors d'oeuvres, each a miniature work of art.

"Katherine, this is Angélique," François said kindly. "She has been a valued member of our family for over thirty years."

"I'm pleased to meet you," Katherine said to her as Angélique bowed shyly and backed out of the room.

"Years ago, it was not unusual for many families to have such valued staff. Our apartment is enormous, and she has her own quarters at the end of the hall," he said, indicating a long corridor.

"I want you to know," he added, to Katherine's amusement, "that Angélique chooses to wear that uniform. It's a bit embarrassing for me, but she likes it and feels it shows her chosen career. Interesting, isn't it? How nice to have such pride in what you do."

Katherine agreed heartily.

Philippe had already confided in Katherine that Madame Sophie Fortier, the wife of François, had been an invalid for many years and required constant care. A refined, educated woman of many accomplishments in spite of her challenges, she was beloved by all who knew her.

Sadly, she had succumbed to the grips of Alzheimer's disease a few years before and was now in a hospital a half hour away. He had said that François visited her every day when he was in Paris, unwilling to let go of the great romance they had shared for such a long time.

François was bright and engaging, a delightful host. He regaled Katherine with tales of life in Paris, the good and the bad sides, and she was thrilled to have this personal perspective.

Time passed quickly. The delicious *salade Niçoise* served for lunch was followed by an indescribably subtle but richly flavored *crème brûlée*. When coffee was served, Katherine sensed her host was tiring and after an appropriately courteous amount of time began to say her good-bye.

"François, this has been a pleasure. I am thrilled to see you on the road to recovery, and I know everyone is awaiting your return to Sainte-Mathilde."

"Merci, ma chère," he replied with a sparkle in his eye. "It has been my pleasure to receive you and to be able to thank you."

"And Picasso," she reminded him with a grin.

He laughed. "I will invite him for lunch when I am back in Provence."

François asked if Katherine had enjoyed her stay in France. "Many North Americans do not understand much of the French way of life," he commented.

"I have had the good fortune, as you know, of meeting such wonderful people. That combined with the countryside of Provence and the beauty of Paris has made my trip as perfect as it could possibly be."

"And did you have time to truly see this magnificent city?"

"Thanks to the list Philippe made for me, I have seen special places I would otherwise have missed. I have been a *flâneur* as much as I could and it has been *fantastique!*" Katherine explained, her eyes sparkling.

Noting the flush of her cheeks when Katherine mentioned Philippe, François's voice softened and his face took on a serious look.

"I have learned an important lesson as a result of my little episode, and I feel compelled to share it with you—*mon Dieu*, with *tout le monde*, everyone! Life is short, no matter how old we become. Sometimes we get caught up and forget to pay attention to little things."

Katherine nodded.

"I have had a successful life, as you can see. But truly I realize now that I need none of these trappings. My happiness comes from the calm I feel and the beauty I see in Provence. When I am there, I am at peace with myself. I have decided to close my apartment here and settle Angélique with a small pension so she can live comfortably. She will continue to visit my Sophie on a regular basis, and I will come up on the TGV once a week."

Katherine shifted with a hint of discomfort as his disclosure became so personal.

"I'm sorry. I do not mean to make you uneasy. We don't know each other really, but for some reason we became connected, and I am a great believer in fate. That is why I feel I want to share this with you, this advice, or whatever you call it. Life is full of choices. Don't be afraid to make them when you know they are right for you. You are so much younger than I and have so much life to live. Live it well."

Nodding, Katherine said, "It often takes an experience such as yours to remind us of what is important. How good that you see your path so clearly now. I wish you much happiness with your choices. Everyone will be pleased to have you back down there."

Taking a deep breath and smiling, as if his disclosures had somehow invigorated him, he said, "I know too that everyone in Sainte-Mathilde enjoyed your company and is sad to see you go. We all hope you will return for a visit some day."

"I hope so too," she replied. François reached out for her hand and graciously brushed it past his lips before escorting her to the door that Angélique was already holding open.

Back at the hotel, catching up in her journal, Katherine thought long and hard about his words.

Life is full of choices . . . live it well . . .

Contemplating how she had connected in such a meaningful way with the strangers that befriended her on this trip, she kept trying to put it into perspective. *Perhaps it doesn't need to be. It simply was. Maybe Lucy will have an answer.*

⚜

There was one stop on Philippe's list that Katherine had not managed to see yet, one that François had instructed she not miss.

The medieval Gothic royal chapel, Sainte-Chapelle was across the bridge and a few blocks from her hotel. Gasping as she entered, she understood their insistence and why both men had used the word "jewel." She immediately knew this was the highlight of all she had seen in Paris.

Completed in 1248 for Louis IX, its soaring stained glass windows and vaulted ceiling gave an almost heavenly sense of weightlessness. The gemlike colors of the glass and the richly decorated walls left her enthralled as she sat quietly absorbing the effect of this small but magnificent treasure. In spite of desecration during the Revolution, it was amazing to read that two-thirds of the spectacular stained glass windows were original.

At 8:30, she took her time walking through the narrow lanes of the Latin Quarter to Le Procope, which Joy and Mirella had recommended.

Opened as a café in 1686, it had served as a gathering place for men (no women) of arts and letters for centuries beginning with Rousseau, Voltaire, Benjamin Franklin, Thomas Jefferson, and other luminaries of the time. During the Revolution, the Phrygian cap, soon to be the symbol of Liberty, was first displayed here, and the Cordeliers, Robespierre, Danton, and Marat were regulars.

Refurbished in the late 1980s, the elegant setting oozed atmosphere. Luxuriously draped windows, sparkling chandeliers, and large oil portraits of the ancient writers, philosophers, and politicians created an air of important history.

A *foie gras* entrée and traditional *coq au vin* main course were completed with a selection of some of the finest cheese she had ever sampled.

A couple from Montreal at the next table chatted with her throughout the evening, providing good company and interesting conversation.

Being alone is not such a bad thing. I can do this.

The words of François rang in her ear.

⚜

Tuesday morning, she had one plan left.

After settling her bill, she left her luggage in a small room off the lobby. The Musée d'Orsay opened at 9:30, and after a quick taxi ride, Katherine was one of the first inside. She had an hour to make the most of it and so she did, heading straight for the Impressionist collection.

Better than nothing. Another item checked off the list.

By 11:00 a.m. she was in a taxi en route to Charles DeGaulle International Airport. There was no avoiding it now.

28

"Kat! You look fantastic! I can see this trip agreed with you as much as you were telling us!"

"Andie, I'm so happy to see you!"

"And I, you . . . I was afraid you might not come home!"

The two rocked in a tight hug, laughing.

"Everything was fine with the flight?" Andrea asked.

"Couldn't have been better!

On the way home Katherine insisted that Andrea catch her up on all her family's news before anything else.

"Once I start talking about this trip, it's going to be tough for you to get me to stop!"

They chattered on for the rest of the afternoon, and Molly and then Lucy called to say welcome home. Katherine was going back to work the next day, and afterward Molly was going to pick up Swiss Chalet chicken and bring it over to Kat's.

In her usual fashion, Andrea brought dinner with her and left shortly thereafter so Katherine could fall into bed early.

Very familiar with jet lag, she warned Kat, "You will probably be wide awake at four a.m., so be ready for it. Jet lag always seems worse coming this way, and you can expect it to last a week or so."

Saying good-bye with warm embraces, Katherine promised to spend a weekend in St. Jacobs soon. "I'll either come this weekend or the next one," she said. "Let me just get a handle with what's going on here."

Checking her e-mails before she turned in, she was excited to see several exchange inquiries. Scotland, Germany, and Spain were offered. She knew her next exchange would be a year away, but it was such fun to consider the possibilities.

She smiled to see an e-mail from Philippe saying he hoped she had arrived safely.

Katherine's return to work the next day meant no one accomplished anything for the first hour as they drank coffee and listened to her recount her adventure. At their insistence, she promised she would put together a slideshow to share with them.

She had never before been so open at the office about details of any vacation, she realized. She also realized she was enjoying the experience.

On the subway after work, Katherine felt a change to her outlook. Rather than anticipating being back at her job, she was relishing moments of her trip instead. She had noticed it in the morning too.

She couldn't recall a holiday in the past where she had not been very happy to be back to work when it was over.

Setting the patio table for dinner, she mixed a pitcher of Bloody Caesars, keeping the vodka on the side. The evening was warm, there didn't seem to be any mosquitoes taking over the garden, and she felt in the mood for a celebration. Molly could decide whether she wanted the alcohol or not.

Katherine was looking forward to seeing her more than she could remember.

Texting Molly to come around to the backyard when she arrived, Katherine busied herself refilling the bird feeders her father had built through the years.

He had enjoyed the continuous parade of feathered visitors in every season. She smiled now as she recalled how he had even made peace with the pesky squirrels and found a way to keep them all happy.

Simple pleasures are always best, he liked to say.

"*Plaisir,*" she thought. *This trip has impressed that in my mind like no other.*

Her calm was interrupted as Molly arrived in her usual flurry.

"Katski! Welcome home! I'm so happy to see you!"

Setting the takeout bags on the table, Molly wrapped her arms around Katherine and squeezed her tightly.

"Sit down and tell me frickin' everything, right this minute!"

Laughing, Katherine opened the bags. "Let's get this food out before it gets cold and then I'll begin. What about a Caesar? Virgin or otherwise?"

"Virgin will be just fine, thanks. I can't tell the difference when there's vodka in them anyway, so why waste it?"

"Well, I'll put your vodka in mine then," joked Katherine. "I'm feeling like a party."

They clinked glasses, and Katherine took a bite of the roasted chicken. "Y'know, I ate so much amazing food while I was away, but it's still good to come back to good old SC—yum!"

"Okay, enough about the chicken. Let's have the deets about the trip," Molly urged.

A smile spread slowly across Katherine's face. "Moll, without exaggeration, it was truly life changing. I think I have fallen in love."

"What? You never said a word about meeting any hot guys!"

The smile didn't change as Katherine replied, "Nope. It isn't about hot guys—you know that's not remotely on my agenda—but I have fallen in love with what I saw of France."

"No kidding?" Molly asked in a more serious tone.

"Truly. Madly. Deeply."

"Ho-o-o-ly shit," Molly muttered, examining her friend's face closely.

"No shit," laughed Katherine. "Remember how I've always told you I loved that country when I was there over thirty years ago?"

"Mm-hmm."

"Well, the feelings were even stronger this time. I can't stop thinking about it. The farmhouse and property were like something out of a beautiful story. Every room breathed character and history. The property, the gardens—it was magic."

The conversation went on long into the evening, with Molly interrupting every so often to ask for more details. She listened raptly as Kat described her experiences with Joy and her family and Mirella and Philippe, but her greatest enthusiasm showed when Katherine told her about Picasso.

"I can see that was a big part of your love affair. You should see the sparkle in your eyes."

"Well, here he is—gorgeous or what? Who would ever have guessed that a dog would become so important to me? I miss him!"

With her laptop set up while they ate, they flipped through just enough photos to show what Kat was talking about.

"Those are great shots. Wow! I get it. What a sweet-looking Lab. And that countryside, those villages. It's a stunning part of the world, that's for sure."

"I'll get a proper slideshow organized and we'll tuck in for an evening to watch it."

"I'll bring the wine and cheese," Molly offered.

Katherine told her about François and how having to hurry to get help for him brought her back to biking. They laughed uproariously at some shots of the rusty Peugeot bike.

"It looks like a crappy piece of junk," Molly said, giggling.

"Exactly! What a surprise it turned out to be. I'll never ever forget that!"

Then she went on to describe her mini-Mayle motor trip.

Seeing a shot of Katherine, Hubert and Lucille, and Matt on their hike, Molly commented. "So who's this dude? He isn't bad-looking."

She was wide-eyed with shock as Katherine related her experience with him in the pool at Le Mas des Oliviers.

"For Chrissakes, that's a goddamn sexual assault—and could have been worse! You should have reported him!"

"Honestly, I just wanted to get out of there and not see him. It would have been his word against mine. There were no witnesses, and you know, most of the time the woman is accused of asking for it. Nah, I didn't want to put myself through that."

"Well, I'm sorry you had to experience that. What a frickin' asshole he turned out to be."

"It still makes me twitch," said Katherine. "It was something I never imagined having happen."

"Stupid prick," agreed Molly. "What is it with some guys, anyway? And that's strictly a rhetorical question—no answer required."

"Well, just to prove the opposite of that, here are some shots from the lunch that day I Skyped you from Joy's manor house. Everyone here was charming, and none more so than Philippe."

"*Oo-la-la*, Kat, he looks like a sweetheart."

"And so he is," Katherine agreed. "Intelligent, warm, and unbelievably considerate. Fun too!"

"This is sounding good. So? Did any sparks fly?"

"Moll, it simply wasn't like that. He's a widower who is very set with his life, but as a friend, he was a lovely part of my holiday. Kinda renewed my faith in men."

"But—"

"No buts. You know I didn't go there looking for anything but a change and a bit of an adventure that didn't include anything like that. Besides, I'll never see him again. He was just a super-nice guy and reminded me there are some out there. On the other hand, I barely got to know him."

"With a sexy French accent to boot? I would have seriously been thinking of jumping his bones, if I'd been you."

Katherine shook her head and laughed. "You crack me up, girl. You really do! Such a big talker!"

Molly wanted to see more shots of Philippe, and Katherine was surprised at how many she had taken.

"Holy crap, Kat, he's so hot he's making my feet sweat! Seriously, there's a certain *je ne sais frickin' quoi* about that guy!"

Katherine insisted now that it was Molly's turn to fill her in on everything.

"First off, did the police find out anything about your Zipcar being keyed? Any clues?"

Shaking her head, Molly explained that even though there were cameras in the parking lot—

"Where aren't there these days?" Katherine interrupted. "Sorry."

"Yeah, well. Nothing's perfect. Those cameras are controlled by the security company hired by the school, and apparently there was some kind of malfunction that afternoon with the wiring or something, and the cameras were off for a while."

"Hmm, strange coincidence," murmured Katherine.

"Goddamn right it was strange!"

The phone calls were still coming but not as often.

"I'm spooked every time it happens, but I can't stop hoping . . ."

"Still nothing from Shawn?"

Molly shook her head sadly.

Katherine had noticed Molly check her phone a couple of times during the evening, but it turned out she was now addicted to Words with Friends.

Even though Kat's eyes were starting to close by nine o'clock, she convinced Molly to stay until ten. She was adding an hour to her bedtime each night for the rest of the week to work through her jet lag.

Molly filled Kat in on what a delightful couple the Lalliberts were and how they had enjoyed their time in Toronto.

"They loved the fact they could just walk up the street to the subway, and they couldn't believe the selection of restaurants they could stroll to here in the Kingsway. The house is in great shape, right?"

"Like no one had been here," agreed Katherine. "They left me three bottles of fabulous wine from their vineyard. I can't believe they packed that in their luggage. Thanks for helping me out with the exchange."

She handed Molly a package with gifts for her.

"Merci beaucoup, mon amie!" Molly said with a grin as she unwrapped a bright tablecloth and napkins in the typical Provence blues, greens, and yellows, as well as some soap, a bottle of lavender honey, and an olive-wood cheeseboard.

They laughed as Katherine described how she'd had to sit on her much heavier suitcase to close it for the trip home.

"Thanks for all of your help, Molly. I really appreciate everything you did."

"No worries, Kat. It was my pleasure, and it's such a blast to see how well this home-exchange concept works. If I ever live in a frickin' decent apartment again, I may just give it a try."

That comment led to talk about Molly's financial situation, which remained restricted.

"Molly, I have to say, I'm so impressed with how you are handling this. You are budgeting and cutting back with such a positive attitude."

Molly shrugged. "Hey, it is what it is. I'm managing. And the more changes I make, the more I'm okay with the way my life is. I think I've always been a minimalist at heart."

As they parted, tentative plans were made for the weekend.

29

As Kat settled back into her old routines, the week passed quickly.

Lucy organized her life so she and Katherine could have a quick bite after yoga, and there was no end to her questions. Katherine seemed to have been living her dream, she said.

Lucy had consulted her astrological charts, and everything was aligned in Kat's sphere. She assured her that the trip to France had been the right thing to do, based on her readings. Katherine knew Lucy truly believed the stars were in command.

There was the usual catching up to do with her work: studies to read and assess, and her own papers to work on. Much of this, Kat was able to accomplish in the evenings at home.

She mailed a card to the Lalliberts, expressing her appreciation of sharing their very special home and of course their even more special Picasso, for whom she slipped a packet of treats into the envelope.

Thank-you notes were posted to Joy, her son, Henri, and his wife, Sylvie, as well as Mirella, François, and Philippe. The latter she had sent in care of Joy's address, knowing it would be forwarded on. She did have Joy's e-mail address as well as Philippe's but felt it was more personal to handwrite her thanks.

Every minute her mind was not consumed with other things, it was filled with thoughts and images of France. She wondered how long it was going to take for the fantasies to fade.

In the meantime, she had a good time responding to several more exchange inquiries. Norway, Wales, Costa Rica, and Dallas. The possibilities are endless, she thought as she began to consider what her trip next year would be.

She planned to take Andrea and Terrence two of the bottles of wine the Lalliberts had left to thank them for pushing her into the whole idea of home exchange in the first place.

On Saturday, Katherine lifted her bike off the rack in the garage. She had covered it with an old sheet when she moved it from the townhouse, and now—almost ceremoniously, she noted with a chuckle—she pulled that cover off.

She knew her bike maintenance well, trained under her perfectionist ex-husband. After a wipe-down, along with a few drops of lubricating fluid, she placed the bike on a stand and turned the pedals to check the gears before she examined the brake pads and cables. Everything seemed to be in order. It was ready for the road, and so was she.

Going to the basement, she retrieved the storage bin in which she had placed her biking clothes. Pulling on the skin-tight shorts and jersey, Katherine was pleased to see they fit better than ever in spite of her baguette, cheese, and wine diet. *To say nothing of the* fondants *and* crèmes brûlées, she giggled.

Lying on top of the clothes was a piece of paper. Katherine recalled Andrea had sent it to her shortly after "la Katastrophe," when Kat had announced she was never cycling again.

It read, "When the spirits are low, when the day appears dark, when work becomes monotonous, when hope hardly seems worth having, just mount a bicycle and go out for a spin down the road, without thought on anything but the ride you are taking." Written by Arthur Conan Doyle.

Trust Andrea to find a quote that was so right, although she did not appreciate it at the time.

Slipping her feet into the clip shoes and putting on her helmet, her anticipation mounted. The day was perfect for a ride, with no obvious breeze. Pleasantly surprised that she felt nothing but excitement, Katherine rode the few minutes over to the Old Mill, where she hooked up with the Humber River Trail. Pedaling leisurely down to the Martin Goodman Trail, just beyond Humber Bay, this popular paved bike and walking path along the lakeshore would take her right through the city and across to the Beach area on the east side. It was a route so familiar she felt she could ride it blindfolded, and she loved it every time.

As Katherine reached Lake Ontario and headed east, she was reminded that her favorite time for this ride was in the early morning to catch the sunrise over the water. She filed a mental note for the next time.

A completely different landscape surrounded her than in France, but the cycling feelings were the same: a sense of freedom and strength offered by the swiftness of motion and the rapid rush of air. She felt her pulse dance as she picked up speed.

"Yes!" she shouted, feeling the euphoria of liberation. "Yes, yes, yes!"

⚜

Molly dropped by late Sunday afternoon on her way to choir practice.

"Hey, I see your bike rack on your car. What gives?"

Katherine grinned as she explained, "I'm taking it up to Chain Reaction later today to leave it for a tune-up. I rode it to the Beaches—"

"The Beach," Molly interrupted with a cynical look.

"It will always be the Beaches to me," Katherine stated firmly.

"I think it's great news that you are back riding, girlfriend!"

"Yeah, that's another bonus from my trip. I was forced over that hurdle in a fairly dramatic way!"

"I'll say," said Molly. "Have you heard anything more about that guy? The one who had the heart attack? How's he doing?"

"Other than when I had lunch with him in Paris, I really don't expect to. He was doing well. I didn't tell you about the words of wisdom he imparted to me before I left his apartment, though."

Molly looked interested.

"As we were saying good-bye, he suddenly said he felt he had to share something with me. He told me how deeply he had been affected by his 'episode' and how he felt fate had connected us. He told me of major personal changes he had decided to make. He wanted to counsel me not to fear change in life and to make choices that would bring me happiness."

"Hmmm, kinda, sorta spooky. I mean, like, he barely knows you."

Katherine nodded her head slowly. "I have to say it was a fairly profound moment. Seriously. Not that we don't know those sentiments, but just coming from him, there, in the moment, and considering how I got to be there in the first place, it did feel meaningful." Looking off, her eyes welled up as she added, "I've been thinking about it a lot."

"I can see that," said Molly. "I could use some change in my life right now!"

Shaded by the patio umbrella and serenaded by a chorus of birdsong, they talked for some time about the possibility of change for each of them.

Molly felt stuck where she was, financially and emotionally, but on the other hand admitted to Katherine that she was reasonably happy.

"Two things I want to change in my life? First, finding my brother, and finding him well. Second, these goddamn phone calls and weird shit that's happening. That's got to stop. Really, that's all the change I need."

"Truly? Wouldn't you like to have your relationship with the mysterious—to me, at least—Antonio out in the open?"

"Nope, that's never going to happen, and I can deal with it. I've worked through that."

"Molly, you've had me stymied on that one for years, and especially now that we spend so much more time together. I don't get it."

"I know, and you've been considerate by not pushing me to talk about it. Unlike some other folks, you don't live in Judgmentistan, and I truly appreciate that."

Katherine burst out laughing as Molly put her own quirky humor into a reasonably serious conversation.

"As I've said before," Molly continued, "trust me. He's not married. It's just the way this has to be. The love is real and we know that and it's enough for me. And most important, there is respect. This works."

"One thing I get from you, Molly, is that everyone doesn't necessarily have to have perfection in their life. As embarrassing as it is to admit this, I think I had a warped view of perfection when I was married. I thought my life was as good as it could possibly be and never looked beyond that."

"Well, what's wrong with that? Isn't that kind of the way it should be? If you're happy, why look beyond?"

"I guess, but since that seemingly perfect bubble burst, my world seems to be opening up and offering opportunities I never considered. I'm actually feeling a kind of happiness I don't think I felt in my marriage. At least, that's how I think I'm feeling. I'm changing, and I'm realizing that my old life wasn't really perfect after all."

"Well," Molly agreed, "I didn't get to see you that much then, but always felt that James was pretty frickin' controlling. Turns out that's how he was!"

"Exactly. So how do you think my ego feels about accepting that for all those years?"

"I'm guessing that part of it sucks! But it looks to me like you made a gigunda breakthrough on this trip."

30

Her bike loaded on the car rack, Katherine drove up the long lane to Andrea's farmhouse. The trip through the lush countryside around St. Jacobs, with crops established and pastoral views of grazing sheep and cattle, left Katherine with a sense of well-being.

She never ceased to be surprised when she passed someone working a field with horse and plow and admired the loyalty to tradition the Old Order Mennonites displayed.

The plan was for a cycle with Andrea along some of the back roads they had biked throughout the region since they were teenagers. Special routes they felt were their own secret discoveries.

None of the kids were around, and Terrence was helping out at a neighbor's farm, so they had a day just to themselves. Andrea was eager to hear more details of the home exchange, and Kat had brought her laptop for more photo viewing.

Wasting no time, they headed out right away to the St. Jacobs Farmers' Market, where the famous homemade sausage and sauerkraut stand was the first stop.

"I'm starving, Andie! I saved myself for this."

"Me too!"

They merged into the bustle around them and patiently waited in the long line at the popular food stall. A fine warm June Saturday was peak time for the market. Katherine entertained with comparisons to the markets she had visited on her trip. The lineup of wood-and-canvas horse-drawn carriages in the parking lot was one of Katherine's favorite photography subjects.

The ride along quiet rural roads, some paved and others packed gravel, took them through rolling countryside and eventually across the Kissing Bridge, the only original covered bridge left in Ontario, in the hamlet of West Montrose. Pausing to drink some water, Kat took a few shots as she commented on the exceptional light.

Andrea gave her a sideways glance. "Kat, I'm so, so happy you are cycling again. I know how special this spot is to you. Is it a problem being here now . . . y'know . . . without . . ."

"Without James? See, I can say his name, although it sounds better if I say 'without James the Asshole'."

Andrea laughed. "That sounds more like Molly."

"Right! But it has a certain ring to it. And no, the answer is no. It's not a problem. Honestly, Andrea, I've really made progress in dumping the baggage. What I have reaffirmed is that I do love cycling and that's that. In fact, I'm loving that I can decide where I'm going without having to consult anyone. That wasn't an option before."

"Good news, girl! I'm constantly amazed. You've opened up more and more about how controlling that guy was."

Kat shrugged. "So am I. I'm amazed that I never saw it that way."

Setting up for another photo, Katherine was suddenly overcome with melancholy. As much as this landscape pleased her, she felt a deep longing for the countryside of Provence and the images so deeply etched in her memory.

On the ride back to the farm, she struggled with putting her thoughts into perspective. *That was then and this is now.*

Over a green salad with juicy cherry tomatoes fresh from the vine and some warm flax bread straight out of the oven for dinner, Katherine shared more of her travel experiences. She thanked Andrea multiple times for helping to make it all happen.

"Kat, you have no idea how thrilled we all are that you went through with this! And guess what? We've got an exchange organized for October in Vienna! Cool, huh?"

Opening another bottle of wine, they spent hours looking at Katherine's photos as she supplied a running commentary and Andrea plied her with questions.

"And you truly didn't mind being on your own?"

Katherine's face clouded. "Anyu's words to me about being alone, about finding strength in being alone, live inside me all the time. They're empowering."

Andrea nodded and squeezed her cousin's hand gently. "For sure. If she did it, why on earth can't anyone?"

Terrence joined them just after ten and added his questions to the mix. It was approaching midnight when they decided another bottle of wine was in order.

Katherine argued successfully with them about opening one of the special Côtes du Luberon bottles she had gifted them.

"Good idea, Katherine. How better to toast your return home?" Terrence enthused.

"It's amazing there are around four hundred eighty growers within that small area, along with fourteen cooperative wineries and fifty-five private wineries such as the Lalliberts'," Terrence commented, reading from a brochure Katherine gave him.

They enjoyed her descriptions of living in the midst of a vineyard, and her intimate photos of the vines, the grapes, and the soil, especially with their experience working the land as they did.

"It sounds like you have a lot of reasons to want to return there," Terrence said.

"The list is longer than you can imagine! I loved everything about the small taste of France I had, and I will return sometime for sure, but who knows when. I'm receiving exchange inquiries from so many interesting places. I know you told me this would happen, but I never imagined it would be like this."

Covering her mouth as she yawned, she continued, "But I'm done for this year, so now it's time to focus on making plans at home. Speaking of which, I've got to hit the sack. That's my immediate plan!"

Sunday morning Katherine was up early and busy helping with chores, in spite of a dull headache from being slightly overserved.

By early afternoon, she was taking back roads home instead of the highway, reminiscing about her drives in Provence.

This countryside is peaceful and picturesque, but its beauty simply does not compare.

The following Tuesday, Katherine was surprised to receive a last-minute "hot list" exchange inquiry. She had taken to checking her e-mails at lunchtime since she had signed up for home exchange. It was just too much fun to wait until she got home.

This one was from a British couple, George and Mary Brown, living in a small coal-mining town in north England with grown children still at home. However, they also owned a small house in the town of Antibes on the French Riviera, and they were hoping to find an exchange in Toronto.

"Our oldest daughter is expecting our first grandchild in Toronto, and we have just learned she must have bed rest for the duration of her pregnancy. We are hoping to go and help for the next three or four months, but they have a small apartment, so if we can find an exchange our prayers would be answered."

Through Google, Katherine had looked up Antibes and discovered it wasn't all that far from Villefranche, where she had been so many decades before. On the Côte d'Azur, between Nice and Cannes, the photos and virtual tours on the Internet showed a beautiful old town right on the Mediterranean with a history dating before the Romans.

The artistic history was amazing too with an impressive roster of artists and writers having spent time there. She bookmarked a bunch of sites to read later.

Knowing she certainly could not consider such an offer, it was great fun to entertain the fantasy. She forwarded the request to Andrea in case they knew someone through their exchange connections.

Katherine also told everyone at the office about it.

"You never know," Lucy said to her as they talked about it on the way to yoga, "somebody might just know someone else who would do something like that. That's a long time, though—three or four months."

"Exactly. They would probably be better off to look for a rental. Maybe that's what they will end up doing."

31

Checking her cell phone as she walked home from the subway after her yoga class, Katherine was stunned to see Molly had called five times in the past hour.

"Molly, what's up? Are you okay?"

"Yes and no," Molly replied, her voice shaky. "Can I come and stay with you tonight?"

"Of course! What happened?"

"Someone broke into my apartment today and totally trashed it. The cops just left. I'm actually sitting outside my place in my Zipcar. I knew you were at yoga."

Katherine shook her head and shuddered slightly. Poor Molly.

"I'll be home in five minutes. Come now. Remind me to give you a key to the house. This is crazy!"

As she hung up, Katherine was horrified by this latest event and thought Molly sounded quite calm considering what happened. She hadn't even sworn. That in itself was strange.

Putting on the kettle for tea and checking the liquor cabinet, Katherine considered all the frightening and mysterious incidents Molly had been subjected to through the last few months. She wondered when it was all going to come to an end.

Fifteen minutes later Molly plopped herself down in a kitchen chair, running her hand through her hair and blowing out an enormous sigh.

"Tea, wine, or scotch?" Katherine asked.

"Tea, please. That's all I can handle at the moment."

Katherine set the teapot on the table next to the china mugs already there and sliced a lemon.

"So, tell me what happened."

Leaning forward, Molly put her face in her hands for a few seconds and then sat up. She stared at Katherine in silence, shaking her head.

"So . . . ?" Katherine asked again, wrinkling her brow and spreading her hands wide. Molly continued shaking her head, wide-eyed, her lips pressed firmly shut. Putting her hands on Molly's shoulders, Katherine shook her gently. "What's going on in there, girl? Are you sure you are okay?"

Molly nodded yes, but still said nothing.

Katherine poured their tea and dropped a slice of lemon into both mugs, placing Molly's next to her. She sat down in a chair, staring back at her friend.

"Are you going to talk?"

Molly nodded affirmatively again.

"Soon?" Katherine said with a smirk, sensing now that Molly was fine in spite of the weird behavior.

Reaching for her tea, Molly took a sip and slowly swallowed. "You are not going to believe this. I can't believe this . . ."

"I'll try my best. Start at the beginning of what happened today," Katherine said.

"I walked into my place after work and it was a disaster—stuff was thrown all over, bookcase toppled, my drawers emptied on the floor. Fortunately I had very little in the fridge!"

"Oh my God, how horrible. Weren't you afraid someone was there?"

"Yes, I was. To be honest, I waffled between being terrified and totally pissed off! So I ran right down to the super's office and we called the police. I gave them the number that one officer had given me, and he was one of the pair who responded."

"Oh, that's good."

"Yup, I was glad I didn't have to start at the beginning again. The officer took charge right away, and he knew something I didn't."

"Which was . . . ?"

"After the flower-delivery fiasco, the building owners installed security cameras, but the tenants were not told. So they went right downstairs and looked at the tape.

"I knew who it was right away . . ." Her voice died off and she shook her head again. "Un-fucking-believable, Kat, un-fucking-believable."

Katherine sipped at her tea patiently while Molly collected herself again.

"It was Pauline."

"Who is . . . ?"

"Pauline! The secretary at my school."

"You're right, Molly, un-fucking-believable. You could recognize her from the camera?"

"Not right away. She wore a hat and glasses, but I knew it was someone familiar. There was just something about the way she walked. The kicker was that they had a camera on the outside of the building too, and it showed her getting out of her car. The license plate was clear as a bell, and the police pulled it up."

Katherine shook her head. "I'm confused. Why?"

"I couldn't believe it, but it explained a lot of things, like my lost purse and a few things that happened at school that I didn't mention because I thought I was becoming paranoid."

"Oh, Molly!"

"Plus she left the school at noon, saying she was taking the afternoon off because she was sick. Duh!"

"Why on earth was she doing those things to you? Have you ever had words with her?"

"No—in fact, we always got on just fine. You'll shake your head at this story. Since last September, I've secretly been giving the vice principal, Terry Murphy, piano lessons. He wanted to surprise Kit, his wife, by playing something at her birthday next month. So a couple of days a week we would go into the music room and I would lock the door so we wouldn't be disturbed. Frickin' Pauline apparently has had a huge crush on him, and there was a little hanky-panky a year or so ago before he cut it off. She thought he was getting it on with me. And she flipped."

"Um, to say the least!"

"I know! It's bizarre! I'm mad at her, but I feel sad for her too. How pathetic to be so desperate. But then I want to pop her one right in the nose for all the crap she put me through."

"Well, the feeling sad part is awfully big of you," said Katherine. "I just say thank goodness that's over with."

"Holy Mary, Mother of God, you are so flippin' right, and I'm relieved it wasn't some weird, smarmy dude."

"Right. Yeah, me too. It was pretty scary there for a while."

"I have to go to the police station tomorrow to fill out some more papers. They are going to lay charges."

Both sat quietly for a moment. Molly shook her head, saying, "How do these things happen to seemingly normal people? It boggles my mind."

"It's a crazy world these days," Kat agreed. "I'll go to your place after work and help you clean up. Don't go by yourself."

"Thanks, Kat."

She got up and gave Katherine a warm hug.

"No problem. Oh, it's time for *Downton Abbey*. Let's go watch."

"Good idea. Time for a change of pace."

32

The following week Katherine was in Dr. Henderson's office reviewing some new reports with him when he rose and shut the door.

Looking up in surprise, she was unable to recall the last time that door had been closed.

"Is everything all right?"

He shook his head as he sat back down, and a look of sadness crossed his face. "I'm afraid not, my dear. The government has announced we are not going to receive our usual funding this year, and our offices will be absorbed into the hospital's pain research department. The economy is taking its toll on health services, as you know."

Katherine was stunned.

"This is terrible. What will happen to all the work we're doing? All your research?"

"Our work will simply move into the hands of the research department. You know how closely we've worked with them over the years and how much everything we've done is valued."

"Yes," Katherine agreed, "they've always been clear about that."

"They're not happy about losing us, not to mention adding a huge increase to their workload."

Katherine's voice was filled with concern as she asked about the job situation, wondering if they all would be redundant.

He took a deep breath before answering. "Well, that's why I wanted to speak to you before I tell everyone on staff about this. There will be a few positions some of us can move into. However, I've decided it's time for me to retire."

"Really?"

"Absolutely! You know I've considered it from time to time."

Katherine nodded. The subject had come up a few times.

"But I love my work here and just never felt ready to walk away from it," he added. "This is the perfect opportunity, and it feels right."

Katherine sighed, looking down at her tightly clenched hands.

"Dr. Landman, the chair of the hospital department, has already asked if you would be willing to work with them. They're hopeful you will say yes."

Looking up, Katherine shrugged. "This is all so sudden. I don't know what to think. What about the rest of the staff?"

Dr. Henderson stood and slowly paced behind his desk. "Katherine, the position would be a good one, but I have a suggestion for you. This has been a difficult year for you. I think you should take some time off and go on that home exchange."

Katherine's jaw dropped. "Pardon?"

"It's none of my business, but . . . actually, it was Susan's idea."

Katherine smiled. Susan was his wife and one of the most upbeat and energizing people she knew. Confined to a wheelchair and living with MS for as long as Katherine had known her, she had always been very fond of Katherine, and the feeling was mutual.

Susan spent one day a month in the office reviewing the small accounting issues their office generated, and over the years the two women had developed a warm rapport.

"I had told her about the exchange and even suggested *we* might do it, under the circumstances, knowing I would not be working anymore."

"Well, why don't you? That's a marvelous idea!"

"It's a more marvelous idea for you! We couldn't go away from our grandchildren for that long a period. As soon as I mentioned that, Susan realized I was right." He laughed. "Besides, as she so astutely pointed out, there undoubtedly would be narrow, steep stairs involved, although we hadn't actually looked at the listing."

"Stairs and cobblestones," Katherine confirmed. "I know how Susan feels about cobblestones after your last trip!"

The Hendersons had never ceased to be intrepid travelers, often including their grown children and spouses in their travels. Katherine admired their sense of adventure, strong family connection, and the many trips they had taken renting houses in Spain, France, Italy, Costa Rica, and other exotic locations. Throwing a wheelchair into the mix had not slowed them down for a moment.

"So what do you say, Katherine? You have done nothing but rave about France since your return, and the positive effects of that trip on your psyche have been obvious to all of us. This is the perfect opportunity, and what a coincidence all of this is."

Katherine looked off out the window. Everything was happening so fast. The thought of the office closing jolted her. The routine that had governed her life for so long was being seriously dismantled.

It had been one thing when her personal life had shattered, and now her professional one was going to transform. Her whole life appeared to be unraveling. But was that necessarily a bad thing? That thought seemed to be working its way into her head.

Dr. Henderson's voice broke through her distracted thoughts. "Obviously you don't have to make a decision this moment about the job, so think about your options. I'll receive the official letter in a few days and then will break it to the rest of the staff. I'm only telling you now so you can answer the exchange inquiry if you want to."

Then he added with a broad smile, "Susan insisted."

⚜

Done.

Katherine hit "Send," exhaled loudly, and pushed her chair back from her desk. She had gone directly from Dr. Henderson's office to her computer.

Thank goodness it's the end of the afternoon. My concentration is shot.

Her response to the Browns was on its way. She was going to do it.

That's if someone else has not already accepted the offer, she thought with a bit of paranoia.

As she drove home, Dr. Henderson's suggestion was the only thing on her mind. Katherine phoned Andrea and Terrence immediately to ask their opinions. She knew by the time she walked in the front door of her house that she was going to go if the offer was still good. It was no surprise to her when they fully supported her feelings.

"Do it, Kat. Take a chance and step outside your comfort zone again," Andrea encouraged.

"Go for it!" Terrence agreed.

"Oh my gosh!" Andrea exclaimed. "You'll still be there when we do our exchange! We'll come to visit you!"

The thought added to Katherine's already growing excitement.

For some reason Molly was not answering her phone or texts. Katherine sent her an e-mail and then went to the kitchen to make some dinner.

It had been a cool, rainy day, so Katherine decided soup was in order and began clearing out the fridge. Cauliflower, broccoli, carrots, and celery were quickly chopped and tossed into onions and garlic lightly sautéing in butter. After adding chicken broth and *herbes de provence*, her attention drifted.

Three months in the South of France. The French Riviera. La Côte d'Azur. The words tumbled around her mind. *In nine months, my life has changed in ways I would never have imagined. I thought the end of my marriage was the door slamming on my life, but instead it turns out to have opened the door of opportunity.*

Looking out at the garden, she thought of her parents and the hours they had lovingly spent there. She considered where they had come from, what they had experienced, and how they had changed direction with their lives, never looking back.

Why can't I? There's absolutely nothing keeping me here. Andrea and Terrence and their family will always be mine no matter where any of us live. Molly's friendship will always be there. My colleagues at work will move on in different directions. Lucy and I will probably stay connected, and e-mail allows that so easily now—and that's it. There's just nothing to lose by leaving for three months.

When she considered the empowering experience she had in Provence for just two weeks, she was certain much more lay before her.

Giving the soup a stir, she turned it down to simmer and returned to her thoughts.

I'll join a cycling club. I'll have to really get in shape for those hills! I'll go hiking. I'll take French lessons—and maybe even a cooking course.

Now her pulse was racing with excitement.

I'll have to budget, but I know my savings can cover this without a problem. I just have to make sure I have a good cushion when I get back until I find another job.

She tried Molly's phone again and felt a little uneasy that she wasn't hearing back. They had come to rely on each other, and to Katherine's surprise, Molly was extremely dependable about responding. Katherine realized she was Molly's only family, apart from her absent brother. She felt badly now that they had not been closer when she was married.

James had always been clear, right from their early days together, that he considered most people to be duplicitous and untrustworthy. *Obviously he didn't have a problem getting close to what's-her-name.*

He had come from a large family and was completely estranged from all of them since before Katherine met him. In spite of her urging in the early days, he refused to speak about it.

He always said it was so wonderful to have Kat because he could believe in her, confide in her, and never be let down.

Huh! Was I an idiot or what? And guess what, I never did let him down.

Her thoughts went back to their anniversary and all that had occurred in those horrific days. The pain was still there, but it was far less acute.

Taking the pot off the element, she plugged in her food processor. She had decided to make a cream soup today, but it would have to cool for a while before she could purée.

Still with no response from Molly, Katherine decided she must be singing somewhere unexpectedly, since that was really the only time Molly couldn't find a minute to text a few words.

She checked her e-mail, hoping somehow there might be a reply from the Browns, even though she was well aware it was the middle of the night in England. She would simply have to be patient until morning.

33

Katherine was out of bed well before her alarm. The suspense had kept her in a state of fitful sleep, with a single thought repeating: *Don't let me be too late.*

The reply from the Browns was sitting in her inbox. Squeezing her eyes shut, she clicked on it.

They had been thrilled to receive her message. It was a go.

Now they included more detailed information with regard to their daughter and her husband and asked if their son-in-law could come over to see the house. Katherine was only too happy to agree and wrote that she would call him.

Andrea e-mailed to see if the exchange was on and, if so, suggested Kat ask the lawn-mowing company to add garden maintenance to their contract with her for the time she was away.

"That way there's no pressure on the exchange people to do it. It might not be something that interests them. I know you and I would be out there weeding anyway, but not everyone is that crazy. I'll let you know if I think of anything else."

Getting dressed, Katherine was already thinking about being back in France when her cell rang.

"Hey." It was Molly.

"Hey back. Are you all right?"

"Yup, just got home too late last night to call. I was asked to help judge a music competition at the Royal Conservatory when one of the judges suddenly took ill. We actually had to turn in our cell phones. Hilarious or what?"

"Had you planned to attend?"

"I went in the afternoon to support a couple of my students."

"With no break?"

"I'm telling you, it was like a frickin' closed meeting of the United Nations Security Council or whatever! They brought food in. We were escorted to the washroom. No talking. No cell phone."

"What was that all about?"

"Well, these kids were competing for big scholarships and prestige, so they didn't want any results slipping out or any collusion. I've never seen anything like it."

"They must have been talented."

"Awesomely! It was a pleasure to judge them, and you know how music feeds my soul. This was *haute cuisine* at its frickin' finest! But never mind! What's with you and all your messages? Are you okay?"

"Um . . . yeah, I'm okay," Katherine began in a restrained voice, before bursting with excitement. "Oh my God, I can hardly stand it, Molly! I'm going to take that three-month exchange in France, and I'll be leaving in just over a month! Can you believe it?"

"Wha-a-at the . . .? Start at the beginning, please."

Katherine filled her in on the conversation at work and her subsequent decision. Molly's excited and expletive-laced expressions of support put Katherine into an enormous fit of laughter.

"Will you come to visit me if I get you a ticket on points?"

Molly was speechless for a few seconds. "You are such a kickass friend! Are you serious?"

"I still have tons of points, even after my ticket was booked. It would be so much fun for you to come over."

Molly said nothing again.

"Are you crying?" asked Katherine.

Molly squeaked out a weak-voiced reply. "I was the shittiest travel companion ever when we went to Chicago. Are you sure you want to risk it again?"

"This is France, Moll. You can't *not* love it. I'll risk it!"

Katherine had to plead and massage the subject to get Molly to agree to accept her generosity, but eventually was successful.

❧

In the subsequent weeks, everything began to fall into place.

A veil of sadness slipped over the office when Dr. Henderson made his announcement about the funding cut. They had been a good team for a long time and felt proud of the contributions their work had made toward pain management in the hospital programs. Once the shock began to subside, everyone got busy assessing their future plans. Dr. Henderson was determined to retire and actually began to look forward to it now that the decision had been made.

Katherine was relieved that the office was going to be open for several weeks after she left so she would avoid the final inevitable closing-up. They decided to have a farewell dinner before she left, and that would be difficult enough.

Lucy was frantically studying everyone's chart in the hopes of finding encouraging signs about the future. When Katherine announced her plans, Lucy went silent. On the way to yoga that evening, Kat summoned the courage to ask if everything was okay.

"Oh, there's really no problem. It's just that sometimes I'm overwhelmed by the accuracy of my readings, and it frightens me. I knew you were going to be going away again and for a long time, but I didn't want to say anything, and besides that, I couldn't imagine what it would be. I was doing some further exploring to make sure I was right."

"So what else do you know, my clairvoyant friend? Do I have to wait much longer to find out?"

"Not much. But I'm not quite finished. Tell me, is everything good in Molly's life?"

"For sure! Now that the perpetrator has been caught," Katherine told her. "Why do you ask?"

Lucy reluctantly said, "I'm seeing something in her chart that concerns me. The numbers aren't working. Maybe it's just a holdover from what she went through, but somehow I don't think so. You know me, though—I'm afraid to say anything like that. Don't tell her yet. I'll work on it some more and talk to her."

34

One month to go. Thirty-one days.

July began hot and muggy, and Katherine fantasized about the Mediterranean breezes that would cool her in Antibes.

The Browns e-mailed photos of their house, and their son-in-law also offered details, having visited there twice. When he came to see her house, he brought a map and more photos and was able to answer every question she posed.

"You won't believe the location. The house is in one of the oldest parts of the old town, built on what they call the Ramparts. There is just a road between you and the Med and a beautiful little beach. You are going to love it!"

The property was even better than she had first understood, although perhaps not everyone would agree. A three-hundred-year-old *maison de ville,* or townhouse, meant relatively small rooms and narrow stairs—and to Katherine that meant charm.

The ocean view she assumed would no doubt mean hanging your head out a window and craning your neck to see a sliver of blue in the distance. It turned out to be a window on each level that overlooked the sea and a rooftop terrace with a full view across to Cap d'Antibes. Could she get any luckier?

The Browns asked if Katherine's garage was useable, as they intended to rent a car. After discussing the situation with Andrea and Terrence, Katherine decided to include her car with the exchange even though the Browns did not have a vehicle in Antibes.

The truth was, they explained, that you really didn't need one in Antibes. The daily market was literally one minute away, as were the old-town shops and restaurants. The train station was a ten-minute walk, and you could travel anywhere along the coast, including Italy. No car was needed unless you wished to explore the countryside, and then a car-rental office was up the street.

Katherine faced a sudden bout of mixed emotions. As excited as she was about her exchange, she was feeling stressed about her office closing. It had been such an integral part of her life for so long. Feelings of great sadness engulfed her for a few days.

She met with Dr. Landman and the HR people at the hospital, and they agreed to consider holding the position for her until November.

"It would be good to know I was returning to that job," she told Dr. Henderson.

"Yes, it would, but my dear, take it from me when I say that life passes in a heartbeat. There will be other jobs. Take a chance. See this entire situation as a tremendous once-in-a-lifetime opportunity!"

I'm trying to do just that . . . but I'm struggling . . .

Although it hadn't occurred to her before she invited Molly to come to France, Katherine realized how relieved she was that her friend was going to be with her for the first ten days.

As exciting as this exchange seemed, there was now an underlying anxiety as the entire structure and predictability of her life was disintegrating.

"A two-and-a-half-week vacation was one thing, but leaving for three months is a whole different story," she told Andrea, anxiety obvious in her voice.

"Are you going to get in touch with the family you met on your last exchange? You enjoyed them so much."

Katherine paused for a moment. "I've been thinking about it, but then I waffle and think I really don't know them that well. I feel kind of shy about just writing out of the blue. I think I'll wait until I get settled and then let them know. See? I feel unsure about everything right now."

"I really think you should see your counselor," Andrea advised when Katherine called on another day to tell her she was seriously thinking about canceling the exchange.

"I just don't know if I can go through with it. I'm wavering after all my bravado," Katherine admitted, her voice breaking. "I'll call the office in the morning for an appointment."

⚜

Dr. Olson pressed the tips of her fingers together as she leaned back in her chair, carefully observing Katherine. A canceled appointment had allowed Katherine to see her immediately.

"I'm so confused," Katherine confessed, "and don't know if it's because I'm having a delayed reaction to the divorce or something else."

"What else do you think it might be?"

She sat silent for a few moments before answering. "Well, leaving my job after all these years will be a huge adjustment. It has defined me in many ways, and God knows I struggled with losing a big part of my identity when James left me."

Dr. Olson nodded. "Anything else?"

"I'm also feeling as if I'm leaving my mother behind, silly as that might sound. She's been gone for months now, but the act of leaving the house for such a long time makes me suddenly feel her loss more acutely."

"There is logic to that because symbolically you are giving her home to strangers. Even though you did do that for two weeks, this longer period represents something more permanent. The decisions about the house no longer have anything to do with your parents."

Katherine nodded solemnly.

"I would also suggest that accepting the challenge of going so far away on your own—again, for the extended time—very clearly says you are independent . . . on your own. You are in charge of every decision, every choice, you make."

"But I already did that and I was fine."

"You did it for two weeks and could ride along on the euphoria of the adventure during that time. It's almost as if you had something to prove that time and it all worked out very, very well. This longer time means something quite different."

The rest of her appointment was spent discussing all the pent-up anxieties Katherine still harbored over being left by James. She was surprised at the lingering animosity when forced to confront it.

"You are looking at accepting several major changes in your life—the end of your marriage, the death of your mother, and the loss of your job. Even though you may feel you have come to terms with all of these. Bundled together, they are quite an explosive package."

Examining each issue, with Dr. Olson's guidance Katherine began to feel calmer, although she still wondered if it might be best not to do the exchange.

"I may have bitten off more than I can chew," she said sadly.

Dr. Olson gave Katherine some journaling exercises, wrapping up the session.

"Let's meet again in a week," Dr. Olson suggested, but Katherine asked to come sooner.

"If I'm going to cancel this exchange, I have to do it now. Even so, it will be so inconsiderate of me and will cause a difficult situation for the other people."

"Well, that's something you seriously need to consider along with what we have been discussing." Looking at her appointment book, Dr. Olson agreed to squeeze her in three days later.

Long, tearful talks with Andrea and Molly occurred during the next forty-eight hours as Katherine finally let go of emotions she had been storing deeply inside. In return they gave her the gift of honest feedback and opinions she trusted and valued. Katherine was so thankful to have this kind of friendship in her life now. She couldn't believe how helpful it was to talk things through with them. Expressing her thoughts in the journal helped immensely. Finally she sat and looked at the photos of her wonderful two weeks in Provence.

I know I felt like that was the promise of a beginning for me, the acceptance and embrace of change as I move forward. Why am I fearing it now?

Taking a long bike ride, Katherine let the satisfaction this gave her add its healing powers.

She recognized that the emotional turmoil of her divorce and the grief of losing her mother had been abating for months. She understood how the unknown of stepping out of her normal environment and routine for the extended time of the exchange could resurrect anxieties.

I'm not going to let the fear factor kick in here. Talking to Dr. Olson reminded me I can handle the challenges that lie ahead, and I will.

The next day, she returned to the chair in the doctor's office with renewed confidence and resolve.

"You've come a long way in the past few days, Katherine. I actually think you had already come to terms with the issues we discussed. I believe you had an acute case of cold feet."

Katherine agreed, feeling somewhat sheepish. "Our mind does play games with us. I've never made a decision like this in my life, and it scared me. You've explained how change can be positive and a great opportunity to move in different directions. I want to do that in spite of the risks."

"I'm glad to hear that. Talking through these matters, as you have, can be the conduit needed to get yourself to a better place. Remember, you can Skype with me at any time while you are away if you feel you need to."

Shaking hands, Katherine left the office feeling ready to move on as Dr. Olson added, "It's a new world, a new journey. Embrace it, Katherine. Think of it as synchronicity."

Katherine determined to do just that.

35

Merlot was bustling with diners and high energy as usual when Molly and Katherine met for dinner.

Dessert was being served when the call came. Molly's face blanched. It appeared she might faint as she gave one-word responses into her phone. After repeating her e-mail address, the call ended, and she stared at Katherine with a panic-stricken look.

"What's wrong?" Katherine asked with alarm.

Molly swallowed slowly, closed her eyes, and gave her head a quick shake.

"That was the Vancouver police department."

"And . . . ?" Katherine's brow creased with worry.

"They've . . . found Shawn. He's in the intensive care unit of Vancouver General, and that's all they would say, except that I have to go out right away."

"After all this time, it's finally happened," said Katherine as she went around the table to hug Molly. "You never gave up."

"Goddamn it! Why can't they give me more details? That's so unfair!"

"Let's get the bill and go to my house. We can book your flight online and see if we can use my points."

"Thanks, Kat. Do you think we might get lucky? I don't have a god-damn minute to spare, and hopefully I'll get an early-morning flight."

"We'll see. I wish I could go with you, but there's no way with everything that's going on at work and me leaving for France in less than three weeks. I feel so badly. Will you be all right? Do you want to try Andrea?"

"I'll just have to be all right," Molly said, her eyes filled with worry. "No alternative. I'm just praying Shawn is okay."

"Me too. Go home now. You don't need to be with me when I book the ticket. I'll call you when I pull up the flight info, and I'll take care of the bill here."

They hugged each other tightly and Molly rushed off.

When Katherine got home, there was already a message from Molly. She was leaving in three hours at 11:15 p.m. and she was not going alone.

"Father DeCarlo is going to fly out with me and he booked the tickets. He has some business to conduct at the British Columbia diocese office in Vancouver, and he can keep me company. He knows Shawn from way back, and he feels I should not be there on my own. I really appreciate the gesture."

Katherine had to agree. It seemed a little strange, but with what she knew of the priest and his work with the homeless and displaced, she felt certain his presence could only help. There would be comfort no matter what Molly was faced with out there—and with Shawn, you just never knew.

⚜

It was just after Katherine had arrived home from work the next day, and early afternoon Vancouver time, when Father DeCarlo phoned Katherine.

"I'm afraid the news is not good."

"I was worried that might be the case," Katherine said softly.

"We came straight to the hospital from the airport," he continued, "and there were police guarding Shawn's room in the ICU, which shocked us. We both thought he must be in serious trouble."

"Oh, how awful."

"It turned out they were there to protect him. He had been caught in crossfire during an altercation between drug gangs, and the police thought someone might come to make sure he was unable to identify any of them. That was hardly a worry. He was seriously wounded and put on life support."

The ongoing issues with drug wars in the Vancouver area had been in the news for years.

Katherine's eyes filled as she imagined how tragic this would be for Molly to face after living with hope for so many years that she would one day find Shawn well.

The priest continued, "We spent some time with Shawn, and I was able to administer the last rites. God rest his soul. After the doctors explained there was nothing more to be done, Molly made the decision to remove Shawn from life support. She held his hand through to the end."

Tears streamed down Katherine's face.

"I'm so thankful you were there with her," Katherine said, her voice barely a whisper.

"So am I. Her sorrow was overwhelming," he said softly. "She asked me to call you to let you know. Later this afternoon we're going over to his room at a boardinghouse to organize whatever belongings he had, and as things stand now will fly back home the day after tomorrow."

"Thank you, Father. Do you think Molly should spend that night with me?"

"I think so. Yes, I would say that's a very good idea. I will have the limo bring her straight to your place. Would you mind calling the Blue Note to let them know she won't perform this weekend and maybe not the following one either?"

"No problem. I'll call immediately."

"Thank you."

"No, the thanks is all for you! I'm so grateful you are there with her."

When she thought about it later that evening, Katherine considered how the two siblings had responded in such different ways to the traumatic childhood they had shared.

Molly had closed herself off in so many ways emotionally and maintained such tight control of her life with no serious relationships—*just the mysterious ongoing affair.*

Shawn, on the other hand, was always out of control, with his exuberant but lovable personality. In and out of relationships and jobs, he bounced off walls until he slipped into the world of drugs and addiction.

Molly had attempted to be mother, father, and sister to him. Her loss now would be powerful.

⚜

Katherine finished wiping down her bike in the garage on Sunday after a long afternoon ride with her old cycling club. She went over the day in her mind and knew she was glad she had gone. She'd had to push herself, but she had done it.

May McNeilly had sent her an e-mail on Saturday inviting her along, and Katherine had decided it was time to get over the hurdle of facing everyone there. She felt she would want to ride with them regularly when she returned from France, and it would be good to connect with them before she left.

She realized her fears of feeling embarrassed and belittled were unfounded when everyone greeted her warmly. They were all about riding bikes, and that's mostly what they shared, not the ride of life.

The ride had been challenging for her out-of-condition legs and butt. It was fifty kilometers following the Humber River Trail up and back, along mostly paved bike paths except for one short street section. Katherine had joined up at the Old Mill with others who had begun down at the lake. The overcast day made for a more comfortable ride through the forested and green areas that bordered the river. It was easy to forget you were riding through the heart of the west end of the city.

She had taken her cell phone with her but kept it on vibrate in the pouch on her bike, so she checked it now for messages.

Molly had left a voicemail; Kat was pleased to note her voice sounded strong. They were flying back from Vancouver on the red-eye, and Molly would call later on Monday.

"Don't worry about me, my friend. I'm really quite fine—sad but fine. It's not as if Shawn knew this was going to happen, but in a way he anticipated something, and he left me the most amazing letter. Lots to tell you."

That sounded reassuring.

36

Molly called Katherine at the office just before the end of the afternoon on Monday.

"I'll come to your place on my way home from work if you like."

There were tears when she first arrived at Molly's apartment, and they returned sporadically throughout their conversation. Life wasn't fair for some people, and Shawn had been one of those.

"I'm so sorry that this didn't turn out as you had hoped. You held onto that for so long."

Molly sat with her head bowed for a moment, breathing deeply. "Kat, you remember how miserable things were at our house when we were growing up. Our parents smacked the shit out of us and abused us verbally. Dad was a raging alcoholic. But they were our parents and we kept looking for their love and approval when we were young, as kids do."

Katherine nodded, recalling how Molly would often beg to stay at her house some weekends and Kat's parents never refused.

"That stopped once your parents got divorced, Molly, when you were, what, ten?"

"Yup, Mom stopped hitting us then. I think before that she hit us when really she wanted to hit Dad. She was totally buzzed out on prescription drugs most of the time, and I became the caregiver for her and Shawn. I hardly ever saw my dad after that, but Shawn always wanted to go to his place. He got to drink Dad's leftovers after the old man passed out."

Katherine sighed sadly as Molly continued. "Anyway, I don't have to repeat the whole sordid fucking history. You know it for the most part."

"What happened to Shawn? Do you want to talk about it?"

Molly's face was pale and drawn. "Words . . . they feel so brittle right now . . . it's like they crumble and mean nothing. After holding on to a dream for so long, it's hard to accept when it's over."

Katherine slipped her arm around her friend's shoulder.

Molly nodded and continued. "Somehow I always felt it might end badly for him, especially after all his failed struggles to stay away from addiction."

"Was he in a bad way again?"

"Yes, terrible, but typical of him, he met some good people along the way who tried to help him. They filled in the holes of his story for me. I'll give you the short version. He lived cheaply in one room in a sleazy flophouse on the east side of the city. As always, he would get himself going on a pretty good path and in that state used all his energy to help other down-and-outers. He served meals at hostels. He drove around with volunteers to get people off the street in bad weather. He tried to commit to AA meetings until he slid off into a haze of drugs and booze again."

Molly's voice caught again as the pain washed over her.

Katherine swallowed hard. *Shawn was such a sweet guy as we were growing up.*

"He was making a drug buy when he got caught in some gang crossfire," Molly finished, in almost a whisper.

Molly went into her bedroom and returned with several sheets of lined paper.

"He started to write me a letter when he checked himself out of the last rehab center, and he continued an ongoing missive until the week before he died. He said no matter what, he always had me with him . . ."

Her voice cracked as tears slipped down her face. Kat got up and brought over the Kleenex box to put between them after she pulled a tissue out for each of them.

Molly handed her a page. "Read this."

Katherine could hear Shawn's voice in his words. Unbidden, tears pooled in her eyes as a vivid image of the last time she saw him stormed into her mind. He was in bad shape, and Molly was about to drive him to rehab again when Katherine had gone over to say good-bye.

His eyes were bleak, his body emaciated. He had run his hands through his hair as he spoke to her, and the anguish in his voice was barely suppressed. He really did want to turn his life around, but the devil inside him was unwilling to be vanquished. She could see and hear all that now as she read his letter.

There were rambling pages put together through the last few years, but the words on the last page she would never forget.

This will always be the last page of this letter. I'm writing it when I'm clean. Whatever else I add belongs before this page, so if you find it out of order, put it at the end.

I'm clean, Moll, and have been for a couple of months. The relief and the pride are indescribable. But I've been here before and I expect it's not going to last, which is why I'm not phoning you. I've let you down so many times, I won't allow myself to do that to you again.

We could say I have been the poster child for all that was wrong with the 1970s and 1980s. Timothy Leary would have been proud of me. I listened to his message of "turn on, tune in, and drop out" and followed his instructions to the letter. Drugs and booze were my guiding lights. I took the low road and you took the high. Why I didn't go along your route with you has always plagued me. You gave me every opportunity.

I'm not going to search for excuses. We've been through that so many times. I know I have an illness. No matter how everyone else tries—and we know the best have given it all they had—I don't seem capable of being cured.

You are the love of my life, the light of my life. The definition of "sister" begins and ends with you. From the days when we were young, you hugged me and sang me out of my fear and confusion as vitriol and abuse swirled around us in our home, the very place where we should have felt safe and loved—and never did—and through the long and winding road of my addictions. You never let me down, always showed me love, never stopped trying to help, always gave me hope. Imagine where I would have been without you.

Always know how much I appreciate every single act of kindness, love, and support you have offered me. Always know I regret every hurt, always unintentional or beyond my control, I have inflicted upon you.

Don't let my light go out in your heart. Even if I am gone from this earth, somewhere in the universe, the light you have forever given me will be burning brightly.

Katherine buried her face in her hands.

"Oh, Molly."

"Shhh. It's all right," Molly reassured her with a hug as she cried too. "Until I found Shawn's letter in his room, I felt raw and vicious with grief. I was so fucking angry. Knowing how he felt, how he had tried his very best in his own troubled way, really helped me."

"Thank goodness Father DeCarlo was out there with you."

"The depths of support he offered me . . ." Molly bit her lip as she collected herself again. "Taking care of all sorts of details, the cremation, disposing of Shawn's few effects, and . . . just talking and listening . . ."

"Did he get the church work done he had to do out there?"

"Nope. We spent all day Saturday clearing up Shawn's affairs. On Sunday we rented a car and drove up the Sea to Sky Highway to Whistler. He said it was just the drive to take my mind off everything, and he was right."

"For sure! That drive is unbelievable, isn't it? The cliffs, the sea, the light all combine to create such a surreal effect. We had a few biking vacations out there that I will never forget purely for the striking beauty that surrounded us."

They talked about the panoramic views over Howe Sound that took a visitor's breath away, before the drive turned into the richly forested route beyond Squamish.

"We had a peaceful day. Very peaceful. We stopped at a lookout over Howe Sound, took a little walk, and sat on a bench absorbing that splendor. The light was so calming."

Katherine could hear the tone in Molly's voice soften as she recalled the day. "Then we paused later at a few of those amazing waterfalls. Each time I felt something release inside me."

Katherine nodded, remembering.

"At Whistler we took the gondola up to the Roundhouse and ate lunch out on the patio. My God, Katski, those views—mountaintops as far as the eye can see. You know, I have never experienced anything like that. We hiked one of the upper trails, and it was the best place for me to begin to come to terms with everything. I don't know when I've been in such an . . ." Molly paused, searching for the right word. "Such an . . . ethereal environment, almost sacred, you know? I talked. He listened. He talked. I cried until I just kind of came out the other side."

Molly was gaining composure as she spoke about the weekend and its outcome.

"He's still out there for a day or two. Stayed to do what he had to do. That's why I decided to take the red-eye flight home. I just wanted to leave as soon as we left the mountains."

Katherine put her arms around Molly again. They sat like that for a minute.

"There are no words that can express my sorrow . . . none."

"I know, Katski, I know. It's a heavy thing, this thing called grief."

"It will take time to learn how to manage it. That's the main lesson I have gained from this past year. One step at a time," Katherine told her.

Molly stood up and beckoned her to the kitchen. "Actually, I'm feeling kind of hungry. What did you put in the fridge when you got here?"

Kat had stopped and picked up leftover pasta in her fridge from the weekend. She warmed it up and they sat down to eat.

Molly wanted to talk about their trip to France, and a change of topic seemed like a good idea.

"Holy crap!" Molly said. "Less than two weeks before we go. The timing could not be better."

37

Molly slowly stretched and flashed an elated grin at Katherine while she put her seat in the upright position as instructed by the flight attendant.

They were about to land in Nice. After boarding in Toronto the previous afternoon, they had changed planes in Montreal for the trans-Atlantic flight.

There had been a fair amount of turbulence for the first few hours as they skimmed a violent storm over eastern Canada, but both women had managed a few hours' sleep before breakfast was served.

"I'm so goddamn pumped, Kat! The adrenaline is flowing!"

"When *aren't* you pumped? You're going to be buzzed the entire time you are here. I just know it! Although I guarantee the jet lag will hit us later today and we'll crash for a while. Even you."

Katherine had insisted Molly take the window seat for the thrill of seeing the dramatic landing at Nice Côte d'Azur Airport, at water's edge, as the plane came in low over the azure waves of the Mediterranean. The Principality of Monaco and all the towns lining the coast along the way were brilliantly lit by the rising sun as the plane descended. Someone in the cockpit was providing an enthusiastic running commentary of the route.

Katherine still had vivid memories of that landing over thirty years before: the sea a brilliant shade of turquoise as it met the shore along the coast, the colorful buildings of the historic towns nestled against a backdrop of rolling hills with majestic snow-capped Alps behind.

"Pinch me!" Molly whispered. "You weren't frickin' kidding. *Magnifique!*"

"And still virtually no high-rises—except Monte Carlo, of course. Nowhere to go there but up."

The descent into the airport was quick.

"I thought we were headed straight into the water for a minute," Molly commented as they waited for their bags. "You might have noticed me go very quiet and a tad white-knuckled."

Katherine laughed. "I had forgotten the runway is built right out into the sea. That was quite spectacular!"

In no time they were rolling their luggage into the arrivals area of the compact terminal. Searching the waiting crowd, they spotted a sign that read, "Madam Price." Holding it was a tall, sturdily built woman with a mane of wild gray hair. She was wearing a low-cut chartreuse blouse, skin-tight jeans and the highest pink stilettos Katherine had ever seen.

Molly muttered "Holy shit" under her breath while Katherine waved and walked toward the sign.

Introducing herself as Bernadette, the woman explained she operated a taxi service used by the Browns. They had informed Kat, when they confirmed plans, that someone would pick her up. They just hadn't shared the flashy details about her comportment.

The luggage was loaded into the trunk and passenger seat, and they were good to go at 7:00 a.m.

"But it's really only one a.m. for us. We're going to feel a little discombobulated for a while, right?" Molly remarked.

The ride took all of twenty minutes along the Bord de Mer with its stunning scenery, busier with serious cyclists than cars at this early hour. With the sun still rising, the pebble beaches that ran all along the road were filling with early bathers. Long, slim fishing poles, their lines cast and anchored in the stones, were left to do their work. Nearby empty folding beach chairs kept vigilance while their owners clustered around food trucks, drinking coffee, smoking, and chatting with gusto.

Bernadette's personality was as colorful as her appearance. She kept her passengers entertained with a bilingual running commentary on food, wine, and Frenchmen—"Zey are stupid, boring, ugly! *Je préfère les Suédois* . . . Swedish." She looked back at them with raised eyebrows to make certain they got her point.

Indicating the railroad tracks that paralleled their route, Katherine said, "That's why we won't need a car. The train is so easy."

The imposing stone, castle-like Fort Carré guarded their entrance into Antibes. "It's only five hundred years old, one of our modern buildings," advised Bernardette.

Stunning palm trees, a variety of flowering shrubs and bushes, and cacti intermingled to line the streets and border the parking lots next to the yacht-filled harbor. Planted beds of perennials in brilliant colors mixed with fountains welcomed them to the town.

Within minutes, the car passed through an arch in a long stone wall. "These are the remains of the stone walls that made Antibes a fortified village—also five hundred years old," Bernadette informed them.

Before them, buildings of similar vintage and narrow streets were coming alive.

Katherine's face lit up as memories spilled around her. She and Marc-André had taken the train here for a day. She thought so when she saw the photos the Browns sent, but now she was certain.

Molly's eyes shone with excitement as she took in the shops and cafés. Turning a corner—"Look! An English bookstore!"—she pointed out as the car pulled onto a narrow street with a low stone wall. The Med was on one side and buildings on the other.

"*Oui!* Ze only one and I can met you ze lovely owner," Bernadette offered as she squeezed the car around a tight corner. "I can't park, *mais regardez*, your *maison*. We 'ave to go around back to do parking."

The photos had not done the property justice. A blazing purple bougainvillea draped over a thick stone wall that spoke of ancient times. A heavy wooden door with a small grated window offered a glimpse into a tiny courtyard. The house, with its yellow-tinged stone and Provençal blue shutters, looked like a cover shot for a travel magazine. Molly and Katherine simply stared and exclaimed.

The car navigated a labyrinth of narrow alleys and pulled to a stop. Bernadette jumped out, and before Molly or Kat could exit the backseat, she had their luggage piled on a trolley and stood waiting. Once organized, she led the way up a sloping cobblestone lane lined with ancient townhouses, the trolley wheels clattering.

"Oh man, I'm glad the Browns warned me about wearing high heels for my arrival! These streets will take some getting used to!" Katherine remarked.

"Ha!" Bernadette laughed. "Not for French women. We wear stilettos everywhere—even to *la plage*."

Molly was pausing before every heavy wooden door, proclaiming their beauty and charm. "Imagine the stories these doors might tell!"

Stopping in front of a faded blue door with several large ornate keyholes, Bernadette handed Katherine an enormous brass key.

"Voilà, ma chère! Ouvrez la porte!"

They all burst out laughing. "Truly?" Katherine asked.

Bernadette explained that this was the key to a two-hundred-year-old lock that still worked perfectly. However, it wasn't necessarily one you could easily stick in your pocket. The Browns used it just for fun when newcomers arrived. There was another lock on the door that was more modern and could be used.

It took some effort to turn the key. The door opened slowly into a bright and welcoming space of typical Provençal colors. Katherine knew what to expect, from her visit to Provence, but Molly was bowled over.

"It's so beautiful! I love it!"

Those words were repeated as Bernadette quickly and efficiently gave them a tour of the four stories and the roof terrace. Then she bade them farewell, leaving her card and instructions to call if they wanted a ride anywhere or help with anything. Katherine's offer of payment was greeted with a haughty look and a wave of her hand.

Molly hollered down, "Get up here, Katski!"

Kat climbed the narrow stairs from the ground-floor kitchen and sitting area to the second-floor lounge and bathroom and up to the third-floor bedroom where Molly was standing on a small balcony.

"Will you look at this view! We have a beach right there—like two frickin' minutes across the road! Wow, you struck gold with this place, my friend!"

Katherine's grin grew wider as she joined Molly in a happy dance around the room.

"Let's go out to one of those little cafés we passed and have our first French coffee! Can you believe the market is just on the next street—and all those restaurants? I mean, I knew we were near everything. I was told, but I didn't picture it like this."

Molly grabbed Kat in a bear hug. "Thank you! Thank you! Thank you for giving me this gift! We are right in the middle of everything— including the Middle Ages from the look of the neighborhood—and I feel like I'm in a dream! Abso-fuckin-lutely awesome!"

They were soon out the door with the enormous key, Molly having remarked, "It's too cool not to use!" Following their winding lane, they turned left and right and found themselves out of the medieval maze on a more open tree-lined street with a few cars crawling along. Cafés lined the street, and the easily identifiable roof of the market could be seen half a block farther.

"How frickin' convenient is this?"

Molly ordered an espresso. Katherine demonstrated she had learned well from her visit to Provence, ordering *"Un café crème et deux crois-sants, s'il vous plaît."*

Raising her espresso in a toast, Molly said, "The adventure has begun! I'm so grateful."

As they clinked their cups, Katherine replied, "I believe we are both feeling an attitude of gratitude!"

A stream of locals and tourists paraded by, many with their wicker baskets, obviously headed for the market. The Browns' information had indicated the market was open every single day, so it was decided to go on Sunday after they had found some time to think about menus.

A plan was set for the day. Their primary goal was to stay awake until 9:00 p.m. and then crash.

Laughing, they admitted doubts about lasting that long.

⚜

Maison Beau Soleil, as the house was named, radiated charm and history. It had begun as a simple fisherman's cottage, and hooks still hanging in the kitchen on which to dry fish bore testament to that.

Uneven tiled floors, thick stone walls, and heavy louvered shutters kept the interior cool. Fans on each floor ensured good air circulation, and the breeze off the Med knocked the temperature down a few notches. Whitewashed walls inside provided the perfect backdrop for the eye-catching upholstery, cushions, and artwork in classic Provençal patterns and colors. The entire effect left no doubt about which part of the world they were visiting.

Lugging their suitcases up the steep, narrow stairs took some teamwork. Molly claimed the bedroom on the third floor, leaving the master suite on the top floor for Katherine. The rooms were small, but storage was cleverly built in at every opportunity, and—most important—the beds were comfortable.

The two bathrooms were completely updated, and the entire place was spotless.

Off the master bedroom, two steps led up to a large window through which they climbed to the rooftop terrace.

To one side they looked across terra-cotta tiled rooftops to the busy harbor and Fort Carré and beyond, to what they would discover was Nice across the Baie des Anges. Straight ahead was a crescent-shaped cove with a beach and the sparkling waters of the Med stretching away forever with luxurious yachts at anchor or cruising. To the right stretched more of the old town and a high peninsula lush with vegetation.

"That's Cap d'Antibes," Katherine said. "I read about it. We've got to walk up to the top to check out the view."

"This view right here is frickin' spectacular!" Molly exclaimed as Kat grinned.

There was a note on the window with a reminder to always put down the umbrella on the terrace and pile the cushions from the chairs in the bedroom, as strong winds could unexpectedly arise.

Unpacking did not take long, and they both felt energized after showers.

Locking the door with the ancient key again, they set out for a stroll of the town with a small map left for them on the kitchen counter, along with an instruction book about the property and some tourist information.

"There's one thing missing in the house. Have you noticed anything yet, Kat?"

"Um, not particularly."

"No television!"

"Oh, right. Actually the Browns asked if I cared about it and I said no. I thought it would be more interesting not to have one. Wi-Fi was important, though."

"Wow," said Molly. "I don't think I could do that. I mean, I don't have anything more than the basic cable my apartment offers, but how will you live without *Ellen*?"

"Well, I didn't watch television once when I was in Provence and I didn't miss it either. I listened to way more music and read like crazy. It was so good!"

"You know, that may not be such a bad idea. I might be able to do it, but only as long as I could catch the *Ellen* shows online!"

Katherine's mouth was locked in a happy smile as she listened to Molly ooh and ahh her way through the old town. Her friend's reactions were the same as those she had experienced in Provence.

"I predicted you would love it here! France just does that. It makes you fall in love . . . with everything."

"I honestly didn't believe you. I thought you were frickin' exaggerating—in a good way, of course. But you're right, I can't help myself—the buildings, the doors, the windows, the peeling paint, the streets, even that goddamn little train that we keep seeing!"

Katherine snorted. "*Le petit train!* Get used to it, because every town along the coast seems to have one. I remember that from my days in Villefranche. They've been around forever, a traditional French sightseeing custom."

They agreed they would not dawdle but rather get the lay of the land and then spend the next day poking around.

"Apparently there's a flea market tomorrow in another square that we can hit after the regular market," Kat said, catching sight of a poster in a shop window.

She had decided to leave her camera at the house so she wouldn't be tempted to stop every few steps, but there were still plenty of distractions.

It only took ten minutes to walk at a quick pace from one end of the old town to the other, but they could see that the many side streets and winding lanes would offer hours of wandering and stopping.

The transition from old town to new happened seamlessly, and they were suddenly in a more modern environment yet still mixed with ornate old buildings. Place du Général de Gaulle was the main square, filled with plane trees, benches, and fountains. Several cafés bordered the square, and a tourist office was visible at one end.

Using the map, they walked around a corner to the Orange office, where Katherine could buy a new service for the cell phone she had purchased in Provence. Molly was delighted when they discovered it was closed for lunch for two hours.

"How civilized is that?"

"We'll just come back another day. I won't need it right away."

Passing a number of *boulangeries* and cafés with mouthwatering baguette sandwiches stacked in carts or windows, they kept stopping to admire the displays. Molly sighed.

"They all look so delicious, and I don't even eat much bread anymore. I can see that's not going to be the case while I'm here."

"Not to eat bread in France is sacrilegious," Katherine told her, chuckling.

Molly chose a baguette with prosciutto and goat cheese, while Katherine could not resist one with curried chicken freshly prepared as they waited.

Following the same route back to the house, they noted little specialty shops, grocery and hardware stores tucked into the medieval structures along with restaurants, ice cream stands, and some clothing shops. Cafés, outdoor-terrace dining spots, and the ever-present pharmacies with their neon green crosses were in abundance.

"Al fresco dining seems to be the thing to do here," noted Molly. "Love it!"

"And why not, with this weather. Let's come back here for dinner."

"I totally agree! *Bonne idée!*"

⚜

Flowering vines covered the walls of an enclosed tiled courtyard off the compact kitchen. "The perfect spot for lunch, and look, this awning unfolds over it to provide some shade," Katherine said as she unwrapped their baguette sandwiches and Molly brought out a pitcher of iced tea.

The little patio was big enough for a table for six and a few extra chairs. It was outside the front door and surrounded by the stone walls with the stunning purple bougainvillea where Bernadette had stopped to first show them the house. Through the heavy wooden door in the wall was the street.

In spite of the voices of people strolling by and the noises from cars crawling at a snail's pace with tourists distracted by the views, they were both having trouble keeping their eyes open.

"A dip in the Med might be just what we need," Katherine said, stifling a yawn.

As soon as they finished eating, they changed into swimsuits and went out the front door to cross the road. A brief walk along the stone wall led to another archway, the entrance to the Plage de la Gravette.

It was a picture-perfect crescent-shaped protected cove under the watch of the historic old town, with the ramparts of the original village walls keeping it separate from the street. Showers were dotted along the shore, and a Le Snack truck was by the entrance. The beach itself was a mixture of sand and pebbles, and walking into the water was extremely tricky as the stones shifted with each step.

"Forget about looking anything but totally off balance getting in and out of the water," they agreed. Laughing at themselves didn't help. There seemed to be no graceful way to do it, until they spied some people wearing light plastic beach shoes.

"Gotta get us some of those," Molly said.

The water temperature felt cooler than they expected, but once in, it was refreshing.

"Ahhhh," sighed Molly, floating on her back. "*C'est la* frickin' *vie*."

Katherine snorted as she eased into a breaststroke and headed for deeper water.

After exiting the water as clumsily as they had entered, they showered off the salt and slathered on sunscreen. Then they set up the umbrella they had found in a cupboard with some beach chairs. With a blistering sun beating down, they were glad to have shade and sat in their beach chairs taking in all the action.

"I can't believe we're here, sitting on a beach on the French Riviera," Molly kept repeating. They spent the afternoon dipping in and out of the Med, the cool water helping in their campaign to remain awake.

Somehow they lasted through an early dinner of thin-crust pizza at the nearest restaurant they could find. Stumbling back to the house after a couple glasses of wine, they giggled as they admitted they couldn't keep their eyes open any longer.

"Remember, Moll, if you wake up before six a.m., force yourself to turn over and go back to sleep. The later we sleep in tomorrow morning, the better for our body clocks."

38

By 9:00 a.m. sleep was no longer an option for either of them.

"Grab the *panier*, Molly, and let's go to the market. We'll have a coffee and croissant there, okay?"

"Sounds like a plan—as soon as you tell me what the fuck a *panier* is!"

Katherine pointed to the straw shopping basket. "It just sounds so much better in French, doesn't it?"

The daily Provençal market was minutes away and already bustling.

"Let's make a list while we have our coffee, because I can see us totally losing control here," Molly suggested. "In my new world of extreme budgeting, I never shop without a list now, and it sure makes a diff for me. I used to just fill up my basket with whatever struck my fancy, then have a huge bill! No more, *mon amie*!"

Gleefully exploring the stalls, Molly gathered fruit, salad greens, and vegetables, while Katherine followed behind snapping one photo after another.

They returned to the house, stored away the food, and headed out again for the flea market, where they were fascinated by the stalls laden with booty from old homes and families: sterling silver, china and glassware, jewelry, art, linens, vintage clothing, and assorted bric-a-brac.

"Kat, wouldn't you love to be stocking a home here with these goodies?"

"How much fun would that be?" she agreed.

With tourist season in full swing, the town was busy with an atmosphere of relaxed energy. Sidewalk cafés overflowed with patrons enjoying a midday beer or lunch or lined up for ice cream.

Picking up a baguette on the way back home for lunch, they planned to spend the afternoon visiting galleries and exploring some more of the town. As they passed the tourist office, they picked up a brochure of events.

"Somehow I don't think we're going to have to worry about keeping ourselves occupied," Katherine commented, "but let's check out what's going on anyway."

⚜

Taking the coastal train on Monday, Katherine toured Molly around Villefranche-sur-Mer, once a tiny village of fishermen and artists and now, of course, a major tourist stop with a deep harbor for cruise ships to anchor.

With excitement, Kat pointed out where she had rented a room and the language school that was still in operation, although greatly expanded. She was surprised at how little had changed in the old area and how easily she found her favorite haunts.

Grabbing Molly by the hand, Kat pulled her toward the steep stairs leading to the ochre-colored baroque Église Saint-Michel. "There is an extraordinary carving you must see!"

They looked in awe at the life-size figure of a reclining Christ protected by a glass case. The description explained it was carved from a single piece of fig wood by an unknown galley slave approximately five hundred years before.

"That image has stayed with me all this time! Thirty years, and yet it seems like yesterday. Life does have a way of slipping by."

"No kidding," Molly agreed. "And when you have an experience like yours, I can believe you never forget it."

After wandering the thirteenth-century Rue Obscure and other colorful, winding streets, they sat at a lively bar by the water, watching the boaters and drinking Orangina. Katherine revealed the story about her passionate fling with Marc-André in Villefranche.

"Holy shit! You've kept that little secret all to yourself all these years. Let's see if he still lives here!"

Shaking her head, Katherine said, "Don't be crazy! He probably wouldn't even remember me."

"Katski, you didn't forget him, right? Those kind of intense affairs are never forgotten."

Molly confided details of some of her early relationships, most of which were brief and messy. "Nevertheless, there were moments. You're going to be here a long time. You never know what might happen, maybe another passionate French affair."

Katherine looked serious for a moment and explained how she had no interest in having any sort of relationship. "I'm still healing. James hurt me so deeply, I know I will never allow myself to be vulnerable to that again—never."

"Never say never, my friend. I mean, really, wouldn't you at least like to have sex again? Don't you miss it?"

"To be honest," Katherine said ruefully, squinting, "at the moment it's the last thing on my mind. I just want to feel content with myself."

Katherine thought about how her relationship with Molly, and Andrea too, had changed and grown over the brief period of time she had been on her own. A year ago she would never have imagined having this kind of conversation.

Molly, of course, got right to the point.

"You know, Katski, you might be doing yourself a big favor having an affair that's fun and satisfying. I don't mean just falling into bed with anyone, but I bet you're going to meet some cool guys here. Just take a look around. My eyes have been popping out of my head!"

As the conversation continued, Katherine surprised herself by revealing intimate details of her physical relationship with James. How their sex life had kind of slipped off the radar years before.

Feeling her face flush, she described how in the last few years the rare times they had sex was while James watched a porn video. "It wasn't about me or us, just about him. I really felt like a loser, you know—unattractive, undesirable, old. There was nothing romantically erotic about it. To be honest, it was degrading."

"Some guys need that for whatever reason. It probably had nothing to do with you."

Katherine's face looked pained. "Obviously he didn't have trouble having sex with a younger woman who attracted him."

Molly reached over and took her hand. "I know how deeply you were hurt. That entire situation was a horrible shock, but look at how your life has changed for the better in so many ways. You have a whole new opportunity for happiness."

"Maybe so," Katherine replied, looking off over the water, "but I'm not sure it will include another relationship. As for any interest in sex . . ." Her voice broke as her eyes welled with tears. "I really don't think I have any passion left. That part of me just feels dead . . . so I don't think about it."

Molly squeezed Katherine's hand tightly and said nothing at first, her own emotions taking over for a moment.

The two friends looked at each other, their silence speaking for them.

Attempting to lighten the mood, Katherine wrinkled her nose and said, "Besides, I'm getting old. I am heading for sixty, remember!"

Molly's humor kicked back in.

"Oh, boo-frickin'-hoo, girl! Give yourself a shake and get over that! We both know age is just a number. You're a good-looking woman. A lot of men will be attracted to you. Don't be afraid to test the waters, Kat. Don't be thinking you're unfuckable!"

Katherine burst out laughing. "Another Molly-ism! Come on, let's go and take the boat cruise to Monte Carlo that we saw advertised. It's a must to see the coast of the Riviera from the water!"

❧

The next day, they hopped on the train again, this time to Nice. Strolling down the main shopping street to the old town, thirty-year-old memories stirred in Katherine.

"Apart from this ultramodern tram system and some new buildings, things don't look all that different from what I remember," Katherine commented as another sleek tram glided quietly by.

Taking it all in, Molly nodded. "I see why you love it here. Even in a city like this, with its modern stores and offices, you only have to look between the new or down a side street to see the old, to find the charm."

"Exactly," Katherine agreed. "It reminds me of how I felt in Paris, where so much of what is happening today is housed in buildings hundreds of years old. I keep thinking what a testament it is to the builders and artisans of those days."

They cruised the length of the expansive daily market, amused by the calls of vendors who were obviously enjoying entertaining the shoppers. Bordered by sherbet-colored, historic buildings—including an eighteenth-century baroque chapel—the tent-covered stalls filled the length of Cours Saleya.

Stopping for a quick coffee at one of the many bistros and cafés extending down each side of the market, Katherine explained that by early afternoon all the stalls would be packed up and gone. "These restaurants spill their tables into the space, and the entire street becomes one enticing place after another to eat or drink."

There were few stalls, with their artistically arranged displays, that did not beckon them to stop.

"There are vegetables here I haven't seen before—and look, have you ever seen so many kinds of mushrooms and olives?"

Along with the standard produce stands, artists and craftspeople exhibited their work. Vendors of specialty food items tempted buyers with samples as they passed.

The fragrance from the large flower market hung in the air. "Let's come back here before we go back to Antibes. These hand-tied bouquets are irresistible," Katherine said.

"And incredibly reasonable."

"Oh look! Chez Theresa is still here! I ate here thirty years ago, and it had been there for over a hundred years then. Let's share a *socca* pancake—it's a tradition!"

"Crap, look at the lineup!"

"That's part of the tradition too. It will move quickly, though, if I remember correctly."

A labyrinth of winding streets and pastiche of colorful buildings of the old town led away from the market. Kat promised they would return another day to explore them. "We've got to dash or we'll miss the bus, and that's next on our agenda."

They hurried across the Promenade des Anglais to catch the city hop-on/hop-off bus tour.

The overview of Nice was thorough and filled with information. The Italian influence in architecture gave a clear reminder of how this area had been part of Italy until just a century and a half ago.

"Where did that come from?" Molly exclaimed in surprise as a colorful, onion-domed Russian cathedral suddenly came into view. She listened, wide-eyed, as the audio tour explained the long connection between the Riviera and Russian aristocracy.

At the Chagall Museum, they hopped off and spent an hour surrounded by his enormous dreamlike canvases. They found themselves completely absorbed by the beauty and meaning his distinctive figurative art expressed, and Molly was moved to tears at times.

Back where they began, they paused from time to time to look at the different beach spots as they walked along the bustling Promenade des Anglais, mixing with in-line skaters, joggers, and cyclists in their own designated lane. "After all we've read about the color of the Mediterranean here, it does not disappoint," Molly said as they admired the brilliant turquoise water sparkling in the sun.

They agreed they were "starving," as they checked out menus displayed at the beach entrances.

The Browns had recommended the Plage Beau Rivage, with its white-and-blue umbrellas, saying the restaurant there was excellent. Settled comfortably on their lounges after stumbling in and out of the water on the pebble beach, Molly reminded Kat, "Damn! We've got to buy those shoes!"

⚜

Wednesday was a day of rest, casually exploring more of the side streets of Antibes and walking over to the busy, much bigger beach at La Salis on the other side of town.

Sipping refreshing lemonade at one of the beach stands, they convinced each other to resist the tempting orders of *frites* so many others were devouring.

"I wonder why the beaches to the west of Antibes are such beautiful sand and to the east are pebble," Molly noted. "I'm going to google that."

The ongoing high temperatures guaranteed the beach was jam-packed, and it became apparent that the issue of personal space was not a high priority as people parked their towels and beach gear almost on top of each other.

"It's the way they do it here. Take it or leave it, eh?" Katherine said, laughing as several far-from-perfect bodies stretched topless nearby.

Molly rolled her eyes.

As they stopped to watch some of the afternoon *boules* games nearby on their walk home, they agreed that La Gravette was more their style, in spite of the pebbles.

⚜

On Thursday, the forty-minute train ride to Monaco was on the agenda.

"I'm telling you," Molly murmured during the trip, "it's so tempting to get off the train at any one of these beach towns we are passing through. They all look so charming and inviting."

The better part of the day was spent exploring through the old town of Monte Carlo, the harbor, and the stunning casino area. Taking the local bus up to the adjoining town of Roquebrune, they passed the late afternoon visiting the artisan shops before climbing up to the castle ruin to admire the eye-popping view over the hills and the coast.

"This is the thing," said Molly, leaning on a wall and posing for a photo. "Everywhere you look in this part of the world, you see beauty."

"And there are so many places to visit, so many little towns and villages. There's always an option, and that really appeals to me."

⚜

Friday morning bright and early found them on the train again, this time heading for Ventimiglia and the well-known Friday market.

"I'm excited to be getting a little taste of *bella Italia*!" Molly exclaimed as they got underway.

"It will take us over an hour because of all the stops. We could have driven there a lot faster," Katherine said.

"No way! I love this train! It's like going on a scenic trip every time, hugging the coast as it does. I can't imagine a commuter line as beautiful as this anywhere in the world. If there is, I want to see it!"

Watching Molly's reactions to being in France, Kat was thankful she had been able to make it happen and thought about the way her own life had changed in such a short time. Her travel to France was the prime example. First of all, going on her own and proving to herself she could do that happily. Then, being here with Molly and experiencing the fun of traveling with a girlfriend, rather than meekly following where James chose to go.

I honestly don't miss him . . . The thought passed through her quickly with a brief moment of satisfaction at her ongoing transformation.

Her mind wandered as the train rolled by lush palms and exotic flowering trees and shrubs, through seaside villages, and under rugged towering cliffs. Past luxurious villas in elegant gardens and simple cottages overgrown with brilliant blossom-covered shrubs. Past gleaming megayachts with pools and hot tubs on special decks and local fishermen's wooden boats with paint peeling and nets piled. The contrasts somehow blended to create this area of unparalleled beauty.

Her thoughts were interrupted as the conductor walked through the car announcing arrival in Ventimiglia.

Time for more new memories.

The market was a short walk straight down the street from the train station. On the way, they passed what had to be the most enormous fruit-and-vegetable market they had ever seen.

"I could stay all day just taking photos. Look at those eggplants—and those tomatoes!"

"I'm too busy at the chocolate displays," Molly called over.

The rest of the market bordered the local beach and wrapped around a beautiful garden-filled park. Stalls sold much the same merchandise as in the French markets, but there were also deals on all sorts of fragrances and Italian leather goods: purses, luggage, belts, gloves, and clothing.

Most stands were fronted by enthusiastically vocal vendors, creating a carnival atmosphere. Laughter filled the air.

"I actually think I can easily stick to my budget here," Molly commented as they determined it was time for some cautious retail therapy.

There were bargains to be had on locally made clothes, and some stalls had rock-bottom prices on leather goods. They each purchased small Prada purses that came with certificates of authenticity.

Bernadette had warned them about the issues around knockoff luxury goods coming into France. At border crossings you might very well have your purchases checked by police and be charged if you have phony goods.

"No joke. Luxury goods are an important part of ze French economy," she had explained.

Lunch was authentic and delicious, perfectly al dente, pasta in a lightly fragrant marinara sauce—after which they happily put their feet up for the train ride home.

"Loved my taste of Italy, Katski," Molly said with a happy grin.

The Italian theme continued in the evening in Antibes as they strolled to a restaurant in the tree-lined open square of Place Nationale for wood-fired thin-crust pizza.

As they sat enjoying their meal and the warm evening air, two men at the next table passed the occasional friendly comment to them. While Katherine was initially quite cool in her response, Molly quickly engaged in good-humored chatter.

Nick and Graham were easy company, with typical Australian humor and casual friendliness. Tall and tanned, Nick had an air of sophistication about him, while Graham, stockier and slightly rumpled, was warm and personable. Conversation and laughter soon flowed among the four of them.

Nick was a businessman who owned a boat anchored in the harbor, and his friend Graham had come over to spend some time with him but was returning to Sydney in a few days. Explaining they were seriously in vacation mode, they soon had the women laughing with tales of their exploits, most of which centered around food, drink, and some disastrous attempts to communicate in French.

"Even when we know the correct words to say, our Aussie accent messes things up!"

Another bottle of wine was ordered as Graham mentioned they were actually celebrating his sixtieth birthday that evening. "Join us in a toast, ladies," he invited. "A toast to remind us to live every day as though it might be our last."

"*Santé!*" they replied.

By the end of the evening, Molly had accepted an invitation to join them for lunch and an afternoon on the boat the next day. She simply ignored Katherine kicking her ankle under the table.

"Bring your bathing suits if you like, and we can go out on the open water. The sea is the perfect temperature these days with the blistering heat of the past few weeks."

"You know, we thought we were just going out for a simple pizza and a glass of wine this evening. Who knew?" Molly said as Katherine launched another attack on her shin.

The men laughed and joined her as she raised her wine glass in a toast. "Here's to tomorrow." Katherine feigned pleasure.

"We'll walk you back to your house," they offered as the evening was winding down. "It's on the way to our mooring, and it's a beautiful night for a stroll."

"It seems to me that every night here is beautiful for a stroll," commented Katherine, to unanimous agreement.

Once inside, Molly knew she would have some convincing to do.

"Kat, what are you so paranoid about? We aren't teenyboppers, and they are not lecherous guys looking for an easy lay or they wouldn't have been talking to us. Have you noticed the vast selection of hot young women around here?"

Katherine nodded as Molly continued.

"Let's trust our judgment too. Just relax and enjoy their company, because they seem like decent guys to me."

39

At noon on Saturday, Graham was waiting for the women in front of the fish market stands by the harbor.

"G'day ladies! Nick is busy preparing lunch, so I hope you're hungry. He tends to get carried away. We stopped by here this morning and picked up some sardines and the catch of the day."

The fishermen, their catch, and their customers were long gone. Fishing nets were neatly piled on the boats after hours had been spent in the morning untangling and cleaning.

Walking down one of the many docks in the Marina Port Vauban, they were astounded by the number of luxurious yachts moored in the large harbor.

"This is your . . . boat?" Molly called up incredulously as Nick stood at the bow of a beautiful black one-hundred-foot motor launch named *Searendipity* waving to them.

"Nah. I just rented it for the day to impress you," he shot back.

Graham assured them it did indeed belong to Nick.

"Holy shit . . ." Molly muttered. Katherine was speechless.

Nicholas Field was a successful IT businessman, based in London, England, when he needed to be. Most of the time he operated from his floating home in Antibes. He and Graham had been school chums in Sydney and best friends all their lives, even as their destinies carried them in completely different directions.

Graham operated his family's sheep farm in the outback of Australia and barely had enough money to pay his bills.

"Nick's an incredibly generous chap, and each year he insists I come to visit. He always offers to fly my wife and children over as well, but they were busy with school commitments this year. We're on a different schedule down under, as you know."

Both men were gracious hosts, relaxed and good fun to be with, and Nick's suggestion they go for a cruise was met with enthusiasm. Katherine was feeling comfortable now too. The sun was high and hot and there would be a beautiful breeze, he assured them.

Going up to the bridge, he called to someone who apparently was a captain, and after a low rumble of engines, they were under way. Standing at the stern, watching their exit from the harbor, both women marveled at the precision, quiet, and ease of movement of the enormous motor launch. Passing the medieval walls, Katherine commented she could almost feel the sense of history that permeates the port.

"Life in Antibes has always revolved around this port, from as far back as 500 BC, when the Phoenicians used it as part of their trade route," said Nick. "Did you know that the name Antibes is derived from Antipolis, which means 'the town on the other side'? This harbor mirrors the Nice port on the other side of Baie des Anges. That's my history tidbit for today."

Graham added, "And this fort we are passing right now, Fort Carré, is from the sixteenth century. You should take the guided tour while you are here, Katherine."

"I will. I love this—the history that surrounds us here," Katherine replied.

"There's an excellent English tour of the town from the tourist office, but they only have it once a week, so you should check that out too," Nick told her.

Graham had not been exaggerating about Nick's lunch.

After a glass of champagne, they sat in the luxurious off-white upholstered seating area one deck up, shaded by beige sun umbrellas. Later they moved to the dining terrace.

On a long earth-toned granite sideboard was a sumptuous buffet looking like something from a photo shoot, Katherine commented as she took out her camera. Most of the offerings had been prepared on the biggest barbecue grill the women had ever seen.

Grilled sardines, full of flavor and perfectly seasoned. Escargot in a simple mouthwatering garlic butter sauce that demanded the fresh baguette be dipped into it. The tantalizing tomato, onion, and olive oil salad Kat had first tasted in Provence. A huge bowl of grilled veggies—eggplant, zucchini, leek, carrot, parsnip, peppers. A whole grilled local whitefish stuffed with fennel, garlic, and lemon. A simple green salad. The inevitable cheese platter with some of the most flavorful tastes, accompanied by an array of fresh fruit, put the finishing touches on the meal.

"What an impressive meal, Nick," Katherine exclaimed.

"I spent years toiling in restaurants and actually achieved being a sous-chef while I was in uni and first working. In another life, I think I would be a chef," Nick told them. "I love to cook!"

"You have some cheese here that I've never even seen before, let alone tasted," said Molly as she helped herself to seconds. "I mean, every one I've tried has been fucking remarkable. Oops, pardon my French."

Nick looked at her with a raised eyebrow and laughed. "How is it I knew you were going to come out with something like that at some point?"

Graham chuckled as he explained they had discovered one particular cheese vendor in the market who was truly a connoisseur. "I mean, this guy talks to you about cheese like a sommelier does about wine."

Nick continued, "I've received quite an education from him through the past four years. I'll have to introduce you to him if you enjoy cheese, and you should while you are here, Katherine. It's like a religion in France, you know!"

Laughing, Katherine nodded, explaining how she had learned this lesson well during her two weeks in Provence.

This in turn led to her answering their questions about home exchange. Graham in particular was very interested and said his wife had spoken about it, but they had not looked into it.

"It's something that might work very well for us, even though we live on a farm."

Katherine assured him it was worth a try through stories about Andrea and her success in exchanging with her farm.

One thing led to another in the comfortable ambiance of their setting, and gradually each spoke about their careers and lifestyles. Nick told them he had been a workaholic most of his life and his marriage had dissolved as a result. He did not have any children and had been single for almost twenty years. "Married to my work, you could say," he admitted, a grim look crossing his face, "until four years ago, when I had a heart attack and a triple bypass. That was my wakeup call. I sold my business and just work as a consultant now—no pressure and a schedule I make as I wish."

"That's a frickin' big change!" said Molly.

"I'm discovering it takes work. Doesn't come easily to a type A like me—"

Graham interrupted, "Let me tell you, he's making a good effort. Every once in a while he's tempted to start up another business, but then he manages to talk himself out of it."

They cruised westward past Cap d'Antibes, Nick pointing out various estates and the beautiful beaches and restaurants of La Garoupe.

Beginning to veer away from land by Juan-les-Pins, Katherine asked about the difference between Antibes and Juan-les-Pins, since they were considered the same town.

"Juan is the glitzy beach resort sister of historic Antibes, and they are separated by the Cap d'Antibes."

Both men commented on the nightlife there and the Jazz à Juan festival in July.

"That's an exciting time to be here and it's right after the Nice jazz festival, so you really get a full month of the most fantastic music—artists from all over the world."

"Concerts on the streets. Musicians just wander around and start to play. It's *so* good! Even if you can't get tickets to concerts, which sell out early on, you still get to hear great music."

Molly was very familiar with the information. "It's on my wish list. I've listened to music by relatively unknown artists who have gotten their start at those venues."

Katherine apologized to Molly and then went on to tell the men what a talented singer she was. Molly modestly waved the compliment away with her hand.

"She's shy about it until you get her on stage, and then look out!" Kat assured them.

Next along the coast was Cannes and beyond that the red hills of the Massif de l'Esterel.

"It's amazing how quickly the landscape changes along here," Nick said. "That's part of the incredible appeal of the South of France—of all of France, really. It's a country that has so much to offer."

"Are you ladies on a schedule today? Any rush to get home?"

Molly looked at Katherine, who had an ambivalent expression on her face, not quite knowing what was being asked.

Nick took that as a positive response.

"Since we're talking about jazz, I have to tell you about the piano bar at the Hôtel Belles Rives. It was originally Villa Saint-Louis, the home of F. Scott and Zelda Fitzgerald during one of their stays in these parts."

"*Les années folles!*" said Katherine. "I've read everything about Scott and Zelda. He's one of my favorite authors, and they were mad about jazz!"

"That's right," Nick agreed. "They did have a wild time here, that whole gang—Hemingway, Fitzgerald, Picasso—the Lost Generation, as Stein called them. The bar has an amazing pianist, and it's always a good time. When we go back, you can go home and change and we'll pick you up to take you there for dinner. How does that sound?"

Nick was obviously an organizer. No stone left unturned.

"It sounds like fun. What do you say, Kat?" Molly answered, while Katherine suppressed her anxieties. Her memories from Provence and Matt were too fresh.

We really don't know these guys.

"Great! Let's do it! Right now, though, we will drop anchor and test the water. We've got Jet Skis and Windsurfers, if that interests you. Pick any suite down below and make it your change room. I'll let Tim know we want to stop. He's driving this ship."

❖

Back at the house later that afternoon, Kat expressed her concerns to Molly.

"I hate to be a party pooper, but do you think Nick is too pushy? He's been organizing us since we met last night!"

Molly smiled warmly at her friend. "Lighten up, Katski. I'm not getting any bad vibes. I think he's a very nice guy with pots of money and he likes to enjoy life. I mean, today was pretty frickin' fun, wasn't it? No one made any untoward moves. Graham is a sweetheart who loves his wife and is proud of it. I got that."

Bent over, rubbing her wet hair with a towel, Katherine mumbled from underneath, "I guess you're right. It's the paranoia in me coming out."

"Well, we both know I haven't always been the best judge of character in my life, but I have learned a lot about trust more recently."

"From the mysterious Antonio?"

"In a word . . . yes."

Katherine sighed. "Someday I hope there will be an unveiling of that relationship, and I will be first in line to meet this man. He seems to mean the world to you."

"On the first part of your comment—not bloody likely. On the second—he means everything." Changing the subject, Molly continued, "Singing at the Note all these years has definitely sharpened my perceptions and observations of people in general and men in particular. I feel I could write a goddamn thesis on that now."

"Well, I hope you're right about tonight. I don't want to have to deal with any awkward situations."

"Strength in numbers, my friend. We'll be fine, but hey, let's google Nick and see what we find."

⚜

Katherine's anxiety was fueled when Graham knocked on their door to walk to the parking area and she saw they had hired a taxi. Feeling overly suspicious, she immediately sensed they planned on some heavy drinking.

Molly gave her the evil eye and mouthed, "Lighten up."

"That way we can drink as much as we want and not worry about getting home," Nick explained with a wink, as if reading Kat's mind. Her stomach knotted recalling a somewhat similar wink from Matt.

The Hôtel Belles Rives oozed charm and history. The ambiance in the piano bar was exceptional with a wide terrace overlooking the sea toward the Îles de Lérins and Cannes, backed by the Esterel.

Molly wore a fairly low-cut green silk dress, her hair pulled back into a sophisticated chignon. "I hate to tell you how old this dress is, Kat, but I still love it."

"And it still looks beautiful on you," Katherine replied. She was wearing a more conservative pale-blue linen sheath, complimenting her slim stature.

Both men were turned out in crisp shirts, blazers, and beige linen slacks—Nick's sharply creased and Graham's appearing well lived in.

Molly's prediction turned out to be spot on. The men were nothing short of good company and, discovering a dance floor on the terrace, great dancers.

Nick refused to slow dance, explaining, "I've got two left feet when it comes to a slow song. Give me swing or a rockin' jive number and I'm your man."

Katherine had loved to jive since high school. She grudgingly had to admit that James had been an exceptional jive dancer and they had enjoyed that together.

Graham was a good all-around dancer. Snuggling close to both women during slow songs, he thoughtfully asked permission, saying, "Trust me, it's the wife I have on my mind, but it feels so stilted to dance slowly two feet apart. I even dance like this with me mum!"

"You have to love him," Molly said to Katherine as Nick laughed and Graham blushed.

The sultry evening air combined with the moon's reflection on the water, created a relaxed atmosphere. From time to time, someone would whisper a request to the pianist and pick up the microphone to serenade the patio guests.

Conversation flowed easily amongst the four of them and before long, Nick and Graham cajoled Molly into singing.

Once Molly held the microphone in her hand, any hesitation slipped away. Nick and Graham were astounded by her talent, as were the rest of the patrons. Katherine felt very proud of her.

The bar was only half full and the guests were enjoying the show, calling out requests as the night went on. From Billie Holliday, Carmen McRae, Ella Fitzgerald, Etta James, Peggy Lee, to Diana Krall.

Katherine's fears of an out-of-control booze-a-thon were completely unfounded.

"Thanks for an amazing day—and evening," both women said as the men bid them goodnight at the door.

The men agreed, complimenting Molly on her singing again.

"Why don't you come up to our roof terrace for a nightcap?" Molly suggested. This time, Katherine swallowed her knee-jerk anxiety. *Why not?* she thought.

Admiring their cozy quarters on the way through, it was a perfect night to be perched on the roof with the still air and a sliver of a moon creating just enough light.

It wasn't long before Katherine announced she was exhausted and had to go to bed. Nick made a lighthearted comment about tucking her in, which gave her a bit of a chill, but she chose to ignore it.

As the men were leaving, Nick issued an invitation back to the boat for the next afternoon with a group of friends he was entertaining. Katherine explained they had other plans.

They did agree to meet at the market on Monday morning so Nick could introduce Katherine to the cheese vendor.

"I am so looking forward to that!" she exclaimed.

After the guys left, Molly said, "See? Not all men are jerks. I had a good feeling about those two, and I was right. They are decent guys and there are lots more out there, Katski. Trust me."

"You can keep working on me, but to be honest, I still feel I would just like to be on my own."

"You have a lot of life ahead of you. Why wouldn't you want to share it with someone? It doesn't mean you have to get married again, y'know."

"Molly, look who is talking. You've told me since you were a teenager that you would never get married or even live with a guy—and you haven't."

"Kat, Kat, Kat, you know why, and have I been happy? Until Ton—I mean Antonio—no, a big fat, un-fucking-qualified *no*. If you'd had the childhood and the parents I did, then I might accept what you are saying. I have a good excuse for my choice, but you don't. Really, you don't."

"I have to tell you that my home exchange in June, and now being here and knowing I'm staying for three months, seems to be giving me strength. I like it. I feel independent and not vulnerable in any way. I like being on my own more than I ever imagined. Even dealing with Matt the Asshole ended up being an empowering experience for me. I handled it!"

"I am woman, hear me roar," Molly sang as they both flexed their biceps and burst out laughing. "That's the wine singing. I think I've had my quota for the year this week."

"We were getting way too serious," Katherine said.

40

Katherine was lying on the bed with Molly on Sunday morning, guide-books and maps strewn about. Molly's bed had the best view, and nei-ther of them felt like getting up just yet.

"Isn't this just one of the best things that girlfriends do?" Molly said to Katherine.

"So good. Why didn't I realize what I was missing? Who says you can't still have girlfriends when you are married?"

"Um, well, I guess your husband said so."

"Why was I so accommodating? What the hell was wrong with me?"

"Let it go, Kat. What's done is done and here you are—here we are—and we are having some quality girlfriend time. Woohoo!"

They both laughed and jiggled closer together.

"Which we haven't done since we were teenagers," Katherine said. "And now we're, ahem, aging girlfriends."

"I'll tell you one thing, girlfriend, this view is frickin' better than the one you had from your bedroom—just sayin'," Molly said, and they both laughed again.

They looked straight out between their feet, watching boats glid-ing by on the sun-kissed waves that sparkled like diamonds. The rich deep azure of the sea harmonized with the blue of the sky, which they agreed was a shade only an artist could describe. The ceiling fan slowly circulated the warm sea air wafting in through the open French doors.

"Ahhh, breathe in that air," Katherine sighed, inhaling deeply.

"Mmmm. I'm thirsty, though. I'm going to get some OJ. Want some?" Molly asked as she rolled out of bed.

"Great idea. I guess we should think about getting up soon."

"It's only eight," Molly said as she arrived back with the juice. "Let's go for that walk up to the lighthouse you mentioned. I'm realizing I only have two more days here, and I don't want to miss a minute."

"Good plan," Kat agreed as she sipped her juice. "That might take an hour or two, and we can talk about what you want to do this afternoon and tomorrow. I've dragged you all over the place this week and you may not want to do anything."

"Are you crazy? I can't get enough."

Not quite an hour later, they were briskly walking along the ramparts over to the big public beach of La Salis where they began the climb up the stairs of the *Chemin du Calvaire* on the east side of the Cap.

"Oh crap! I wish my legs were in better shape," Molly complained. "These steps are killing me!"

"I'm glad I got back into cycling before I came over," Katherine admitted.

"Speaking of cycling, I keep forgetting to ask why you didn't bring your bike with you."

"I decided I'm going to buy one over here. I talked to Ben at Chain Reaction and he gave me some brand names to look for that could still be serviced at home."

"Well, that's exciting!"

Katherine grinned. "It is! My bike is eight years old and the advances have been phenomenal since then, so why not? Besides, it's another vestige from my old life that I can shed."

Reaching the top of the climb, they were glad the church was open.

Notre Dame de la Garoupe had been the traditional fisherman's church for centuries and was filled with all manner of marine memorabilia. Touching handwritten notes to St. Pierre, their patron saint, were left on the walls of the church—many with photographs attached—and spoke of heartbreaking loss at sea as well as miracles.

Katherine noticed Molly wiping her eyes as she read one of the notes.

"Are you all right?" she asked, slipping her arm around Molly's shoulders.

Molly nodded and accepted Kat's offer of a tissue. "I know I said I didn't want to talk about Shawn while I was on this trip, but these messages of hope and despair are bringing memories flooding back. His story is all about just that."

Katherine steered her into a pew at the front of the church and listened as Molly recalled Shawn's struggles, her vain attempts to help, his honest desire to be clean, and broken promises when he weakened. The pain and heartbreak they shared for so many years. Her sorrow at losing him forever, but also her relief at knowing his torment had ended and he was at rest.

"We can't win every battle, Kat. It's not like I didn't know that, but somehow I believed we could win his—and we couldn't."

Katherine was staring ahead at the simple altar and hand-painted walls, which somehow offered calm healing. Listening was often more important than speaking, and at that moment the comfort was coming from their surroundings, not her words.

"I'm so glad we came here this morning," Molly continued. "There's something inexplicably authentic that is truly bringing me peace. Shawn wrote about how he loved the sea in Vancouver, and maybe there is something to that, which I'm feeling here. I'm going to write a note and leave it."

"If it feels right, do it," said Katherine. "That's the most important part of coping with grief. It's a lesson I've learned too."

"What doesn't kill us . . ." Molly said.

The rest was understood. Hugging for a moment, they stood to leave.

On a table by the entrance, a notebook and pen sat on a wooden ledge, where others had written notes or requests for prayers. Molly took a page from the back and began to write.

"Take your time. I'll be outside taking some shots."

Wandering the grounds later, they exclaimed at the brilliant colors and exotic planting combinations, bending over to breathe in heavenly scents.

"The growing conditions in this part of the world have to be among the best anywhere," Katherine said, describing to Molly the prolific displays she had seen in Provence as well.

Moving around for the perfect light, Katherine's shutter worked overtime. The view was a spectacular 360-degree panorama.

"This was worth the frickin' leg cramps I'm going to have tomorrow," Molly muttered as they began the descent in the midday heat. The path was shaded by tall pines giving off a clean, fresh scent that hung in the air.

⚜

"Let's stop here for a *croque-monsieur*," Molly suggested. "Ever since we had one the other day, I've been thinking about the next one!" The classic French take on a grilled cheese sandwich, with a slice of ham added, also appealed to Kat.

Lingering over lunch, they decided to pop back into the Picasso Museum just up the street from the house on the way home.

"We've been intending to go all week and I know if we don't do it now, I'll be on the plane on Tuesday regretting I missed it."

Housed in a five-hundred-year-old castle where Picasso had kept a studio for a time in 1946, the collection had grown to more than two hundred pieces. With an information-filled audio guide, they had no trouble spending well over an hour taking everything in.

Next on her request list was beach time at La Gravette.

"I'm going to miss this special place," Molly sighed, waving her hand around the intimate cove as they stumbled over the rocks and grumbled about still not buying the beach shoes.

Katherine nodded, agreeing the settings in Antibes were so much more beautiful than the already beautiful photos she had seen before they arrived. "It's just *so* different here! I'm going to wear out the words 'visual feast,' but it's all I think when I look around."

"Katski, I can see you wanting to stay here forever. I mean, why not?"

"Well, apart from having a house to look after and a job waiting for me, I do have to earn a living."

"You could rent the house. Maybe you could find a job here. I wonder how hard it is to do that. I mean, I guess you would need a special visa or something."

They continued to daydream about the possibilities until Katherine suggested she would probably be ready to go back to Toronto after three months.

Molly yawned, "You never know . . ." and drifted off into a sun-induced afternoon snooze.

41

The alarm clock had been set by mutual agreement for Molly's last walk around town before they met Graham and Nick at the market.

The men were waiting at the appointed spot by the market, drinking coffee and looking undeterred that the women were a little behind schedule.

"Sorry, guys, we got caught up in a few stores. I'm into that last-chance souvenir-shopping panic!"

"No worries! Will you join us for a coffee, or should we dive into the *marché*?"

"We're coffee-ed out at the moment. Let's go buy cheese!"

The Monday-morning crowd had begun to thin, and it was easier to walk up the aisles without the early-morning crush.

Nick pointed out the particular stall with a large yellow banner proclaiming *Artisan Fromager.*

"Oh, we bought some cheese there this week," said Katherine.

"Yes, but I happen to know that the guy we're introducing you to was not there this week. He was away. He's the one you need to meet."

Graham was pointing out some of their other favorite stalls when Nick said, "Katherine, I would like to introduce you to the finest cheese expert I have ever known—and thankfully he speaks English!"

Katherine turned around and was stunned.

The man waiting to greet her was none other than Philippe, the nephew of François. Equally stunned, he cocked his head to one side and looked carefully at Katherine, blinking. Nick looked at both of them, wondering what on earth was wrong.

"Katherine?" The answer was like a reflex action. "*Katherine! Quelle surprise!* What are you doing in Antibes?"

"Philippe, I might ask you the same," Katherine said, gasping to catch her breath.

Wiping his hands on his apron, he quickly came around the stand to *bise* her and take her hands.

"*Non*, I live here. This is my shop," he said, waving his arms to take in the entire market. "But you . . . you live in Canada."

"It's a long story, but . . ." she stumbled over her words, flustered. "I had no idea you lived here. You only mentioned you lived on the coast . . . near Nice . . ."

They stopped speaking for a moment, looking intently at each other.

"Well, Antibes is where I live," he said, a broad smile spreading across his face.

"I am staying in Antibes for three months, and I'm very happy to see you."

"*Oui, moi aussi.*"

Nick watched this exchange, his head turning from one to the other as if attending a tennis match.

"You know each other, obviously . . ."

"Oh, Nick, sorry. Yes . . . this is so unreal . . . Philippe and I met in Provence in June, when I was there for two weeks. We spent some time together . . . it's another long story."

The lineup was quickly growing behind Katherine and Nick, with customers beginning to shuffle and mutter with impatience. Philippe hurried back around to the other side to conduct sales.

"Let's meet for coffee or a drink," Philippe suggested. "I am busy this afternoon, but later today? Say, five p.m.? The perfect time for a *pastis*. Nick, come too, of course. All of us!"

Katherine hesitated. "I don't know if we will be back by then. We're going to Eze and hiking down the Nietzsche trail this afternoon. I'm not certain how long it will take."

Philippe handed her his card. "Here's my cell. If you aren't there at five, just call me when you do get back. I will keep this evening free. Really, it is incredible to see you here!"

The muttering of irritated voices was becoming noticeable in spite of a coworker's efforts to pick up the slack. Katherine turned and offered a *désolée* to the people in line. Waving to Philippe, the four hurried off.

Stepping out of the market into the less-crowded square, Molly took Katherine by the arm. "That was *the* Philippe?" she asked, wide-eyed. "The gorgeous dude in your photos?"

Katherine nodded, still in shock. Then she briefly told Nick and Graham the story of François and Philippe.

"It's the 'small world' syndrome at play again," Graham commented. "It's amazing how often that happens!"

"How are you planning to get to Eze?" Nick asked, changing the topic rather abruptly.

"We were reading about it in a guidebook yesterday and can take a train to Villefranche and then the 81 bus up to Eze Village," Katherine said.

Nick chuckled and shook his head. "That bus goes once an hour, and if you miss it, you are out of luck."

"Especially if there's a cruise ship in Villefranche harbor. If the bus is packed, the driver won't even stop for you," interrupted Graham, making a face.

"Do you really want to do that trail?" Nick asked.

Molly nodded enthusiastically. "We have a special connection to Nietzsche going back to when we were kids. We *must* do it! Right, Kat?"

Kat grinned and nodded. "And Molly is leaving tomorrow, so we have no choice but this afternoon."

"Connection to Nietzsche as kids? That's pretty damn heavy stuff!" Graham said.

Molly laughed. "What doesn't kill us makes us stronger. Katherine's amazing mother gently drilled that into us. It was a message I sure as hell needed in those days."

"When we read about the Nietzsche trail, we knew we had to hike it. We're taking the easy way, though—down, not up."

Nick thought for a moment and then offered to drive them up to Eze. "It's not a long drive from here and will take a lot less time than the train and bus. We'll drop you off."

He and Graham exchanged a few words while Molly and Kat agreed with each other that would work nicely.

"Nick, that's really kind of you. We don't want to put you out."

"Nah," Graham answered. "In fact, you've just given us a good excuse to roll on into Monte Carlo and play a few hands of poker at the casino. That's our plan."

Nick continued, "Then we can pick you up in Eze-sur-Mer, which is where you will end up. Right by the train station."

He gave her the name of a beach bar just down from the station, saying they would wait there and have cold beers on order for their arrival. "You're going to be ready for a cold brew after that. It's going to be stinkin' hot coming down that cliff. Make sure you take your cell phone, and lots of water. Go get ready and meet us at the boat."

⚜

The narrow, winding drive up to Eze had some white-knuckle moments of its own.

An eleventh-century village perched atop a rocky cliff, it was now an artisans' colony and tourist attraction with boutiques and galleries lining its narrow, cobbled streets. How anything was ever built there was remarkable.

Dropping them at the parking lot just below the entrance, Nick gave strict instructions to walk through the little village to the Exotic Garden and climb up to the castle ruin before they began their hike.

"It's one of the most magnificent settings on the Riviera. Katherine, I guarantee you will go there again, but Molly must not miss it!"

He was so right. The sensational view stretched forever along the coast, offering a faint outline of Antibes's ramparts in the distance. The garden, filled with exotic succulents and cacti, bore witness to the dedication of those who had moved every stone and plant up the steep hilltop by hand. In spite of the many photos she took, Katherine promised herself a return for more.

The hike down, on a well-marked trail free of litter, took just over an hour and a half. Typical of the French commitment to their hiking *sentiers*, there were concrete stairs on some steeper sections.

They walked briefly in the shadow of cliffs and through forested parts, stepping aside from time to time to allow hikers to pass them on their way up the trail.

"I'm darn glad we are not them," Katherine commented.

"Down was definitely the right decision," said Molly.

The two friends talked incessantly, pausing only when the path demanded they save their breath for a more strenuous section.

Molly had some thoughts she wanted to share before she left.

"As much as I've teased you about having a fling and getting a man in your life, I also want to tell you this. In spite of what the song says, one is not necessarily the loneliest number. Seriously, Katski, I'm proof that living alone can be a very good thing. Don't feel you can't be happy staying on your own."

"I'm always glad to hear you say that. You know I'm feeling more and more comfortable with that."

"Having some good loving on the side doesn't hurt, though—just sayin'."

"You are determined to make me agree that sounds like a good combination, aren't you? I'm just not convinced at this point that I need or want that side dish. One day at a time—that's my mantra now."

Dripping with sweat in the heat of the afternoon, they paused for long draws from their water bottles and to spritz themselves with canned water sprayers.

"Here's to Elisabeth," toasted Molly at one of their stops. "She gave us more than she will ever know."

"To *Anyu*, forever in our hearts," Kat responded.

In unison, they laughed as they repeated, "What doesn't kill us makes us stronger."

In some places, the worn dirt path opened up to expansive views.

Turquoise water lined the coast, changing to shades of green and deeper blue before becoming lost in the rich azure of the deep sea. The *basse corniche*, paralleled by the rail lines, snaked its way along the water's edge.

Lush vegetation grew around the earth-toned cottages and luxurious mansions that covered the hillsides right up to the cliff tops. They stopped several times to picture how it must have looked when only simple fishermen and farm cottages dotted the landscape.

Imagining Friedrich Nietzsche pondering his philosophical puzzles as he labored up and down this ancient goat trail, they wondered, "Do you suppose these stunning views relieved some of his torment? Or made it worse?"

The remainder of Molly's last day and evening flashed by in a blur.

The cold beer at the bottom of the trail was a welcome prize. The drive back to Antibes was slow, the road jammed with traffic.

Katherine called Philippe to say they would not make the 5:00 p.m. rendezvous, and they agreed to meet at eight for dinner at Le Brulot.

"I'll book a table for five of us and it will be Molly's farewell dinner," Nick suggested.

And so it was.

⚜

Bernadette, in her flamboyant attire even at this hour, collected Molly and Katherine at 6:00 a.m. for the 8:30 a.m. flight to Montreal. Katherine had insisted she was going right to the gate to see her friend off. "I wouldn't have it any other way, Moll. No arguments!"

With the check-in completed, they went to the espresso bar.

"My last caffeine blast in France," Molly sighed, smiling at Katherine. "How am I ever going to thank you for everything? This visit has been like a fantasy."

She dropped her eyes for a moment before looking back at Katherine. "There could not have been a better way for me to begin to heal over losing Shawn. Thinking about him while surrounded by the sea and all of this beauty was so meaningful. It helped me to focus on the important and sweet things about him."

"I'm so glad to hear that. I've thought about him a lot too," Katherine said, taking Molly's hand.

"Thanks for always being my friend, Katski. This year we've sure as hell made up for a lot of lost time."

"It's like a gift for me. Having you come with me was one of the best ideas I've ever had," Kat admitted. "These were without a doubt the most fun-filled ten days of my life! None of this would have happened if you had not been with me. I wouldn't have met Graham and Nick—that's for sure!"

"Sometimes good stuff happens for a reason. Then sometimes shit happens for no good reason at all, as we know! Whatever, now you know people here and you are all set to carry on with your adventure.

I can't wait to Skype and hear what is going on, especially with those two hunks in your life."

Katherine laughed again. "Don't get your hopes up, Molly."

"One is *not* the loneliest number you will ever know," Molly sang.

Katherine chuckled.

Molly continued with a gleam in her eye, "But, if I were you, I'd be getting to know Monsieur Philippe better, *ooh la* fuckin' *la*, he seems like a sweetheart. The strong, silent type. And those eyes. He had me at *enchanté*."

"Oh, Molly, who makes me laugh more than you?"

Tearful good-byes were said, and after waving until Molly disappeared from sight, Katherine took the shuttle from the airport to the train station to go home alone.

42

Strolling back to the old town from the station, Katherine decided to swing by the market and invite Philippe over after he closed up shop. He had been quiet at dinner the previous evening. With Nick and Graham in top gear, it was hard to get a word in edgewise.

He smiled shyly as she waved, walking up the aisle to his stand.

"I'm on my way home from the airport. Would you like to come by for lunch when you are finished today?"

"I would like that. I should be there by two p.m., and I know Maison Beau Soleil. The Browns are good customers."

Turning the key in the lock, Katherine entered slowly. The house felt quiet and empty after the nonstop energy of the previous ten days.

As she climbed the stairs to her room, she paused in what had been Molly's bedroom and smiled.

Taking the last few stairs two at a time, Katherine was surprised to discover a gift bag sitting on her bed.

That Molly. She snuck up here just before we left!

Sitting on the bed, Katherine pulled the tissue paper from the bag to find another wrapped item and three books tied together with a ribbon. Taking the books out of the bag, Katherine laughed out loud.

Fifty Shades of Grey. She and Molly had seen these books at the airport bookstore when they were leaving Toronto. They had a hilarious conversation about them, and Molly told her they were selling like hot-cakes everywhere. Apparently, while they weren't literary masterpieces, they were very juicy female erotica. When the heck had she purchased them? Molly had suggested she should read them, and Kat told her she was not the least bit interested. Typically, Molly ignored her opinion.

Unwrapping the other gift, Kat dropped it back into the bag and fell backward on her bed, shaking with laughter.

Oh, Molly! Only you. A vibrator? Those books?

She opened the note card.

Ma Chère Katski—Merci! Merci! Merci!

I will never be able to thank you enough for this amazing time together. I could not have imagined the fun we have had. Thank you for showing me why you love this beautiful part of the world. I get it.

Remember my suggestion that you have a fling or two while you are here! This gift is to remind you of that and perhaps help you to change your mind and heat up the libido. What else are girlfriends for?

Thank you for being my bestest friend ever.

Love,

M xoxo

Lying on the bed for several minutes, Molly's note in her hand, Katherine sensed that her crazy friend might have a point. Maybe a fling was just what she needed. She just as quickly dismissed the thought.

I'm a long way away from believing that.

Taking a pitcher of water from the sink in her room and picking up her Kindle, she settled on the roof terrace and watched the surf breaking against the rocky outcropping past the beach. The rhythm of the waves was hypnotizing, and she could feel the comfort it offered on this calm day. Contemplating the reality of how she might spend her days during the next three months, Katherine knew she wanted a plan with some structure.

She also became suddenly aware that she had just invited a man to lunch with her alone, something she had not done for thirty years.

Focus on the waves, the comfort, the calm . . .

❧

When he arrived at her door, Philippe had a paper-wrapped wedge of cheese in one hand and a chilled bottle in the other. "Brie de Meaux is an ancient cheese dating back to the sixth century and apparently Louis XVI's last wish was for a taste of this. I thought I would introduce you to one of France's oldest and most popular cheeses—and here's a bottle of champagne, which is the perfect accompaniment. We need to celebrate our reunion!"

Katherine blanched at the thought of champagne, hoping it wasn't noticeable. *I thought I was over that,* she told herself, as a lingering unpleasant memory resurrected itself.

She handed Philippe a corkscrew.

Looking at her with a quizzical expression when she hesitated as he handed her a glass of the bubbly, he asked if everything was all right.

"Someday I may explain," Katherine said.

Just as he had been in Provence, Philippe was good company— quiet but interesting—and Katherine was happy to have him all to herself. She felt nervous, but not overly.

All was well in Sainte-Mathilde, he told her. Joy was busy as usual and thrilled to hear Katherine was in Antibes when Philippe called to tell her. François had rented his flat in Paris and moved to his simple home just outside the village.

"Pico is thriving but misses you," Philippe said with a twinkle in his eye.

"I miss him terribly too. I still cannot get over how attached I became to him in such a short time."

"Dogs can do that to you. They steal your heart before you know it."

"I'm planning to go up to see everyone once I have my life organized here."

"Joy is hoping you will do that. She was sad you did not tell her you were coming back to France."

Katherine explained she had planned to contact her once she was settled and that since Molly flew over with her, she had not been in touch with anyone.

"My goal is to take care of all that this week, now that I have some time on my hands. My first task is to buy a bike."

"Well, you are talking to the right person for that," he told her with a wide grin. "There are several excellent bike shops all along the coast, and I will be happy to introduce you to them and tell you which one is my favorite."

"That would be wonderful—thanks!"

"They will treat you well, and their prices are fair. You can join my cycling club, if you wish."

Katherine was pleased at the thought. *Check that off my to-do list.*

She put her hand over her glass as Philippe moved to refill it. "No more for me, thanks. You were right, though, it does go well with this Brie. Nick told me you have provided him with the best education about cheese," she said. "Do you think I could sign up for some lessons too?"

Philippe chuckled and assured her it would be his pleasure. "It may sound odd to some, but I have to tell you, I have a passion for cheese— for the tastes, the history, the process, the pleasure it offers. Like a fine wine, cheese can be very seductive."

Katherine heard something in his voice, saw it in his eyes, and thought, *There we are again, pleasure and seduction.*

⚜

Katherine shopped at the market almost daily. Two mornings a week, a half hour before it officially opened, she sat with Philippe behind his counter as he offered tastes, explanations, history, one type of cheese at a time. Some mornings Nick joined them.

❦

On Wednesdays, she took the train into Nice and wandered through the Cours Saleya market before meeting up with a group of women from the International Women's Club.

Mirella had sent her an e-mail introducing her to a friend who was a member, and Kat was immediately welcomed into the organization that consisted of many expats as well as locals. She signed up for the Wednesday hiking group, women who also practiced their French at the same time. Through them she discovered a number of women in the Antibes area who had started a beginner's bridge group in Juan-les-Pins. A local bus took her right to the street. That took care of Monday evenings.

Tuesday evenings and Sundays, the cycling group had organized rides.

It seemed she quickly had a plan with structure, and as August was ending she realized that she had not missed her job for a moment. She thought often about her colleagues. Susan Henderson, Lucy, and Laura all sent e-mails keeping her updated.

The office had closed with less emotion than everyone had anticipated. Dr. H. was enjoying retirement and busier than ever. Lucy and Laura were happy with their new positions.

Life goes on, and mine is unfolding in a different way every day.

43

Nick had become attentive and a regular presence in her life after Graham and Molly left. He had a lot of friends in town, most of them younger, and could frequently be found at the Blue Lady Pub, which drew the sailing crowd and many English-speaking regulars. It was a happening place, with lively conversation and mingling, not the sort of place in which Katherine was accustomed to spending much time. She was surprised to discover how much fun she had. She was even more surprised to discover that she could be fun in that setting.

Kat straightened up the kitchen one night as she waited for Nick to pick her up for dinner. She gasped when she opened the door to see him holding an enormous bouquet of pink roses.

Her immediate reaction was to shut the door in a panic. She stood there mute as she pulled herself together. Nick must have assumed she was speechless with pleasure.

"Hey! Beautiful roses for a beautiful woman."

Accepting them in spite of the sick feeling in her stomach, she invited him in and poured them each a glass of wine.

Taking the flowers to the sink, she filled a vase. As she trimmed each one and placed it in the water, she spoke with her back to Nick.

"These are gorgeous flowers. Thank you. But I feel I need to make something clear between us. Forgive me if I am reading something into this that isn't there."

She felt his hand on her shoulder as he came to her side and turned her to face him.

"You are reading something into this, and it is there," he said, his eyes searching hers.

Katherine swallowed hard. "You are a fine man, and I enjoy your company very much . . ."

"Ah, here comes the 'but.'"

"Yes, but the 'but' is my issue, not yours. We haven't talked about my situation, and it's complicated—for me, anyway. All you know is that I'm fairly recently divorced."

He nodded, took her hand, and led her over to the couch. "Let's sit down and talk about this then."

"I'm not going into all the sordid details, but my husband left me suddenly, without any warning. Not quite a year ago. I can't tell you how painful it was for me. Debilitating at first."

Nick put his hand to her cheek sympathetically. Katherine gently moved it.

"I'm still damaged, and I'm trying to put everything in perspective. I'm not ready for any romantic involvement."

Nick put his fingers to her lips. "Shhh. It's okay. Say no more."

Katherine continued. "While Molly and Graham were here, we all had great fun together. You're a kind, thoughtful, and very handsome man—"

Nick made a face and waved away her words, but she persisted. "Don't argue. You are! I know there are many women who would be thrilled to have a relationship with you, but I can't. I'm just not ready. And I don't want you to waste your time."

She blew out a big sigh, blinked hard, and looked directly at Nick.

Taking her hand again, he said, "We're not kids. I understand, sort of. My divorce was very different. It was long and slow and a big relief to both of us when we finally agreed there was nothing left between us. I buried myself in my work and had fling after fling. It was quite a bloody good time!"

The look of pleasure on his face and his booming laughter made Katherine smile in spite of herself.

"I like you a lot, Katherine Price. I think we are a good fit in many ways, but I also understand what you're saying. We still have a lot to learn about each other."

Katherine nodded.

"I would love to continue seeing you. No pressure. Let's keep doing what we've been doing, and I will attempt to keep my hands off you." He laughed again and pulled her into his arms in a friendly way, giving her a quick squeeze before he let her go. "No worries, mate! I'm good with it, for now anyway, and we shall see what we shall see. How's that?"

"That's great, Nick. Thanks for understanding."

"All right, let's go get some grub. I checked the catch of the day at Le Don Juan and it sounds de-e-e-vine! I'm starving because the cleaning crew was on the boat today and I can never stay out of it. I've been polishing and shining all bloody day."

Katherine was glad she had cleared things up. They continued to have the odd night out and some beautiful days on the boat, always with a group of his friends. She wondered if he was avoiding being alone with her, and she was cool with that. Relieved, actually.

44

Apart from their cheese rendezvous—the thought of which always made her smile, but which were, in fact, fascinating and delicious—Katherine and Philippe met occasionally for a meal or a drink. Often the talk turned to cheese making again as Katherine discovered the whole subject was surprisingly interesting. It reflected the French history dating back to Roman times as much as nature.

To her astonishment, under Philippe's careful tutelage, she discovered she loved the *bleus*. Her favorite was Bleu d'Auvergne, crumbled into piping hot fresh pasta, as he had recommended.

It wasn't just the tastes but also the history of the cheeses and the often intricate methods of the craft whether from the milk of sheep, goats, or cows. She began to be aware of flavors such as those resulting from the diet of Alpine grass and spring flowers the special Tarines cows graze on to produce the Beaufort cheeses, or the sprig of savory that adds the scent of Provence to Tome de Banon.

There was so much to absorb, so much history that also included intrigue and secrets and family feuds. For centuries in ancient times some of the oldest cheese-making methods were kept alive in remote mountain monasteries. *Who knew?* Political involvement was an ongoing issue; so-called health regulations interfered with successful methods used for hundreds of years. Philippe became passionate about the discussion at times, his eyes fiery and his voice full of emotion.

Katherine was surprised and pleased to see this other side of his normally calm personality.

He sometimes dropped by in the afternoon after the market closed, bringing her a portion of a new or special cheese. It occurred to her that this was his equivalent of flowers. She liked that.

They also saw each other twice a week at the cycling club and began to ride nearer to each other as Kat's endurance grew. Her new bike was a dream to ride, and her excitement and pleasure was immense at the diverse routes they traveled, always with spectacular views. For the most part the rides were far more challenging than any she had experienced, and she pushed herself to the limit on every ride.

Her muscles ached, but in a good way. The endorphins were working overtime, bringing her to a calm, happy place.

Socializing after a ride was a big part of this club's regime, and it wasn't long before Katherine began to feel accepted. She knew her connection to Philippe helped that along.

Most conversations were in French, although several members spoke English and were happy to assist with translations. She could see how those who spoke English loved to show it off. Whether they realized it or not, they made her feel she was welcome and not *l'étranger*.

The last week in August, Philippe mentioned he was going to Sainte-Mathilde.

"I'm just making a quick trip up for the day on Friday. Would you like to go with me?"

"I would love to," Kat answered with no hesitation.

Joy e-mailed her an invitation to spend the day together. She said the request was also from Picasso, which Kat loved, and the plan was set. Katherine had been feeling guilty about not going back there, so this suited her perfectly.

Walking back from a quick dip at the beach the day before, she thought how lucky she was to be living this dream.

I know this can't last forever. In another two months I will be back in Toronto and going to work in an office somewhere, and the dream will be just that, a wonderful memory.

She also reminded herself to sign up for the cooking class she had seen advertised in town.

While I'm at it, I might as well make the dream the best it can possibly be.

⚜

At 7:00 a.m. on Friday, she walked through the relative quiet in the still-empty market hall as vendors were organizing their displays. The camaraderie of the less-established vendors was evident as they picked numbers to determine their stall placements. She had witnessed this on one of her early meetings with Philippe, and the laughter and joking between those involved was a refreshing start to the day.

In fact, she had felt this on all her early morning walks through the old town as it was just becoming alive. There was always laughter, whistling, singing, and banter. In her month of almost daily walks, she had not heard one cross exchange. She often wondered if she was applying selective hearing to the lanes and alleys that provided such pleasurable sounds, but she felt this was her true experience.

Perhaps it is the weather, so perfect now. Maybe in the winter with a bitter mistral blowing, the cheerfulness diminishes.

Philippe had arrived much earlier to set up his stalls, which were stored in a building across the street each day after the market closed. Gilles had been working with Philippe for several years and would be in charge today. Philippe had no concerns about that, although he knew some customers might be disappointed.

Setting off on the *autoroute* in his aging Citroën, they soon passed through the rugged red hills of the Esterel and turned north. Sitting in the car together for two hours felt so much more intimate than having a meal or cycling, and Katherine felt a slight shyness at first.

Philippe's calm, gentle voice and easy manner soon erased Kat's reticence. Before long they were speaking easily and ventured into more personal territory than ever before. He quietly described his wife's long battle with cancer and his commitment, after losing her, to being both father and mother to their daughter. She disclosed the sudden jolt in her life. To her surprise, she found herself relating the essence of the note James had left and her shock at the sudden end to what she had thought was a good marriage. They both conveyed the loss, the despair, the aloneness, and the pain they experienced, the struggle to regain their footing.

Katherine found the timbre of Philippe's voice soothing and his ability to express his feelings quite extraordinary. "Grief," he said, his voice gently halting but not hiding the depth of the emotion he shared, "can enter your life through many doorways, but there really is only one exit, and only you can find it. Most of the smothering, consuming pain eventually begins to fade, but part of it remains forever."

Katherine reached over and put her hand on Philippe's arm. "I am so sorry for your loss and your daughter's. I truly am."

He nodded slightly, placing a hand on hers for a moment. "And I too, for yours."

It was easier, when Kat thought about it later, for them to have the conversation when they weren't sitting across from each other, when eye contact didn't become so intense that the thread of the subject had to be snipped.

Their eyes met from time to time, but the demands of the road broke the connection. She thought that was a good thing.

They rode in silence for a while after the heaviness of their chat.

"Let's listen to some music," Philippe suggested. "Do you like this?" he said as some soft jazz began to play.

Their topics switched to music and cycling, familiar to both and easier to share.

⚜

The countryside began to bring back memories. Vineyards, orchards, olive groves, and fields stretched toward the backdrop of rolling hills. Hilltop villages perched on rugged peaks appeared and disappeared as the road twisted and turned.

"It's so dramatically different from the coast," she commented.

Suddenly they were turning into the lane of the manor house, and Katherine's heart jumped as she caught sight of Picasso's golden coat and wagging tail. "It feels like coming home."

She could barely contain her excitement and opened the car door the moment it rolled to a stop.

"Pico, Pico!" Katherine whispered as she knelt to pet him and receive his happy nuzzles. She was surprised as tears sprung to her eyes. The dog moved excitedly from Katherine to Philippe and back again.

The front door opened and Joy appeared, grinning with delight, followed by a couple who were unfamiliar to Katherine at first glance. As they came up to her, she recognized them from previous photos online and at their farmhouse.

"*Bienvenue, ma chère Katherine.* Please say hello to Madeline and Jean-Pierre Lallibert, your exchangers!"

Enthusiastic greetings were shared all around.

Philippe stayed for a coffee and then made to leave, planning to have lunch with François and run some errands.

"I'm concerned about dear François," Joy told him. "He is very slow to recover. Perhaps you can convince him to go for some physiotherapy, as he is getting very stiff with no exercise. We all think it would help."

Philippe assured her he would try his best. "We know what a stubborn old goat he is. Just like the elders in his beloved herd!"

They laughed affectionately and waved good-bye to him before walking to the back terrace to chat. Joy told Kat they would be going to Roussillon for lunch. "Henri and Sylvie insist on seeing you as well," she explained.

❧

The day passed quickly. The Lalliberts were eager to talk about their enjoyable stay in Kat's house and their visit to Toronto and the surrounding area. They were a quiet couple, doing home exchanges for over ten years. As Molly had told her, they loved Toronto.

Their English was limited, so Joy acted as translator.

"We would be happy to do another exchange with you any time," she interpreted for Madeline.

Katherine agreed she felt the same. "As you know, this was my first exchange on my own, and I feel so fortunate that it was here. Staying in your farmhouse and meeting your family, and Picasso, was very special."

They explained how Picasso had always stayed at Joy's house during their other exchanges and how surprised they were to hear he had settled in with Kat.

A smile lit her face, and Katherine leaned down to scratch behind Picasso's ears as he snoozed by her feet. Feeling at a loss for the right words in French, she said to Joy, "Please tell them that I was just as surprised and that spending that time with Picasso was one of the nicest experiences of my life. I learned a lot from him."

The Lalliberts showed their pleasure as Joy passed on her words. They declined the invitation to come along for lunch, and Katherine felt a tinge of sadness as she said good-bye once again to Picasso. After one final nuzzle from him, she watched him happily follow his owners into the vineyard for the stroll home.

The midday crowd in town was busy, and the lunch service was even slower than usual. She was reminded how no one complained about the slow service except the tourists. *It's the French way. Mealtimes are to be savored and enjoyed. No rush.*

Katherine was greeted warmly by Joy's son and his wife, and she enjoyed their lively company.

After lunch, Joy and Katherine went to Sainte-Mathilde to meet Mirella at Le Petit Café.

"For old time's sake," Joy said with her twinkling laugh.

❧

Philippe arrived back shortly after they returned from the village.

"Oncle François sends his best regards to everyone and especially you, Katherine. He chastised me for not bringing you to see him. I promised I would another time."

"Bonne idée," Joy agreed. "Why don't you plan to come back for *les vendanges*? It will be a great experience for Katherine, and I'm certain François will be even stronger by then."

Philippe looked questioningly at Kat.

"I would love to be here for the grape harvest," she agreed. "I've read so much about it."

They relaxed in the shade of the awning over the terrace for a while longer, since the evening had yet to bring relief from the heat of the day. Talk centered on the extremely hot summer and how the semi-drought conditions were causing havoc with some of the crops.

Joy attempted to convince them to stay for dinner, but both Kat and Philippe agreed they would not be hungry for some time.

After promises were made to return in a few weeks, they began the drive back to the coast.

Philippe spoke about François and the small but charming cottage he was slowly having restored now that it was to be his permanent home.

"It has been in his family for over two hundred years, and he feels very connected to it. He never really bothered to fix it up before, but since he has made these changes in his life, he has an interest to do that. Also, young Philippe—"

Katherine interrupted, "Surly young Philippe, the young man I thought was you?" she said with a grin.

"Yes, one and the same. He is a rather confused and angry young man but has been extremely helpful and stays with François when he wants to visit his goats. Otherwise he is looking after the herd himself for now, and that is a huge assistance to all of us."

"Your uncle has no regrets about his decision to leave Paris and settle here permanently?" Kat asked. "He had a philosophical talk with me when I visited him in Paris. It was inspiring, and certainly part of the reason I'm in Antibes now. He got me thinking about my life, and then highly coincidental things happened at my office as well. It was crazy—like it was all meant to be."

She explained about the government funding being cut, and Philippe asked questions about her career and life in Toronto. Somewhat shyly, he asked if she was serious about going back for the grape harvest.

"Yes! I would truly love to do that."

"And, uh . . . this is all right with Nicholas? He does not mind?"

Katherine was taken aback by the question. "Nick has nothing to do with it."

Philippe's face flushed slightly. "Sorry. I had the idea you were more than just friends. He speaks of you as more, and I assumed—"

"We are nothing more than friends. He's a very nice man and good company, but we are simply friends. To be honest, I can't imagine being more than friends with anyone right now."

Philippe was quiet for a few moments. "I do understand. Even after six years, I often think nothing more seems possible . . . although you are causing me to feel like I might want to try."

Startled, Katherine looked over at him. Their eyes met briefly. Surprised, she quickly stared straight ahead again but, when she finally spoke, felt something quite different than her words implied.

"Would you put on that jazz station again?"

They talked intermittently, listening to the music, immersed in their own thoughts. They seemed to be back down on the *autoroute* in no time.

"Katherine, if you feel ready for dinner, please join me. I have a favorite restaurant, Nounou, on the beach in Golfe-Juan. It would be my pleasure to introduce you to it. The fish dishes there are *fantastique!*" Kissing his fingers to make his point, he grinned.

Wedged between the busy road bordering the coast and a thin strip of sandy beach, Nounou was surprisingly elegant inside with an impressive marine mosaic by the artist Jean Marais on the wall of the entrance.

Katherine smiled with pleasure. "I don't know what I expected, but not this."

Philippe chuckled. "What's that you English say—don't just look at the book's cover?"

Amused, Katherine gently corrected, "Don't judge a book by its cover. So true."

"Next door is Tétou restaurant. They earned a Michelin star last year and have become one of the hot spots. Brad and Angelina ate there during the film festival, and that made it even more popular."

"That would do it," Katherine agreed.

"But the owners of Nounou have been family friends of ours since the early 1900s. Like most places along here, it started as a fisherman's kitchen. If you like bouillabaisse, you must order it here. It's a *spécialité*."

"Um—I can't take the fish faces staring out at me! But I love fish soup, and I see that on the menu."

"Well, it's a good second choice, with no eye contact from your bowl." Philippe smiled as Katherine laughed easily and often during the meal.

By the end of the evening, Katherine was aware of the comfort she felt with Philippe. His soothing voice and thoughtful philosophy mixed with humor kept her engaged and relaxed.

She found herself captured by his eyes more than once during the evening and allowed herself to enjoy the pleasure this gave her, wondering what it all meant.

45

September continued with a visit from Katherine's nephew, Andrew, on his way to Elisabeth's birthplace. He had arranged to spend time at an organic farming cooperative just outside the town while he also hoped to learn some of his family history in the area.

"Actually the town is now part of the Ukraine," he explained as he showed Katherine the file he had compiled on her mother's family history. "I've got some of Grandad's and Uncle Jozsef's information as well, but what I really want to find is the grave of the man who betrayed Grandad's father. I want to see if the rat poison worked!"

Katherine grimaced. "I can't believe my parents did that! It was a shock to read about it."

"Different times, different circumstances. They were my age. When I put myself in their position, I would have done something too," Andrew exclaimed. "I'm determined to find that guy's gravestone."

"Don't get your hopes up," Katherine cautioned. "It's been a long time, and there will be few people left who even remember those days. I suspect the war years will not be a popular topic there."

"I understand, Aunt Kat. There's just something fulfilling about someone from our family actually going there and seeing the town, feeling the history. It's like I have to do it. I want to add my experience to the story your mother left for us. After all, if she hadn't written that story for you, we wouldn't know any of this, because my granddad and your father said nothing about it. Nothing!"

"You're right. It's a terrible shame to lose these stories forever. Even though they are full of tragedy, they're so important. I'm so proud of you for doing this. I haven't been able to stop thinking about it, Andrew, and I've decided I'm going to go with you."

"Are you serious?"

"Never more. I checked to make certain I don't need a special visa, and it all sounds quite simple. The only warning I read was not to try to drive across the border, because they won't let rental cars in, and the lineup may be horrendous to make other arrangements."

"I read that too," Andrew agreed.

"Give me your flight information and I'll book my ticket. It's a go."

Andrew gave his aunt a very long hug. "You are something else."

"So I'm discovering," she said, chuckling. "I don't plan to stay long but, like you, I feel the need now to discover where Mom and Dad came from. You are making this happen, though. Your mother and I vaguely talked about doing this after we read Anyu's story, and we decided there would be too much sadness. I'm still a bit afraid of that, but if you are brave enough to do it, so will I be."

They spent three full days hiking the *sentiers* along the coast with their bathing suits in their backpacks. Beginning early before the heat reached its peak, they visited beaches that were new to Katherine as well.

"I can see why you love it here," he told her.

"And I love that you are finding all these amazing beaches! This is the best I've been to."

Plage Mala. Tucked into a cove at the foot of towering cliffs, the turquoise water shimmered in the sunlight. Public and private beaches staked out their spots. The vibe was young and hip, and it looked as though you needed to get there early to score a good spot.

Looking around, though, Katherine noted there were plenty of people her age in spite of the energy.

"Young and hip can be a state of mind, y'know," Andrew told her as he lifted his beer to toast her. "Don't forget that, my favorite aunt."

Katherine laughed loudly. "And your only aunt!"

Philippe joined them for dinner one night, and Nick took Andrew on the boat for an afternoon of scuba and windsurfing. Both men drove them to the airport for their afternoon flight to Budapest, wishing them luck and giving strict instructions to keep in touch.

46

Arriving in Budapest, Katherine and Andrew checked into a hotel near the train station. Venturing out, they discovered they had time to catch the last circuit of the city tour bus.

"It's more beautiful than I expected," Katherine commented. "Somehow I expected it to be darker and less inviting."

By the time the tour was over, their stomachs were grumbling and they asked the driver to recommend the best place to eat *Weiner schnitzel* and *spaetzle*.

"It has to be that," said Andrew, "and we will see how it compares to your mom's!"

The following morning they were on a train to their destination.

"Aunt Kat, I still can't believe you are here with me. This is so awesome!"

"Well, you were awesome for making this happen in the first place. Now we will have each other to hang onto when things get emotional—and I have no doubt they will."

The train rolled through unremarkable flat countryside, and from time to time Katherine struggled to banish macabre haunting thoughts. Images from *Schindler's List* and other movies about the Holocaust invaded her mind, and there were moments she squeezed her eyes tightly shut in an attempt to block them.

The few villages they glimpsed appeared poor and lightly populated, and to their amazement, most of the plowing and field work was being done by people rather than machines. Romani families traveling with ramshackle horse-drawn wooden carriages were as common as cars in some areas.

"It feels like we're doing some serious time travel backward," Andrew commented.

He had booked rooms at the Hotel Imperial. Recommended as the best accommodation in town, its name hardly reflected the interior. Tiny beds and worn carpets did nothing to warm up the stark effects of their adjoining rooms. Poor lighting and terribly outdated bathrooms added to the dismal ambiance.

A guide had been booked to meet them the following morning, so after a short walk around the drab neighborhood, they chose pierogies and salad for dinner at a nearby restaurant.

"Mmmm-mm! Bingo! We got lucky here," Andrew exclaimed as he loaded his fork. "These are delicious!"

Katherine nodded, her mouth full.

It was apparent that North American tourists were a rarity in the area.

"You are here to find the roots?" the jovial waitress inquired, leaning in conspiratorially and lowering her voice. "That is reason most English here."

"We are Canadians," Andrew replied, "and yes, we are looking for our family's history here."

"You have guide?" she whispered.

Andrew nodded and told her the guide's name.

"Very good! You must be careful, but I know this man is good one," she assured them.

At 8:00 a.m., after Andrew and Katherine both admitted to a fitful sleep on the thin, hard mattresses, they met Benedek in the lobby. A tall, frail-looking man with a weathered face, he still farmed a small garden while his sons had taken over growing crops and raising poultry. To supplement their meager income, he had been acting as a guide for the past few years.

In broken English, he explained that for a long time only the relatives of missing people came here, in the hopes of discovering some information or possibly retrieving family property. Now a younger generation was coming, searching for their roots or bringing grandparents one last time.

"I am eighty-two. I was young man during war, but I remember. I wish not."

Benedek told them he lived in a neighboring village and really did not know anyone from this town until long after the war. This news dashed Andrew's hope for the possibility that the guide would introduce them to some people who knew his family. Since his father and uncle had not been Jewish, he had considered the possibility.

When they arrived at the town hall, housed in one of the few surviving historic buildings, Katherine commented on the stark interior. Benedek explained how poverty stricken the populace was after the war and how every bit of decoration had been removed from such buildings, to be used to fuel fires or as building materials.

"Beauty was not important then. Communists frowned on excess."

With the names and dates they had, Benedek looked through records to see where Elisabeth's family had lived.

"That street was *Juden*. It was ghetto. All gone now."

He described how the ghetto area had been bulldozed in the 1950s as the town attempted to wipe out reminders of the terrible crimes of the Nazi regime. New, wider streets and a simple green park replaced it.

They had more luck with the home and plumbing store taken over by the father of Jozsef and his brother, Andrew's namesake.

The building that housed the business was still there and in commercial use, but the spacious apartments above it that had been their home were now open warehouse space. Life had always been simple there, and the apartment had never been richly appointed. Anything of value had been stripped out by the Russians in the months after they liberated the area.

The setting of the town was peaceful, on the banks of a wide river, overlooked by a hilltop castle, with rolling hills on the horizon. Katherine tried to imagine the happy youthful days her mother had described before all hell broke loose. She was struggling.

The original eighteenth-century Jewish cemetery had been desecrated by the Nazis, they were told, reduced to a shambles with the headstones used for filling potholes and road repairs. The few postwar graves had eventually been transferred to a new location, along with a portion of the original wall that was set with broken pieces of ancient headstones and tablets that had slowly been retrieved.

Cows grazed across the overgrown area of the original burying ground. In one corner, inexplicably, the remains of an entrance gate stood intact as a ghostly reminder.

A commemorative plaque at the new cemetery and another on a building that once housed a former synagogue spoke to the memory of those who perished. Hardly enough to begin to honor the thousands murdered from this small town alone.

Benedek led them next to the main village cemetery on the other side of town. Andrew gave him the name for which they were searching, and after several minutes he located a number of headstones. An elderly woman—stooped but sturdy, with a kerchief tied securely around her head—raked around the graves. She appeared puzzled as the visitors approached. Benedek spoke briefly to her and then listened at length, as the woman apparently had a lot to say. He informed Andrew that these particular graves belonged to her family going back many generations.

Beckoning them to follow, the woman stopped and pointed to one aged and cracked headstone. It was the name they sought. The year of his death conformed to the year Elisabeth had indicated they left the town.

When Benedek asked, at Andrew's request, if the woman had known the man, her animated response went on for several minutes with much head shaking from both.

Benedek translated. She had not. She was a baby during the war, but he was her great-uncle and known in the family history as a man much vilified.

When Benedek paused, the woman poked his arm and spoke some more, in disgust, before ending with a cackling laugh.

The translation was rough, the sentiment clear. "He was bully, mean. He brought shame to family during war. He was fat pig. He was eat favorite *palachinta*. He choked and died. That is family legend."

Andrew barely suppressed his grin and moved to knuckle-bump his aunt. Katherine, appearing momentarily horrified, smiled weakly.

They visited the new synagogue built on the site of the original main shul. Somehow the current efforts Benedek described to encourage a Jewish return to the area felt wrong to Katherine. She couldn't get past the pain.

Everywhere she saw what once had been: lines of Jews, yellow stars on their clothes; German soldiers on street corners yelling insults as their dogs snarled and lunged; the fenced ghetto with sunken faces staring out; bodies hanging in the square; young and old being herded onto cattle cars; steam rising from train engines, slowly leaving town, as others arrived with empty cars. The visual was relentless.

As the day passed, she became increasingly morose.

"Andrew, I feel such a burden of sadness. Every time we cross the railroad tracks, I get chills and feel nauseous. I'm seeing things that aren't there, but I know only too well that they were. I think I'm going to have to leave tomorrow."

Putting his arm around her shoulder, he empathized. "I'm feeling a lot of strong emotions too. Anger, for sure, and frustration. But I'll be here for a while and will find a way to process it somehow. I'm glad I'm staying, even though I can't explain why right now."

"I think your mom and I were right when we felt there was no point in coming here only to feel sadness. Sometimes you simply can't go back in life; you need to move on. That was always a message our parents imparted to us, and only now do I feel a sense of that."

"But these stories need to be told," Andrew stated emphatically.

"Absolutely, and in a manner that helps us understand and accept each other. To be honest, I sometimes wonder if the world really learned from this tragedy. We hear the words 'never again,' and yet we see genocide happening repeatedly . . . oh man, I'm getting depressed."

Andrew gave her a gentle hug. "Let's pack this in."

After paying Benedek—who was confused at the brevity of their tour but immensely grateful for being paid in full anyway—Andrew said he would be in touch another day.

"I thought I saw a decent restaurant by the river. Let's go . . . you look like you could use a stiff drink!" he said to his aunt.

Later in the afternoon, they bumped a short distance out of town in a taxi, along a road in terrible disrepair. The farming co-op where Andrew would be spending several weeks consisted of an expansive collection of fairly new buildings. Staffed by an international team, the British farm manager introduced them to a few colleagues who showed them around and spoke of the experimental work being undertaken. The hope was to revive and improve the long-established agriculture of the area.

Andrew's quarters were spartan, but several of the staff assured him that mattresses had been shipped over from England so at least the beds were comfortable.

"There is still a shortage of basic comforts in the small towns of these countries. You're going to find this an enlightening experience in that regard," Andrew was cautioned. "But the crew here is great, and the local people truly are warm and welcoming, although that's not always evident at first."

Andrew and Katherine were invited to join the staff for dinner after their tour; the cook appeared to be a magician in the kitchen.

"Andrew, I guarantee you're going to pack on a few pounds while you are here, even though we'll keep working you hard," the manager warned him. "Gaspar, our cook, is a priceless asset, and all the ingredients used are from our fields and livestock."

Andrew laughed. "Somehow I didn't anticipate finding gourmet dining here. Got that right!"

❧

That evening, attempting to make themselves comfortable in Kat's hotel room, Andrew and Kat sat on the floor on extra pillows scoffed from a linen closet down the hall after a little reconnoitering.

They spoke more of the positive experience Andrew was about to have at the co-op and less about how they had reacted to the tour of the town.

Katherine wanted to be strong in front of her nephew. Andrew feared he could not adequately comfort his aunt.

Still later, alone in bed as sleep eluded her, tears fell—for her parents, for their parents, for the children, for every persecuted person during those terrible, unfathomable times.

She thought about her mother's beautiful carpet. For the first time she felt a true understanding of the emotional connection that must have passed through Elisabeth's fingers to and from the threads.

As they parted at the train station the following morning, Andrew thanked her for coming with him. "It meant a lot to me to have you here. I'm sorry it was so painful for you."

Katherine nodded. "It's far worse than I considered it might be, but in retrospect I think I will see it was the right thing, even this brief a visit. Most important, it was so meaningful being with you. I've never really given it much thought, but here with you I've felt how life really does go on, through you kids. My generation did that for our parents, and now you are surviving and living for those who did not. Maybe your generation will do a better job than ours."

They hugged each other tightly before she stepped up into the train to leave behind the horror of what once had been.

47

Katherine texted Bernadette from Budapest and was happy to find her waiting when the early evening flight arrived.

In her typically inquisitive manner, the flamboyant chauffeur peppered Katherine with questions about her trip, interrupting with some highly unflattering remarks about the problem of immigrants from Eastern Europe. ". . . in my 'umble opinion," she said.

"This EU is for *les oiseaux*," she said. "It has caused nothing but *mal de vie* for la France!"

Katherine remarked how friendly and helpful she had found the people she encountered on her short trip.

"That's because the nice ones are staying there! But I did know a very handsome man from Poland once." She went on to relate an amusing story about a brief interlude she had shared with this fellow.

By the time they arrived at the house, Bernadette had caused Katherine to laugh out loud several times. She was appreciative of having her heavy mood lifted as she walked into the cozy familiarity this home away from home offered.

Opening the doors and shutters on each floor, she breathed in the soothing salt air before pouring a *pastis* and wandering out to the roof terrace.

Scraping a chair lightly on the tiles as she pulled it over, she sat down and placed her feet on the wrought-iron railing of the deck. Heaving an enormous sigh, she leaned back, taking in the star-filled evening sky.

Her thoughts returned to the previous forty-eight hours and all she had seen and felt, knowing it would take a very long time to process it all, if indeed she ever could. She wondered how her mother would have reacted to the trip after all the years of protecting her daughter from the horrendous details.

At least she would finally have known their palachinta *plan worked.*

Tears came again. She longed to go home and press her hands and face to her mother's carpet as she had watched Elisabeth do so often. Now she understood.

There will be time for that.

She heard her mother's voice. *Every day is a gift.*

Drifting off to sleep a short time later, Katherine resolved to live more by her mother's words. She wondered if she had been closing doors that she shouldn't, and she questioned if she knew how to open them.

⚜

Wakening later than usual the next morning, Katherine felt an overwhelming urge to stay in bed. Coincidentally, it was raining—in fact, it was teeming: thunder, lightning, the whole package. Nick had once described the rainstorms along the coast as brilliantly spectacular, and this one certainly packed a powerful punch.

Realizing she had left all the windows open, she dashed through the house, closing the shutters.

There was very little water on the floors thanks to the thick walls and sloped ledges of the window openings.

Clever builders, those ancient craftsmen.

Boiling a cup of hot water and adding lemon, she went up to the guest room and climbed into that bed. From there she could look out through the French doors and watch the normally calm sea roil in the storm.

Ghosts from her visit to her mother's town continued to haunt her. Her heart felt heavy and sad as she struggled to work through the pain that had accompanied her return. Running through the classic questions of how and why, she knew there were no answers.

She heard her mother's voice saying, "What doesn't kill us makes us stronger" and knew better than ever what she had meant. She sent e-mails to Andrea and Molly, telling Andrea she would be there to Skype at 6:00 p.m. Antibes time. A talk with her might help. Within the hour, the rain had stopped and the sun was already drying the streets. Kat knew there was one sure way to bring herself into balance as she put on her cycling clothes.

The small front courtyard had turned out to be the perfect spot to store her bike. Once out the front gate, she had to ride the wrong direction and turn back down the market street to get on her route. Stalls were being dismantled and several vendors were already closed, including Philippe.

"Katherine! Katherine!"

Braking, she turned to see Philippe waving to her from the front of his storage space.

"You are back so soon!"

"I couldn't take it, Philippe. I had to leave."

Philippe moved closer, as if to hug her. Feeling inexplicably shy, Katherine quickly positioned herself to ride off. "I know a ride will clear my head."

"I'm so sorry for your sadness," he said, his dark eyes piercing hers. "*C'est difficile* . . . but a ride helps everything. You are right about that. What route?"

She described her plan.

"Faites attention," he said. "The road may still be slick in places. Take your phone. I can go with you if you want to wait while I finish here."

"Thank you for being so thoughtful, but I really need to be by myself," she replied, touched by his offer.

"D'accord. Please call me to say you are home safely."

She rode along the Bord de Mer toward Nice, then cut up through Cagnes into the hills, a route familiar to her from the Tuesday-night rides. It was a straightforward and moderately challenging route, and she had no qualms going on her own.

Thoughts of her parents' painful past fought against the rhythm of pedaling as she pushed herself harder, muscles straining. Tears streamed down her cheeks. Sobbing loudly at times, she was helpless against the emotions demanding to be released.

Gaining speed as she flew downhill, the switchbacks keeping her barely under control, a long gut-wrenching cry escaped from deep inside her heart.

After careening dangerously on the next corner, she began gradually braking and at length pulled onto the almost nonexistent shoulder. She leaned her bike against the rock wall and climbed up to a large boulder, where she sat with her arms wrapped around her legs and her forehead resting on her knees, her chest heaving.

Weeping, she thought not just about her parents, but also about James and the end of their marriage and everything that had occurred in the past year to lead her to where she was now: sitting on a boulder in the South of France looking down over hillsides and rooftops cascading to the endless blue sea, still alluring under an overcast sky.

Finally her tears abated.

The torment that had filled her began to dissipate as her thoughts cleared. The lessons learned from her parents, the integrity they demonstrated throughout their lives—in spite of the early suffering—had shaped her values and her spirit. This would be part of her forever. The shocking end of her marriage and the painful realization it had never been what it might have been, had opened her to seeing new possibilities in life . . . little by little, in ways she could never have imagined. Ways that brought her here.

She knew she had to let go of the past and give herself permission to move forward.

Always the obedient daughter or the accommodating wife or the dutiful employee. Now she was in charge of taking chances and deciding her next step.

She had felt the promise of this during her exchange in Sainte-Mathilde, and it was reinforced during her visit with François in Paris. Now she sensed a release.

"Finally I can just be me," she said out loud as she climbed back on her bike.

She slowed her speed and focused on the ride. Gradually a semblance of peace overcame her as she gave in to the cadence and flow of her body and bike.

Skyping with Andrea later, as planned, they shed tears together while Katherine described the visit to the Ukraine and the ghosts that would not stop haunting her.

"The emotions were powerful. I felt like I was being sucked into a dizzying vortex of images and sounds from those horrific years. I had no control."

Andrew had also spoken about their visit with his mom, so she was well aware of the difficulties Kat had experienced, and offered what comfort she could.

"Kat, you did what you thought was right, and I think in time you will be glad you went. You won't have to wonder about it anymore."

Then Katherine told her about the bike ride. "I believe this ride was a turning point, Andie."

Next she surprised herself as she added, almost with a small laugh, "It was so powerful I'm betting Lucy has received a karmic message about it."

"You have no idea how good it is to hear you say that and to feel the change in your voice!"

They chatted about other family news until Katherine was interrupted by knocking. "Hang on a sec, Andie. Let me just get the door."

Nick stood outside the open door with another bouquet of flowers. Holding up his hand, he quickly said, "These are not a testament of love, but a bouquet of sympathy. I ran into Philippe, and he told me you had a difficult time. Please let me take you to dinner."

Katherine smiled and graciously accepted the flowers. "I'm just Skyping with my cousin, so let me finish that. Come on in and pour yourself a *pastis* or whatever you want," she said, pointing to the bar.

Signing off from Skype, Kat promised she would call her back the next afternoon. Before going back downstairs, she remembered Philippe had asked her to call him. She quickly did so.

"I'm back and I'm fine. It was a good ride, but you were right—there were some slick spots—so thanks for warning me to pay attention."

"*Très bien*. I'm glad the ride helped you feel better. Would you like to have dinner with me?"

"Thank you, but I can't," she replied awkwardly.

⚜

After a light salad at one of the nearby cafés, Nick suggested they stroll to the port.

Katherine was aware of a nagging guilt at turning down Philippe's offer. She hoped they would not run into him and wondered why it bothered her so much.

At the end of the ramparts, they stepped inside the white stainless steel sculpture that faced the sea and dominated the harbor of Port Vauban. Lit from the bottom in the unfolding darkness, there was a sense of a shimmering diaphanous embrace.

"The artist crafted his vision well," Nick observed.

"I've been mesmerized by this from my terrace," Katherine said, sighing. "It's as if he's a guardian, almost like a mirage from a distance."

"This part of the ramparts is Bastion Saint-Jaume. Originally constructed in the 1700s, it was blown up by the Germans when they retreated in 1944 and rebuilt according to the original plans," Nick said, ever the historian.

"This sculpture is so unique, almost magical." Katherine studied the outline of a person squatting, arms around knees, constructed entirely of letters joined together.

"*Le Grand Nomade*, but tourists refer to it as the 'Man of Letters'— for obvious reasons," Nick continued. "Oddly, the Spanish sculptor's name is Jaume Plensa."

Katherine smiled at the coincidence.

Nick's voice softened, reflecting the intimacy he craved.

"I love looking out at this from my boat and seeing how so many people are drawn to come near the sculpture. Plensa left the front of this piece open so people can stand or sit inside and be surrounded by letters, words, thoughts. And of course you can see through it to the stunning scenery that makes it even more powerful. It's so much more than simply metal."

They sat for some time in the warm evening air, talking intermittently, with Katherine sharing some details of her trip with Andrew. Nick listened with empathy, putting his arm gently around her shoulder.

"The war was such a different experience for us in Australia. Terrifyingly threatening, but we didn't live it in the same manner they did here. I've heard some inspiring stories and many tragic ones since I've been staying in this part of the world."

Walking home later, Nick took Katherine's arm and slipped it through his, giving her an affectionate smile. Patting her hand as he felt a slight resistance, he said, "It's okay, Kat, it's okay."

Looking straight ahead, she smiled shyly and nodded, a silent admission that she felt a warm response to his touch.

As they neared her house, she took the ancient key from her purse. Nick laughed. "I can't believe you keep using that key!"

"I love it! I love the idea it has been turned in this same door by so many hands through two centuries."

"You're a funny bird, Katherine Price, a sweet, funny bird. I'm so sorry for the sadness you experienced on your trip." He put his arms around her as they stood in the intimacy of the narrow street and pulled her close, something that had not happened to her in a very long time.

Resting her head on his shoulder briefly, she said, "Thank you, Nick, for being such a comfort. It was good to talk about this tonight."

He kissed her gently on each cheek, lingering long enough to give a clear message of his feelings. Katherine caught herself almost ready to slip her arms around him just as he gave them a quick squeeze and pushed open the heavy door.

"I'll call you tomorrow."

A sudden panic overtook her, and she decided to be busy for the next little while to spend some evenings on her own.

⚜

An e-mail message from Joy to both Katherine and Philippe reminded them of her invitation to come to the *manoir* for *les vendages*, the grape harvest. It was going to be held in three weeks' time.

At the market for her morning *leçon sur les fromages*, Philippe asked Katherine if she was truly interested in going.

"I wouldn't miss it for anything!"

"Will you drive with me?"

Katherine hesitated. "Do you mind if I go with you?"

"*Avec plaisir*. I did not want you to feel it was a foregone conclusion."

Katherine smiled as she thought about it on the way home. For all the time they spent together in the cycling club, the two mornings a week she had her cheese lesson, and the odd meal or drink they shared,

Philippe never stopped being a classic gentleman. She was discovering he had a great sense of humor and was thoughtful and courteous, but there was always a little edge of restraint. That was fine with her. She understood where he was coming from.

❧

Walking home from the bus stop after her bridge lesson the following Monday, she heard Nick call her name.

"Katherine! Where are you going? Have you been avoiding me?"

"Hey, Nick, I'm just on my way home from bridge. What are you up to?"

"I'm heading over to the Blue Lady for a nightcap. Didn't feel like drinking by myself. Want to come?"

One drink turned into a couple, with Katherine getting caught up in the convivial atmosphere of the pub and the banter among Nick's high-spirited friends. Feeling a little unsteady on the way home, she didn't object when Nick put his arm around her as they walked.

After opening the door to her house for her, he pulled her back gently as she began to step inside, and she slipped into his arms, her lips meeting his.

This time, he did not suppress his desire for her, and to her surprise, Katherine responded. They kissed several times, saying nothing as his lips brushed her face and neck before finding hers again, the caress of his mouth soft but demanding.

Katherine moaned lightly, her eyes closed, unsure if her head was spinning from the kiss or the martinis. "I think I better lie down."

"Good idea," he replied, the tone of his voice clearly implying he would join her.

"I mean alone. I'm feeling a little drunk," she said.

Nick kissed her again, more passionately, before Kat eventually pulled away.

"Katherine Price, I'm going to kiss you into submission one of these nights. I'm warning you right now. Prepare yourself. You are a beautiful woman and I want you to be mine."

Katherine gently pushed him away and waved good-bye. "Thanks for being so much fun. I needed to laugh! You're a good kisser too—really! G'night."

"Goodnight, gorgeous! Just remember, I'm going to be all over you. Consider yourself warned," Nick said as he pulled the door closed.

Nick was taking it slow for her sake. She knew it and appreciated it but was beginning to think he might be the fling Molly wanted her to have.

Much to her surprise, Kat had been sharing all the details with Molly during their Skype conversations. "Spill, girlfriend!" Molly would say, and spill Katherine did. Molly continued encouraging Kat to have an affair. She had seen enough of Nick to feel he was a decent man and was convinced Katherine would only benefit from feeling some love from him. She believed Katherine had something good in her future, and the sooner she began taking baby steps toward it, the better. Molly wanted Katherine to recognize that her own sensuous, physical self still existed. Tony had certainly given Molly the gift of that belief.

"You know I'm not suggesting you turn into frickin' Sally Slut! That would never be you under any circumstances."

Kat laughed. "Got that right."

"Trust me. There is love waiting for you. Love from a good man. I feel it. I'm not saying that good man is necessarily Nick. But he might be the right place to begin. It's a new world, girl. Go for it!"

Katherine still struggled with whether she really had a place in the "new world," whether she really wanted a place there.

She also knew Nick was a man with a history of relationships. He had never been secretive about it when some gorgeous younger woman sidled up to him at the Blue Lady and looked at him in a way that could only mean they had slept together.

Looking sheepishly at Katherine, he would shrug his shoulders and say, "Hey, I've been on my own for a while."

They shared another evening of serious kissing on Katherine's terrace after splitting a pizza at the café around the corner. Katherine was discovering more pleasure from Nick's lips than she could recall. Certainly it hadn't happened like this in her marriage. James had been a hasty kisser, wanting to get right down to business.

"Kat, that's it. If I don't get out of here right now, there will be no stopping me," Nick whispered before getting up to leave.

She realized Nick could sense her hesitation in moving their physical relationship along, but she was beginning to think she wanted more.

I've got to stop acting like a modest schoolgirl and listen to the passion that is building inside me.

Her dinners with Philippe were filled with easy conversation. He took pleasure in introducing her to all manner of fine dining in unobtrusive little hole-in-the-wall cafés that only a local would know. Their interaction became more animated but never moved beyond friendly, although she often caught him studying her carefully.

She also caught herself doing the same and began to wonder how it would feel if he kissed her.

There were several times when she shared dinner or a coffee or drink with both men. At those times she found herself fantasizing more than once about them, but then she would remind herself she was no spring chicken.

Why would either one be interested in me with all the beautiful young women around this town? If I were ten or twenty years younger, choosing between these two men would be a lovely dilemma.

48

This weekend might be the test, Katherine thought as she packed an overnight bag. Nick had invited her to cruise along the coast and over to Saint-Tropez. The distance itself would normally only take a few hours, but he had some stops planned, so they would make a weekend of it.

In spite of the sumptuous luxury of designer everything on Nick's yacht, each area felt comfortable and easy to live in. There were three bedrooms besides the master, and Nick suggested she pick whichever appealed to her.

"Sharing the master bedroom is your best option," he said, squinting slightly as he cocked his head and gave her a long look.

"I love this one," Katherine announced, standing in the doorway of a small stateroom decorated in shades of turquoise and aqua like the sea itself. Nick smiled stoically as he placed her weekend bag inside.

Tim, the captain, and his wife, Twig, were on board, although Nick had told them no help would be needed in the kitchen. They had their own crew quarters and would be seldom seen. It was an odd feeling for Katherine, but she soon adjusted.

Leaving early Saturday morning, they cruised slowly, stopping first at Île Saint-Honorat in the Îles de Lérins, just minutes off the coast of Cannes.

Although the current monastery and vineyard were not open to the public, they were able to see the stark abbey with its medieval vestiges and the ruins of the fortified monastery, stunningly set on the sea edge.

"It is so peaceful here, Nick. So quiet . . . very Zen."

Nick, turned tour guide once again, described how the monastery was founded in the fourth century and that Saint Patrick supposedly studied there in the fifth century.

"The fortified structure was built between the eleventh and fourteenth centuries, but of course, during the Revolution, the monastery was confiscated and became the property of the state. I shudder to think what happened to the poor monks! The church regained ownership in the mid-1800s and built this modern building then that is used today. I've heard there are about thirty or so Cistercian monks here now."

Katherine smirked as she was reminded of the European definition of the word "modern."

As they entered a small gift shop, he said, "For centuries, silent, humble, and ecologically minded, these monks have divided their time between prayer and sustenance. Today they produce all of this stuff—their own red and white wines, lavender oil, honey, and this"—he picked up a bottle—"an herbal liqueur, Lérina."

"It looks kind of like Chartreuse," said Katherine.

"It's similar. Tastes a bit like Galliano too, but it can pack quite a punch! I've got some on board—the older, the better."

"Look at these," Katherine pointed to CDs for sale.

"They are well known here for their Gregorian chants, beautiful and haunting," Nick said, selecting two to purchase.

Watching a few monks slowly walking in the distance in their distinctive bleached-white hooded habits, Katherine thought how the image gave a mystical feeling to the surroundings.

"It's one of my favorite places to stop," Nick told her.

"I can see why. I'm glad you brought me here."

They returned to the boat for lunch, which Nick had already prepped.

"Here, Kat, you can help by shaving the parmigiano onto this beef carpaccio," he said, placing two plates with scrumptious-looking paper-thin slices of meat arranged in a circular pattern with a clump of arugula in the middle.

"Mmm, looks delicious!" Katherine noted as she reached for the olive oil.

"That's the secret," Nick said, nodding at the oil.

The yacht slipped away from the dock and moved westward as they ate.

Along the Côte de l'Esterel with its rocky, red hills, west of Cannes, there were many beautiful, quiet coves.

After putting on bathing suits, they anchored midafternoon to snorkel and swim in a hidden inlet, free of any other boats, and unreachable by land.

Katherine had to admit, Nick looked pretty good in a bathing suit for a man his age. He had the kind of solid, compact body that wore clothes well, and there was something very sexy about his graying blond hair and tanned body.

Did I really think 'sexy'?

She was enjoying the feeling that was growing stronger as they stood at the railing, their arms touching lightly. Taking her hand, Nick helped Katherine down to the platform at the stern of the boat, where they put on flippers, masks, and snorkels. Laughing at each other's appearance, they slipped together into the sea.

The turquoise-edged deep blue water contrasted in the most striking way with the red sandstone rocks and hills of the massif behind that were dotted with brush and deep green pines.

Swimming in the warm water of such a protected lagoon was a sensuous experience, Katherine quickly realized. The salt water was liquid silk, as Nicked called it, and its crystal clear quality gave the fish and coral below a vivid clarity.

Resting her elbows on a floating mattress and slipping off her mask, Katherine shook the water from her hair and turned her face up to the sun. Swimming up from behind, Nick put his arms around her. Katherine quickly ducked underwater to the other side of the mattress. Nick's action had brought back a very unpleasant memory of that night in the pool in Provence, and she had reacted with fear. Foolishly too, she thought.

"Whoa, what was that all about?" Nick asked. Embarrassed, Katherine was successful in laughing it off as nothing more than being playful.

"I was just being silly." She knew her fear this time was the reaction to the exhilaration she felt from his being so close to her. She wanted it.

Nick leaned across from the other side to kiss the tip of her nose, her chin, and finally her lips, and Katherine leaned into each one.

"Is this paradise or what?" he asked.

"It has got to be pretty close," she agreed. "Simply stunning."

Back on an upper deck of the boat, they relaxed on soft-cushioned lounges as the course shifted across the bay. After bringing them each a large glass of water, Nick sat on the edge of Kat's lounge and leaned across her. His eyes slowly worked their way up from her toes to her hair, desire clearly written on his face.

Katherine was wearing a white strapless suit that emphasized her toned body and smooth bronzed skin. She had to admit she felt good when she put it on.

"Do you know how gorgeous you are?"

Katherine smiled. "Nick, I'm heading for sixty. With all of these nubile young women around, I can hardly qualify as gorgeous."

"It's all in the eye of the beholder—and youth isn't everything. You are a beautiful woman, Kat. You're in great shape, and you've got a way about you that is incredibly enticing."

She put her hand up to his lips, but he simply held it and continued. "You know how I feel about you. I don't want to just be friends."

Pulling her up by her hand, he slipped his arms around her and made his point with a kiss that was too good for Katherine to resist. The warm sun washing over their almost naked bodies only fueled his passion.

They continued to kiss while his hands caressed her body. She didn't even think about stopping him, and kissed him back with increasing pleasure. His fingers lightly skimmed down her torso until they rested close to the warmth between her legs, sending a tremor of excitement deep inside Katherine. After a few minutes, he gently laid her back on the lounge, kissing the crest of each breast before he stood.

"We just passed second base, gorgeous."

She smiled, pulling him close to her again, her voice thick with emotion. "I'm glad we did."

His tongue traced a line from her chest to her ear, where he whispered huskily, "To be continued, sweet woman."

Katherine felt pleasure rush into the pit of her stomach and did not want it to stop.

The moment was lost as Nick's phone rang. Hesitating, he checked the call display and then excused himself, looking annoyed at the interruption. With Nick distracted by his Blackberry—something she had noted was a constant part of his routine—Katherine picked up her camera. Leaning on the railing, she carefully planned her next shot and tried to calm her still trembling hands.

Nick's eyes followed her, but he remained caught up in his phone call.

As the village of Saint-Tropez seemingly began to rise out of the sea ahead of them, Katherine went to a higher deck to take photos of the colorful jumble of ochre, yellow, and pink village houses overlooked by the church tower and the hilltop citadel.

From a distance on the water, it still appeared to be the unassuming fishing village it once was. Drawing slowly into their mooring, that image was quickly dispelled.

Side by side all along the dock were yachts like Nick's. Some smaller, some larger. All reeking of extravagance.

"It's a different world," Katherine observed quietly. "I'm not sure it's mine."

"Just put a cover-up over your suit now and bring a casual change of clothes. I've ordered a water taxi to take us to La Voile Rouge. We can swim there, have dinner on the balcony, and watch the sunset. I reserved two lounges, so we're good to go. Okay?"

"You're the guide. I'll be ready in a minute after I throw a few things in my bag and fix my makeup."

As the water taxi headed out on the short run, Nick filled her in. "This is the original beach club in Saint-Trop, as the locals, the Tropéziens, call it, and it's still the hottest ticket in town. It's very French, and the clientele likes everyone to acknowledge that, so North American behavior really isn't tolerated. The beach is small and beautiful. The food is outstanding. The parties can get wild."

Katherine looked at him and raised her eyebrows in a questioning way.

"Don't worry! You'll see everything from kids to grandparents loving it there. If I'm going to show you what it's like in Saint-Trop, this has to be our first stop."

⚜

Nick was right about everything, Katherine thought to herself as they stumbled back down to the water taxi well after midnight. *The beach, the atmosphere, the food, the sunset, the party. All* magnifique.

The champagne certainly helped.

She giggled and put her finger to her lips to shush him, as Nick helped her onto *Searendipity*'s gangplank, singing loudly. Whirling her around the deck in a mock waltz step, he lost his balance, and they collapsed in a heap on a suede-covered couch.

"Oh Christ, Kat. I want you so badly," Nick's voice was muffled as he pressed his face into her neck and ran his hands through her hair. Without giving her a moment to respond, Nick kissed her passionately, his tongue seeking hers.

Katherine felt her last vestiges of resistance melt away. Her lips responded, parting.

The stars, the moon, the gentle lapping of water around the boat created the perfect ambiance.

Their mouths and fingers explored each other, and he guided her hand to feel just how ready he was.

Their clothes dropped to the floor as they fell back on the couch, Nick's body covering Kat's. His hand gently parted her legs as he kissed her breasts. His fingers stroked her, slowly at first and then more urgently.

The electricity of skin on skin, so foreign to her for so long, heightened Katherine's passion as she ran her nails down his back and thrust her hips forward, inviting him in. *Hurry*, was all she could think. He slipped on a condom with obvious skill.

She hadn't meant *Hurry and finish*, though. His deep thrusts had her burning with desire. After a quick explosive orgasm for both, they lay quietly entangled in the sweat of each other's embrace. Moonlight spilled across them.

Katherine's alcohol-induced languor kept her drifting in and out of sleep, but her foot rubbed along Nick's leg as her desire grew again and she waited for him to respond.

Slowly she became aware of his deep breathing, which quickly turned into loud snoring. She sighed in frustration and, slipping quietly out of his arms, fumbled her way to bed, where she instantly passed out.

49

Kat was surfacing from a deep sleep when the commotion of voices reached her. Thanks to being overserved the night before, she took a few seconds to realize where she was. Opening her eyes slowly, she quickly shut them again as bright sunlight streamed through the porthole directly into her face.

Her body was reminding her of what had occurred just a few hours before. She squeezed her legs together as a warm sensation spread through her. It felt good. It was time.

She was jolted back to awareness by a loud knocking. Wrapping her housecoat around her, she opened her door to find Tim, the captain, with a worried expression.

"I'm sorry. Can you come up on deck, madam?"

"Is something wrong?"

"Just get dressed and come up, please."

In a few minutes, Katherine climbed the stairs. Nick was standing at the end of the gangplank having a loud conversation with two police officers. A German shepherd on a lead stood beside one of them, looking strong and vigilant.

She watched Nick throw his hands up in exasperation and step aside as the officers and dog walked onto the boat.

"Kat, I'm sorry about this, but the *gendarmes* need to search the boat. Come and sit in the café across the street with me until they're finished."

"I'm just going to get my purse."

One of the officers stopped her, took her arm, and shook his head. Nick stepped in and after much arguing, Katherine was allowed to get her purse, which was then thoroughly examined by the officers and sniffed by the dog before they returned it to her—minus her passport.

Nick took her hand as they walked across the street.

Over coffee, he told her he had gotten involved with some of the "wrong people" several months before. He claimed he hadn't known they were part of a group running drugs out along the coast. After surviving a number of wild parties and observing some clandestine behavior, he suspected what was going on and actually went to England for two months in an attempt to break the connection.

"You know, they weren't the skuzzy types you might imagine. They were an educated, refined, and good-looking bunch. I had a great time with them until I began to see beyond the surface. There were a few times when it became quite dangerous, and I was an idiot not to get out faster than I did."

Obviously his name and boat information were still in the police computer. They made it clear they did not want him docked in their jurisdiction and were not going to let him leave until the boat had been checked thoroughly. He was also going to accompany them to the *gendarmerie* to deal with the inevitable bureaucratic paperwork.

"I swear I'm not involved with any of that shit in any way. I'm confident we'll be able to leave soon. I'm really sorry we haven't had time to explore the village."

Katherine just shook her head and looked at him. "Don't worry about that, Nick. This is terrible. I'll feel better when I have my passport back."

He nodded, repeating gruffly, "I'm very sorry."

Following the officers off the boat some time later, Tim and Twig told Nick they were going to take a stroll through the village while he went to the station. Nick introduced them properly to Katherine, and they invited her to join them.

In spite of feeling fragile from her hangover, she found the hour wandering through the atmospheric old town to be a helpful distraction from the current unpleasantness. The couple knew the village well and regaled Kat with all manner of inside stories.

Tim and Twig were a cool couple with fascinating stories to tell of the years Tim had freelanced as a captain on the megayachts. Twig would go along as a cook or steward when the post was available. They had sailed the world, observing lifestyles most people could not even imagine. Twig suggested she and Katherine get together back in Antibes for some girl time. It was a pleasant interlude, but an undercurrent of forced casualness prevailed, causing Kat to wonder if there was more to the altercation with the police than Nick was letting on.

Nick called Tim from the *gendarmerie* to say the police wanted to speak with Katherine and they should report there immediately.

After a quick five-minute walk, Katherine was a bundle of nerves as she was gruffly ordered into a small room containing a desk and two chairs. Her lifetime of being a completely law-abiding, rule-following citizen had not prepared her for this type of experience. Knowing she had nothing to hide did nothing to relieve her instant anxiety. The questions were routine and straightforward, the interrogator speaking English with very little accent, yet Katherine felt threatened.

Tapping his hand with Katherine's passport, he asked, "Where are you from, Madame Price? Where are you living in France? Why are you there? How do you know Monsieur Nicholas? When are you leaving France?"

Apparently satisfied with her responses, after what felt like an agonizingly long pause, the officer handed her passport back to her.

"Be very careful, Madame Price, who you choose as your friends," he admonished with a stern look.

Feeling as though she had done something wrong, Katherine nodded slightly, her mouth locked in a tight line. Making a hasty exit, she hoped her fear did not show.

Back at the bar by the harbor, Nick ordered a beer. The thought of alcohol made Kat feel nauseous after her overindulgence, combined with the episode with the police.

Observing an exchange between Nick and Tim, she was surprised by Nick's uncharacteristic anxiety. Something wasn't quite right. Kat felt a sense of unease with the way the men looked at each other.

The voyage back seemed to take forever. Nick was in a fury over the incident and showed a side Katherine had never seen. He was constantly on his phone and on several occasions ended the conversations yelling at the top of his lungs.

Katherine tucked herself into a lounge chair on the upper deck by the hot tub and took out her Kindle. Concentration was impossible. Her simple, straightforward life in France momentarily seemed complicated.

Or is it really? she wondered.

What's going on now is Nick's problem, not mine. Just because we had sex last night—and that's exactly what it was, sex—doesn't change things. A fling is a frickin' fling, to quote Molly. I just have to get my head around that.

She smiled, contemplating how Molly's unique expressions of her life philosophy could be right on the mark. It also dawned on her how open she was, in her current single state, to actually listening to what Molly had to say. "Molly the Moaner," James had called her, but Katherine could see now that was a complete misnomer.

Watching Nick move around the boat with his Blackberry pasted to his head, she had no trouble telling herself she was not falling in love with him. He was basically a nice guy, attractive, living in a completely different reality than most, and a friendship with him was all there needed to be.

Or maybe not, after this experience. This is a bit too scary for me. His lifestyle was not for her. She had partied in a champagne fog at La Voile Rouge, but if she never did that again, it would be too soon. *Last night was alcohol-fueled lust, pure and simple, but it did feel good.*

Feeling another aftershock from the fiery climax of their brief frenzy, she allowed the bliss to wash through her, momentarily erasing the confrontation with the police.

Looking out across the calm sea, as Saint-Tropez faded into the horizon, she had an epiphany of sorts about what really mattered in her life at this point: freedom to be herself, do as she pleased, and be content with her choices. Because of the controlled, seemingly safe world in which she had lived until the past year, she had always maintained a certain skepticism about the unfamiliar.

I can't continue to blame James for that. I obviously bought into his way of doing things, for whatever reason.

In the space of mere months, she had thrown herself headfirst into the unfamiliar and discovered it to be a wonderful place.

⚜

Carrying her bag, Nick walked Katherine back to her place. He was still steaming and indicated he was going to contact his lawyer and get the harassment cleared up.

"I can't have this situation hanging over my head indefinitely. It's annoying, embarrassing, and could possibly get quite complicated for no good reason. I've got to see my lawyer and get to the bottom of it."

Katherine nodded.

Taking her face in his hands, Nick kissed her gently. "What happened between us last night was beautiful—in its own crazy way. I'm sorry I fell asleep. Christ, am I sorry about that!"

Katherine started to speak, but he put his fingers to her lips.

"Shhh, let me finish. I'm sorry our trip had to end as it did, and I hope I can make it up to you. I'll call you this evening and we can make some plans."

"Nick, I'm hungover and need to go to bed this minute. Come for breakfast tomorrow, or brunch, lunch, whatever. Okay?"

He called early the next morning, saying he had some unexpected business he needed to address immediately and was flying to London that afternoon for a few days.

"I'm so sorry, Kat. Man! I seem to be doing a lot of apologizing all of a sudden! I'll call you from London, and I'll miss you."

Katherine wasn't so sure she would miss him. She felt a pang of guilt over her loss of control that weekend. On the other hand, she was feeling more alive and in tune with her body than she had in years.

50

Kat was on Skype with Molly late Thursday night, dinnertime in Toronto. They had already discussed the Saint-Trop weekend in detail a few days earlier.

"I'm glad you finally broke through and had a fling, Katski. Don't worry about how it all went down. Obviously the police realized you were an innocent bystander."

Katherine admitted wrestling with some guilty feelings. "I just keep reminding myself I'm not sixteen years old and to get over it, and basically I am over it. And you're right—it did feel good! But that business with the *gendarmes* did cast a definite pall over everything else."

She remarked that she had a good time hanging out mainly in women's company this week without anything that looked or felt like a date on her calendar.

"Of course, I've spent time with Philippe cycling and at the market, but that's just kind of been our normal stuff. We haven't gone to dinner or anything this week. I think he's holding back a bit because we'll be going to Joy's for the weekend. He's really careful about not appearing overbearing, and I like that."

"Yeah," Molly agreed. "Nothing is going to happen there anyway from all you have said."

"For sure," Katherine agreed. "There's no pressure."

"Who would ever have guessed there was so much that was actually really frickin' interesting to learn about cheese?" Molly asked. "That just cracks me up!"

⚜

Nick had been in London all week, and Kat had not found his absence an issue. In fact, she liked having her life entirely back to just her choices again.

She had kept the week low-key. On Monday evening she had her weekly bridge lesson with seven women whose company she was beginning to enjoy very much, as well as a dour, strict teacher.

Tuesday morning brought a lesson on Roquefort and intriguing details of the centuries-old caves in which it ripens. Philippe knew of Kat's weekend trip on Nick's boat and asked, in a reserved voice, if she had enjoyed visiting Saint-Trop. Katherine hoped he didn't notice her face reddening. "It's a beautiful setting and town, but not my kind of place," she replied before quickly returning the chat to cheese. She wondered if she imagined a more relaxed tone in his voice after her unenthusiastic comment about the weekend.

Cycling that evening was followed by a cold beer with the group, including Philippe, who walked her home. As they parted, they confirmed the details about the departure for Joy's on Friday.

Wednesday was her international women's hiking and French conversation group. During the half-hour train ride along the coast, Katherine thought how her life was feeling full. *Living on your own doesn't mean you have to be lonely*, she mused almost with surprise.

For the past two weeks, she had been taking an afternoon cooking course in town on Thursdays. There were two more to go, and she was feeling inspired to cook again, but now a Mediterranean-style cuisine.

Ever since Molly's departure, practically every day began with an early-morning yoga session, no later than seven, followed by her walk around the village. Her camera was stashed in her *panier*, along with her dictionary. The number of shots she took had certainly lessened, but inevitably something new would catch her eye: angles, light, shadows, fine details that only the passage of hundreds of years could create.

The thrill Kat experienced from these quiet walks, with the village just beginning to come to life, never diminished. In the almost empty maze of narrow cobbled streets, the centuries seemed to unravel.

Even though this historic old village is a popular tourist destination now, if you free your mind and stop to listen, you can still hear echoes of its long and storied past.

After making her market purchases, she would stop in at a nearby *tabac* and pick up the morning edition of *Nice-Matin*. With her trusty dictionary close at hand, reading the newspaper from cover to cover was her daily French lesson, along with language podcasts on her iPod.

The *boulangerie* lineup, tastings in the wine shop, the curmudgeonly waiter at her favorite café, chats with the delightful owner of the English bookstore—all were feeling so right; like it was the way her life was supposed to be. She felt surprisingly connected to the rhythm of the routine she was establishing. *I'm doing things for me—no one else.*

⚜

Driving up to Sainte-Mathilde Friday evening, Katherine and Philippe had almost reached Joy's house when she felt her cell vibrate yet again. Purposely silencing the ring before she got into the car, she checked and saw it was Nick calling and chose to ignore it.

"I was not making jokes when I told you they will put you to work! The grapes are hanging in heavy clusters, and *le ban de vendanges* has officially been declared. We'll be clipping the stems from dawn to dusk with a big *fête* in between!"

"Joy advised me to bring old, sturdy shoes," said Katherine, "and she warned me it was hard work—and good fun. Tell me more about the traditions."

"*La vendange* goes back to the Middle Ages, when the local *seigneur* would declare conditions were right for the harvest and *le ban*, the proclamation, would be posted in the village or town square. I assure you in these past weeks there has been much tasting, testing, and checking. *La météo*—forecast of weather—has been closely watched and now, while the sun is shining, the time is right."

Talking about the harvest led them to talk about the importance of traditions in communities and cultures and how such customs were disappearing in today's world. Philippe expressed his pleasure at having these established rituals passed on from generation to generation.

"It's the recognition and celebration of traditions that help each generation remember where they came from. They help ground us even as we are making our own way in life. I believe they really matter, but I know many people don't."

"I feel the same way," Katherine said. She described the Hungarian celebrations her parents taught her and what a meaningful place they held in her heart. "In North America, apart from our aboriginal people, the traditions all come from other places in the world. What appeals to me in Europe is how each country's traditions have been established for centuries and continue to be passed down."

The conversation became increasingly personal as each expressed how good it was to create your own family rituals. Philippe spoke haltingly about his family life before his wife became ill. Katherine spoke of her childhood rituals with her parents and was reminded there were few such memories from her marriage.

Their exchanges lightened, and soon Kat was in stitches as he described other aspects of life in France from a native's perspective. Philippe had an eye for small details of human behavior and a way of interpreting them in an entertaining fashion.

Before they knew it, Pico was prancing around by the car door, waiting to greet them.

❧

Henri and Sylvie were manning the front terrace. "*Bienvenue!* We are the official outdoor greeters, along with Picasso," they said with a smile as Antoine appeared with a tray of filled wineglasses, "and we are particularly thrilled to welcome the two of you!"

The atmosphere in the *manoir* was friendly and festive. The grand entrance hall was filled with people, wineglasses in hand.

"At *la vendange*, no one would consider to drink anything else," Philippe whispered to Kat.

Saying he would bring their bags in later, he was immediately swallowed into the crowd of old friends and family, while Mirella warmly took charge of Katherine.

"We are so thrilled you are here, *ma chère*! Of course you know several people here now, and let me introduce you to the others. Sadly you have missed my husband again! He has made a promise we will come south specifically so he can meet you the next time he is home!"

Again, Katherine felt welcome and comfortable as she was drawn into the lively chatter in the room.

Joy was bustling around making certain everything was going as planned, and after a quick happy embrace with Kat, assured her they would have time for a good visit later that evening. "I'm so interested to hear how you find life on the coast and in Antibes in particular."

Kat's smile revealed her delight when François appeared at her side, his balance assisted only by an ornately carved walking stick. He was feeling much improved since he had arrived back in the village, he told her. They found two chairs and sat chatting at length before he said he must call it a night.

"I only came to see you. I've decided I'm too much of an old man for such grand parties, and I'm very comfortable with that. Promise me you will come to visit again so I might show you my humble abode that is bringing me so much peace."

"I promise," Katherine vowed, appreciating even more the company of this wise man.

Finally having a moment when she could politely do so, Kat went upstairs to the ladies' room. On her way back down the grand staircase leading into the party area, she happened to catch sight of a very attractive young woman who made her way across the room and swept Philippe into a tight embrace. It was not the French way to greet someone, and Kat was taken by surprise when Philippe appeared to respond with equal pleasure, covering the young woman's face with kisses. Several people standing near them were applauding and smiling warmly.

Feeling a response she could only identify as jealousy, Katherine stopped on the stairs to watch.

Speaking with great animation, Philippe embraced the woman several more times as many people stepped up to kiss her cheeks and exchange greetings.

Obviously I haven't known everything about him, but why am I reacting like this? she wondered, surprised at the strength of her emotion.

She was startled out of her thoughts by a hand on her elbow. Joy introduced her to some old friends, and Katherine attempted to stay engaged in conversation. The couple had visited Toronto and were delighted to speak about their experience with someone who knew the city. Struggling to look like she cared about the chat, she desperately wanted to turn around to see if Philippe was still with the beauty. She felt warm and slightly nauseous.

After what felt like much longer than it actually was, she excused herself and turned to see if she could find a way to go to her room. The sudden urge to remove herself from the presence of Philippe and any young woman was overwhelming.

Looking around the great hall, his eyes bright and face flushed, Philippe noticed Katherine on the stairs, waved, and made his way toward her, bringing the woman with him, his arm comfortably around her shoulder.

Katherine jolted herself out of the moment, walking to the bottom of the stairs with a forced smile.

Philippe deftly had the two women face to face. "Adorée, please meet Katherine Price from Canada."

With a warm look back at Philippe and a bright smile, the beautiful young woman took Katherine's awkwardly outstretched hand to shake.

Kat felt as though an obviously phony smile was betraying her confused emotions.

"Katherine, I want you to meet my daughter, Adorée. I had no idea she would be here!"

Laughing, the young woman with long chestnut-brown hair leaned in to greet Katherine with *bises*.

"I'm so thrilled to meet you! I have heard lovely things about our family's new Canadian friend," she said.

Katherine smiled sincerely now and hoped her sigh of relief was inaudible.

"My father should know I would never miss *la vendange*!" Adorée explained to Katherine. "But I always give him my flight arrangements, and this year I thought I would play a trick and tell him I was just too busy at work to get away."

The surprise only added to the festivity of the evening, but at 11:00 p.m. Joy rang a bell and announced everyone had to leave and go to bed immediately. *"Dormez bien,"* she added with a twinkle in her eye. "We begin at dawn tomorrow morning, which will be precisely 6:27. *Bonsoir! Bons rêves! À demain!"*

❧

The morning began with coffee and the usual croissants, *pain aux raisins*, and *pain au chocolat.*

"Allez vendangeurs!" rang through the air, and the backbreaking work began. The air had a healthy coolness at that hour, and everyone attacked the vines with careful but vigorous efforts, clipping bunches of grapes and placing them in baskets at their feet. The contents of the baskets were emptied into bins placed along the rows, and others were assigned to load these bins into trailers attached to tractors. The tractors would then begin winding their way along the narrow country roads to deposit their cache at the wine co-op.

Katherine was amazed at the parade back and forth along the bordering roads she could see from the field. Tractors of every size pulling bins and wagons were accompanied by massive mechanical harvesting machines. The procession was endless through the entire day.

She was told that until the early 1970s, every grape in France was picked by hand. As well as the friends and family, who might only pick on the weekend, at the other end of the vineyard, grape pickers from Spain were employed until the job was done.

Picking grapes all day was no easy task, Katherine realized as the hours passed, and she congratulated herself on remembering to bring Advil with her. Straightening her back and stretching on a regular basis, she was thankful for the benefits of the yoga sessions on her terrace most days.

Toward the end of the afternoon, Philippe and Adorée found Katherine, who had been picking with the Lalliberts. They instructed her to turn in her clippers and basket for the day and whisked her over to the co-op so she could see, smell, and hear the excitement of watching the grapes go into the machines for processing.

After being carefully emptied from their box or basket, bad or unripe grapes were removed before the rest went into a de-stemmer/crusher. Stems and leaves were separated from the grapes in that machine before they dropped onto a sorting tray and then onto yet another tray to wash any airborne particulates that may have adhered through the growing season.

"No bird poop, please!" Adorée exclaimed.

Philippe explained how the grapes then go into a grape crusher to separate the skins and begin the juicing process before it all went into the grape press to extract any remaining juice from the skins. The juices ran through hoses into barrels and vats to begin the fermenting process.

"It's all done with such military precision!" Kat observed as her camera shutter clicked away, capturing the deep rich colors of the enormous mounds of grapes. The satisfaction of the growers' smiles as they watched the process and congratulated each other on a fine harvest provided wonderfully authentic portraits of grizzled faces at the end of days of hard labor.

Musty sweet smells of fermenting grapes filled the air.

Philippe and his daughter laughed as Katherine insisted on getting as close to the action as possible, her shoes sticking to juices that covered the floor. "An occupational hazard," they explained. "Now the next best part begins, as we will feast tonight back at the *manoir*. Antoine and Hélène and their kitchen army have been cooking all day."

Adorée took Kat's arm as they walked back to the car. "If you thought last night was a party, just wait! Here's the drill—shower, snooze, and be ready for *une grande fête*!"

"Then be ready to do it all over again in the vines tomorrow," Philippe added.

Driving back to Antibes on Sunday evening, Katherine was barely able to keep her eyes open.

"I'm sorry, but I know I'm going to fall asleep any minute," she said.

Philippe chuckled knowingly. "I would be amazed if you didn't.

This weekend was hard labor and hard partying. Go to sleep and don't worry about it."

⚜

Philippe took the key from Kat's hand and opened the door to her house. Much to her embarrassment, she had slept during the entire drive. Turning down her invitation to come in for a drink, Philippe said, "Now it's my turn to, as you say, crash. I need to lie down very quickly."

They both laughed.

"But I want to invite you to come with me tomorrow afternoon for a few hours. There's something I would like to show you."

Without hesitation, Katherine agreed, thinking she would cancel her bridge commitment in the evening just in case she was not back in time.

"I will meet you at two o'clock at the statue in front of the market. Wear jeans and running shoes and bring a light jacket, even though it will be warm. And bring your camera."

Standing in the doorway, he leaned in and kissed her on each cheek. Katherine wondered if it was simply her imagination or whether there was something different about his touch this time.

She was intrigued by his invitation, but he would offer no further details.

"Thank you—for everything," she said, her voice strangely full and throaty. "This weekend was an amazing experience in so many ways. It was great fun to see everyone and spend such a happy time together— exhausting but happy! Your daughter is a beautiful young woman, and I'm so pleased I had the opportunity to meet her."

She suddenly was aware she had taken his hand in hers, and she felt her face flush. Their eyes met as he told her how much he enjoyed her company, how easy she was to talk to. Raising her hand to his lips, he kissed it lightly, his eyes never leaving hers. Then he backed out the door and was gone.

Katherine stood for a minute, still holding that hand in front of her, staring at it as her heart raced.

Going straight to her computer, she sent Molly a message marked "Urgent" and hoped her friend would check her mail when she got up for work. Stunned by the change in the dynamics with Philippe, Kat felt like a lovesick schoolgirl who needed to confide in her best girlfriend.

Her phone beeped again as she climbed into bed, and she remembered that Nick had been calling her. She let it go to voicemail. In the excitement of the weekend, she had completely forgotten about her phone. Listening to the messages—days ago he had left three—she was almost pleased to hear he was still in London with no firm return date, due to "complicating factors." And he missed her.

She didn't miss him.

Lulled by soothing sounds from the sea, she fell asleep, feeling fortunate to have shared another unique experience of *plaisir*.

One month left. It's not going to be easy to leave, but what memories I'll be taking with me.

⚜

Katherine was wakened the next morning by loud knocking on the front gate and her name being called through the open window.

Grabbing her robe, she poked her head out to see Twig and Tim looking up.

"Sorry! I guess we woke you?"

Katherine dashed down to the courtyard and unlocked the gate.

"Hey, come on in. What's up?"

"Nick asked us to come and let you know what is going on. He doesn't want to call anyone now, as things suddenly are heating up."

Katherine offered coffee, but they said they wouldn't stay long.

"Nick wanted us to reassure you that he hasn't done anything wrong, but he's in a bit of a pickle," Twig said in her delightful British accent that took the edge off any conversation.

"He won't be traveling anywhere for a while," Tim said. "He has been warned he may be arrested if he sets foot back in France, and the boat is under a travel restriction until further notice."

"It's all about an unfortunate association that has become extremely complicated."

"Here's a different e-mail address for him. He would like it if you got in touch, and he sends his apologies for his rather abrupt disappearance."

Katherine assured them she would think about it. Her session with the *gendarmes* had left a sense of unease.

"We're going to be staying with the boat to take care of things here, but let's get together for a drink before you leave."

❧

Molly Skyped Katherine as soon as she read her "urgent" e-mail. She caught Katherine just after noon and listened as Katherine breathlessly recounted her weekend. There was a different timbre to her voice today.

After the Saint-Tropez weekend, Molly had celebrated Katherine's breaking through her "fling fear factor," as she put it.

"You stepped outside your comfort zone. Good for you," she had congratulated her.

Now Katherine's voice was full of passion and excitement, combined with apprehension, as she described her feelings about the weekend with Philippe.

"Something changed, Moll. I can't precisely pinpoint what it was, but we both seemed to respond to each other in a more intimate manner. When he introduced me to his daughter, there was something different in his voice. I didn't know who this beautiful young woman was when I first saw her with him, and I can't begin to describe how jealous I felt!"

Molly listened carefully. "It sounds to me like romance may be in the air, girlfriend! Perhaps that little roll in the hay with Nick opened you to other possibilities."

Katherine chuckled. "I don't know about that, but I do know, whatever it is, it feels good. I have no idea where this is going, but I just had to tell you!"

"Let the good times roll, Katski. I can hear the happiness in your voice, and that's frickin' wonderful. I've got to dash, but I'm glad I caught you."

"Me too! Let's try to talk while Andrea and Terrence are here. By the way, I'm not telling Andrea what happened with Nick. I feel sort of embarrassed."

51

Just before the bells in the Hôtel de Ville tolled 2:00 p.m., Katherine stood next to the statue in front of the market.

The village seemed a little quiet for a Monday, and she wondered if everyone was recovering from the same type of *vendanges* weekend that she had. She had to admit, some muscles were still feeling rather stiff and sore.

Sitting on the steps next to the statue, she watched a lively group of men, women, and children arriving for a civil wedding in the town hall. That procedure had become very familiar to her, living so close by. She had enjoyed many moments over a cool drink or a *crème*, feeling the happiness floating in the air as the wedding parties and their guests celebrated. In the beginning she had been reminded of her own small wedding and suffered pangs of sadness, but that had passed. Now it made her smile to join the applause with everyone else who happened to be walking around the area when the bride and groom exited the hall.

Some couples would then go around the corner to the cathedral to follow up with a religious ceremony. Kat had noted most did not.

A vintage white Rolls-Royce was parked in front with the traditional large and beautiful floral arrangement attached to the hood. The bride and groom would be driven around town, followed by the guests, horns honking incessantly. She noticed too that guests dressed far more casually, and there was much less attention to extravagance. On Saturdays in particular, the bells of the Hôtel de Ville and the cathedral rang their joyful songs as one wedding after another moved through the process.

Directly in front of her was a small parking lot for motorcycles, a popular and sensible means of transportation on the narrow twisting roadways all along the coast and in these cramped villages. Katherine watched as an immaculately polished vintage Ducati pulled into a spot. The driver—*looking very seductive in those leather chaps*, she thought—removed his helmet.

Philippe grinned and beckoned her to come.

Greeting him with a look of astonishment, he spoke before she could ask. "Yes, we are going for a ride on this, my other bike! If you don't object."

Katherine was speechless for a moment and simply shook her head.

He handed her a helmet.

"In all the time you have been here, you haven't been up in the hills yet. I want to take you there—that is, if you want to go."

"Let's do it," Katherine said, not even trying to conceal her excitement. "I've never been on a motorcycle!"

He explained there were communication headsets built into the helmets so they could talk to each other in normal voices. No shouting necessary. They talked for a few minutes about safety—how to hold on, how to respond to his movements on corners, how to trust him.

"Put your arms around my rib cage and grab onto your wrist. If you feel comfortable, lean against my back and I will lean slightly into you. It makes us more aerodynamic. Be sure to hold even more tightly when we accelerate from a stop. But if you are uncomfortable with that, I can put on a bar for you to hold."

Assuring him she felt perfectly comfortable holding on to him, she climbed on behind him. A sudden surge of pleasure rose from the pit of her stomach as she slipped her arms around him.

Where did that come from?

Reminding herself he was ten years her junior, she tried to focus on not falling off, but his closeness kept intruding on her thoughts. Her face was so close to his neck she couldn't help but breathe in his clean smell, a smell that made the backs of her knees tingle. He smelled strong, safe, sexy—as if he had just stepped out of a shower.

His dark hair curled out under the back of his helmet, mesmerizing her.

Watch the scenery . . .

Leaving town was a slow process with many stops and starts, but within fifteen minutes they were out in the countryside and climbing.

The switchbacks were exciting and terrifying and Katherine felt all her senses firing. Looking down, the views became increasingly stunning, and she drew a sharp breath as images of perched villages presented themselves, dotting the hills.

As they rode, Philippe spoke to her about their surroundings. Not in the voice of a tour guide, as had Nick, but in a thoughtful and philosophical way, mentioning the artists and writers who had fallen in love with the places they were passing. He had stories of the lives they lived there and the legacies they left.

She could feel his passion for the land.

Pointing to one of the first spectacular hilltop villages, he said, "Saint-Paul de Vence is very special. I don't want to stop there today, as it will be full of tourists, but I will bring you back if you like. La Colombe d'Or is now a fancy inn and restaurant, but it was once a hangout before and after World War II for Picasso and other broke young artists, who paid their bills to the owner with paintings and sketches and original written work. Imagine! He eventually owned one of the most comprehensive art collections in the world, and of course, inevitably, celebrities took over. Now a reservation in the summer is essential."

"I'll look forward to that," Katherine said, trying not to acknowledge the carnal thoughts she was having as she listened to his sensuous voice with her arms wrapped around his taut body and the power of the motorcycle vibrating between her legs.

They continued to climb and settled into an exciting rhythm on the switchbacks, with little traffic interrupting the flow of the ride. As much as she loved to ride her bike, she had to admit this was an altogether pleasing alternative. She had always thought motorcycles such loud, intrusive annoyances, but now she could feel how the rider becomes one with the machine in a powerful, thrilling ride. The noise fades into the whole sensation.

Slowing down as they rode into a typical scenic square shaded by plane trees, Philippe suggested they stop for a stretch and a cold beer.

"This is Tourrettes-sur-Loup, famous for growing violets for the perfume makers in Grasse for hundreds of years," he said. "The ice cream maker in the village serves violet ice cream, if you want to try it."

They decided to have a cone and save the beer for later.

Strolling the village, they savored the mellow coolness of the pale-mauve ice cream. Katherine was again taken by the ancient stone houses and the contrast of the restoration of one next to another that was crumbling in disrepair. Both displayed their own unique beauty. And then, of course, there were the doors.

"I love, love, love it," she repeated as she kept working her camera shutter. "It's such a buzz knowing that these same dwellings have been inhabited for hundreds of years. I'm absolutely fascinated by it, as you know from Provence—the history, the atmosphere . . ."

A half hour later they were back on the road and climbing again.

Philippe told her to look up, way up, where she could see a medieval village clinging to the top of the highest peak.

His words brought alive a love story between a noble who once lived in the castle that hung off the cliff and the daughter of a shepherd who tended his flock in the fields below. Fable or fact, no one really knew any longer, but it was a passionate tale that brought the countryside to life as the hills flashed by.

"I am constantly astonished at how these perched villages were ever built on such remote rocky crags," Katherine gasped.

When they stopped in Gourdon, their beer was refreshing, with the late afternoon still hot without the cooling breeze from the ride. They were seated in a quaint square, surrounded by fairy tale–type architecture and a panorama that stretched down across the hills to the coast. It was easy to pick out the iconic Baie des Anges Marina. The multi-tiered design of the massive condo development gave the appearance of an ocean liner. That controversial landmark signaled Nice to the east, Antibes to the west. The Mediterranean glistened beyond.

Katherine felt on top of the world.

She had endless questions about the communities in the area, and Philippe explained how recent development was creating great change but the history of towns such as Gourdon would always remain alive. The government was putting in strict controls to ensure such treasured heritage was not lost.

Watching his face, Katherine allowed herself to appreciate what she had noticed about him at their first meeting at Joy's family lunch. His deep-set, intense dark eyes flashed with emotion as he spoke. Damp curls fell across his strong, high forehead, released as they were now from the restrictive helmet. The strong profile of his nose caused her to fleetingly fantasize of Roman ancestry, and when she got to his lips she gave herself a shake and attempted to focus back on the conversation.

Back on the road, the talk became more personal. Their physical closeness combined with the inability to have eye contact somehow offered the right combination for disclosure.

Katherine spoke about the feelings of independence her trips to France had given her.

She confided how the breakup of her marriage had caused her to worry about being alone and how she had come to realize she had been alone in her marriage.

"My two weeks in Sainte-Mathilde were the best thing that could have happened to me. I had never done anything like that on my own—never done anything alone, really! This may sound strange, but the more time I spent on my own there, the more alive I felt."

Katherine could feel Philippe's response as he put a hand on her clasped fingers across his chest.

"I had a bit of a relapse just before I came to Antibes. I almost canceled."

"I'm glad you did not," he said softly. She tightened her grasp ever so slightly.

"So am I."

Philippe spoke again about the overwhelming grief he had battled for several years after the death of his wife. "Had it not been for Adorée, I don't know how I would have survived. Grief is so raw, so consuming and painful. It turns light into dark and strangles hope . . ."

Katherine gulped back tears at the depth of his sadness. "I'm so sorry."

"Time has helped me to come to terms with everything. I owed it to both Adorée and Geneviève to be the best father I could, and that is what I became. The rest of my life really didn't matter. Gradually my love for my work came to the surface again. So that was good for me when Adorée became older and then went off to school."

They could feel each other's pain.

"It's good to be able to talk to you about it," he said. "Really, to be honest, I resisted all these years in opening this door to anyone."

Katherine felt herself lean more deeply against him and sensed the response of his body to hers.

"This is the first time I have taken anyone except Adorée on this bike in six years," he said softly.

Her eyes filled again as she swallowed hard.

The ride down was even more thrilling. By the time they arrived back in Antibes, Katherine was beaming. *The only negative is that I have to unwrap my arms from his strong body that feels so very, very good.*

She shook her head and ran her hands through her hair, trying to eliminate some of what she was certain was unattractive helmet head.

"You look just fine, Katherine. Don't worry."

From the first time she met Philippe, the way he said her name sounded special, beautiful even. She had never thought of her name that way before him. In fact, she had preferred being called Kat or Katica. *Katherine*, from Philippe's lips, sounded quite wonderful to her.

And now this afternoon, bringing them so physically close, creating an intimacy that surprised and excited her. She tried to hide her confusion with enthusiasm.

"I loved this, Philippe. Thank you! The motorcycle ride was truly thrilling and the villages, the views—*magnifique*!"

"If you have time, we will go to back Saint-Paul another day."

"Definitely!"

"If you like we can also go to one of the goat farms that supplies my *chèvres*. That ride is different, much farther into the hills, to where it becomes rocky and rugged. A different world again. They serve a hearty lunch with everything from their own farm."

"I would love that too!"

He laughed, giving her a perplexed look. "Is there anything here you don't love to do? I've met many excitable tourists, but you are a different breed altogether."

Blushing, Katherine said, "I'll take that as a compliment."

"I meant it as one," he said with a smile, his eyes holding hers hostage.

She invited him for a light dinner, and he promised to come over after he slipped home to shower and change.

Katherine found herself thinking how she would like it if he showered and changed at her place. Her fantasies were suddenly expanding when it came to her *fromager*.

52

Philippe arrived an hour later with a fresh baguette, a block of delicious-looking *chèvre* sitting in golden olive oil and herbs in a container, and a bottle of Bandol rosé, which he knew was Katherine's favorite.

"Save the *chèvre* for tomorrow," he suggested, as he placed a small, wrapped packet on the counter. "I have something else for us tonight."

Katherine had mixed a salad of arugula and spinach with cherry tomatoes and green onion.

At the market that morning she had purchased plump, local white fish, which she planned to pop on the grill and serve with oil and lemon.

The peach tart at the *boulangerie* had been too tempting to pass up. The menu was complete.

The grill was in the intimate, stone-walled front courtyard. Bright flowers tumbled from the large earthenware pots that she religiously watered. With the massive purple bougainvillea cascading down one wall, Katherine felt it was her secret garden. She set the table with her bright Provençal tablecloth, Biot glasses, and warm light glowed from a Biot glass candleholder, a brilliant shade of blue, as the centerpiece.

"Magnifique," Philippe commented, taking in the setting. As he opened the wine, Katherine felt proud of the warmth she was creating in her temporary home.

Philippe lifted his glass of rosé to Katherine's, looking deeply into her eyes. "Here's to a beautiful day with a beautiful woman. Thank you for going with me."

Katherine flushed, feeling a flutter of emotion. "Thank you for asking me. That was such an adventure! There's still so much for me to see."

"Less than a month left. What will you do when you go home?" Philippe asked.

"Ohhh, I don't want to think about leaving."

"Then don't."

Katherine laughed. "Well, I have to face reality. I have a home to take care of and a new job to begin."

Philippe nodded slowly, saying nothing for a few seconds. Then he asked about her new job.

Katherine described, in greater detail than ever before, the type of work she had been doing and what she would continue to do in her new research position with the hospital.

"Do you enjoy this?"

"I find it interesting and challenging. We are involved in interpreting studies, so there is always something new to consider. I work with nice people who I really didn't get to know very well until this past year. Funny how we can live within a bit of a bubble sometimes."

Philippe nodded. "I know that bubble. I stayed in it even when friends wanted to introduce me to women. They were just trying to be kind and thoughtful, but I wasn't ready. In fact, I thought I would never be ready."

This time Katherine nodded. She got it.

"*Et bien*, we should be laughing and smiling after our beautiful day. Let's do that!"

"*D'accord*," Katherine said with a grin.

Philippe offered to do the grill work, which took just a few minutes. Katherine poured more wine.

"*À ta santé*," Philippe toasted. Katherine smiled and raised her glass, as their eyes met once again.

Philippe continued, "It's so important to look into the eyes of the person with whom you are toasting; otherwise, the sentiment is lost."

"That makes so much sense, and yet many people don't even think about it and just clink glasses. This will be another lesson from France."

Philippe chuckled, turning back to the grill.

The meal was ready in minutes, but more than an hour later they were still at the table, slowly relishing each taste of the Reblochon Philippe had brought. He entertained her with the story of how the cheese was first invented by farmers in the thirteenth century. They would pay their rent in milk and then secretly milk their cows a second time, keeping the much richer product to make this cheese.

Kat laughed as he explained, a sly look in his eye, "This is what I call a sexy cheese. It creates stirrings of *fromage* passion that are almost inappropriate."

Here's another French lesson, Katherine thought as they lingered over the simple meal. *Eating is such a social experience here, savoring the food as well as the conversation. They seem to know so much more about what they are eating than I have ever imagined. Even food has a colorful history here.*

His voice took on a deeper tone of rapture as he described a *tartiflette* famous in the Alps consisting of potatoes, bacon, onion, and cream smothered in melted Reblochon.

"Riding up into the Alps on my Ducati is another experience you should put on your list," Philippe suggested, his voice filled with a different type of desire.

Their eyes met in a gaze that seemed to surprise them both.

"I . . . I would like that," Katherine finally sputtered, a bit awkwardly, before she stood and tried to look like she knew what she was doing. Her head was spinning.

"Those little fish were full of flavor, just delicious," Katherine said as they cleared the table together.

"The trick is in the timing of the grilling, and the oil, always the oil—that's it."

"I've never eaten as much seafood as I have since I arrived here," Kat said. "It's all so good. My education in fish, bread, wine, and of course *les fromages* has been outstanding!"

Philippe laughed. "I hope I haven't been . . . too *pédant?*"

Katherine reached for her dictionary, never far away. "Aha, pedantic, are you kidding? I never would have guessed in a million years what there was to learn about cheese, and somehow I feel we aren't finished!"

Looking up at the moon from where they sat in the courtyard, Katherine suggested they go up to the terrace for dessert.

Standing at the railing, Katherine described her fondness for *Le Grand Nomade.*

"He looks so magical, especially bathed in moonlight, standing sentinel over the harbor."

"It was a source of controversy at first," Philippe said. "But then everyone seemed to fall in love with it."

"I have heard the story behind it. Quite delightful," Kat replied.

His voice softened. "And the artist, Jaume Plensa's philosophy?"

"No, not that."

Philippe continued, his voice becoming quietly intimate. "I read an interview with him that touched me deeply. The feeling he expresses through this work is that letters are like bricks. They help us to construct our thoughts. He described his belief that our skin is permanently and invisibly tattooed with the text of our life experiences, and then someone comes along—a friend, a lover—who is able to decipher these tattoos."

Biting her lip, Kat looked out over the calm sea. "The text of this year of my life would call for quite the tattoo."

Philippe gazed at her, his eyes soft. A nuance of a smile hovered at their corners. His arms slipped around her and she responded instinctively, sinking into his embrace. She knew she had missed that, and suddenly she was feeling vulnerable.

After leaving lingering kisses on each of her cheeks, Philippe pulled his head back, keeping his arms around her. Once their eyes met, Katherine was unable to look away.

He kissed her lips gently. Feeling a long-forgotten quickening deep inside her, Katherine lost herself in the moment.

They remained embracing, as if each was wondering what would come next.

Gently pulling away, Katherine moved clumsily and began to clear the dishes.

Consumed by the wave of emotion, she felt almost in a trance.

I've felt this before, and it was never with James . . . Villefranche . . . Marc-André . . . a desire I've not known since, until now . . .

Philippe gathered the wineglasses. As he handed them to Katherine, he held her gaze with a warmth and intensity she allowed to wash through her before he spoke again. "It's a beautiful night. Let's walk down to the beach."

Katherine felt the pulse in her neck beating madly as they walked out the door.

Is his heart pounding like mine?

The old town had a slower feel to it these evenings as the crowds of August had gradually filtered away. The warm evening air was less humid now, inviting lingering strolls.

Stopping to listen, faint singing and music could be heard.

"I'll bet that's the tavern in Safranier! Do you want to pass by?"

There always seemed to be a festival of some sort in this special community just a few twists and turns through the maze of streets from the market. Traditions and ancient customs were celebrated with gusto.

Stopping by the tavern terrace that bordered the flower-lined square, they were engulfed by the high-spirited atmosphere. Singers and dancers were performing in colorful folk costumes while children of all ages ran around or bounced on knees.

Philippe was hailed by friends to join the table. The conversation and ambiance were pure good fun. People sang along with the entertainers, who laughed and encouraged their participation.

Katherine felt Philippe's eyes on her through much of this time, and after a glass of wine and a polite time visiting, they said goodnight to the rowdy group and carried on to the beach.

When she stumbled slightly on a crumbling curb, Philippe caught Katherine by the hand. Their eyes met briefly when neither let go, continuing to walk hand in hand until they reached a secluded bench by the sea.

As the tranquil moonlit waves gently lapped at the shore, Katherine spoke of the thrill she felt having the opportunity to live right on the sea. "The smells, the sounds, the movement of the sky and water . . . I look out and can't help thinking of the history that has crossed these waters . . . the ancient Greeks, the Romans, the Moors. I see billowing sails, tall masts, the wooden ships transporting their goods, warships coming to resupply, Napoleon's armies. Somehow my fantasies stop short of thinking about more modern times and the bad history."

"You see all that in among the luxury yachts?" Philippe teased. "You're a romantic, Katherine, *une vraie femme romantique*. This sea can be cruel and dangerous at times, especially to our fishermen. People who make their living from her do not necessarily share such romantic notions. Violent storms appear out of nowhere and rage for days."

Katherine nodded.

"I'm going to miss the Med."

Still holding her hand, Philippe continued, "And I'm going to miss you. You have helped open my soul again in so many ways, to see a side to life I had stopped appreciating."

Katherine bowed her head, feeling much the same without voicing it, and then turned slowly to look at him.

Philippe's voice had stilled. His eyes studied hers in a way she could not remember experiencing. The feeling was strangely powerful and extraordinary.

It seemed there was no thought, but rather simple reflex, that brought their lips together for a very long time, tender and loving. A kiss that touched Katherine so deeply that she could barely keep from bursting into tears.

They pulled back briefly, eyes meeting as their arms slipped around each other into a gently passionate embrace, their lips saying everything once more.

"Katherine, sweet, sweet Katherine," whispered Philippe, brushing his cheek in her hair. "What are we doing? Where are we going with this?"

"I haven't allowed myself to think about it. I never thought you saw me this way," she answered softly.

They held each other in that embrace for several minutes.

"I have only a little over three weeks left," Katherine murmured, pulling her protective forces around her ever so slightly. "We don't know what this is and don't really have the time to find out."

She was hearing Molly's comments about flings echoing in her head and wondered if this was the one she was meant to have.

What if I'm wrong, and this is nothing more? Perhaps the interlude with Nick was just a warm-up. I mean, what do I know about all this?

Arms around each other, they walked back to her place, each knowing precisely how they wanted this night to continue, each unsure of where it would go from there.

Philippe opened the door for her. They stepped inside and were immediately caught up in slow, deep kisses full of erotic desire. Their lips and bodies moved together in a sensuous dance, responding naturally to each other.

Finally they leaned against the wall in an embrace that conveyed all the emotion they were feeling.

"I'm going home," he whispered in her ear, his voice deep and low.

"Go home," she whispered back, unconvincingly.

"I don't want to."

"I don't want you to either, but I don't want our beautiful friendship to change. I'm afraid."

She felt him nod his head.

They parted slightly, their eyes locked. Seeing the same depth of feeling, the same desire, the same connection.

Nick might have been the warm-up, but this doesn't feel like just a fling.
Pulling her close, he kissed her forehead.

"I'll see you tomorrow for dinner then at Nounou, right?"

Katherine sighed, feeling confused but sensing they were doing the right thing. Her body was screaming otherwise.

"Yes, I'll pick up my cousins at the airport tomorrow morning. They are just flying from Vienna, so no jet lag to deal with! I'm looking forward to dinner."

They laughed awkwardly, knowing what they really wanted at this moment, and with a determined nod, he turned and left.

Katherine remained leaning against the wall of the narrow entrance-way. Her entire body throbbed with desire. She could not recall feeling anything so intensely—not even in Villefranche.

This is so completely different from what I felt with Nick. When Nick got started with me, I wanted what he would do to me. This time I want what Philippe and I will do to each other.

Feeling happiness and surprise mixed with confusion and appre-hension, she climbed up the stairs, stripping her clothes along the way.

Stepping into the shower, she closed her eyes and felt Philippe's soft, strong lips on hers. The water matched his tender touch, making her entire body feel alive and sensuous. She arched her back and felt some-thing of the pleasure she now suspected they had the power to give to each other.

Where did I put those gifts Molly left me . . .

It was a while before she could even think about sleep. Eyes wide open, she lay looking at the ceiling, realizing it would take some time to sort out her emotions.

At length, her excitement over Andrea and Terrence's arrival for a quick three-night visit replaced all other thoughts as sleep found her.

53

Katherine spent the morning cleaning Maison Beau Soleil from top to bottom. She knew her burst of energy was directly linked to the sexual exhilaration of the night before. Philippe had ignited fires that were refusing to go out.

The iPod speakers had been on full blast while she worked, and much of the time she put one song on repeat. Molly had gifted it to her from iTunes earlier in the week, and she couldn't stop listening to it.

"Stronger," by Kelly Clarkson, seemed to have been written just for Katherine, Molly said in her e-mail. It was quite remarkable, Kat had to agree. The chorus began, "What doesn't kill us makes us stronger . . ."

Go figure.

The song was about a breakup in a relationship and how the woman was now much stronger, feeling liberated and a great deal happier. This was Katherine today. No question about it.

⚜

Bernadette picked her up at noon. Depositing Katherine at "Arrivals" at the Nice airport, she indicated where she would be waiting with the car.

There were shrieks of delight as Andrea and Katherine leaped into each other's arms and bounced around. Terrence grinned broadly before scooping Kat into a bear hug.

"I can't believe you're here!" she cried with joy.

Katherine was entertained watching their reactions as Bernadette delivered her standard routine driving along the Bord de Mer. Like most first-time visitors to the Côte d'Azur, they marveled at the scenery.

Terrence exclaimed, "You certainly weren't exaggerating!"

They told Katherine how they were enjoying their exchange at a small farm property just outside Vienna. The house was an ultramodern contemporary style, completely different from their farmhouse in St. Jacobs.

The farm was a hobby for the retired owners. The manager who helped oversee the work had taken a shine to Andrea and Terrence, and he and his wife had invited them to dinner and spent another day touring them around.

"So we have a good source of support if we need help with anything, and they are great folks. Our communication is mostly smiles and hand gestures, but it works," Andrea commented with a grin.

They compared how this exchange of Katherine's was quite different from the one at the Lallibert farmhouse in Provence.

"This time I haven't had the same kind of family involvement. Bernadette was my contact person, and she has been terrific, but I've hardly needed to bother her except for driving at times—and that's her business. I've really been on my own, but of course Molly was with me at the beginning, and we met Nick then. Then it turned out Philippe lives here, which was a huge surprise, and of course Mirella, from the last exchange, put me onto the International Women's Club in Nice, and before I knew it, I had a life here!"

"It's surprising how easy it is to slip into a different world, isn't it?"

"Truly an eye-opener for me," admitted Katherine. "Life changing, really. Speaking the language a little bit definitely makes it easier, though. I even found a hairdresser here, through the ladies in my bridge group, and I like her better than the one I go to at home."

"I guess they speak English?" Andrea asked.

"As a matter of fact, not much! But listen—I love how this happened. The first time I went, there was one other customer, very friendly and just so much fun. Her name is Christiane and she does speak some English. She is a longtime friend of the proprietor and the other sweet young stylist. I had such a good time in their company that when Christiane said she had an appointment every Saturday, I made all my appointments on Saturday too. I can't tell you how much I learned from the three of them about living here and French attitudes and humor and things like that. I'll never forget those women, and we plan to keep in touch!"

"It just proves that people are friendly no matter what country," said Terrence.

"We're always happy to go home, though," Andrea said.

"No place like it," he agreed.

Katherine was quiet for a moment. "Well, you know how much I love Toronto. And I'm proud to be a Canadian, but I have to tell you, I feel so at home in this country. There is something about the surroundings and the culture that speaks directly to my heart."

"Just from the little we've seen from the airport to here, I can understand—and of course, this house is a little piece of paradise. But perhaps it's the novelty of it all too," Andrea replied.

⚜

As it had Molly, the town of Antibes captivated Andrea and Terrence.

Their first stop, as Katherine had promised, was Félix Café, immortalized by author Graham Greene during the three decades he lived and wrote in a nearby apartment.

"Hmm, somehow I thought it would be a more colorful place," Andrea commented.

"And didn't he call it Chez Félix?"

"Never mind," Andrea continued. "I'm loving just sitting where he sat. He's one of our all-time favorite authors. This is very cool, isn't it, Terr!"

Terrence smiled broadly.

"Did I ever tell you that apparently Pablo Picasso swilled down more than a few beverages in Maison Beau Soleil?" Katherine asked them.

"Wha-a-at?" squealed Andrea.

"You'll see that my place is just down the street from the Musée Picasso, a part of which was once his studio, and Bernadette says he partied with everyone in those days, often just dropping in unannounced."

"Those would have been amazing years to live in the South of France. The arts have always been such a vibrant part of the life here."

Finishing their beers, they continued exploring the village and fantasized about who had hung out there before them.

"The old town has such an atmosphere, Kat, with this blend of shops, restaurants, and homes. It's so inviting! All of these patios tempting us to sit and relax, eat, drink, talk. It doesn't just feel like a tourist town," Andrea said as they strolled.

"Exactly. There is such a mix of residents, ex-pats, and locals who work in town. Some families have occupied these homes for generations. The town feels lived in and authentic to me."

"It reminds me of St. Jacobs in a way," observed Terrence, adding with a chuckle, "in a French way, of course."

⚜

Dinner at Nounou was the fine evening Katherine knew it would be.

Philippe gave them a short tour of Juan-les-Pins beforehand, showing them Jardin de la Pinède and the concert venue La Pinède Gould, as they were well aware of their importance in the jazz world. Then he drove the short distance into Cannes to see the famous walk along the sea, La Croisette, pointing out a few hot spots of the International Film Festival before doubling back to Golfe-Juan and pulling into the restaurant's parking lot.

As Katherine had done, her visitors gasped when they stepped into the unexpected elegance of the restaurant. Philippe had arranged the best beachfront table, and the evening was filled with comfortable conversation while they dined on seafood, blazing *crêpes Suzette*, and cheese that truly offered them a fine example of French cuisine.

After Philippe dropped them at home, Andrea, eyebrows raised, looked at Katherine. "Now, there is a fine man!"

"No question," agreed Katherine, a little too hastily. "Now let's get to sleep. We've got a busy day tomorrow."

Andrea's eyes widened and she opened her mouth, about to push on about the subject of Philippe, but Katherine was already on her way up to her room, giving a clear message the exchange was over.

⚜

The four-day visit flew by. In Nice, Katherine had her very own tour organized after her day with Molly.

After exploring the market and old town, they strolled the pedestrian area and had a *pastis* in the bar of the famous hotel Le Negresco before dinner. Katherine had chosen La Merenda, a shoebox-size restaurant on the edge of the old town with a celebrated chef, serving traditional Provençal cuisine. She had been taken there first by Philippe, and they had returned more than once.

"No reservations. No credit cards. No cell phones," Terrence read aloud from a sign outside where the simple menu was printed on a blackboard.

"Yes," Kat explained, "we just have to poke our heads in and see when they can take us."

The next day featured a stop at the market to visit Philippe. When they dined at Restaurant Nounou, Terrence had been intrigued by his conversation with Philippe and wanted to see his business.

Philippe took them to Biot in the afternoon to see the glassblowers and then up into the hills. A late afternoon drink on the bar terrace in Eze, hanging over the spectacular view, was a must before they ended up at a funky beachside bar in Eze-sur-Mer, drinking beer and snacking on *la friture du jour*, tiny fried fish.

Up early on the last day, Andrea was in full tourist mode. "Let's go! Kat says we can squeeze in Monaco. I love how so much is so close!"

Arriving home midafternoon, they packed their carry-on bags and then sipped rosé on the rooftop terrace one last time. Later, Philippe and Katherine were going to drive Andrea and Terrence to the airport and carry on to a concert at the Nice Opera House.

"I can't believe how much we've packed into our stay," Andrea exclaimed. "I never imagined it would be so easy to get around and that there would be so much to see so close by. This has been heaven—a very busy heaven!"

"Philippe is a great guy, Kat," Terrence said. "I like him very much."

Andrea gave Katherine a narrow-eyed stare. "I like him very much too. Do you like him very much, my darling cousin?"

Katherine laughed, her color changing to the brightest shade of crimson. "I've been wondering when this question would come up from you two. Yes, I like him very much too, but I'm coming home very soon. Plus, he is ten years younger than I am, and there's nothing going on beyond some semi-serious flirting."

"Methinks she doth protest too much," countered Terrence, chuckling gently.

"Seriously," Andrea added.

"Another time, another place," said Kat. "It's an unrealistic scenario here."

"You don't have to come home, you know," said Andrea. "You could stay if you wanted. The electricity between the two of you is almost dangerous to anyone in the vicinity!"

"Well, let's get real here. Now you're being the romantic," Kat exclaimed. "I've got the house to take care of, a new job to begin, and . . ." Her voice trailed off.

"And, nothing—my point exactly!"

"Andie, dear Andie, I love it here, as you can see. I'm sure I will return on another exchange or whatever, but the fact is that I came for three months and my exchange is almost over. It's time to get back to reality. I need to earn some money again, for starters."

Andrea looked at her and smiled. "Your mother would have loved to see what you're doing and how you're doing."

Nodding, Kat told her how much Elisabeth had been in her thoughts during the two exchanges, especially this one with her visit to the Ukraine. "If nothing else, that trip with Andrew—brief as it turned out to be—brought her words back to me loud and clear. I do believe I have lived this trip waking up every day appreciating what a gift it is."

"Yup," said Andrea, "an attitude of gratitude is what it's all about."

The talk turned to reminiscences of childhood days and the long history they shared.

"I wish we could stay here longer! But we have another week left in our Austrian exchange, and then it's back to the farm for us. We'll only be back a week or so, and then you'll be home."

Saying good-bye at the airport was easy, since they knew they would see each other in just a few weeks.

Shaking his hand, Terrence couldn't stop exclaiming how their visit had been unforgettable, and they both thanked Philippe sincerely for all he had done.

Philippe stepped forward to *bise* Andrea.

"I do believe that's my favorite French custom," she announced.

54

From the airport it was just minutes to the old town. Parking in the underground garage below Cours Saleya, the pink-toned ornate *belle époque* opera house was a block away.

Puccini's *La Bohème* was opening the season, and Katherine was excited to hear it. James had hated opera, saying the voices spoiled the sound of the orchestra.

Settling into elegant chairs in a small balcony framed with silken drapes, the red and gold decor evoked images of a golden age. The costumes, sets, and performances—especially Mimi's classic death scene—did not disappoint.

This was the first time they had been alone since the night they were in each other's arms at the beach. Both were aware of the intense connection between them whenever they inadvertently brushed against each other.

Partway through the second act, during a particularly moving aria, Philippe took Katherine's hand and kissed it before tucking it into his for the remainder of the performance.

Afterward they walked hand in hand to the car, having decided to have a nightcap back in Antibes. The night was unusually warm and muggy as September, and now October, were turning out to be the hottest on record.

"Let's go and sit on my little beach," Katherine suggested, assuming ownership of La Gravette, as they finished their drinks at La César Café.

"It will be cooler there, for certain. I have towels in the car, so I'll get them as we pass by."

"I guess everyone who lives in this part of the world is prepared for a dip in the Med at any time."

"Exactement!"

Slipping their shoes off, they walked barefoot in the sand. Philippe spread the large towels close to the water's edge. The moon was a mere sliver, allowing the darkness to wrap around them. It was still hot, even by the sea.

Katherine began wading, holding up her dress and struggling to maintain her balance on the pebbled bottom. Philippe rolled up his slacks to join her. Suddenly she lost her footing, and Philippe quickly reached to help her. Pulling her up by her hands, he slipped in the shallow water as well, and they both sat laughing.

"Well," she said, "we might as well go for a swim now." Pulling off her simple linen sheath, now soaking, Katherine threw it onto the sand before diving underwater toward the center of the cove. Philippe stripped off his shirt and trousers, tossing them on a towel before he followed.

The calm sea was refreshing as they swam to the large rocks that formed a breakwater at the mouth of the cove. Treading water and floating on their backs, they studied the night sky, picking out constellations and outdoing each other as they made some up.

Soft lighting fell across the water from some of the luxury yachts anchored nearby, and a few small fishing boats out for a night catch could be seen, red rigging lights bobbing in the distance.

When their feet could touch bottom, Philippe pulled Katherine into his arms, and they made love with their lips. Long, slow kisses that were at the same time, tender, romantic, intense. Katherine's heart raced as the seductive kisses seemed to touch her soul.

Something prevented her from pulling him out of the water and onto the towels to make love right there.

She recognized what was stopping her. Fear. Falling in love was not on her agenda, but what she was feeling did not fit into the category of a fling.

Catching their breath as they stumbled back onto the sand, Philippe wrapped a towel around Katherine's wet body and another around his.

Scooping up their clothes, he took her hand and they ran back to the house, trying not to make too much noise with their laughter.

"Let's get the salt water off," he said, and Kat led him to the shower on the guest-room level. She leaned in to turn on the water and turned back to where he was standing. Undoing her towel, all resolve vanished. She stripped off her soaking-wet underwear and stepped into the stall, leaving the door open and not taking her eyes from him.

Philippe dropped his towel to the floor and joined her.

Naked, they pressed together as the warm water washed over them. Reaching for the soap, he ran it over her neck, her back, her shoulders, her arms, her breasts, her stomach, and on down. His lips followed, kissing her body as the soap ran off.

Katherine did the same, her fears banished by the sheer intensity of the moment. A fire burned up her limbs and into her very core. Their lips found each other again.

No words were spoken as Philippe picked her up and carried her to the bed. Pulling back the duvet, he laid Katherine softly on the bed. Their wet bodies fused as she wrapped her legs around him. Nothing existed but the sensation of being loved.

Taking their sweet time, the lovemaking was cautious at first—a slow sensual symphony as she moaned, softly urging him on. Philippe gently nibbled her ear and neck. Discovering how to excite each other, there was no rush to reach the peak of that pleasure . . . *le plaisir*.

His touch felt like he was reading her body by braille, interpreting the messages it was telling him. His fingertips traced lightly at first before his strong hands pressed slowly up to her face and into her hair.

Looking into each other's eyes, Katherine had only one thought as she gasped with anticipation. *Desire—this truly is desire.*

Touching him, Kat was drowning in the response of her hands on his smooth skin, his strong body, his tight buttocks.

Giving themselves to each other with total abandon, desire drifted from lingering rapture to urgent hunger and back again through the night, until finally they lay entangled in each other.

His warm tears mingled with hers as the realization surfaced of all they were sharing, still without words. His hands brushed her hair. Her fingertips gently wiped his tears as he kissed hers away. Then they slept.

❖

Katherine awoke alone. She had been carefully covered with a light sheet and lay with the sun streaming in, feeling fulfilled and confused.

What the hell have I done?

But she knew what she had done. What they had done. The question was, what would they do with it now?

Stretching slowly, she closed her eyes and luxuriated in the lingering memory of their lovemaking. A light smile played across her face. *It's still there. I'm not too old. That spark of excitement that ignited the fire . . .* She felt her body move sensuously into the sheet as she recalled the bursts of pure pleasure that had surged right to her toes . . . *time after time . . .*

She thought about Andrea's words at the airport, about not having to go home.

Trust Andrea to see past what is holding me back. She's so calm and logical and willing to take risks. Everything she said is what I feel but can't give myself permission to accept.

Philippe appeared in the doorway with fresh croissants. She could see he had even gone to Choopy's to pick up her special caffe mocha.

Wearing a slightly abashed expression, he placed the tray on a side table and sat on the edge of the bed. Taking Katherine's hand, he kissed it lightly on the back and the palm. With the back of her other hand, she softly rubbed the light stubble on his cheek before pulling him to her for a brief but tender kiss.

"It was a beautiful night," he murmured, his eyes and voice full of emotion. He spoke slowly, as if hearing the echo of each word and confirming his voice was expressing what his heart was feeling. "You are a most special woman, Katherine. I never thought I would meet someone like you."

She put her fingers to his lips, as if afraid of what he might say next, while she responded in close to a whisper, "It was so beautiful. Oh yes, it was. And you are special to me too. We have so much to think about, so much to work through—in our hearts, in our heads."

Philippe nodded. "*Oui, c'est vrai*. It's true . . ."

"I don't want this to change the friendship we share. I'm leaving in just over two weeks—that's the reality here. Can we just keep going and see where this takes us?"

"I want you to know I have not been with anyone since Geneviève. It's important to me that you know this. You know there is nothing to worry about. We did not take precautions . . ."

Kat had not even considered that aspect, she realized with an internal admonition, and appreciated his concern that she might worry.

She assured him that he too had nothing to fear.

"It's okay. Let's not talk about it anymore now. Let's just be."

"*Oui* . . . let's just be."

He brought her a robe that was hanging by the shower. "I'll take the tray to the rooftop and we can have a quick bite. *Désolé*, I must get back to work, but I will come back after we close up—if you like."

"Of course I would like that."

As she reached for the robe, their hands touched. It took only a second for Katherine to pull him to her, wordlessly stripping off his T-shirt as he unzipped his jeans and kicked them aside. Their kisses were strong and fiery. Quickly he straddled her and felt her hips rise to meet him as they both groaned with pleasure. He hungrily kissed her neck, her hair. Katherine felt a hot streak course deep into her pelvis and she pushed him back, this time climbing on top of him.

All reserve was gone. She felt strong, sexy, desired, knowing what she wanted to give and to get.

Later, Philippe held her face for a long time as they lay together. Then he drew it to him. "You are beautiful," he whispered, covering her cheeks, her nose, and her forehead with small kisses. "You are such a gift."

Breakfast could wait.

55

He did come back after work. Katherine had been counting the minutes.

"You have never seen where I live, Katherine. Did you not think it odd that I never invited you to my place?"

"To be honest, I never really thought about it because we were always going off to somewhere interesting or out of town. But now that you mention it, where do you live, anyway?"

"Two places," he answered. "Let's go on our bikes."

The first ride was not far: along the ramparts, past the anthropological museum with its impressive display of artifacts and the park where afternoon games of *boules* are played, to Rue Albert Premier.

They stopped in front of an elegant white early-twentieth-century apartment building, locked their bikes, and climbed an elegant staircase to the third floor.

He showed Katherine around a spacious, comfortably furnished four-bedroom apartment with a large terrace. "This is where my parents lived when they were elderly, and Adorée and I moved in here after we lost Geneviève. This is what Adorée calls home."

Back on their bikes, they cycled along the road bordering the sea, past Pointe Bacon, and then turned uphill onto the Cap d'Antibes. Large estates adjoined lots with smaller simple homes and then there was everything in between. Many properties were hidden by tall hedges, and at one such lot, they stopped before a locked gate.

Opening the gate, they rode their bikes down a long dirt lane, apparently infrequently used as grass and wildflowers grew tall in the middle. Overgrown flowering shrubs and bushes tumbled into their path and brushed against them before they arrived at a rambling villa, partially in disrepair.

"This property has been in my family since before the Revolution. Originally part of a much larger piece of land, it was an orchard and farm for over one hundred years. The orchard was eventually sold to several other families who built homes. My great-grandfather built this house and kept a small farm garden. The house was added to over the decades. That's why it rambles as it does."

"It's such a beautiful property—and the view! How did it come to be abandoned?"

"France has some archaic inheritance laws. After my grandfather died, my uncles fought over it and tied up the case in the courts for the rest of their lives. How smart was that?"

Katherine shook her head. "I've read about situations like that in novels but never imagined it was that bad."

"About ten years ago, everything was finally resolved and the property passed to me. Geneviève and I had plans to fix it up and open a small inn. We had just begun to clear the overgrowth and restore the house when she became ill."

Katherine put her hand on his arm. "I'm so sorry. You don't have to talk about it if it's painful."

He took her hand, pressing it to his lips.

I could get used to this.

"It's painful, but I do want to talk about it. You make me want to talk about things I haven't mentioned in years."

The house had an intricate alarm system; he explained squatters could be a problem in the area.

He continued to tell her about his hopes for the hauntingly beautiful house and property as he carefully led her through areas where beams had fallen and walls crumbled.

"After I met you in Provence, you were so full of life, so in love with France. You got me thinking. I began to come back here and slowly do work. You see—you inspired me."

"And I had no idea."

The kitchen area was barely useable, and in one corner there was a cot.

"I sometimes stay here when I'm working on the property. Now I want to be here again."

They walked out through fragile French doors into what must have once been a vast and magnificent garden. Gasping at what she could see was splendor begging to be rescued, Katherine identified many plant species among the woody and brambly overgrowth.

Climbing rosebushes had a stranglehold on a rotting arbor that now tipped to a sad angle but still was an ornate piece of workmanship. Massive twisting trunks of wisteria were hidden behind intrusive, shallow-rooted wild pepper vines that she knew could be so easily yanked from the soil.

"Let's work on this before I go back home. I would love to help you begin to recover this garden."

He looked at her, saying nothing at first. A slow smile transformed his face, and his eyes shone with contentment.

"Allons-y!" he said.

"Let's do it!"

⚜

She would never have believed two weeks could simply vanish in bliss.

The mornings were hers, as Philippe left at 7:00 a.m. to organize his stand at the market and tend to his customers.

Joyfully laborious afternoons were spent working in the gardens and planning how the final outcome might look. There was a small semblance of order appearing around the grounds and an impressive collection of empty wine bottles gathering on the pantry counter.

Lying squashed on the cot in the kitchen or sitting with their legs dangling off the wooden counter, they talked long into many nights. Conversation between them flowed easily as they shared their thoughts and interests and swatted mosquitoes. They were surprised to discover they shared similar tastes on topics like books, history, and concern about world affairs. Simple pleasures made them both content. Philippe's quiet humor was ever present, and Katherine was aware of the absence of sarcasm—something she had heard from James on a regular basis.

Philippe revealed his dreams, once buried along with Geneviève, for the property and the possibilities he envisioned of transforming the house to a small inn. He encouraged Katherine to share her ideas as together they began to bring it all to life.

As he listened to her, Philippe knew he wanted only to be with her, to have her body leaning into his, their arms around each other.

Other afternoons they took liberating motorcycle trips into the hills, riding far and fast and feeling such a sense of freedom.

"Trust me," he encouraged as he took her on steeply winding climbs. She thought about how she was beginning to trust him in so many ways that had nothing to do with the motorcycle.

Spreading a blanket under ancient abandoned olive trees on secluded hilltops along their routes, they made love or simply talked, their silences often just as meaningful. The panoramas stretching before them were as memorable as the moments they gave each other.

After the first exciting and out-of-control nights, their lovemaking felt comfortable and satisfying. They knew their desires were arising from mutual respect and a deeper caring that comes with age as well as from physical attraction and stores of passion that had been hidden away for a very long time. Listening to each other, they were equal partners in this passion.

This intimacy felt new to Katherine and brought into focus how she and James had been more like roommates for a very, very long time.

At one point she realized she had stopped being concerned about her age. She felt strong and confident and recently had smiled as she looked at herself in the mirror and recalled the old skin-care advertising campaign—"You're not getting older, you're getting better." Her skin glowed. Her blue eyes had a brightness that had been lost for years. The fact that more white and gray hair was mingling with the blond didn't seem to matter. Most of the time she simply lost herself in moments where age faded away.

One day they rode to the goat-cheese supplier and ate the most basic and delicious meal: green salad with toasts covered in melted *chèvre*, prosciutto made from the farm's own stock and sliced so thinly you could almost see through it and served with fresh baguette, followed by the newest of *chèvre*, accompanied by lavender honey and an apple *tarte*. Everything was served simply on rustic slabs of olive wood.

Philippe explained the differences between the new and old *chèvre*. To hear the farmer describe it and watch the actual process, handed down for generations, was fascinating. The men spoke of the frustrations cheese makers were suffering with many unnecessary changes the European Union regulations were demanding.

"Who says the old ways are not the best?" the farmer asked.

Some of the structures on the farm dated to the sixteenth century, and with the seemingly isolated and wild setting, high in the hills, one had a sense of time travel.

The goats displayed a certain beauty, with majestic curved horns and coats of burnished copper and rich brown tinged with beige. They wandered freely along with some of the most gigantic pigs Katherine had ever seen.

Philippe smiled knowingly when she described how captivated she was by the place. She could tell it pleased him to see she appreciated his world.

Mirella and her husband brought Joy to Antibes for a day. The visitors stayed overnight with Philippe at his apartment, and their dinner at a favorite bistro featured a few champagne toasts as they celebrated the happy reunion.

Joy confided in Katherine that she had not seen Philippe so happy in all the years he had been alone. "I think you have been a very good tonic for him, *ma chère*. How I wish we could keep you here."

Katherine nodded. "I will miss all of you, and I promise to return. How could I not? I feel torn, but I know I have to get back to my real world. I have a new job waiting for me."

That night, Philippe remained at his apartment with his guests, and Katherine became painfully aware of how quickly she had accepted his presence in her bed, in her thoughts, in her heart. This had not been part of her new life plan. She never wanted to be vulnerable to the hurt and deceit she had endured with James. She hadn't been certain she could trust anyone again, and she had reached a point of feeling happy alone before she met Philippe. Now she felt even happier with him and acutely felt his absence.

It's just as well I'm leaving before I get in any deeper. Wait, could it get any deeper?

As the lovers had agreed after that first night of passion, they had not spoken much about what was happening between them. In their most intimate moments they had, at first with hesitation, expressed feelings and whispered desires, but never projected into the future.

There were looks and touches that transmitted signals so deeply they simply could not be missed. Each time something held one thought captive.

In spite of the emotional expressions, soft voices, passionate responses—*why does every word sound so beautiful with a French accent?*—the words "I love you" had not been heard.

Katherine had blurted this to Molly during one of their Skype chats, and Molly's raspy chortle and words had stayed with her. "Katski, in my humble opinion, saying 'I love you' is so yesterday. Don't get hung up on it. The way Philippe behaves with you, respects you, hears you, and makes you feel—that's what really counts. That's where the love shows. If you feel that love when you have your clothes on, then I'm betting what you feel when you get physical is magic. Here endeth the gospel according to *moi*."

"You know, Moll. I sometimes remember how James would say he loved me even though I know now he was cheating on me. So, yeah, really, how important is it?"

Philippe did make her feel respected and special. She felt she offered the same to him. They had not tried to determine if they were taking down the protective walls each had put up after their own particular disasters. They had just been.

There were moments she shivered with delight and embraced completely the joy of what they shared. There were other moments she felt paralyzed with fear that this was too good to be true.

In her final week, Katherine bade good-bye to her bridge group, which had a laughter-filled surprise party for her. She *bised* her hiking and conversation group and thanked them for making her so welcome. The cycling group also had a festive send-off for her after the last Tuesday-evening ride, teasing her about how she would miss her friend Philippe. She wondered how they would feel if they knew he was spending every night with her.

56

Katherine had requested fish soup for lunch at Nounou before they spent her last afternoon at Philippe's property.

She filled load after load into a wheelbarrow as she clipped and dug and cleared another swath of overgrown flowerbeds. Philippe emptied the brush on the fire burning in the large open area behind the house, along with larger tree limbs he was attacking.

The mellow, smoky smell of the wood fire brought back childhood memories to Katherine of blissful weekends spent with her parents and Andrea's family on their farm.

Who can predict where life will take us? As a child, I had dreams. As an adult, I thought my life was settled. It was what it was. I looked forward to things like holidays, times with family, but I stopped dreaming. Now, like a child, I'm filled with dreams again. Here everything fills me with . . . le plaisir . . .

When he returned the empty barrow this time, Philippe removed his work gloves. She looked at him and smiled, smudging her face slightly as she brushed her hair back.

"Time for a break?" she asked, pulling off her gardening gloves and stretching her back as she rose from her kneeling position in the dirt.

He gently laid a hand on each side of her face, his eyes determined and sure. "Stay here, Katherine. Don't go."

Somewhere deep inside, she knew these were words she longed to hear. Something deep inside could not let her say the words she longed to say.

"I'm afraid."

He pulled her into his arms. "I'm ready to take a chance."

They remained like that for several moments.

"I want to stay with you. I can't imagine being without you. But I'm so afraid."

"We are battling the same demons."

Taking her hand, he led her down to a point where they had placed a dilapidated, sun-bleached wooden loveseat discovered buried in over-grown brush in a remote corner of the property. Overlooking the spectacular bay and beaches of La Garoupe, the turquoise water shimmered in the late October sun. The warmth of summer still lingered in this year of unusual and unpredictable weather patterns.

This year of unusual and unpredictable life patterns.

Holding nothing back, they laid bare the fears that haunted them from the past. Their exchange was raw and honest about the hurt, the damage, the struggle, the need to feel protected from any remote chance of recurrence.

"I want so much to trust what we have found together," he said. "I'm beginning to feel I can do that in a way I never believed I would."

"I have to go back home. I have a new job waiting, a house to take care of . . ." Tears streamed down her cheeks as her words stuttered out. "This has been like a dream, and I'm afraid dreams don't come true. I don't really know how to believe in them. Maybe we need some time apart to see how we feel then."

Philippe sat staring at the ground, his hands hanging between his knees.

"I don't want to let go of this. I'm afraid if you go, we will lose what we have."

Katherine could barely speak now. "I don't want to lose what we have either . . ."

They sat in silence, lost in their thoughts.

"Promise you will come back—soon," he whispered.

Katherine nodded silently. First . . . yes. Then . . . no. "That . . . that will be difficult with my new job—at least until the spring. Perhaps you can come to Toronto."

"I will."

Side by side, bodies molded, gazing at the movement of the sea and the boats gracefully gliding by but seeing none of it, Philippe and Katherine sat; his fingers lightly caressed her back.

Katherine's mind kept replaying everything that called to her about this part of the world, about the person she was here, about the way she was learning to love like she never had before.

I've been a different person during this time, but somehow I feel like I have never been more myself. Whether it's forever should not be the issue. I want to keep living in the moment in a way I never have before. Why can't I take one more step and do it?

Their plan had been to cycle to a favorite secluded cove with a picnic they had decided upon the day before and prepared after an early-morning stop at the market, where Philippe had left his associate in charge.

Putting away the gardening tools and tidying the villa one last time, they were lost in their own thoughts and acceptance of the reality of this day. Soon they were on their bikes, riding a short distance along the coastal road.

At the side of the road, there was a plaque on a stand showing a print of a painting by Claude Monet that captured Antibes across the bay. The artist had worked in that very spot. Katherine loved how there were such plaques all along the Riviera.

This was a popular place for the fortunate few who arrived before the space was taken. Down a narrow, barely visible path and around a slight bend was another small cove with just enough room for two people to sit on rocks smoothed by waves during more turbulent times.

Sitting unseen from anywhere else, the view was that of Monet's painting with the glistening water of the sea leading the eye to the stone buildings and ancient towers of the old town, appearing golden in the late-afternoon sun. Set against the backdrop of rolling hills behind which the setting sun would slowly sink in a blaze of pinks and reds, Katherine knew it was her most favorite view.

Even today, confused and conflicted as I am, this view fills me with such a sense of beauty and peace.

They shared a light menu and slowly sipped champagne. Katherine had banished the painful memories long before. Baguette, *foie gras*, with a decadently creamy Délice de Bourgogne. Succulent figs followed, accompanied by a Roquefort Papillon Noir, the clean and forceful flavor Philippe had once declared was "an emotional experience."

Between bursts of conversation and moments of silence, they wished time would stand still.

Reminiscing about their first meeting in Sainte-Mathilde, both chuckled at the memory of Katherine thinking the other Philippe was the one who left the flowers. They expressed amazement again at the coincidence of Katherine finding herself in Antibes and discovering each other once more.

"I felt your special qualities in Provence," Philippe told her, "but I also knew we would never see each other again."

Katherine confessed that she had experienced similar thoughts.

"Whatever this is, whatever we have found, we have to hold on to now. We have to see how this will fit into our real worlds," Katherine said at length.

"Perhaps fate put us together to show us we can take down our walls. We can find happiness again. Maybe that is what this was . . . *une affaire de coeur*," Philippe said, sounding unconvinced.

They had agreed a few days earlier, during a ride in the hills, that they would not spend this last night together. Katherine had insisted it would be far too difficult to say good-bye to each other. She wanted

Bernadette to drive her to the airport so she could begin her trip, possibly, without being a total mess.

The night before had been their last together. They had moved the mattress onto the roof terrace and made love bathed in soft moonlight under the stars, the quiet rhythm of the waves lulling them. Knowing how to please each other, they still found ways to surprise in some tender and other wildly passionate moments. They held back nothing, and everything felt right.

Each wondered how they could walk away from what they had found. How everything that had become so familiar to them together would fade away.

Now Philippe leaned his bike against the front wall, under the brilliant blossoms of the cascading bougainvillea. He held the gate open for Katherine as she wheeled her bicycle into the garden, then she went into the house to get the travel carton.

Together they securely packed the bike away.

"*Ma chère Katherine, mon petit chat, mon amour, c'est le temps.* I will go now."

Sweeping her into his arms, they kissed until they were almost breathless and clung to each other. Finally, with great reluctance, they released each other amidst promises to talk as soon as Katherine arrived in Toronto.

"Some people search all their life for what we have found together. This is not good-bye, I promise you," he declared, his voice husky and breaking as he gathered her to him once more.

Katherine nodded into his shoulder, unable to speak. Her face wet with tears.

And then he was gone.

⚜

Katherine slowly climbed the stairs to her room. Her bags were packed, with the exception of her nightgown and toiletries. Putting today's clothes into her travel laundry bag, she tucked that in her suitcase and stepped into the shower. Water mingled with her tears.

Crying would change nothing. They would have to work things out. The fact neither of them had said "I love you" was no longer a concern. Molly had helped her with that. Kat had felt the love they shared in every other way.

Perhaps Philippe was right and this was simply a lovely affaire de coeur *that allowed us both to discover we were capable of more.* That thought was quickly banished.

Katherine slept one floor down so she could lie in bed looking at the strip of moonlight reflected in the waves one last time. She did not want to be in the same bed where, for so many nights, they had made love, slept in each other's arms, and felt sensations and emotions they thought had been lost forever.

The sea air was not soothing her now.

Her mind replayed the reasons she had convinced herself she needed to return home. A house. A job. *Really?* True friendships and treasured memories would remain with her no matter where she lived. *This I am learning.*

As she tossed with anxiety over her decisions, from the depths came her mother's calming words.

Every day is a gift, Katica. Try to live your life knowing what matters most and always, always remember . . . what doesn't kill us . . .

Finally she slept.

⚜

Katherine turned the key in the lock, rubbing her hand over the worn wooden door as she pulled it closed for the last time.

This has begun to feel like home.

A gray drizzle added to the somber mood in the car. Katherine said a silent good-bye to her familiar neighborhood before she and Bernadette passed through the arch in the ancient wall. In the harbor, the local fishermen were unloading their catch, preparing for their first customers.

As they turned onto the Bord de Mer, she leaned her head back against the seat.

"Not a nice way to remember this route," Bernadette muttered. "You should 'ave one last beautiful sunrise, not this rain. It was to know you, *un plaisir*. Please say you will visit Antibes again."

"The pleasure was mine. With all my heart, I hope to return."

With few cars at that time of the morning, they were soon approaching Nice. Bernadette's cell phone rang, and Katherine swallowed hard as she turned her attention back to the route she had driven and cycled so often.

She fought back tears, thinking of everything she was leaving behind. *Philippe.* Passing a cluster of cyclists caused her heart to wrench.

"You are so fortunate to live in this beautiful part of the world," she told Bernadette when the brief call had ended.

Bernadette grumbled yet again how it would be even more beautiful if they could replace the French men with Swedes.

Katherine smiled briefly and then tears came, in a way she could not control.

I do not want to leave.

Bernadette handed her a box of tissues from the front seat.

I can always come back. This doesn't mean the end to anything. I may be happy to be back in Toronto. I may love my new job.

Bernadette apologized before she pulled the car to the shoulder of the road and raised the hood. "*Excusez-moi,* there is a little problem with the engine, and I know we 'ave enough time before your flight. May I stop *un moment?*"

Katherine shrugged. A few minutes wouldn't matter.

She took out her phone, hoping to see a text from Philippe, even though he had told her he planned a very early cycle to take his mind off her leaving. She had promised herself she would not text him until she was safely checked in—beyond the point of changing her mind.

Closing her eyes, Katherine considered the woman she was now compared to the day she arrived. It seemed like a lifetime ago. She was going home changed. Stronger.

Bernadette's *moment* turned into several and then they were on their way again in a flurry of *pardons* from her. As they arrived at the airport, Katherine straightened with resolve.

Stopped in front of the international departure entrance, Bernadette helped load the bags on a cart. They *bised* warmly, and Katherine handed her an envelope with a generous tip inside, ignoring the protests.

With a deep breath and with one last backward wave, Kat entered through the automatic doors to the check-in area.

This is it. It's the way it has to be.

Taking her passport and boarding pass from her purse, she stepped into line. The reality would be easier to accept once she was through security and settled at the gate.

A curt announcement over the loudspeaker informed there would be a delay at the counter. After a few words of commiseration with the people next to her, she took out her Kindle and read until the line began to move once more.

"Katherine."

Startled, she turned and watched in astonishment as Philippe strode through the terminal toward her. In his cycling clothes, drenched from the rain and the sweat of his race to the airport, he hurried along the line as the other passengers stared wide-eyed.

With the velour rope barrier between them, he stopped.

His eyes told her everything before she heard his words.

"Ne me quittes pas."

Katherine was rooted to where she stood.

"Please stay with me." He reached for her, still struggling for breath from the exertion of cycling against time.

They folded into each other's arms across the barrier. Their embrace was gentle and loving. His lips tasted salty and sensuous on hers. Katherine felt overcome with the desire to be with him, to trust everything she believed that promised.

She ran her fingers through the damp curls clinging to his neck as his arms pulled her tightly into him. Every nerve of her body was on fire.

He is what matters most to me.

Oblivious to the looks and smiles and gentle applause swelling around them, their long embrace left Katherine soaked too.

Philippe's lips brushed her ear. "Let's take a chance."

Katherine felt joy surge through her with no fear, no anxiety.

Still speechless, her feelings raw and exposed, Katherine reached for her carry-on.

The passenger behind her unhooked the rope while Philippe took Katherine's hand and her bag as she stepped out of the line.

Their gazes remained unbroken. Smiles spread across their faces.

"Let's go home," he said.

"*Allons-y.* Let's go."

EPILOGUE

Katherine's impulse to ignore her flight home and leave the airport with Philippe felt *magnifique* at the time. After weeks of soul-searching, she knows in her heart this is the right choice.

This is love.

However, life doesn't always turn out as expected.

Who can predict what the future holds?

AFTERWORD

Dear reader,

Thank you for your tremendous response to Katherine's story!

I've been overwhelmed by requests for the story to continue . . . and so it shall! *The Promise of Provence* has now become Book One in the Love in Provence series, and two more novels are to follow.

Promises to Keep (Book Two) will be published by Lake Union in October 2015, and I'm busy writing the next. I'm excited myself to see how this adventure unfolds.

All these books will encompass Katherine's love of everything in the South of France that appeals so much to those of you enjoying her story. Your enthusiasm makes my work a pleasure.

To bring these stories to life even more, the Womens Travel Network in Toronto has worked with me to develop a tour of the Côte d'Azur and the countryside of Provence. For women only, in small groups of twelve to sixteen, this is a fabulous trip that I get to lead. Details can be found on my website. Join us!

If you would like to receive updates on the progress of the next novel through my monthly newsletter, there's a sign-up link on my website as well.

patriciasandsauthor.com

facebook.com/AuthorPatriciaSands

twitter.com/patricia_sands

À bientôt!

AUTHOR'S NOTE

Family, writing, and travel are my passions—okay, and chocolate—and I'm seldom without a camera. Toronto, Canada, is home for me most of the time, Florida some of the time, and the South of France whenever possible. There are benefits to getting older!

Beginning with my first Kodak Brownie camera at the age of six, it seems I have told stories all my life through photography. With our happily blended family of seven adult children and, at last count, six grandchildren, life is full and time is short. Becoming an author in my—gasp—sixties was not on my agenda. But here I certainly am, and writing is what I will continue to do.

Writing offers me the opportunity to examine the rewarding friendships and bonds women share and the challenges life often throws in our paths. I prefer to celebrate the positive friendships most of us experience rather than perpetuate the stereotypes of bitchy, negative connections, full of angst and drama, that are so often featured. That is why I was motivated to write *The Bridge Club*.

My greatest reward has been the many messages I have received from readers describing the valued friendships in their lives and saying how the story was a reminder to celebrate each one. Many thanks to all of you, and please do keep talking to me!

Inspiration for *The Promise of Provence* came about after supporting some friends when their long-established marriages fell apart. It also seemed the perfect chance to write my love letter to France, share my appreciation of home exchanges (my husband and I did our eighth exchange in September 2013), and to offer a message that we are never too old to begin again.

I based the character of Elisabeth, in this story, on my late mother-in-law, Elizabeth Landman. The carpet described in this novel hangs in the home of one of our sons. The history of how it survived, as written in these pages, to finally arrive in Canada, will be treasured and will live on, as will the memory of Elizabeth and her family.

One of the great pleasures of being published is receiving requests to speak with women's groups on the subjects of writing and self-publishing as well as the importance of valuing our personal stories. I encourage women of all ages to embrace change and see challenges as opportunities. I live by the philosophy that it's never too late to begin something new, to seize each day and be a "possibilitarian." As the saying goes, just do it!

ACKNOWLEDGMENTS

It would be impossible to thank all the people who have, in large and small ways, inspired and assisted me in publishing this novel.

My large and loving family deserves my first thanks—in particular, my patient and supportive husband.

I am grateful on a daily basis to the writing community and the collegiality we share. It's an exciting time to be a writer. I am so fortunate to have the support of honest and critical beta readers and excellent editors, proofreaders, and cover designers.

Thanks to Heidi Lee, owner of the English Book Shop in Antibes, for her friendship and observations about living in that part of the world. It was a thrill to see my books on her shelves. It was sad to see this iconic bookstore close in January 2015, but good news to hear the new Antibes Books is open at 13 rue Georges Clemenceau.

Jacques, a *fromager* at the daily Provençal market in Antibes, was generous with his friendship and the time he took to enlighten me about his work, *and* I am grateful for every taste of cheese we enjoyed from his stand.

Of equal importance are the readers who enjoy my work, visit my blog, write reviews, send messages, and offer tremendous support on a daily basis. Knowing that my writing is meaningful to you is the greatest reward, and I look forward to ongoing conversations with you. Thanks!

I realized as I was writing *The Promise of Provence* that, as well as celebrating the idea of hope and change as we age, this novel is also in many ways my love letter to France.

I feel I owe a debt of gratitude to France—the country, the culture, the history, the language, the people I have met . . . just everything. How I loved writing about the stunning *departement* of Provence–Alpes–Côte d'Azur and Paris . . . indeed, the entire culture of France that has captured my heart for over four decades. In particular I want to share my love of the town of Antibes–Juan-les-Pins, where my husband and I lived for five months in 2011. To be specific, thanks especially to *La Vieille Ville*, which took hold of my imagination with its atmosphere, beauty, and vibrancy and provided the perfect setting for this story.

ABOUT THE AUTHOR

 Patricia Sands lives in Toronto, Canada, when she isn't somewhere else. An admitted travel fanatic, she can pack a bag in a flash and be ready to go anywhere . . . particularly the South of France.

Her award-winning debut novel *The Bridge Club* was published in 2010, and her second novel, *The Promise of Provence*, the first in the Love in Provence Series, was an Amazon Hot New Release in April 2013, a USA Best Book 2013 Finalist and a 2013 Finalist in Literary Fiction, National Indie Excellence Awards.

Celebrating the rewarding friendships and bonds women share, her stories examine the challenges life often throws in our paths. Location features prominently in all her novels.

For book club discussion questions or to contact Patricia, please visit patriciasandsauthor.com.